RUN, GIRL, RUN

A THRILLER

ALEX C. FRANKLIN

Perago Press

Published by Perago Press

ISBN: 978-0-9950692-1-3

Visit the author's website to sign up for news of the next release and lots of other cool, free stuff: www.AlexCFrankin.com.

For Bhim & Otta

Prologue

JOURNAL ENTRY:

Friday, March 11

My mother fled the confinement of a religious and deeply dysfunctional home, shortly after turning seventeen, and her shadow never crossed the threshold of a church, ever again. Nevertheless, I still think of her as a profoundly spiritual person.

She saw the operation of a divine hand at work in everything around her, from the rising and setting of the sun, to the ebb and flow of the tides, and the birth and death of every living creature.

So many years after she's gone, I remember two of her observations as particularly astute.

The first concerned destiny. In her understanding of life, a divine will offered each one of us a greater and a lesser destiny. She would say that what may seem to small, finite minds as chaos in an irrational world is often the spiritual alignment of people and circumstances in a manner that manifests destiny.

"There's no such thing as luck, neither good, nor bad," she would tell me. "There's only Life presenting a moment of opportunity and asking you whether you have prepared yourself to make good on your greater destiny."

The second observation my mother made was that the world has a habit of underestimating women.

Many men, and even some women, fail to appreciate the ambition to a greater destiny that may throb in the heart of a woman. They do not see a woman's potential because they look at all women through the lens of the limitations they place on the female of our species.

"A smart woman will use this to her advantage," my mother would often tell me.

People's lower expectations allow such a woman to fly under the radar, quietly growing in wisdom and strength, until the moment arrives when she can strike, and claim her higher destiny....

PART I

Seven months earlier

Chapter 1

The hit job — if it was to happen at all — was just over forty-eight hours away.

The Russian assassin wound his way on foot through the narrow streets of Beausoleil, France, down toward Monaco. It was late August, the last Thursday of the month, and dusk had brought the cooler temperatures that suited him. He kept his gaze on the precise spot where he knew the rooftop of Villa St Eustace was. He couldn't see it. The leafy branches of a giant jacaranda blocked the building completely from view.

That pleased him.

His eyes were hidden behind mirrored sunglasses and his appearance was distorted by a latex nose and a false beard. He pulled his New York Yankees baseball cap lower down on his brow and crossed the street which marked the border between France and the micro-state.

The avenue descended behind a tall retaining wall and took him to Villa St Eustace, a yellow, five-story building with a typical Mediterranean roof of terracotta tiles. It was the headquarters of the privately-held international mining giant Magrelma Mines, and home on the Riviera to its American principals.

The killer-for-hire walked on briskly, surveying the villa's service entrance as he went. This narrow annex stood in the shadow of the windowless rear of two taller commercial buildings.

In his mind, he went over the blueprint of the villa, the security measures in place, and the routine he had worked out that would give him entry.

Getting in would be the easy part. The job, itself, would be a hell of a challenge.

No weapons were to be used. The chic, ultra-wealthy principality was not the kind of place where you went around gunning people down, or slashing their throats.

If the order eventually came, the client wanted this to look like an accidental death.

The Russian followed the quiet avenue around a bend and found himself suddenly in the bustling heart of Monte Carlo. He bristled at the thought of the security cameras pointing down onto the streets from every angle in this section of the principality.

He paced his steps behind the throngs of tourists in their summer shorts and broad-rimmed hats, ducking and weaving so that their bodies shielded him from the electronic stare. He hated being recorded, even when in disguise.

"Can you believe this place?" said the male half of a slow-moving couple in front of him.

"Like a Disneyland for adults," the woman said.

He had no time for gawking and paid no attention to the window displays of dresses that cost more than cars, and wristwatches priced higher than four-bedroom houses. Spending money was far from his thoughts. Making it — using his particular skills — was all that occupied him.

He had already received the promised fifteen grand just for showing up. If the job fell through, he would walk away with the free money. But if his services were indeed needed, and if the job were accomplished cleanly, a million dollars would be wired to his Swiss bank account.

He wanted this gig.

The Russian cut through the Casino gardens. He walked past the brasserie of the Café de Paris and ignored the perfumed and trendily-coiffed diners who stationed themselves under broad, white umbrellas to watch the tourists parading the Casino Square, and, more pointedly, to be watched by them. He stopped only when he arrived at the foot of the staircase of the famous Casino de Monte Carlo.

He looked back up the hill from where he had come. All that showed of Villa St Eustace was a small, yellow rectangle consisting of the far right corner of the top two stories, and one skylight of the red-tiled mansard. The service annex was completely hidden behind taller buildings.

This pleased him.

He had seen all that he needed to see, but he would linger a few moments.

As he pretended to merge with a cluster of day-trippers from the cruise ship in the harbor, he looked at his watch. He expected William Mahler, the owner of the top floor apartment, to show up at Le Bar Américain just about then, as was Mahler's custom almost every summer evening.

Mahler did not disappoint.

His silver Maybach, which would have made a one-minute journey from the garage of Villa St Eustace, crawled to a stop in front of the Belle Epoch confection known as the Hôtel de Paris, just yards away from the Casino.

On cue, a liveried doorman trotted down the steps of the hotel and removed a red, velvet cordon from a pair of bollards. The Maybach eased into the now free parking space closest to the hotel entrance.

The chauffeur — in all black, from cap to glistening shoes — emerged and removed a wheelchair from the trunk, which the doorman promptly whisked away to the top of the staircase. A stocky man dressed in a white, short-sleeved uniform — evidently a male nurse — exited the front passenger side.

With much deference and obvious pride at being part of the spectacle, the two men eased their silver-haired and slightly portly employer from his place in the backseat. This took some time as there were two legs in plaster casts to fuss about. Each man draped one of Mahler's arms over his shoulders, and they ferried their precious cargo up the stairs.

Tanned, wearing a cream, bespoke suit and carrying the air of a man of enormous means, Mahler settled into the wheelchair with a smile. The doorman unlocked a rarely-used glass door and the nurse wheeled Mahler's chair through it. They paused at the statue of Louis XIV mounted on a horse, and then disappeared in the direction of Le Bar Américain.

"Was that some old movie star or something?" a middle-aged man among the cruise ship passengers said.

"Heck if I know," someone replied.

"If ever I become wheelchair-bound, *that* is the way I want to go," the first man said.

"Sure, Gary; all you have to do is win the lottery first," a voice rang out, and the clutch of passengers erupted in laughter.

The Russian circled around to the back of the casino. The dark blue Mediterranean stretched for miles before him. A dozen triangular, white sails bobbed in the distance, but his eyes focused only on the Monte Carlo Bay Hotel, which practically squatted in the sea on a plot of reclaimed land at the farthest southeastern edge of the principality.

Fran Mahler, William Mahler's wife, was there now. She had spent the previous day in Milan, and, to the casual observer, it would have appeared that she had been preoccupied there with meeting the Milanese event management firm she had hired for the gala dinner she was to host at the Monte Carlo Bay on the coming Saturday. The Russian, however, had arranged for her to be watched; word had got back to him that a beefy, young Italian male model had trailed a discreet distance behind Mrs Mahler, and had eventually entered her Milan hotel room.

Carmela Greene, the owner of the apartment below Mahler's, was off on a luxury cruise in the South Seas and was not expected back for several weeks. Daniel Greene, her son, who lived in London, would have landed in Nice a short time ago. Mrs Greene's chauffeur had taken her late husband's Lamborghini out to the airport. The Russian expected Daniel Greene to arrive behind its wheel for a meeting with Mahler at the bar in about twenty minutes.

To the right, in the harbor below, sat the massive, white cruise ship which had disgorged the hordes of tourists who scurried about the principality. Ironically, it dwarfed the scores of boats lining the marina, the irony being that among them were some of the largest superyachts on the planet.

The last of the occupants of Villa St Eustace, Henry Maitland, was a guest aboard one of those boats, the dark blue one with the canary yellow deck chairs, which belonged to a New York media mogul. No doubt Maitland was somewhere close to the bar on the lower deck getting himself completely hammered, as was his daily habit.

From not far off, came the sound of a roaring engine. The beast-like growl was unmistakable to the Russian's ears. He strode back to the Casino Square, and arrived in time to see the red Murciélago crawl by a wall of admiring spectators. It found a place at the lawn-covered traffic circle in front of the Hôtel de Paris.

The scissor door rose and the driver emerged. Tall, lean, clean-shaven, and in his early thirties, he cut a striking figure in his denim jeans and a crisp, white shirt. Without making eye contact with anyone, he shut the door, slipped on a navy blue jacket, and bounded up the stairs to the hotel.

The Russian checked his watch. Daniel Greene had arrived fifteen minutes earlier than expected.

Either his flight had landed early, or, more likely, the Lambo had zipped like a bat out of hell along the rugged and treacherous cliff-hugging road known as the Moyen Corniche, which was Greene's preferred route into the principality.

The Russian pictured Greene charging along as if on the last lap of the Monte Carlo Grand Prix, disregarding all manner of traffic regulations, and leaving angry or — very likely — envious drivers in his wake.

"Never been this close to a Lambo before," said a young man who grinned and posed in front of Greene's car. "And look at all the other whips in this one spot — three Ferraris, a Maserati, and a Rolls! Just crazy man!"

"God, I wish I could live here," said the young woman who snapped pictures of the fellow with her cell phone. "Must be like waking up in a dream every morning."

The Russian glanced at the couple as he headed back toward Beausoleil. In their early twenties, he figured. He shook his head. They should have been old enough to realize that all that glitters is not gold.

A dream? The place ran on the greed and treachery that made his chosen profession viable.

And in little more than forty-eight hours — if granted the opportunity — he would become the worst nightmare of someone at Villa St Eustace.

Chapter 2

Daniel Greene stepped into Le Bar Américain.

His rather prominent nose cast a shadow on a just barely perceptible scar, which bore testimony to years of seemingly endless surgeries to correct a cleft lip. His light green eyes searched the room.

From his wheelchair, parked at a table behind the unoccupied piano, Mahler had a clear view of Greene. He had long felt sorry for the young man. He imagined those childhood years spent in and out of hospital must have been rough on Greene, especially given the circumstances which caused the boy to battle his medical challenges practically on his own. And he knew growing up as Isaac Greene's son would not have been any walk in the park, either.

But the one thing Mahler would not endure from anyone was intrusion into his turf at Magrelma Mines. The whiff of competition that he had caught from Greene was enough to wipe out the smattering of sympathy in Mahler's breast for the younger man.

For three decades, he had slugged, schemed, and schmoozed in order to steer the company to the plateau of success. His partners had learned early to bow to his sway; the kid would have to learn to fall in line, too.

Over the past few weeks, Mahler had disregarded Greene's calls and emails. And now, here was Greene, his eyes searching the room, his face telegraphing his determination to no longer be ignored.

Two companions at Mahler's table helped themselves to a platter of wafer-thin potato chips. The company and the glass of cognac he had already imbibed served to heighten Mahler's natural congeniality. He began on his second drink and made up his mind not to let the inevitable encounter with Greene kill the spirit of the evening.

His eyes met Greene's when the younger man finally turned in his direction. Mahler waved him over.

"Daniel, you haven't met Richard Pimms and George Crawford have you?" Mahler said above the din of the bar. "Richard,

George, this is Isaac's boy. Taking up at Magrelma where his father left off."

The men got up and extended their hands toward Greene.

He, however, kept his stare firmly on Mahler.

"I didn't come to socialize."

Unfazed by the brusqueness of youth and warmed by the extra old elixir, Mahler dismissed his companions with a tilt of the head. He motioned Greene to sit.

"Did you remember to stroke the horse?" Mahler said.

"What?"

"The statue out front. They say stroking the horse's knee brings good luck."

Greene said nothing.

Mahler continued. "Your father and I used to do it almost religiously. Except he only did it if he was going to the Casino afterward. But I stroke the horse every time I pass through those doors. Been doing it since the first day I moved here. Sure has worked for me."

"I make my own luck."

Greene's eyes were cold disks topped by thick eyebrows and underlined by dark lower lids. There was no goodwill there, Mahler thought.

He waved to beckon a waiter from the opposite corner of the bar.

"What will you have?" Mahler asked Greene.

"Nothing."

"Hey, kid, relax. You've got to learn to take things easy. Enjoy life. Enjoy the *good* stuff. Look, I'll get you one of what I'm having."

The waiter arrived and Mahler ordered another cognac.

"So, how's your mother?" Mahler said. "You know, this is so typical of Monaco; we live in the same building and I never see her. How's she doing?"

"Haven't seen her in a while."

"I know how it is. The women around here, when they start on their soirees, and lunches, and whatever the hell it is that they get up to, they become so busy, they have no time for anybody."

Mahler leaned in conspiratorially toward Greene.

"Take Fran as the prime example. I can't remember when last we exchanged two proper sentences between us. Seems like months she's been planning this bloody dinner she's having this weekend. Got the prince, himself, to be the patron. But it's a ruse, I tell you."

Mahler lifted his glass and winked before taking a sip. "This business about the dinner to raise funds for some charitable cause or the other, it's all a ruse. I think her real plan is to try to seduce the prince and take off behind him."

Mahler threw back his head and chuckled.

"Can you believe such a thing? I've given her everything money can buy these last nineteen years — the jewellery, the clothes, the properties around the world, a life of unending vacations. And yet, in a heartbeat, I promise you she'd leave me to run off after him — if she had the chance. The lucky thing is she has so much competition, and younger competition, too, from all–"

"Can we cut the crap?" Greene growled.

Mahler stared at him.

The waiter reappeared. Tension hung thick in the air as a white-gloved hand placed the balloon glass of golden liquid before Greene.

Mahler fingered his own glass and looked around the room.

"Syron Lake," Greene said after the waiter left.

"What about it?"

"Did you read the report I sent you?"

Mahler sighed. He brought his glass to his lips and emptied it slowly.

"It's been more than a month now," Greene said.

"Look, kid–"

"Do I look like a kid to you?"

Mahler observed the flared nostrils, and felt the cold steeliness of Greene's eyes.

"Fair enough. Look, Daniel, what that report calls for is impossible. It simply can't be done. Not with the kind of regulations that are in place."

"Since when did Magrelma Mines let rules and regulations stop it?"

Mahler let out a sharp breath. "Syron Lake is in Canada, damn it."

Greene narrowed his eyes into a piercing stare.

Mahler shook his head. "Look, forget about whatever leverage we may have elsewhere. Government controls are shaky in Africa and the former Soviet Union. Canada's different. And besides, you're talking about a former *uranium* mine. That's a whole different ballgame. You just can't do whatever you want with those things."

"But did you read the projections in the report?"

Mahler rapped his fingers on the table.

"Did you even get the potential of this thing?" Greene said.

"Listen to me, and listen carefully." Mahler leaned in toward Greene. "The only reason we bought that Syron Lake company was to get its operating mine in Saskatchewan. But as for Syron Lake, itself — the original property in Ontario — that's worthless.

"In fact, it's worse than worthless. It's a damned albatross around our necks. Just a pile of bloody uranium waste that has to be kept under protective cover for all eternity."

Mahler leaned back. "The only saving grace is that we get to pass it off to the government, eventually. And I tell you, as soon as the chance to do that comes up, later this year, we're grabbing it with both hands."

"But if you read the report-"

"Enough!" Mahler slapped the table. "That report is pure, unadulterated bull!"

Greene's jaws tightened.

Mahler shifted in his chair as much as his leg casts would allow. "I don't know who's feeding you these things, but this Syron Lake project is going nowhere as long as I head this company."

Greene stared ahead in silence.

Mahler looked around the room. He caught several hastily averted eyes and continued in a lower voice.

"Listen, Daniel, in this business, you get all kinds of people coming at you with all kinds of plans and projects. But you have to sniff them out. You can't jump at every report and all the fanciful projections that pass under your nose. No! Even if that report had any merit to it, if we acted on it, it would stir up so much hell, this whole company could blow up."

Mahler looked at Greene's chest rapidly heaving and falling, as if the younger man, himself, was about to explode.

"Look," Mahler said in a mellower tone, "I know you're just trying to jump in there with two feet and do your part. I realize you and Isaac didn't always get along, and maybe your father didn't give you enough credit for your abilities. But *I* know you're an intelli–"

Greene stood up abruptly and his chair screeched as it shifted away. He leaned over the table toward Mahler and spoke through clenched teeth.

"Don't patronize me."

He straightened himself, turned on his heels, and marched off.

Mahler watched him exit the bar, then reached over for the untouched glass.

The two companions from earlier returned.

"That one sure seems wound up," Pimms said as they sat.

"Bloody cokehead," Mahler said.

"Oh, one of those." Pimms nodded to Crawford.

"I don't understand it," Mahler said after a sip. "The kid grew up wanting for nothing. Isaac near killed himself working to build this company. Isaac, his cousin Bernard, Henry, and I...we all worked our tails off.

"We were young renegades. Sure we bent some rules here and there. We did what we had to do to make a name for ourselves and give to our families the best in life. And for what? For a young punk like that to thrash everything we worked so hard to build by going off on some coke-fueled fantasy?"

"It's a different generation, Bill," Crawford offered.

"Different is right," Mahler said. "With that attitude of his, that kid won't survive in this business."

Chapter 3

The bush two feet ahead on the forest trail shook, and I froze.

It wasn't the work of the wind. In fact, the morning air was still.

Something was there, moving among the shrubs.

My first thought was to dash back to the motel where I'd parked the rented cargo van. At the front desk, the receptionist had said the shortcut through the woods would lead straight into the town. I'd been driving for five hours that morning alone, so I had relished the idea of stretching my legs.

But now, the inescapable truth filled me with panic: I was in a real forest, and within two feet of some wild creature.

Ironically, this was what I'd wanted when I had decided to move two thousand miles from Vancouver to this remote town, deep in the Northern Ontario forest — *to be close to Nature.*

For the last month as I'd thought about relocating to Syron Lake, I'd pictured myself camouflaged among the bushes, watching in awe as moose, elk, or deer foraged before my eyes in their natural environment.

But what if it was a great, big, angry black bear lurking in the bushes?

I hadn't expected to meet such danger, and certainly not within minutes of arriving.

The branches rattled again. My heart slammed against my ribcage.

A tiny, brown limb poked through the leaves. I screamed and jumped back. The rest of the ball-like body came into view, and, immediately, my fear began to ease.

A hare: it was nothing but a hare.

"Phew!"

The sound that escaped my lips seemed to startle the animal. It made as if to dart off, but got nowhere, and the bush near it shook violently. Sunlight glinted off a translucent, blue ring around one of the hare's back legs. Some carelessly discarded plastic bag had snagged it.

The hare bucked, cracking brambles and tearing off leaves.

Its thrashing had me shaking, even though it was just a tiny critter.

I'd always been a scaredy-cat. I was nothing but a mousey slip of a girl who was squeamish about the sight of blood and would run from the scene if she saw people do as little as raise their fists against each other. And I was scared now. What if the hare bit my hand or jumped and scratched my eyes? What if it was diseased?

But I couldn't leave the poor thing trapped like that to starve and die, or to be eaten by some ravenous predator.

My trembling hands grabbed the plastic even as the hare pranced about. Its soft body brushed against my knuckles and made my insides go cold. I held my breath and tugged at the plastic with everything I had until, finally, it burst.

The hare didn't hesitate for even a second. It shot across the trail, and disappeared in the undergrowth.

I fell back on my buttocks. My mind rewound the adrenalin rush of last few moments. I'd been terrified of some unknown creature lurking in the bush, and it turned out to be a tiny fur-ball that had been even more scared of *me*.

I threw my head back and laughed.

My eyes welled up, and the laughter soon turned into sobs.

It was bound to happen.

Tears had been streaming down my cheeks almost non-stop since I'd loaded up the van with all my worldly possessions and set out from the west coast, six days earlier.

Four weeks before that, I had been told I was out of a job as editor of the website and newsletter of a small non-profit that fought to protect B.C.'s salmon. It was the downturn in the economy, my boss had said. Funding had dried up and the organization had to shut down.

It seemed everything had been pushing me out of Vancouver, anyway.

My uncle, who lived in California and whom I'd never met, had suddenly called to say he was selling my grandparents house from under me. I'd lived with my grandparents since my last year of high school, when my father had died, and I became an orphan; we'd got on so well that I'd continued to stay with them after graduating from journalism college. When they died in a car crash and my uncle inherited the place, he had let me stay on for a nominal rent as he'd had no plans to return to Canada. The arrangement lasted almost three years, until he, too, got burned in the global financial meltdown. He needed to liquidate assets in a hurry. He'd given me mere weeks to pack up and leave.

And then, there was Peter.

I'd told myself this was *The One*. Third time's a charm, I'd thought. My first two romances had both been like wet fireworks that sparked at first and died quickly without ever going anywhere. But Peter and I had been together for fourteen giddy months, during which my mind had constantly conjured up images of our future — of him getting down on his knees with a ring; of us strolling barefoot on a beach on our honeymoon; of him changing diapers or fumbling with a bottle, and of me giggling and giving encouragement and instructions.

Since the middle of spring, though, every time we met, we inevitably ended up fighting. Even something as stupid as whether he'd used the term "vegan" correctly had blown up into an argument that'd killed all romantic possibilities the last time we'd seen each other.

We hadn't officially broken up. But he'd talked on the phone about needing some space. Well, fine. I would take what he'd said literally. I would show I was strong enough to be the one who created that space.

I would run away from him.

But in the convoluted logic of a love-addled mind, I felt I was running *to* him when I left Vancouver and headed off to Syron Lake.

It was his home town, after all.

After he'd left to attend university in Vancouver, he had never returned, not even at Christmas, although his father still lived in Syron Lake. As the media relations officer of a large environmental organization in Vancouver, Peter could hardly see himself settling back home where there were no such job prospects. But he and I had bonded in our early days over our mutual hatred of big city life, and our common desire to move to a small town where we could live at a slower pace, and be close to Nature.

Everything happens for a reason, my grandfather used to say. And, trying to make sense of the previous hellish month, I figured

I'd been pushed out of Vancouver so that I could live that quiet, small town life I'd said I really wanted.

Deep down, I hoped that if Peter realized I'd established myself in Syron Lake, and that if I got to know his old man — who I imagined would probably be going down in age — well, I hoped that Peter, too, would come to choose the lifestyle *he* had said he really wanted. And, maybe, when he did, he would come to decide that what he really wanted included me, too. Maybe....

A chorus of birds chirped in the trees overhead. The only other sound was my jagged sobbing.

At that moment, I felt completely broken and alone in a big, unfriendly world.

But crying couldn't change a stitch.

Eventually the sobs turned into sniffles. I dried my cheeks with the ends of my sleeves and pulled a small mirror from the sling bag I carried. Bloodshot eyes stared back at me, their dark brown irises dull, their pupils soulless. Dark, puffy eyelids called attention to themselves on an ashen face.

No, that wouldn't do for my morning's mission.

I slapped my cheeks, and put on a coat of lipstick. I took several deep breaths of the cool, pine-scented air. Finally, I felt ready to move on.

I followed the trail out of the forest and abruptly found myself in what looked like a slice of suburbia.

Neat bungalows and a row of cheerful, redbrick townhouses lined the street. Dusty pickups and shiny sedans squatted in the driveways. Garden gnomes watched over late summer blooms of blue monkshood, pink turtleheads, oxeye daisies, and baby's breath. Almost all the front lawns were trimmed low and many bore small, plastic signs urging anyone who noticed to vote for someone or the other for mayor or council.

But it was another type of sign that I was interested in. My eyes honed in on anything bearing the magic words: "For Sale."

Houses were dirt cheap in this town. The real estate section in an old copy of the *Syron Lake Beacon* that I'd once seen at Peter's place had sent my pulse racing when I'd realized that for less than a down payment on a rundown Vancouver starter home, I could have an entire, three-bedroom house in Syron Lake.

My plan was simple: get a nice two-story, take in tenants on the upper floors, and use the rent to pay the mortgage while I lived — at no cost — in the basement.

I calculated that I had just about enough from a small inheritance from my grandparents and from my own savings for a down payment and for food and necessities for one and a half, maybe, even two (very) frugal years. I wouldn't have to work. I could finally get a start on that romance novel that I'd been dreaming of writing since childhood.

At age twenty-six, it was about time for me to give it a shot.

The street descended to the commercial part of the town, marked by nondescript two-story buildings. I found the office I was looking for and a bell tinkled as I pushed through the glass door.

"Mr Ada?"

"Mrs Jacob?" A short man with a shock of white hair bounded from behind his desk and stretched out his hand toward me. "You're in good time."

"Actually it's 'Ms.' But, please, call me Stella."

"Okay, Stella. Good to meet you in person, but you're nothing like I imagined from your phone call."

I raised my eyebrows.

"I was expecting someone older. It's mostly retirees who move up here." He grabbed a pile of papers and a bunch of keys. "I made a list of places that might work for you. Shall we get going?"

In the car, he had all the conviviality of a seasoned salesman.

"So where are you from?"

"Vancouver."

"Ah, but I hear a slight accent. I'm thinking somewhere in the Caribbean. Jamaica, perhaps?"

"Actually, I was born in Toronto, but grew up in Trinidad."

"Trinidad? Is that the one with the Carnival?"

"Yes."

The island — home to the descendants of British, French, and Spanish colonists; African slaves; East Indian, Chinese, and Portuguese indentured laborers; Jewish, Syrian, and Lebanese later arrivals; and the original Amerindian settlers — was best known for the annual festival that brought its people out into the streets to dance and party together, regardless of race, religion, or social status.

"I've always wanted to go for Carnival," Ada said. "Heard it's lots of fun."

"It is. You should go."

"One of these good days, I will. But how come you're coming all the way from Vancouver?"

"After my mom died, my dad married a Trinidadian and we moved to the island when I was five. When my dad passed away, I went to live with his parents out West."

"Well, you'll find that Syron Lake's a lot different from the pace of life in a big city like Vancouver, and it's no tropical paradise, that's for sure. But it's alright."

"It's surprisingly civilized for a former mining town the middle of the forest."

"That's thanks to the retirees. They sell their homes in Toronto, move up here, and get something for a tenth of what their old house was worth. And that leaves them with a pile of cash to fix up their new place."

I bit my lip. Hearing about retirees and their piles of home renovation cash made me suddenly embarrassed about my own plans, which now seemed rash and vague.

"I'm afraid only the first two places we're going to look at actually have a mother-in-law suite," Ada said. "It's just not something people around here are into, I guess."

Those first two houses were way beyond my budget. Still, I'd read up on creative financing and egged the agent on to call the owners to see if they'd let me take over their mortgages. That was a non-starter.

We spent the rest of the day crisscrossing Syron Lake. Ada took me to more than a dozen other places that were less expensive, but their unfinished or moldy basements made them unsuitable for my purpose.

By late afternoon, we had exhausted Ada's list. The hope that had earlier seen me bound into the agent's office was now replaced by a sinking feeling.

"Okay, Stella, I know you've said you don't want to limit yourself." Ada's voice seemed to strain to maintain a cheerful friendliness. "And I know you think that, as you say, with creative financing, anything is possible. But you've got to give me a figure to work with, otherwise we could just be wasting a lot of time here."

I didn't like being pushed. But I could tell the agent had reached the end of his patience.

"Thirty. Thirty-five, max," I said.

Ada snorted. "We haven't seen that kind of price in years."

My Syron Lake dreams were quickly shriveling.

The real estate agent tapped his thumbs on the steering wheel. Perhaps what he really wanted to do was kick me out of his car.

"Actually, there is this one place," Ada said after a while. "I'm not sure it's suitable for you. It's kinda out of the way. But we might as well give it a look before we call it quits today."

He drove for several minutes out of town and then turned off on a narrow road. We continued on another few minutes, during which I saw only two other houses in between the trees. Ada pulled into the driveway of a long and somewhat shabby bungalow, and parked beside an old pickup.

"Looks like the owner's here. Built this himself. There's no mortgage on the place. He just put it up, bit by bit whenever he could afford it."

Despite the dented, faded siding and curling asphalt roof tiles, the place had a certain charm, mostly because it was nestled among gorgeous maples and majestic pines. If I lived here, all I had to do was look outside the great, big bay window at the front of the house for all the inspiration I needed to write.

Through that window, I saw a gaunt figure shuffle across the room. "You said he owns the place outright?"

"Uh-huh. A former miner. Lived here by himself; no wife or children. When the mines closed, he moved to an apartment down South and rented out this place. But he's had a string of bad tenants the last few years and now he just wants to sell up. I listed the house for him fifteen months ago. Not too many takers, even though he's asking forty for it."

My pulse began to race.

The price was still too high, but I would negotiate. I would beg, grovel, and do whatever it took. I was even ready to use the weapon I most hated resorting to: my womanly wiles.

It was the editor at my first job at a tiny Vancouver paper called *The Sentinel* who had showed me how to smile and lower my head and look up with vulnerable eyes. He'd taught me the words to use to appear like a damsel in distress who admired a man's strength and wisdom, and needed him to save the day. Then he had unleashed me on the cops. He would laugh at editors on bigger newspapers who would meet him in the bar on Friday nights and wonder aloud how *The Sentinel* consistently scooped them on the crime beat with a rookie reporter. I worked those womanly wiles on the cops and got the stories, but felt cheap and exploited. That's why when I'd heard of the opening at the salmon non-profit, I had immediately jumped for it.

Now, my mind tried to retrieve all that I'd learned from my old editor.

I went full throttle. Beamed at the house seller. Played with my shoulder-length, jet-black hair, and nonchalantly stroked my collarbone. Touched the old fellow lightly on the upper arm, and leaned into him as I spoke. Asked about his life, and laughed at anything he said that was remotely funny. Told of how I was just starting out in life, myself. Of how I found the place he had created to be unique and enchanting, and of how I would treasure it, as a hopeful, young writer....

Three hours later, I walked out the door with a signed agreement.

"So you beat his price down to thirty-two grand and got him to give you a vendor take-back mortgage," Ada said as we got into his car. "That's some kinda negotiation skills you've got there, young lady."

"Oh, I don't know about that," I mumbled. I knew it was all down to pure desperation.

As we pulled off, the house seller came outside and shuffled around to the back.

"He's in a bad way," Ada said pensively. "Thinner and frailer than when I last saw him."

"You're not trying to imply that I took advantage of an old man, are you?"

"No, no. I've seen him become cantankerous with buyers who tried to lowball him. He seemed to have taken quite a shine to you."

I remained quiet.

"My commission may be lower because of that deal, but, actually, I think it's a lucky thing that you showed up today to take this place off his hands," Ada said. "At his age, he needs to let go of that house, stay down South, and just take care of his health."

Lucky for him and lucky for me. It turned out that I wouldn't even need tenants as I could more than manage the monthly payments we'd agreed to. I now had a whole, big house in the woods to myself, where I could comfortably and happily write up a storm.

Moving to Syron Lake felt like the best decision I'd ever made.

Little did I know how quickly all my expectations would be turned upside down.

Chapter 4

At half an hour before midnight on Saturday, Monaco was alive and buzzing. Throngs looking for a grand time on the Riviera filled the Casino Square, and flooded the waterfront bars and lounges. Euro techno and American hip-hop blasted out of jam-packed clubs and mingled with the sound of the Mediterranean rolling in and crashing on the rocky shoreline.

The Russian parked his motorcycle high on the hill in Beausoleil. Dressed in all black fatigues and tabi boots, and carrying a bulging, black backpack, he made it on foot down to Villa St Eustace. He encountered not a soul.

There were no glamorous nightspots here, only villas, apartment buildings, two office towers, a dental office, a jewelry repair shop, and a stationery store. No one would be in this street at this time unless they had a good reason to be there.

The assassin slipped into a narrow passageway and stood before the service entrance of Villa St Eustace. Behind the door was a staircase that went straight to the top, to the mansard where the servants' quarters were. That was where he needed to be.

Picking the lock would have been easy; for him it was a minor, low-level skill. But there were cameras inside, one on the ceiling of every floor.

The only safe way to enter was from the roof.

He knew every inch and all the innards of the building. The client had supplied the blueprints.

It was a century-old villa built by a Russian merchant who'd been ordered by doctors to "take the waters" on the Mediterranean in his dying days. Knowing that his offspring rarely got along with each other, the old man had designed the villa to contain five separate apartments, each one occupying an entire floor. The property had remained in the hands of the merchant's descendants until sold to Magrelma Mines almost two decades prior.

Originally, each of the four founders had had an apartment, and the company's office had occupied the ground floor. Upon the death of the oldest among them, Bernard Ellis, whose wife returned to New York, the office expanded to two floors.

The third floor belonged to Henry Maitland, who was divorced and kept no domestic staff. Carmela Greene owned the floor above that. Mahler had the top-most apartment, with the best view.

And just above him was the mansard. Divided into eight hutches for the servants, each room was so small there was little space for anything other than a twin bed.

The assassin aimed a REBS compact grapnel launcher at the roof and fired. The rubber-coated hook shot into air and landed with only the slightest thud on the terracotta tiles. He tugged on the rope until it snapped taut.

He checked the street again. All clear.

The split of his tabi boots allowed him to grasp the rope with his toes as well as his hands. In less than a minute he had climbed up onto the roof.

Intermittent reminders of the nearby revelry in the Casino Square floated up to his ears: loud laughter, a screech of tires, someone calling out to someone else. But he snaked his way across the roof with the assurance that he was shielded from view by the giant jacaranda and the taller commercial buildings around him.

He stopped at the skylight of the room belonging to Mrs Greene's maid. He took a radiator hose pick out of his backpack, and with deft flicks of his wrist, he worked past the skylight's weatherstripping until he caught hold of the latch and popped it open.

The room was the closest one to the stairwell. It was empty. According to the client, there would be no one in the mansard that night. Mrs Greene had left the week before with her maid for her cruise. Fran Mahler had given her servants the weekend off as she would spend Sunday at the Monte Carlo Bay after the gala finished in the wee hours of the morning. Three of the rooms were used to store extra files and equipment from the Magrelma office; but it was highly unlikely that anyone would be working that late on a Saturday to have any cause to come up to the mansard.

The killer had the floor to himself.

The first order of business was the security camera.

It was a stationary unit, which pointed down the stairwell, and was trained on the back door to Mahler's apartment. There was no device surveying the other direction — the corridors of the servants' floor. The inherent snobbery of this arrangement was to the Russian's advantage.

He placed a chair from the room as close as possible to the security camera. He climbed up on it, pointed a Fujifilm Instax 210 Instant Camera in the same direction as the security camera, and clicked. In seconds, he had a printed replica of the scene.

Working quickly, he passed a black card before the lens to mask the act of mounting the picture directly in front of the security camera. If anyone was actually monitoring the camera feed in the security post in the basement, it would have looked as if the equipment experienced a momentary lapse. It would easily have been taken as an unremarkable blip, after which the normal view was restored.

He returned the chair to the room, packed away the instant camera, and took out a smaller sack with gear for the next stage. Footsteps coming up the stairs made him dart to the door. He closed it and breathed silently as he listened.

The client had stipulated no guns. But the Russian was wearing a piece. He had to be prepared for all eventualities.

The footsteps were slow and shuffling. Whoever was out there passed right in front of the door, then continued to the corridor on the opposite side of the stairwell.

Keys jangled; a lock tumbled.

The assassin cracked open the door just in time to see what looked like a female figure disappear into a room at the far end of the corridor opposite. The door closed behind her.

She could be in there all night. Or she could re-emerge at any moment.

He couldn't dwell on this unexpected complication. There was no time to. He would continue as planned. If she got in the way, he just would have to eliminate her and get rid of the body.

He sprinted past the security camera and down to the landing where the stairs changed direction, just above Mahler's back door.

He would not attempt entry through the back door. The state-of-the-art double locks were nothing he couldn't handle. The problem was that any attempt to pick them would set off the alarm.

Once inside the apartment, he expected to find the security code written down and kept on Mahler's nightstand. The client had said Mahler had promised the rest of the villa's occupants that he would keep the code handy after one too many incidents in which Mahler had stepped out to the back stairwell for a smoke only to have a piercing alarm rip through the building because he hadn't remembered the numbers to punch in to turn off the system.

The code would quicken the Russian's exit after he completed his mission. Now, though, his whole focus was on gaining entry.

The blueprints had exposed the building's internal vulnerability, and now he would exploit it. The garbage chute was a solid steel tube which ran from the vent in the roof to the trash compactor in the basement. It gave an access point to every apartment.

The Russian swung the side-hinged door open and affixed two switchable magnetic welding clamps to the steel walls of the chute. He climbed through the door and slid himself, feet first, into the narrow shaft.

Strapped loosely to his ankles were two more clamps. The split-toe tabi-boots gave him flexibility and control. He positioned the dangling devices against the wall and used his toes to turn on the magnets.

Having created a foothold, he straightened himself. He grabbed onto of one of the upper clamps with one hand, and, with his free hand, pulled the door shut.

Darkness engulfed him. A lesser man would have been deterred by the pitch blackness, the claustrophobic space, the awkward, suspended position, and the sure knowledge that failure of the magnets or a misstep would send him hurtling some fifty feet into the jaws of a merciless compactor that would close in and crush the life out of him.

The Russian, though, would let no obstacle stand in the way of his million-dollar payment.

His muscles were tense. Beads of perspiration formed on his

brow. But he controlled his breathing and allowed only thoughts of successfully completing his progress through the shaft to play across his mind.

Switching the magnets on and off and shifting them down, each in turn, he lowered himself. Nothing else in the world existed at that moment other than each inch of patient descent. Finally, he was at the opening to Mahler's apartment.

He pushed in the chute door, squeezed through the opening, and rolled onto the floor of the dark utility room.

According to the client, only Mahler and the male nurse would be in.

The plan was to take out the attendant first.

The nurse was a former green beret who had been kicked out of the Army for misconduct on account of a heroin addiction that once nearly cost him his life. The man had cleaned up after some years and had retrained for a new career, eventually landing this gig in the Disney World for the wealthy. He'd been on the job for six months.

The drug abuse may have done some damage, but who could tell what an ex-green beret's reflexes might be. The Russian knew he would have to be fast, and precise.

Hidden in the darkness at the end of a long corridor, he scanned the scene.

The drapes were closed and all lights in the cavernous living room were off, except for track lights over the home bar in the alcove to the left.

The nurse sat on a stool at the bar with his back to the Russian. A television on the wall behind the counter showed a baseball match. The volume was turned down.

The man paid no attention to the screen. He kept his head bent, focusing on something on the counter. An open decanter and a half-empty glass were to his right.

From what he knew of ruthless, corporate warriors like Mahler, the Russian figured the drink was not courtesy of Mahler's largess. The illicit enjoyment of his employer's grog would be the nurse's last experience on the planet. How in character for an ex-officer who'd dishonored his green beret, the Russian thought.

The attack from behind was swift. The killer caught the nurse in a headlock and pressed a rag soaked with Deslurane over the man's nose. The nurse barely had a chance to react. His hand reached up, but his fingers could only weakly wrap themselves around the Russian's gloved hand. The ether knocked him out cold.

The substance was not intended to cause the final exit. However, it bought the Russian time. He let the nurse slump forward onto the counter.

He had originally planned to place the nurse on the long sofa which sat near the voluminous drapes. All would serve as good tinder.

But the bar now presented a better opportunity. It was closer to Mahler's room. And, on the counter, stood a wine rack in the form of a twisted wire sculpture that suspended six bottles at impossible angles. All good fuel.

The killer emptied paraphernalia from his sack onto the counter: a syringe, a spoon, a lighter, a vial of water, and a packet of white power — the purest heroin. He emptied the packet into the spoon, added a few drops of water, and lit the lighter under the spoon. Then he filled the syringe.

Finding a suitable spot to inject was a challenge. The nurse's hand was riddled with needle marks. The Russian had to roll the man's sleeve way up above the elbow.

He plunged in the needle and squeezed the syringe. Whatever the ex-green beret's tolerance level before, the stuff that now coursed through his veins was so potent, there was no way he would survive.

Sighs and moans from the television were the only sounds in Mahler's bedroom. The lights were off, but the chamber glowed and went dark as porn scenes flickered on the giant flat screen on the wall. Mahler was fast asleep in his bed.

The titan had spent a lifetime battling foes and ordering around the men under him as he built the monumental, globe-spanning empire that he now controlled. The sense of being in control was the one thing corporate warriors like Mahler craved most, the Russian thought. They hungered for it more than money itself, more than love, more than physical pleasures. The assassin was sure the idea of being so powerless, so completely vulnerable in his final moments would have been utterly abominable to Mahler.

All the same, the man would have a beautiful death, the Russian thought.

He placed a breathing mask over Mahler's nose. Attached to a canister of carbon monoxide, it delivered enough of the toxic gas to choke more than half of the oxygen out of his blood.

Mahler would continue to breathe for a few minutes again, but he would never wake up.

The Russian found the alarm code scribbled on a Post-it note that was stuck to a cigarette case. He memorized it and returned to the living room.

Setting the fire was his final task.

He picked up the decanter from the bar counter and sniffed. The aroma of caramel and vanilla pleased him. It was a fine bourbon, and, with an alcohol content of at least forty percent, it would make a fine fuel.

He placed the decanter to the left of the nurse's body. Then he shoved the deadweight along the counter and straight into the bourbon and the wine rack.

All hit the floor with a terrific crash. Glass splintered, and amber and red liquids streaked the plush, beige carpet.

A paperback novel, *The Broker*, which the nurse had apparently been reading, had slid off the counter as well.

The Russian took a half-smoked cigarette out of his pocket. He re-lit it and placed it beneath the alcohol-soaked cover of the book.

He waited.

The embers died.

He lit the cigarette again. This time, the pages ignited. He watched the flames grow wilder and begin to travel the course of the spill.

His work was done.

He entered the alarm code, shut the back door behind him, and bounded up the steps. It took less time to remove the photo from the security camera than it had taken to install it, mostly because the thought of the spreading flames and the fire alarm they would soon trigger propelled his every muscle. He packed all his equipment, and climbed out through the skylight.

Back down on the street, the coast was clear. He skipped up a flight of stairs that led to the French border and noiselessly bounded up the hill to his motorcycle.

The bike would be left in a garage in Nice. He had arranged

for it to be picked up before dawn to be melted down as scrap.

He, himself, would be on a plane bound for Macau within the hour.

It was the perfect crime; it would never be detected, and he would never be caught. The client would be well pleased.

As the assassin donned his helmet, his lips spread in a faint smile at the thought of the string of zeroes that would soon be added to his bank balance.

Chapter 5

Spike Simmons straightened his tie and tamped down the lapels of his jacket as he stepped into the elevator. He pushed the button for FBI Director Robert Hutton's floor and scanned the notes he'd scribbled on a small pad. In his mind, he rehearsed what he would say and exactly how he would say it.

He'd been in group briefings with the director a couple of times before, but this would be his first one-on-one with Hutton and he wanted to come off looking good.

The man was a legend. A decorated Army intelligence officer-turned-lawyer who later spent years abroad as a diplomat, Hutton had been running the Bureau with a steady hand for twelve years under three different administrations. And he had another two years left before retirement. The four years' extension to what would normally have been a ten-year term had come at the special request of the president who shared his predecessors' implacable faith in Hutton's leadership.

The timing of the meeting with Hutton that Saturday afternoon, however, could not have been worse.

It was Simmons' weekend with his son, Reg, and the two of them were supposed to have been at the cinema right about this time, watching *Lottery Ticket* and laughing their heads off at the antics of Bow Wow and the gang. That outing, itself, was supposed to have made up for having to cancel their trip to the Redskins' training camp a couple of weeks before, again because of work.

His ex had been decent about taking the boy back at short notice, though. She'd even refrained from giving that look, the one by which she would usually let Simmons know she was relieved they weren't together anymore.

Now, he would have to try to think up some fantastic, mind-blowing activities to keep himself in the good books of a super intelligent nine-year-old. He had let things slide as husband, but he was sure as hell not going to strike out at being a dad.

Still, his job came first.

It was all he'd ever wanted to do, growing up in the tough

neighborhood of Capitol View. And it was all because of Mammy. His mother had been a receptionist with the FBI and would come home and fill his head with stories of the fine folk in spiffy clothes who checked in at her desk and dropped hints about the important and sometimes dangerous work they did to keep the nation safe.

She'd made up all of those stories, of course. Simmons quickly realized when he joined the Bureau right after college that nobody spilled such details to a lowly front lobby receptionist. But Mammy's deception had worked to keep him off the streets and dreaming in a different direction from his peers.

He was glad she had lived to see him get his badge. If she'd still been around, she would have clapped her hands and giggled to hear that he was to sit down with the great Hutton, himself, in his office.

He had barely set foot in the doorway when the low bass voice boomed in his ears.

"Simmons, what have we got on this William Mahler case?"

"Not much, I'm afraid, sir."

This was definitely not how Simmons had imagined things would go.

For a thirty-nine-year-old, he was pleased about having climbed a rung or two in the department that handled crimes committed abroad against US citizens. But it was by a fluke that he'd landed in the director's office.

There were four others in the chain of command above him who should have been in that meeting with Hutton. However, Callahan, his immediate superior, was in the hospital with a ruptured appendix; Baldwin was on vacation, and incommunicado at some fly-in fishing lodge; and Reginald and Tubman were off separately attending conferences in far-flung corners of the world. It was a groggy-sounding Reginald who'd called and ordered him to get his butt into the office, pronto, to brief the director on the death of a wealthy US businessman in Monaco.

Simmons had thought there'd first be an exchange of pleasantries and that, maybe, he'd have a chance to talk about how he enjoyed being part of the Bureau before he would ease into confessing his near empty-handedness on the Mahler case. But he understood; Director Hutton was a very busy man whose time you didn't waste with small talk. Even on a Saturday.

"Shut that door, will you," Hutton said.

Simmons obeyed, almost robotically.

The silver-haired director, at six feet, nine inches tall and with two hundred twenty-five pounds that gave only a hint of sagging on a seventy-two-year-old frame, was intimidating to the average person, and more so to a kid from Capitol View who sometimes still pinched himself to ensure his entire career with the Bureau wasn't all just a dream.

Dressed in his customary dark suit as if it were any ordinary workday, Hutton pointed his chin toward a chair in front of his desk. He leaned back in his executive chair with his fingers clasped over his broad chest and waited for Simmons to settle himself.

"So?" Hutton said.

Simmons cleared his throat. "It happened around midnight, Saturday, Monaco-time. Monaco is saying it looks like there was an accidental fire after Mahler's nurse OD'ed on heroin."

Hutton nodded.

"A former addict, it seems." Simmons found himself suddenly dependent on his notes. "Looks like he went off on some kind of suicidal binge. He was apparently drinking at the time, and smoking too. Cigarette ignited. Er... flames spread quickly before the fire service arrived. Mahler died of smoke inhalation. The nurse had major third degree burns. That's it; no further details."

"So, just a tragic accident?"

"Yes, sir."

"Well, that's what Monaco would say, wouldn't they?"

"That's the information they've given us, sir."

"Well, they have an image to protect. Nothing out of the ordinary ever happens there. Ever."

Simmons adjusted his tie. He felt Hutton's eyes scrutinizing every inch of his being.

"You know Mahler had his fair share of enemies among rival companies, don't you, Simmons?"

"Yes, sir."

"Mining is a cutthroat business. Any one of a number of his competitors could have wanted him dead."

"It's quite possible, sir."

"And you also know it's said that for a long time Magrelma Mines occupied, let's say, a special place among US business interests abroad, don't you?"

"I got clearance to access the files on Magrelma only this afternoon, sir. Didn't have the time to go through them fully before our meeting. But from what I understand, there's been speculation over the years that the company was a channel for the CIA to support opposition groups in certain countries where Magrelma had operations. Some of those groups came into government and that activity is said to have died off by the end of the nineties. But as far as I can tell, all of that is only speculation. The CIA has never confirmed any of this."

The director tapped his fingers on the armrest of his chair.

Simmons felt a knot form in his stomach. Okay. Big mistake. Never contradict the boss, or even give the slightest appearance of doing so. And especially not a boss like Hutton. As FBI Director, he was privy to secrets about everyone and everything that mattered. And it was quite conceivable that in his past life as a diplomat, he could have been in on the truth about Magrelma. Simmons knew well enough that all kinds of foreign service postings were used to mask the fact that a person was actually working for the CIA.

He coughed. "Of course, there could be some truth behind the speculation."

Hutton kept him in a steady gaze.

"Let's just suppose it were true," the director said. "And let's say Magrelma's support of opposition forces led to the ouster of some two-bit despot or the other. Well, Simmons, power is a very intoxicating thing. It elevates a man's sense of potency. Makes him feel invincible. It even deludes some into believing that they've somehow become immortal. Those who find it suddenly snatched out of their hands feel the sting for the rest of their lives. They may spend all their remaining days in a desperate fight to climb back to the lofty heights they once enjoyed. And if they get the opportunity, some will hound down and seek to destroy those they believe are responsible for their fall from grace."

Hutton sat up.

"So, you see, we can't assume, like Monaco, that things are as they seem. If we continue to suppose that Magrelma was a covert channel to promote a US agenda abroad, then there are serious implications if some person or some forces came after Mahler because they found out about his company's clandestine political role. It could even mean current US operations abroad have been compromised."

Simmons swallowed hard, but remained silent.

"So?" Hutton said.

Simmons knew the right answer was that he would report back to Callahan, or Baldwin, or Reginald, or Tubman and let them take things from there. But, at this moment, in the pregnant silence of the director's office, with the stern eyes of his ultimate boss pinning him, Simmons knew that that was also the wrong response.

He cleared his throat. "I'll contact Paris. Our legal attaché there could dispatch a couple of people to Monaco to collaborate on a full investigation."

"Good." Hutton stood up. "Stick with this file, Simmons. We must leave no stone unturned."

Simmons nodded and got to his feet.

"Keep me posted," Hutton said.

As soon as he closed the door behind him, Simmons yanked his tie loose.

Sure, he wanted to be known and to move up in the Bureau. But this case, which had landed in his lap simply because he was the only able-bodied man available on a weekend, had taken on an importance he hadn't remotely expected.

The director seemed to be into this case in a big way. Simmons wasn't sure he could survive this level of scrutiny.

Chapter 6

The state dinner for the Canadian prime minister was winding down. Having gorged and tippled, the guests were in high spirits as they floated out of the dining tent and sauntered to the entertainment tent on the South Lawn.

Robert L. Hutton detested such occasions for their pomposity and feigned congeniality. He had hosted his own share of them, on a smaller scale, of course, during his time at the missions in Cairo, Ottawa, and London. He had arrived tonight as late as was socially acceptable, and would slip away soon. But first, he had to take care of the real reason he was there.

His eyes narrowed as he scanned the stream of bejeweled and tuxedoed bodies passing by. After some time, he saw her: Secretary of State Angela Roseau.

She was headed his way, walking and speaking with Alfred Danforth, the Canadian deputy prime minister, and two other members of the visiting delegation. Hutton was glad that her almost eternal shadow — her fastidious chief of staff Kathy Wang — was nowhere in sight.

Dressed tonight in a long-sleeved, floor-length, teal gown, instead of her usual austere pants suit, she appeared more feminine and less like the formidable political animal she was known to be. He had been aware of this softer side to her going back twenty-five years to the time when she had arrived as a fresh-faced articling student at his law firm in New York, the year he had made partner. Even back then, the ever upward-moving internal force that drove her had been palpable.

He positioned himself in a corner close to the exit of the dining tent, in front of a row of tall, potted plants.

"Angela," he called out in a half-whisper.

She turned to his direction and caught his eyes. She excused herself from the Canadians and walked over to him.

"Robert! Where have you been all night?"

She reached up and kissed him on either cheek. There was nothing more than business to it. She had always been so with him.

"How's Valerie?" she said.

"She's fine."

"Give her my regards."

Hutton nodded.

"Well, this has turned out to be a fine evening." The Secretary of State looked about her with a broad smile.

"I noticed, earlier, when I'd just arrived, that you had the president's full attention," Hutton said.

"He may be smiling, but he's having an awful night."

"Is he now?"

"With this being his last term, everyone in his orbit with even an ounce of ambition is jockeying to get his endorsement for *their* bid to take over from him. People have been approaching him to whisper in his ears all evening. This event was all my idea and he blames me for his woes tonight."

She laughed.

"On the positive side, though," she said, "Prime Minister Peabody is in his glee. The man looks like he's about to explode with his sense of importance. It's almost farcical.

"Of course, I told the president it would be so. Invite him for a state visit, I said. Let's massage his ego. See what we can wring from him after.

"You know he's not been budging on this softwood lumber issue, and it's been souring relations between us and Canada. But his ego is his weak point and we'll work on it. The man is such an amateur in this game."

She dropped her voice to a whisper.

"Do you know what they nicknamed him at his first G20 meeting?"

Hutton shook his head.

"Shirtsleeves!" She chuckled. "It started with the staff, then moved up to the ministers and even some of the leaders were using it at the end. Not to his face, of course. But it was clear to everyone that the man can't control his emotions. Can't properly govern himself. I found out tonight in just how low a regard he's held by his own cabinet.

"But you know the story. Two years ago, Peabody's opposition party was in disarray, and he became leader almost by default, and soon after that, the previous government had to call an election because of a spending scandal. So, with a low voter turnout, those who were most disgruntled with the past administration ruled the day. And voila, there you had it; by an accident of fate, Canadian Prime Minister John J. Peabody."

She was in her element. Hutton enjoyed seeing her animated like this, but he nodded and raised his hand to stop her.

He reached for her left elbow and led her closer to the potted plants. He positioned himself so that when she faced him, her back would be to anyone passing by.

"Angela, I need to tell you something."

She raised her eyebrows and tilted her head quizzically, but her eyes strayed. It seemed she was itching to get back to the schmoozing.

"Angela, there was a fire at Bill's apartment in Monaco, yesterday."

"What did you say?" She gave him her full attention now. She frowned as she seemed to try to catch the significance of his words.

Her face relaxed, then she chuckled. "Poor Bill. Seems he's having a string of bad luck these days. Did you hear about the skiing accident? Broke both legs.

"I'd meant to ring him up and rib him about it. Heli-skiing at his age! What does he think he is? Some sprightly twenty-year-old? But I've been so busy lately, it slipped my mind.

"I must call him and ask him what jinx is following him around. Maybe some kind of curse from one of those African countries where Magrelma has mines."

"Angela, I'm sorry to tell you this," Hutton said, "but Bill didn't survive the fire."

Her eyes remained fixed on him, her body immobile.

Silent seconds slipped by.

"Look, I know how much he meant to you—"

"That was a long time ago, Robert."

Her face appeared calm, almost emotionless. The news of the death of her former fiancé seemed not to penetrate her. Hutton thought he knew better.

"He didn't suffer, Angela. Monaco officials say he died in his sleep. Smoke inhalation. The fire didn't touch him."

"And Fran?"

"She wasn't home."

"I'll send her official condolences and have someone from the Paris mission attend the funeral."

The actions were only faintly perceptible, but he had seen them – the micro-movement of the chin upward, the rolling back of the shoulders a smidge, the stiffening of the spine. She was shifting into full Secretary of State mode.

Hutton wished she would allow herself to be vulnerable, to show she felt this loss, and, perhaps, lean on his shoulder, even if for just a brief moment. But deep down, he knew that was expecting too much.

"They say the fire was accidental," he said. "But I've asked for our people to look into it, just in case."

She nodded.

At the corner of his eye, Hutton saw someone approaching, and he looked up. Bounding with determined steps toward them was Steve Roseau, former congressman and scion of an old Louisiana family. Hutton would have preferred if Angela Woodward, as she had been known before her marriage, had ended up with Mahler instead of this silver-spooned buffoon; at least Mahler had been a fairly decent guy from a solid, upper middle-class background who had worked hard to make his own way in the world.

She turned at the sound of the footsteps.

"There's my girl," Steve Roseau said. "I was wondering where you'd disappeared to." He looked at the director. "Robert," he said with a stiff nod.

"Steve," Hutton said with an even stiffer nod.

Steve Roseau offered his arm to his wife. She curled her hand around it. As they were about to leave, she turned back to Hutton.

"You will keep me informed about the investigation, won't you?" she said.

Hutton bowed deeply.

Chapter 7

In the dim light, just off from the entertainment tent, the Canadian prime minister shook hands with Kees Verhoeven, chairman of a global heavy machinery company that had been started by the Dutchman's great-grandfather.

Peabody drew on a cigarette. The protocol officer had made it clear that no smoking was allowed on the White House grounds. But Peabody was hyped up tonight. He had to have *this* smoke. There was no way they would come after the guest of honor for lighting up, he figured.

"Where are you these days?" Peabody pulled out a cigarette case and lighter from his breast pocket and offered them to Verhoeven.

"Oh, here and there. London mostly." Verhoeven looked around at the stony-faced security types who stood not far off. He exchanged glances with one of them, then shrugged and lit up.

Peabody and Verhoeven had been at the University of Toronto at the same time. They never had much in common to begin with. The Dutchman, older by several years, had been finishing up a Master's in engineering when Peabody became an undergraduate law student. They'd met only because they served together on the student council. They had never been fast friends, but their paths had crossed so often over the years, the association felt enduring.

"How are things working out with Derek at your Hong Kong office?" Peabody said, accepting back the case and lighter.

"He's doing just fine."

"Thanks for letting me know. I don't hear from him myself these days. Now that he's got a job, he's too busy to talk to his old man."

"That's kids for you. They can't wait fly the coop and, when they do, they become complete strangers. Unless you keep them in the family business, of course." Verhoeven thrust his chin in the direction of a muscular young man who had followed two steps behind him all night. "Hans, my youngest."

"Good grief he's got big since I last saw him. What have you been feeding him?"

"He likes to take care of himself. Doesn't have much of a business mind. But he's good to have around." Verhoeven sucked hard on the cigarette, then expelled a long, white stream into the cool, night air. "Listen, John, I'm glad to catch a moment with you. There's something I wanted to talk with you about."

"Go ahead. Shoot."

"This Syron Lake hearing."

"Syron Lake hearing?" Peabody cocked his head; his eyes darted from left to right, as if rifling through a mental filing cabinet. "You'll have to remind me of that one."

"Syron Lake, Northern Ontario. From what I understand, four or five companies had uranium mining operations there until the market bottomed out in the nineties. All the mines closed. They've been managing the toxic waste left behind ever since. In November, a regulatory panel will review plans for the government to assume control of the waste."

"Oh yes, that matter." Peabody smirked. "Getting into the mining business now, Kees? Haven't got enough on your plate already, eh?"

"I'm only inquiring on behalf of a third party. Just repaying a favor from years back."

"What about it then?"

"How far can you ensure that the panel will be, let's say, *friendly* toward the mining companies?"

"I can't. As far as I know, the chairman of the nuclear regulatory authority is set to handle that proceeding himself. He's as straight as an arrow. Believes in transparency and all that kind of crap. You know, when I go to social events, mining executives come up to me all the time and complain that he refuses to even shake their hands when they run across him during a hearing."

"Is there any way he could be persuaded to hand the hearing over to Ben Dromel, then? You remember Dromel, don't you?"

"Hmm, Dromel? Dromel?"

"He's also a U of T man. Did a double major in law and engineering. He was in the debating club when you were president."

"No. Coming up blank on the name."

"Well, he's been with the nuclear regulator a couple of years now. I understand that he's, let's say, *malleable*."

"The chairman isn't one of my appointees. And he's very vocal in asserting that the nuclear regulatory authority is supposed to be an independent, arm's-length body. I can't force him to do anything. Sorry, Kees. You know I'd love to, but I can't help you there."

Verhoeven held up his hands in mock surrender. "Okay. Just asking."

Approaching footsteps caused the two men to look up. Angus Firestone, the prime minister's chief of staff, walked briskly across the lawn toward them.

"They're looking for you, John," Firestone said. "They're about the start the entertainment."

Verhoeven slapped Peabody on the shoulder. "Go on in and enjoy it," he said. "The night belongs to you, after all."

Chapter 8

Benoit T. Dromel had hardly had a chance to settle in at his desk for the morning when the phone rang.

"You heard about Stan?"

It was the deputy chairman. Dromel had always found the man's voice irritating; but then again, he had found the man himself utterly uninspiring. The two of them had just never hit it off.

"My secretary mentioned something about him being in the hospital, just as I walked in."

"Oh yeah. He's in the hospital alright. I went to see him before I came in."

"How bad is it?"

"Very. Get over to my office. I need to talk to you."

Dromel put down the phone and took a few moments to straighten papers on his desk that didn't need straightening. He didn't appreciate being ordered about like that.

The deputy chairman, a bear of a man with a unibrow and hunched shoulders, sat behind a desk cluttered with binders, manila folders, envelopes and stacks of loose sheets. Dromel took the mess to be an indication of a weak and disorganized mind. He wondered, now, as he'd often done, why this guy was sitting pretty as the deputy chairman instead of him when they'd been appointed to their posts within weeks of each other.

He took a seat.

"Well?" he said.

"It was ugly. He was sedated. He's all black and blue."

The deputy chairman focused on Dromel's completely bald pate. Dromel found this disconcerting. He wasn't sure the deputy chairman was avoiding his eyes out of weakness or staring at his cleanly-shaved head out of contempt.

"What happened, exactly?"

"Volleyball."

"Again?" Dromel shook his head.

Three months earlier, the entire executive floor of the Canadian Nuclear Regulatory Authority had been shocked to see the chairman walk in with a large purple welt under a reddened left eye. His weekly volleyball game had been a little more exciting than expected, the chairman had joked.

Dromel liked the man. Small in stature and good-natured about it, the chairman was affable with fellow commissioners and his staff, even if a little too earnest about regulatory matters. Oddly for a man so keen about his job, the chairman was at the same time altogether too casual about his position and the status it carried. Dromel had teased him not to play with the "big boys" – he knew if *he* were chairman, he wouldn't be mingling with just anybody and everybody in weekly drop-in volleyball games at his local community center, even if the facility was in a mostly upper middle-class neighborhood.

"Nobody saw what happened," the deputy chairman said. "Police questioned two Serbian cousins who were nearest him when he went down. Nobody had seen them at the center before. But everybody had signed injury waiver forms. So nobody was held responsible."

"I bet Stan's learned his lesson now. He shouldn't have even put himself in that situation."

"The doctors say two months, maybe three, for recovery."

Dromel shook his head.

The deputy chairman opened a thick folder.

"Anyway, that means all of his duties fall to me, and I'm delegating some of them to you."

He went through a list of meetings, planned announcements, and reports that had to be signed off on. Dromel frowned as he noticed a pattern: anything that had the least possibility of press or involved top executives in the mining or power companies went to the deputy chairman; he got the grunt work.

"As for the public hearings, there are only two, both out-of-towners." The deputy chairman cleared his throat. "I'll chair the one in Saskatoon next month, and you'll do the one in Syron Lake the first week in November."

It was the last straw.

Syron Lake was way up in the bush in Northern Ontario. The chairman may have been worked up about it; but he was zealous about everything. The hearing was about long-closed mines that most people had forgotten. There was zero chance of media interest. And it meant traveling to what was certain to be a crummy, dilapidated, near-ghost town in the forest for a whole week.

The Saskatoon file, on the other hand, was sexy. A handful of environmentalists and First Nation activists had clashed with police while protesting plans to expand one of the biggest uranium waste management sites in the country. Blood had been shed and the incident had made national headlines. The reports all mentioned that with tension remaining high, restoring peace hinged on the upcoming hearing before the Canadian Nuclear Regulatory Authority. Whoever chaired that panel was almost certain to make a career-boosting appearance in front of the television cameras.

"Shouldn't we at least discuss this?" Dromel crossed his arms and tried to catch the deputy chairman's eyes.

"What's there to discuss?"

"Oh, I don't know. How about a bit more balance in the apportioning of these duties?"

The deputy chairman slapped the folder shut, then rested his clasped hands on it.

"Balance?" He forced a smile.

"Yes. I'm seeing a huge difference in the significance of the duties assigned to me and those you'll be handling."

"It seems you've failed to grasp that there's no symmetry between us, Dromel. In Stan's absence, I'm in charge."

"Sure you are. But how about an effort to give at least an appearance of fairness?"

"I've made my decisions, Dromel."

The two stared down each other.

"Fine." Dromel stood up abruptly.

"I'll have my secretary send you an email with all that we've discussed," the deputy chairman said.

Dromel was already out the door.

In the evening at his regular watering hole overlooking the Rideau Canal, Dromel held the third glass of gin and tonic to his lips. He was contemplating how flat his career path had been when a stranger in an expensive-looking suit took a seat, uninvited, opposite him.

His table was in a dimly lit corner since he preferred to drink alone, unseen. It was far from all the other patrons who gathered rowdily around the bar and the billiard tables. Even so, the stranger leaned over and spoke in a hushed voice.

"You're Ben Dromel from the nuclear authority, aren't you?"

"What's it to you?"

"Heard you're heading the Syron Lake panel."

Dromel put his drink down slowly. He had told no one about this. Apart from the deputy chairman, the deputy chairman's secretary and his own secretary, no one else knew.

But then he thought about the fact that his secretary was not his assistant alone; she acted for all seven commissioners other than the chairman and deputy chairman. And she was not exactly known for being the most discreet person in the world.

He remained silent as he squinted and studied the eyes of the stranger.

"You know, the mining companies don't like surprises," the stranger said.

Dromel acted unconcerned. He took another sip without removing his eyes from the stranger's face. But his pulse raced.

He figured he knew where this could be going. He had been here before, more than a decade ago. He'd been working as an engineer back then, and a certain piece of information needed to disappear so a project could move forward. And it did disappear — after a certain thick, brown envelope had been left in his locker at the gym. The contents had come in handy when he needed to make a down payment on a smart, little condo on Riverside Drive.

The stranger continued. "I hear you're a persuasive man, and that the newer commissioners look up to you."

Dromel maintained an air of nonchalance.

"It could be worth your while if a certain company could be assured that the panel will not spring any surprises."

After a long silence, Dromel sniffed. "If, hypothetically, I were interested in any of this, which of the companies are we talking about?"

The Syron Lake hearing involved five mining companies of varying sizes. A couple belonged to publicly-traded global behemoths, and the other three were privately-held. The disparity in their financial resources was enormous.

He would be not so gauche as to raise a discussion about a dollar amount, but, for him, that was the biggest deciding factor.

The stranger seemed to read his mind. He took a gold pen from his breast pocket, wrote on a napkin, and slid it across the table.

Dromel took a brief glance. Involuntarily, he looked again. Yes, the figure was interesting. Very interesting, in fact.

"What do they want?"

"Simply to be sure their request will be granted."

Dromel finished off his drink. All of the mining companies wanted to hand back their licenses for managing the former mine sites. The requests they had submitted, and the hearing for that matter, were more or less a mere formality. The mines had been closed for decades and the active work of cleaning up the sites and building waste holding facilities had been completed years prior. Since there was noting more to be done other than watch over the waste, the companies weren't interested in sticking around forever. The government authorities had made provisions for precisely this kind of exit, which they deemed an orderly transfer of responsibilities.

So if, for some reason, one of the companies wanted to be absolutely certain there'd be no glitch to delay or prevent the hand-over, sure, Dromel could see himself playing his part to make certain the transfer happened.

He looked into the stranger's eyes, and the sides of his mouth turned up in a tightly controlled smile.

The stranger gave a shallow nod. "We'll talk again. I know where to find you."

With that, the man in the expensive suit rose and slipped away through the crowd.

Chapter 9

One month later

The leaves had peaked the week before and I was angry with myself.

I berated myself as I searched among still unpacked boxes for my digital SLR camera. It was now mid-October and I had hardly been out in the woods. What was the use of leaving behind the fast-paced, big city life and moving to the forest if I didn't actually get out and experience the Nature I'd said I wanted to be close to?

In September, while I had waited for the closing on my new home, I had rented a vacant house from Ada, the real estate agent. Since then, and after I had moved into my own bungalow, two weeks prior, I had considered myself chained to my computer.

I no longer had a boss to crack a whip at me. So I had determined that I would act like a responsible adult. I would wake up early and plant myself at the keyboard and churn out at least twenty pages of the novel every day.

I had placed the unvarnished pine table I'd brought from Vancouver — one that my grandfather had made with his own hands — right beside the large bay window in the living room. I'd bought two red, vinyl upholstered chairs from the sixties in a yard sale and placed one at either end of the table, which served as my desk or dining table, according to which end I sat at.

Yes, I had been disciplined. I jumped out of bed at the sound of the alarm by seven every morning. I usually switched on the computer by eight or nine. Except for trips to the kitchen or the bathroom, or to my bed for an afternoon catnap, I would remain at that table until well after the sun disappeared and darkness had caused the maples, pines, and cedars outside the window to merge with the blackness of the sky.

For all that effort, though, there was nothing I felt I could show the world.

I had never made my daily quota but still managed to turn out two hundred or so pages. The printed text was covered with disapproving notes I'd scribbled in with a red pen. The pages were destined for the wastepaper basket — each and every one of them.

This was not working.

I hated the length and rhythm of almost every sentence. But the problem was not only the style. It was also the content.

I had set out to write a romance novel, but now thought of myself as woefully unqualified on the subject.

Who was I to write about the giddy heights of love when I felt stuck in limbo?

There I was, waiting day after day for any form of contact with Peter. It was a constant battle to keep my mind off the ever-present dull pain that had lodged itself in some part of my being that I couldn't name, or see, or touch.

I felt like a broken vessel that had shattered into a million pieces, and I longed to hear Peter's voice; I *needed* to hear his voice. My entire "me," the person I'd been for almost a year and a half and the person I thought I would be for the rest of my life, was totally wrapped up in him. His voice, his eyes on me, his smile...these things bore the magic I needed to glue those shattered pieces of myself back together again. And the romance novel served poorly as a distraction from my restless yearning for that magic.

Trying to reach out to others had only made matters worse.

My feelings of inadequacy in the romantic sphere had grown deeper since I had joined Facebook.

Back in Vancouver, the social media craze had completely passed me by; I had told myself I was just too busy and too tired to be bothered with such things. And besides, I hadn't felt like I had anything to share.

But in Syron Lake I had reached what I'd considered a major milestone in my passage through adulthood: I had bought a house, and I'd done so all by myself as a single woman. So when an email from an old school friend from Trinidad showed up in my Inbox inviting me to join the social network, I didn't hesitate to take a break from struggling to fill a blank MS Word page.

Logging on, however, brought me into the worlds of girls who had sat next to me in school uniforms and pigtails, and whose status now read "Married" or "In a relationship."

There were streams of photos of men with beards, or nose

piercings, or tattoos emblazoned across beefy chests; and there they were, these men, hugging my old schoolmates, or kissing them on the cheek, or grabbing their lower cheeks; acting foolish, or manly, or romantic.

And then there were the babies. Fat, droopy cheeks; eyes filled with wonder; tiny fingers reaching up to touch their mother's face....

And what did I have? A handyman's special in the middle of nowhere, no job, and no prospect for a date in this town, unless I wanted to take up with some widower in his eighties who had a set of perfectly aligned false teeth and a bottle of blue pills.

I was tired of being responsible. If I couldn't have the man and the kids, at least I could unchain myself from the computer and treat myself to an adventure in the wilderness.

The morning had been brilliant and warm, much nicer than it had been since the end of summer. I had walked into town to the car rental agency, picked up some groceries, and now was back at home, packing a tent and my camera.

The leaves were beginning to show some brown, tarnishing their autumnal brilliance. But if captured in the best light right at the start of dawn or just before dusk, they would make for some spectacular shots.

They would be at least *something* to post on my Facebook page. Pathetic, yes. But it was the best I could come up with.

The obvious place to go was the nearby provincial park, where there was a massive outcropping of the Canadian Shield that resembled a turtle poking its head out of its shell. The geological quirk had become the symbol of the region. The old-growth maple forest at its base could be relied upon to be resplendent. And if I was lucky to wake up to a morning mist rising off the nearby lake, the pictures were sure to be eerily enchanting.

This was my last chance to catch such a scene; it was Thursday and tent camping was scheduled to close for the season on Saturday.

The park, deep in the woods north of the town, was an hour's drive if I took the direct route on Highway 103. But I'd heard that *that* road was mostly straight and flat and lined with conifers.

Instead, I chose the scenic way, out onto the TransCanada Highway, and then up the road past the Garter Lake First Nation reservation. The drive would be three times as long, but the crests of some of the hills offered spectacular shots along the way.

The map showed that long after passing the reservation, I would have to take a left turnoff, cut across a hill and descend onto Highway 103; then, with a right turn, I would be a short distance from the entrance to the park.

With the window down and the wind whipping my hair back, I slipped in a CD with nineties music. Singing along at the top of my lungs helped to chase away the qualms that tried to invade my mind about spending the night alone in the woods.

I had done it before, out in B.C., just over a year earlier.

Peter and I had planned the trip weeks in advance. After a fight the night before we were supposed to leave, he had stormed out of my place and didn't call the next morning. He was supposed to have driven us, but I was not about to sit at home moping. I took the bus and hitched a ride for the first time in my life, and I set up camp in the B.C. backcountry, all by myself for a whole weekend.

Now, I had a rented car and I could very well handle an overnight stay in a provincial park just a few miles from my home, I told myself.

I was well on my way, about half an hour past the reservation, and was going over in my mind how to put up the tent when the first flash came.

I told myself it was nothing.

A few minutes later, though, I paid attention.

There was no sound, but the periodic bursts of light had continued.

The clock on the dashboard told me it was only about four-thirty; it shouldn't have been as dark as it had suddenly become.

I switched on the radio and found the local station. Interminable advertisements poured out of the car's speakers. After a few minutes of cheerful, upbeat music, which was annoying just then because it was not the news report, the nasal voice of the host came on.

"That was Bobby Farron with his biggest single, *Cabana Girl*; another golden oldie, right here on Moose FM. And, turning now to the weather, as we mentioned earlier, the meteorological office has issued a severe thunderstorm warning...."

Good Lord, it was about to hit. Wind gusts of sixty miles per hour or greater were expected, along with three inches or more of rain per hour.

The camping was off!

All I could think about now was getting onto Highway 103 and heading back to my warm, dry bed.

Stupid. Stupid. Stupid me for forgetting such a basic thing. *Check the conditions before leaving!* I had been so focused on getting the photos for my Facebook timeline, I hadn't listened to the radio all morning. Didn't Google the weather before I'd left. Such a basic thing!

The next flash blinded me for a second. The air rumbled and boomed.

Involuntarily, I pressed down on the gas. My fingers curled tightly around the steering wheel and I pulled hard on it to keep the car from veering onto the shoulder. A few seconds later, I eased up on the pedal; drew a long, deep breath; and told myself to slow down and stay calm if I wanted to arrive alive.

After driving for what felt like an hour in deepening darkness, I came upon a road to my right. I took the turn, relieved to be heading toward Highway 103.

The rain now came down in a blinding sheet and I had to slow down to a crawl. The flashes came every two minutes or so, followed by peals of thunder. Trees on either side of the road bowed and swayed in the howling wind.

An eternity later, it seemed the unlit highway had narrowed considerably. Nobody else was crazy or stupid enough to be way out here on a night like this. I drove in pitch blackness, except for the narrow, yellow beams from my headlights.

I was only an occasional driver; had been on the road at night only a couple of times; and had never before faced a storm like this. My trembling foot could barely keep firm contact with the gas pedal; my fingers now curled in a death-grip around the steering wheel.

But I pressed on, thinking only of eventually hearing the tires roll onto the gravel of my driveway.

A bolt of lightning forked down altogether too close, above the trees just ahead. It set the sky ablaze and made me blink. Thunder rumbled, then exploded, as if Heaven, itself, was cracking open right above me.

That killed my resolve.

I pulled over and parked beside the guard rail on a high ridge, as far off the road as I could. I turned on the hazard lights, lowered the back of my seat, and lay back with my eyes closed, breathing slowly to calm myself.

I would wait out the storm.

I didn't realize I had fallen asleep until the loudest boom of the night made me fling open my eyes and sit bolt upright. My entire body trembled, and, for a few seconds, I couldn't remember where I was, or why I was there.

Suddenly, I was aware of a continuous roar, louder than even the pounding rain on the roof and the windshield.

Was it the wind? No, this was different from the gusts I'd heard earlier. It was a louder, roaring, hissing, unbroken sound.

I leaned over to the passenger side and peered down, waiting for the next flash of lightning to illuminate the scene.

The strobe that came showed white crests racing away in the distance; a torrent ripped through the land below.

There had been no river there when I had pulled up. I was sure of it. I would have heard it if there had been one.

I was also sure I didn't care to stick around and find out how high or how fast the gushing waters would rise.

Pelting rain or not, I started the engine.

Somewhere in the midst of the terror and the disorientation it dawned on me to check the map.

I flipped on the overhead light, and with my index finger, I traced the route I'd taken. There it was: my big mistake. I was supposed to have made a left turn and then a right to get to Highway 103 if I was going to the park. But as I had decided to go straight back home, it was supposed to have been two left turns. I had taken only a right and had ended up God alone knew where.

I couldn't leave there — wherever that place was — fast enough.

Chapter 10

Back at home, I couldn't get that roaring sound out of my head. I tossed and turned under the sheets, unable to fall asleep.

Finally, I slid out of bed and headed for the living room. I switched on the computer. It was quarter to four.

Outside, the silhouettes of the trees still swayed and bowed. But the violent thunder and lighting had subsided, and the rain was gone.

I should have been appreciating this renewed peacefulness, but I was agitated.

That flood....

What if I hadn't awoken and the waters had risen so high and so fast that it swept the car away?

The rational part of me knew the ridge had been too high and the gully too deep and the raging waters too far away for that to have happened. But still, I was shaken, and the nightmarish what-ifs attacked my mind.

I typed "Syron Lake" into the Google bar and clicked to select the map search. I needed to locate the spot, as if in pinpointing the site precisely, I could somehow conquer it.

The rudimentary research I'd done before leaving Vancouver had told me "Syron Lake" could mean four different things.

First there was the lake itself, a pear-shaped body of water whose basin had been carved into the Canadian Shield at some point between 11,000 and two million years before.

Then there was the Syron Lake Mine, the first uranium mine to be opened in the area in the mid-fifties, just north of the lake.

The company that operated the mine also adopted the name: Syron Lake Resources.

And then there was the town. The first mining camps had cropped up on the north shore of the lake; but as more prospecting companies moved into the area and mining expanded, all living quarters were relocated miles away, to the site where the current town sprouted. Although now far removed from the actual body of water, the town retained the name Syron Lake.

Calculating the time it took to get home, I imagined that I'd been quite near Syron Lake, the actual lake, that is. On the satellite image it showed up as an the inky, pear-shaped blob in the middle of the forest, but the road network on the map showed that my route wouldn't have taken me to the lake.

Northwest of Syron Lake was a much smaller inky shape. It was an almost perfect oval, and a road led to it. There wasn't any river nearby. What was confusing was that from retracing my wrong turn on the road network, the oval was right about where it seemed that I had seen the flood.

Unlike most other lakes on the map, the oval had no name. I opened a new tab in my browser and typed in "Syron Lake," again. But this time, I clicked on the image search. I figured that might turn up some other maps with the name of the oval lake.

There were dozens of them. Maps were attached to company reports, and newspaper reports and linked to a defunct uranium mining protest website. There were also government reports, environmental studies, and transcripts of hearings.

I paid little attention as the dark sky outside the bay window slowly illuminated. I was lost in searching websites, reading reports, and poring over maps.

Finally, I sat back, stunned and trembling.

That inky oval was no lake.

It was a uranium tailings pond that held thirteen million gallons of radioactive sludge left over from the Syron Lake Mine.

Or at least it used to hold that toxic waste.

Chapter 11

He was certain to be concerned; at least I hoped he would be. The issue united two, possibly three, things he cared about. The first was the environment. The second was his hometown. And the possible third was...me.

He was trained to handle environmental crises from the perspective of an activist, so it was quite natural that I'd turn to him first for advice on how to handle the situation. Quite natural, really.

It was eight-thirty, my time; five-thirty, his. As an early riser, he would likely have been just about to start his morning routine of pumping iron.

I sat at the edge of my bed with a sticky palm on the phone. I could almost hear my heart pounding as I tried to compose my thoughts. I would keep things simple, businesslike. Yes, that was the wiser approach; after all, it had been five months since we'd last spoken. Any discussion about *us* would have to wait for later.

His cell number rang seven times. Then, a sleepy, female voice answered.

My heart skipped a beat. And then I realized I knew that voice.

"Oh hi, Jen, can you call Peter to the phone?"

Jennifer, who worked for the same environmental organization as Peter, lived with her girlfriend in the master bedroom of the house Peter shared with four others. Jen and I had met first. We had swapped sandwiches, shared flasks of coffee, and huddled under umbrellas on many an environmental protest rally; and we grew even closer when Peter and I began dating.

"My gosh! Stella? Haven't heard from you in ages. Peter's not here, by the way. He's somewhere in the wilds of Oregon with his cougar. His calls are forwarding to the house while he's traveling. How are you doing, girl?"

"I'm fine."

We played catch-up for a little while, until my curiosity got the better of me. "What's this about a cougar?"

"Oh, that's Lillian, the rich divorcee who joined our board

earlier this year. She and Peter hooked up in March, when you guys split up."

My heart thumped as if it wanted to burst out of my rib cage. Silence was the only response I could manage.

"Hey, Stella, you still there? Did you want me to take a message for Peter?"

"No, no message. It was nothing, really. Thanks, Jen. It was good speaking with you."

I replaced the handset and flung myself onto the bed.

So that's how it was, was it?

It wasn't until April that we'd had our last date. And it was the first week of May that he'd spoken about needing space. But he had begun a new relationship and had been telling everyone we'd broken up way back in March?

I slammed my fists into the pillows. "Why? Why? Why?"

My head was spinning as the possibilities taunted me. Maybe I had not been exciting enough. Was it my "friendship first" approach for the first ten months of our relationship that did me in? Was it because he found her more beautiful? It couldn't have been about the money. Jen said the woman was a rich divorcee, but the Peter I knew didn't care about wealth or status. Maybe I had teased him too often and didn't let him win our arguments often enough. Was it because he ended up thinking that I, with all my Trinidadian ways, was too different to choose to be with forever?

I spent too many minutes curled up on the bed, assaulting the pillows. Eventually, I gathered myself together and slouched off to the shower.

The warm water lashed my skin, but I hardly felt it as my mind became crowded with memories of the laughter and intimacies Peter and I had shared. I also thought, with regret, about the many, many times I'd lashed into him in order to get him to keep promises he'd made. I wondered what this new woman in his life looked like, and I felt anger rising in me as I imagined the fun the two of them were having together.

I'd spent months in limbo, waiting, waiting...waiting for the renewed attentions of that man to restore the shattered person I'd become, and to make me feel whole again.

And all that time, the relationship had been well and truly over, dead, with no hope of revival.

The dreams I'd harbored of our lives together in Syron Lake had never stood a snowball's chance in Hell.

I pounded clenched fists against the wet tiles. A scream forced its way out of me. It pierced my ears and made my throat raw. I let myself slide down against the wall and into the tub.

So that's how it was, was it?

Well, fine.

Who needed a two-timing rat like Peter Redmill anyway?

It turned out that I was a fool to think that relocating here would result in a reunion between Peter and me. But Syron Lake was *my* home now. What I'd witnessed could potentially put the entire town of twelve thousand souls at risk, if it hadn't already exposed us to all kinds of danger. There was an important task at hand, and I could very well handle it without Peter Redmill.

I drove the rental car to town and pulled up to the two-story, redbrick building that served as the town hall.

It was minutes past eight and the doors had just been opened. At the front desk, the generously proportioned receptionist focused her attention on the tiny mirror which she held in one hand, and the lipstick that she applied with the other.

"Excuse me," I said, "I need to urgently report a toxic spill."

"Just a second." The woman didn't shift her gaze from the mirror.

She topped the lipstick with a layer of lip gloss, and smacked both into apparently satisfactory coverage. She dropped the two tubes and the mirror into a small case, which she then shoved into a bulging handbag. Having tucked everything into a drawer, the receptionist adjusted herself in her chair, clasped her hands, and looked directly at me.

"Now, what can I do for you?"

"Who do I see to report a tailings pond breach?"

"A what?"

"A tailings spill, up near Syron Lake — the lake itself. It happened last night, during the storm. Who do I report it to?"

"Wait, you're going to have to explain this to me. First of all, what's a tailing pond?"

"You're kidding, right?"

"Listen, I've been in this job going on six years now and this is the first I've ever heard of this...this tailing pond. So either you explain what you're on about or I can't help you."

The woman pursed her thin, red lips.

I shook my head at the irony that I, a newcomer, a resident for not even a full two months, was the one doing the explaining.

"A tailings pond is a dam with radioactive gravel and sand left over from the old uranium mines."

The woman's eyes glazed over. My words hadn't registered.

I tried again. "When the mines were working, the miners wanted to extract uranium from the rocks, so they crushed the rocks until the rocks turned into gravel and sand. Then they used acid to wash the uranium that they were after out of the gravel and sand. But the process couldn't remove all of the radioactive material. So when the mines were finished with the gravel and sand, that waste material — called 'tailings' — was still dangerously radioactive.

"The tailings now have to be kept underwater in ponds. That's to prevent harmful gases, like radon, from escaping and polluting the environment. That toxic waste can cause people to develop lung cancer or leukemia, or can cause children to be born with birth defects."

The receptionist raised her eyebrows.

"That's why I need to speak with someone urgently," I said. "I think I saw toxic sludge flooding out of the tailings pond up at Syron Lake, last night."

"I see," the woman said, slowly nodding.

She flipped through a binder on her desk, then pointed to a corridor.

"Go straight down to the end. The door to your left. Talk with Mr Drakes."

I was somewhat doubtful when I read the words "By-Law Enforcement" on the door. I was relieved, though, that I didn't have to give an overview of uranium mining waste management to the short, heavyset man who appeared when I knocked.

"Well," Drakes said, "if a neighbor doesn't cut his lawn for months and it looks like a jungle or if someone puts up a fence higher than six feet, I'm your guy. But this tailings breach business, it's got nothing to do with me."

He sent me down a different corridor to the Infrastructure Department.

"I doubt my boss could help you even if he was here," said the young man who was taking apart some piece of machinery. "We do roads, sewers, the landfill...town property only. Check upstairs, maybe the Chief Administrative Officer can help you."

The second floor was all plush burgundy carpeting, marble walls, and low-lighting; the marble was probably fake, but it was all quite fancy for such a small town. A gray-haired woman with round glasses on the tip of her nose sat behind a desk and talked on the phone. The door to her left was closed. A second door, behind her right shoulder, was open; the man in the room rested a briefcase on a chair and shook his arms out of his jacket.

I waited for the woman to put down the receiver. "I'd like to see the CAO, please."

"Sorry, that's not possible today. He's got a full schedule."

"But this is urgent! I think I saw the tailings dam up at Syron Lake burst last night. Somebody in this town must care about environmental pollution!"

"Calm yourself, young lady." The secretary slid her glasses higher on her nose. "And slow down. You said you saw what, where?"

Oh no, not again! I rolled my eyes toward the ceiling.

Footsteps sounded. The man from the room to the right walked out to the foyer. He stood bolt upright and looked me directly in the eyes. "Come into my office a minute."

He tapped on the secretary's desk.

"Margot hold all calls."

"Yes, Mr Demetriou."

Demetriou. The name seemed familiar.

He shut the door and motioned me to sit. He leaned against his desk and folded his arms. He was of average height and average build, but because of our relative positions, he towered over me.

"Now, what's this about a tailings pond breach?"

In the midst of explaining who I was and what I'd seen the night before, the name clicked. I recalled that the majority of plastic signs dotting lawns all across the town read, "Tito Demetriou for Mayor: Safe hands for a fourth term."

Good, I thought. I was getting word to the very top.

"Was anyone else around when this happened?"

"I didn't see any other car on the road. And I was driving

alone. That's how I ended up being there. I didn't have anyone to help me navigate."

"And who else knows about this?"

"I told just the receptionist downstairs, the secretary up here, and a couple of people, in By-Law Enforcement and Infrastructure."

"Good."

The relief in his tone surprised me.

He must have seen the way I had recoiled because, now, the sides of his lips curled upward into what looked like a contrived smile.

"If it was a spill, I'm sure the mining company's already onto it," Demetriou said. "They'd have to do the clean-up. Repair whatever damage there might be. They'd have to inform the nuclear authority about it, too. It's a federal matter, you know."

"But what about notifying the town?"

"Of course I expect they'll send some official communication to the clerk, or the CAO, or to me. If something happened last night, we'll probably hear from them before the end of the day, today. But as it's Friday, we might not. I'd say, Monday, at the latest."

"I was referring to the people who live here."

Demetriou shook his head.

"What are you after, Ms Jacob?"

"Shouldn't there be some kind of public announcement?"

The mayor tilted his head and stared at me, but said nothing. His reticence irritated me.

"Millions of gallons of radioactive waste have spilled into the environment." My voice was now at a high pitch. "Doesn't that call for a public alert?"

"Look, Miss, you don't know for sure if that's the case."

"But *I* saw the gushing water. I checked the map. It could only have been?"

"I'll find out what really happened. I'll call the company, first thing after this meeting."

"But, by the time—"

"Listen, young lady, we need to get the facts first before we go scaremongering."

The word stung like a slap across my cheeks.

I drew a breath and continued.

"And what if it takes days to get the facts from this company? And what if it turns out that the worst actually did happen? Meanwhile, people's lives could be put at risk if they drink contaminated water, or go fishing, or swimming in Syron Lake."

"The tailings pond is nowhere near the town's water supply, Ms Jacob. And nobody goes fishing or swimming in Syron Lake. The only access road runs through private property belonging to Syron Lake Resources, and they prohibit public entry."

"But—"

The mayor's right hand shot up in the air and commanded my silence.

"Listen, if I were you, I'd be careful about talking about this," Demetriou said.

His tone made me jerk back my head.

"The only way you could have seen what you claim to have witnessed was if you were trespassing." Demetriou stepped closer to my chair and narrowed his eyes. "Go running your mouth about this and you could get yourself arrested for trespassing."

He walked to the door and swung it open. The secretary peered into the room, and the mayor bowed with graciousness that was a stark contrast to his tone just seconds before.

"Thank you so much for bringing this to my attention, Ms Jacob," he said. "I'll look into this to see that everything that must be done, will be done."

Chapter 12

I didn't trust Mayor Demetriou.

He was just the type that Adam Levy, my old boss at the salmon non-profit, would have called "a consummate corporate suck-up."

"Do you know what are the most dangerous predators on the planet?" Adam had asked during my job interview. He'd shaken his head at all my guesses: white sharks, piranhas, lions, dingoes.

"It's creatures known as 'corporations,'" he had said, his brown eyes seeming to burn with a century's worth of outrage, although he was just three years older than me.

"They're fictitious beings, but they're treated in law as if they're one hundred percent living, breathing humans, separate and distinct from the men and women who run them. And with the way the system is rigged, they have more rights than any real person."

A corporation was a shield behind which people who had little or no concern for their fellow men or other living creatures could hide and commit dastardly deeds, Adam had said.

"A natural predator seeks food in order to survive, and Nature has programmed it to end the hunt when it's satiated. But a corporate predator has no 'off-switch.' It hunts for wealth and power unrelentingly, even to the point of destroying the very source of that wealth.

"And that's what makes corporations such dangerous predators — they are not restrained by any natural instinct, or by any notion of morality."

Whereas any one of us would be behind bars if we did even a tenth of what some corporations were guilty of, corporate predators almost always got away with their immoral and illegal deeds, Adam had said. "Why? Because so many of the officials who are supposed to be policing them are either too incompetent or too cowardly to do their jobs, or they're only interested in trying to get their snouts in the trough, too."

But throwing up his hands and saying that corporations were too powerful to take on hadn't ever been an option for Adam, or for the handful of volunteers who had rallied around the salmon non-profit; he had said that the havoc corporations would wreak if no one stood up to hold them accountable was too horrifying to contemplate.

So, before we got scattered by the global economic crash (itself brought on by rampaging corporate predators), we'd had a good run of it; I would research and write exposés about overfishing and threats to salmon habitat from logging, mining, and industrial activity, and Adam churned out opinion pieces that nailed company heads, and called out various officials for their inaction or complicity.

Officials just like Mayor Demetriou.

Adam was backpacking somewhere in Australia and unreachable. And apart from Peter, whose image I was trying to scrub from my memory, I could hardly think of who else I could turn to for help. Besides Adam, who was the founder and served as executive director, I had been the only staff at the non-profit. The volunteers, while generous and eager to be helpful, had always looked to *us* for guidance.

Next door to the town hall was the Syron Lake police station, a solid-looking, one-story, yellow building. The glass door of the front entrance seemed to beacon me.

As I stepped onto the interlocking brick walkway that linked the two buildings, I had a vague sense of being watched. My eyes glided up to the second floor of the town hall and caught a glimpse of a figure in a window, just as it moved away.

The anger I felt at being talked down to by Mayor Demetriou propelled my footsteps. But by the time I pushed past the station's door, the force of that rage had almost completely dissipated.

Doubts and fears rushed in to fill its place. What could the police even do in this situation? It wasn't as if I had a crime to report. And what about the mayor's talk about my being arrested for trespassing? Was I about to throw myself to the wolves?

At the reception counter, a slight, young woman watered a pot of English Ivy. From the corridor to the right came the sound of heavy boots. A hulk of a man in uniform suddenly appeared. He tapped the counter.

"Just had an accident back there, Zoe," he said. "Got coffee all over my desk. Take care of that for me, will you."

Without a word, the young woman made haste down the corridor. The man watched her leave, then turned to face me.

"You're the one who just spoke to the mayor about a spill?"

He had the presence of a man who could bat away a black bear, like other people swat flies, and I found myself slipping into my mousey mode under his piercing eyes.

"Yes."

"Right, so we're onto it already."

He folded his massive arms and glared at me.

"Okay. Thank you, then," I said backing away with a bow.

I turned and bolted out the door.

My cheeks burned with shame. The mayor's threat to have the police arrest me for trespassing had undone me completely. With a bent head, I broke into a half trot to put as much distance between myself and the station as quickly as I could.

I never saw the cop coming.

All I knew was that, suddenly, my right arm slammed into something soft, and my entire body buzzed, as if I had been zapped by a bolt of lightning. I lost balance and tumbled into someone, my vision capturing a beard, and the silver buttons and pockets of a dark uniform, and a cell phone clattering onto the ground.

The cop grumbled at the impact.

I righted myself in a flash, and immediately dashed around the corner, out of sight.

Back in the car, I gripped the steering wheel, trembling and feeling utterly foolish. The entire morning seemed like a failure.

I had a couple of hours left before I needed to return the rental. My camera was under the passenger seat. The lens was long enough that I could stay far away and still get good shots. "A picture was worth a thousand words," they said. If I got good visuals, maybe I could get some newspaper or website interested in the spill.

Highway 103 was empty. I pressed down hard on the gas, ignoring the speed limit, and reached the turn-off in under an hour. I got onto the parallel route and made a left into the road I'd mistakenly thought was the highway the night before.

I didn't get very far before I came across two florescent orange wooden horses in the middle of the road. A rope suspended between them carried a sign with a skull that said, "Danger. Keep Out."

On either side of the road were two permanent metal signs: "Private Property. No Trespassing. Violators Will Be Prosecuted."

I hadn't seen the permanent signs the night before. But then again, it was dark and raining and I'd been focusing only on the arc of light from my headlamps.

The camera looked forlorn on the passenger seat where I'd placed it, anticipating that I would need it within easy reach in order to sneak in a few quick shots. It begged to go beyond those barriers, where something was definitely up.

The roar of the flood from the night before came rushing out of my memory and back into my ears. It had filled me only with terror at the time, but, now, the sound made my blood boil, and my heart sink.

I imagined the devastation the gushing waters would have caused. The flood would have cut through the land, uprooting majestic trees and tossing them aside as if they were matchsticks. Any animal that was too young, too old, or too sick to get out of its path would have been swept away. Fish would have been suddenly engulfed by murky waters that turned their natural habitat into a toxic grave.

Osgood was right. Greedy bastards had raped and pillaged Mother Nature and left her for dead.

I couldn't let them get away with it.

The wooden horses didn't seem heavy at all. I imagined myself easily shifting them just enough to squeeze the car through.

And then I pictured Mayor Demetriou's scowl, and the big cop's glare, and my fingers hesitated on the door handle.

I grit my teeth. "I'm *doing* this. Can't be a coward all my life."

The matter, though, was decided for me. In the distance beyond the barrier, headlights snaked toward me. Someone was coming this way from the site of the spill. I did a quick three-point turn and hightailed it out of there.

On foot, after surrendering the rental, I went to the radio station. I had heard from a reliable source that couldn't be named, I said, that the dam with toxic sludge burst up at Syron Lake. The story must have been true, I added, because now there was a roadblock with a danger warning sign.

The baby-faced reporter scribbled notes feverishly. "This is great! Sounds like a major story," he said. He told me to listen for the news, which was carried at the top of every hour.

The newspaper editor was less enthusiastic. "We heard from the mayor's office. We're checking into it." He didn't even assign a reporter to interview me.

Back at home, with the radio going, I called the Ontario Ministry of Natural Resources. I was on hold for half an hour the first time. When the clock ticked past three-quarters of an hour the fifth time I called, I gave up.

Two newscasts passed. Lots of "news" about the upcoming arts tour, and a poker run, and a mayoral debate in a week. But nothing on the tailings.

"My boss killed the story," the baby-faced reporter said when I called. "Said we can't run with anything until we get confirmation that it was a spill."

I suspected that the mayor had gotten to the radio station boss too.

Somewhere in the circuitry of my brain, the uncomfortable sensations I'd felt during my encounter with Demetriou got tangled up with the imprint of what actually happened. So any time I recalled the incident (which was often that day), it was with a vague notion of having been slapped about the face in the mayor's office. Now it felt as if I'd been slapped all over town.

It never felt good to be mousey.

It didn't feel good now. And it certainly didn't in childhood, when I'd flee under the bed whenever my dad came home late from the bar and would raise an angry fist at my stepmother, who, having downed a few glasses of rum while waiting for him at home, would put up a screaming, raging fight that often left housewares and furniture broken, and, occasionally, brought concerned neighbors rushing over. Nor did it feel good when I was cowering and trying to shield my face from lashes from a leather belt, which my stepmother reserved for teaching me lessons about how to behave properly.

What had felt good was hanging on to Adam Levy's coattails as he had fought his battles. It was he who had sent me out to all those environmental rallies, where the mass of bodies and the fiery voices supplied me with courage I'd never known before as I joined whatever fight was on.

How could I tap that courage again?

I flipped through the local phone book. There was only one listing in the community groups section under the heading "Environment."

I rang the number.

"I agree with you; the mines shouldn't be allowed to hush up something like that," the woman with a frail voice said after I'd explained all.

"So can we get some kind protest going?" I said.

There was silence on the other line. "I'm sorry, dear, but that's not really our thing." The delicate voice practically dripped with politeness. "We're all retirees in the Syron Lake Field Naturalists Club. We put up bird feeders, go on walks, have monthly meetings, that kind of thing."

I sighed.

"We're having a meeting tonight at the Moose Lodge," she said. "Starts at eight. Why don't you come? You could talk to Osgood. He's on our board and he's running for mayor. Maybe he could help you."

I didn't hesitate. "I'll be there."

Chapter 13

The meeting with Angus Firestone was at two-thirty in the afternoon. The venue was a sandwich shop at the end of a street lined with tiny, rundown former loggers cottages. It was in Hull, on the Quebec side of the river, across from Ottawa.

Benoit Dromel drove across the Alexandra Bridge thinking the encounter would be a little too close for comfort to the bachelor pad he kept secret from his common-law wife, Bernice. But, as he was quite sure his clandestine life there was unknown to anyone other than his paramours and the tall, skinny kid he jokingly referred to as his majordomo, he had agreed to Firestone's request.

The appointment had been arranged and canceled at the last minute twice before in the last month. Things had come up on both their parts. Now, he was determined that it should happen. He was curious to know why the prime minister's chief of staff wanted to see him, and at such an out-of-the-way location, too.

When he arrived, Firestone was already seated on a tall stool in the empty eatery, studying his Blackberry. Dromel had come across his fair share of political operatives over the years in Ottawa, and he knew this type. At thirty-seven, Firestone was just under two decades younger than Dromel; he had risen fast in the world and exuded the cockiness Dromel associated with a power-behind-the-throne syndrome.

They introduced themselves, then ordered vegetarian wraps, which they took to the most isolated booth in the joint.

"How's your chairman coming along?" Firestone said.

"Slower than expected."

"When does he get back?"

"Not sure. It's looking like his recovery might take longer than first thought."

"Your deputy chair's got the Saskatoon hearing, right?"

"Yes."

"So you're doing Syron Lake?"

"Yeah, sure," Dromel said after a pause.

For the first time since he'd arrived, he began to feel uneasy.

Two weeks earlier, he had tied up talks with the stranger in the expensive suit. He had secreted off to Belize for a quick, little holiday. The agent who registered his offshore company and set up an offshore account in Singapore said neither would be traceable to him.

Half the amount the stranger had written on a napkin had been wired to his account just six days earlier; the other half was promised for when the panel's work was done.

Now the PM's Office was pulling him aside, asking questions. What did they know?

Firestone crunched loudly on cubes of cucumber. "The outcome of your review has great significance to the companies involved."

"That's no different from any of our hearings," Dromel said.

"Look, it's come to our attention that certain entities have certain specific objectives in mind, and it's absolutely crucial that they be realized."

Dromel kept his eyes on the tomato slices in his wrap.

"As you know," Firestone continued, "a chairman of any proceeding usually has enormous sway."

"As someone who's served on many panels, I'm not sure you could make such a claim."

"Well, it looks like that'll be the case with Syron Lake, given that it's a three-man affair, and your colleagues are newbies."

"I wouldn't exactly call Percy Drysdale a greenhorn. He's been with the CNRA for eleven months."

"Yeah, but he's been on a panel only once before. And that other guy...."

"Victor Rigby."

"Yeah, that one. The PM appointed him just four months ago. This will be his first hearing won't it?"

"They're both highly qualified and competent. And they're independent thinkers, too."

"Come on, Dromel. You know very well that every man is subject to persuasion."

Dromel shifted his weight and turned sideways; he stared at the exit.

"What are your plans when your five-year term is up?" Firestone said. He had finished his wrap, and now rubbed his long, bony fingers with a paper napkin.

"That's a couple of years down the road. Haven't given it a whole lot of thought."

"You should."

Dromel stared at Firestone.

"Lots of ends of terms on various boards coming up down the road," Firestone said. "There will be openings. We're talking about full-fledged chairmanships, with all the perks. Or, you might want to consider slipping back into the public service. What were you before you took up this post? Director of something or the other, right? What about going back, but in the upper echelons, this time? Deputy minister, let's say. The possibilities are endless, understand?"

Dromel nodded slowly.

Firestone raised his left eyebrow and leaned toward Dromel. "But possibilities are open to those who can deliver desired results. Those who run against the grain also run the risk of being left by the wayside...or worse."

Firestone stood up. "I trust you'll consider all of this carefully during the Syron Lake review."

Dromel forced a smile. "I always take all important information into consideration."

"Good." Firestone slapped Dromel on the shoulder and left.

On the drive back to his office, Dromel shook his head every few minutes.

Why was the prime minister trying to influence his decision? After all, Firestone was nothing if not the mouthpiece of the PM.

Whose bidding was Peabody doing? Was there a second company out of the five that was looking to get at him? Or was it the same company behind the payment he'd already received that didn't trust him and was trying to send a message through Peabody?

If it was the same company that had wired him the cash, Dromel didn't know which was more disturbing: being doubted by them, or receiving covert inducements on their behalf from Peabody.

He hated the man. He had never forgotten that day from their time at the University of Toronto when Peabody had squeezed him out of a debating team that went to Ottawa for a tour of Parliament.

Dromel always wondered how his career would have turned out if he hadn't missed out on that trip. That particular "what if" inquiry had tormented him for decades. Going there usually resulted in him reaching for a glass or three of gin or vodka.

Back at his desk, he lazily scanned his Inbox.

The email that caught his attention was short, not more than five lines. It was addressed to the CNRA's emergency response department, which had forwarded it to him.

An acute natural event or Act of God — namely, a severe rainstorm the night before — had diminished the effectiveness of a barrier at the former uranium mine operated by Syron Lake Resources in Syron Lake, Ontario.

The situation was under control, the company's email said. Emergency clean-up operations were well advanced. The spill was contained with no discernible environmental impact on the surrounding communities. The company would bear full responsibility for the cost of remediation.

Dromel leaned back and rocked in his chair.

That had to be it.

Syron Lake Resources had to have been the company behind all the clandestine meetings.

Now it made sense that they had sent Peabody as a messenger boy with a bag of goodies even after they'd slipped something to him under the table.

He smelled desperation.

It was not unwarranted. The terms of the agreement his panel was reviewing gave the authorities the power to demand the company pay for and manage a clean-up operation in circumstances such as this. Sure, the company was making the right kind of PR statements about taking full financial responsibility in the initial moments of the crisis. But Dromel had the power to stick the costs to them indefinitely.

Perhaps Syron Lake Resources had cut corners in their maintenance work over the years and saw a disaster like this coming. And, even in the face of it, they wanted to hand back their license and pass the burden of any long-term clean-up operation onto the government and taxpayers.

He had every reason to deny them their request.

Suddenly the balance in his Singaporean account seemed inadequate.

If this company was powerful enough to get the prime minister of Canada to drop hints about plum positions, they would surely be able to cough up more dough.

A payment of the magnitude he had in mind would mean he wouldn't need to be hanging around hoping Peabody would come through with his promises. Dromel hadn't put much faith in Firestone's vague offers, anyway; personal history had taught him better than to bank on anything Peabody said.

With the payment he had in mind, he probably wouldn't even have to serve out his term as a CNRA commissioner.

He could retire early, and leave behind the whole Ottawa lot with their intrigue and backstabbing. He could spend the rest of his days in some warm place on the beach with Bernice at his side, if she wanted to join him. If she didn't, he was sure his fattened wallet would make it easy for him find a replacement, or two.

He clasped his hands and cupped the back of his bald pate. His thumbs massaged the base of his skull, sending a tingle of excitement throughout his body.

Yes, he was due for a bigger payday.

Chapter 14

Director Hutton stood at the window of his office watching the bare trees and the swirling carpet of yellow and crimson on the sidewalk. In past years, the shifting play of colors as the wind tossed about the fallen leaves had provided a welcome distraction for a brain overloaded with the murky secrets of an entire nation. But now, this autumnal tableau brought only thoughts of decay and death.

Hutton sighed.

He hadn't been himself since the summer. Not since he started having those chest pains, the shortness of breath, and those all too frequent dizzy spells. His wife, Valerie, was now near exasperation over his delay in going to see his doctor. Too busy, he kept saying. The truth was that he didn't want to know the truth.

He didn't turn around when Spike Simmons knocked and entered. He had been expecting him. He had found that dealing with this lower level agent on the Mahler case suited his purpose better than consulting Simmons' superiors.

"So we are certain there was foul play?" Hutton said.

"No doubt about it, sir."

Silence ensued.

Simmons cleared his throat.

When Hutton turned around, Simmons pointed to the desk. He held a laptop in one hand.

"May I?"

Hutton was amused at Simmons' eagerness and extreme deference. But he would not let the agent see it. He nodded, then folded his arms and sat on the window sill.

"What have you got?"

Simmons flipped open the laptop and took a wireless mouse out of his jacket pocket. He began to lower himself into the director's chair so he could use the mouse, then seemed to think the better of it. He walked over to a chest-high filing cabinet and manipulated the computer from that awkward height.

"This is the footage from the stairwell leading to William Mahler's apartment," Simmons said.

The silent, black and white video showed a female figure racing down the stairs. She stopped at the Mahlers' back door as clouds of smoke seeped from the creases at its sides and base.

"See, here," Simmons said, "the woman bangs on the door and seems to try to open it with keys. But the keys fall and it looks like she tries to search for them with her foot. Meanwhile, she's covering her nose and coughing. That quickly deteriorates into violent convulsions. Finally, she abandons the effort to open the door and flees down the stairs."

Simmons stopped the video.

"That was one of the Mahlers' maids," he said. "She had the weekend off like all the others, but she'd decided not to go visit her family as she wasn't feeling well enough to travel. She was the only other person we know of that was in the building at the time of the fire."

"A loyal servant; tried to save them," Hutton said.

"The funny thing is that she said she'd left the Mahlers' apartment to go to her room less than half an hour before this scene took place."

"What's so strange about that?"

"There's no footage of it."

Hutton raised an eyebrow.

Simmons continued. "There are recordings of this maid going up and down the stairs three or four times earlier in the day. But there's nothing showing her leaving the Mahlers' apartment that one time before the start of the fire."

Simmons clicked to play another video. "Now, have a look at this, sir."

The screen showed nothing but the stairs.

"Our guys examined the footage carefully." Simmons sniffed with an air of satisfaction. "Just about half an hour before the fire, there's a momentary blackout of the recording. Lasts just a fraction of a second. The same thing happens shortly before the maid ran down."

He stopped the video then showed two pictures of the stairwell, side by side, on his screen. Next, he pulled up a composite image showing one picture with its opacity reduced and overlaying the second picture.

"What we discovered is that the scene from that short block of time and the view that the camera showed at all other times are different. It's subtle, and you'd miss it if you weren't looking as hard as we were. But the two are from slightly different angles. The camera pointing to the Mahlers' door is fixed. These two images are supposed to align perfectly. But they don't."

"Okay, so that suggests the perpetrator or perpetrators entered Mahler's apartment through the back door and made sure there was no record of it," Hutton said.

"That's right, sir."

"But how did they even get to that camera to be able to tamper with it?"

"Through the roof, we believe. The cameras on every other floor all checked out. Nothing was wrong with their footage. So entry from lower floors is ruled out. We asked Monaco to help us check the roof. What's interesting is that the skylight on the room closest to the camera shows some fresh scratches to the weatherstripping. Granted, those marks could have been made by birds or vermin. But it could also have been our killer."

"What about the autopsy reports?"

"They confirmed the causes of death that were originally suspected. The nurse OD'ed on a toxic mix of alcohol and heroin. The heroin, by the way, was so potent that it could have done him in all by itself. As for Mahler, there was some alcohol in his system, but nothing else was found as being contributory to his death other than carbon monoxide. Our guys said Monaco was relieved to hear that."

"I bet they were." Hutton said.

Simmons slipped the mouse into his pocket. He walked over to the desk and shut down the computer. He stood, facing Hutton, spine erect like a soldier reporting to his sergeant.

"We asked our lab to review the samples from Mahler and dig deeper. They, too, reported death from carbon monoxide poisoning. But they found a couple of things puzzling."

"Such as?"

"First, there was *some* soot in Mahler's lungs. But the lab felt the distribution pattern was not right. For the amount of soot that would have been in the air, given the type of material that burned, there should have been much more soot, much deeper in his lungs."

"Interesting."

"They think Mahler actually died too early for Monaco's smoke-inhalation theory to be true. They looked at the concentration of carbon monoxide in Mahler's system. It was way beyond what it should have been, given the time between when the fire is estimated to have started and when it was put out."

"So the lab is saying that the carbon monoxide that killed Mahler appears not to have come from the fire?"

"That's right, sir."

"So it was somehow administered before the fire?"

"The lab thinks that's highly likely to have been the case."

Simmons picked up the laptop, folded it shut, and tucked it under his arm.

"And there's one other thing," he said. "Mahler's wife said there's no way the nurse would have been smoking in the apartment. He loved his job. He'd started just a few months before and often said how thankful he was to be working there. He knew she didn't let even Mahler, himself, smoke in the apartment. And he knew he would have been fired on the spot for smoking in there. Fran Mahler also said there was nothing to suggest that the nurse was depressed or suicidal."

Hutton stepped away from the window and settled into his seat. "Okay, so we have reason to believe these were homicides. What about suspects?"

"As for the killer himself, or herself — can't rule out that it was a 'she,' as you never know these days...." Simmons smiled at his political correctness, but getting no response, moved on quickly. "As for the actual killer, there are none. This was a professional who left no clues as to his or her identity."

The director nodded.

"As for who put out the contract," the agent said, "the field is still pretty much wide open."

"Narrow it down, Simmons."

"For starters, there's Fran Mahler. She inherited practically everything. Mahler had a previous wife and two sons, but those boys didn't survive childhood, and the first wife took sleeping pills to end her life over two decades ago. Fran Mahler is his second wife and they had one child. But that girl is estranged. Lives somewhere in Australia. Fran Mahler is in charge of the trust fund left to her."

Simmons paused and adjusted his tie. "We have some information that there was trouble in the Mahlers' marriage. Reports of affairs. On both sides."

Hutton nodded.

"And it seems there's trouble on the horizon for the business, too. There's talk of Fran Mahler filing a lawsuit to take control. Seems she has ideas for the company to take bold, new initiatives."

"That's interesting."

"But there are other suspects. Mahler's business partners — Daniel Greene and Henry Maitland."

"Where are you getting at with that line of inquiry?"

"Greene was seen arguing with Mahler at a bar in Monaco. Happened just two days before Mahler was killed. Eyewitnesses say the fight was over some business interests in Canada."

The director thought he detected hesitation in Simmons' voice. "But there's a 'but'?"

"Yes, sir. Greene didn't inherit anything from Mahler. In fact, it's Maitland who took over from Mahler and is running the show now. So any motive on Greene's part is unclear at the moment."

"From what I've heard from various sources," Hutton said, "Maitland's not much of a happy man these days."

"That's what we've gathered, too, sir. Seems he's struggling as the head of the company."

"Power comes with responsibilities, Simmons," Hutton said, sitting deep into his chair and leaning his head on the headrest. "No one gets to enjoy the former without tending to the latter. Men like Mahler accept that; they fully embrace the responsibilities, down to every last minute, headache-inducing duty. That's what makes them leaders. If Maitland took out Mahler in order to simply enjoy the status of being head honcho at Magrelma, then he's a fool who didn't pay attention to the warning to be careful about what you wish for."

"Yes, sir." Simmons glanced at his notes. He coughed into his fist before continuing.

"As for others...well, we're checking out business competitors.

And as for political enemies Mahler may have gained as a result of Magrelma's rumored covert activities, so far, there's no indication of involvement by such figures. But we're leaving no stone unturned as far as that's concerned.

"This was a professional hit. Whoever ordered it had the means to hire an expert. Could very well have been some deposed dictator who squirreled away his country's wealth and still bears a grudge."

"Good. Thank you, Simmons." Hutton nodded with finality.

"Thank you, sir."

With his face hidden from the director as he turned to leave, Simmons felt as if the weight of the world had been lifted from his shoulders, and his lips parted in a broad grin. He could get used to playing in the big league like this.

Chapter 15

He had sent for Simmons that afternoon because he knew the Secretary of State would be at the White House later in the day, shortly after he was scheduled to brief the president on some matters.

The FBI director was out of his meeting earlier than expected. He checked with the secretaries outside the Oval Office for some needless information. It bought him some time, but not enough. He felt ridiculous dallying about.

Disappointed at not running into Angela Roseau, he walked down the corridor toward the exit. His gait was slow, but, still, he held his shoulders back, pushed out his chest, and kept his head up. The Army training had been deeply embedded into every fiber of his being all those decades ago and would never leave him.

He heard her voice from behind a slightly ajar door. He smiled. By the time the door opened fully and she stepped out before him, his face was the usual stern mask he showed the world.

She often wore an intimidating mask, too. But hers was a lovely face, he thought. Although the decades had broadened it, added wrinkles, and caused it to sag here and there, he still saw the beauty that had so often made him toss and turn at night, even as he lay in bed alongside Valerie.

Their eyes met, and though he wanted to deny it, her sparkling baby blues made his pulse race.

"Angela, we're running late." Kathy Wang, the infernal shadow, stepped out the door, clutching a notebook computer.

"Go ahead, I'll catch up with you," Roseau said without breaking eye contact with Hutton.

He told her all he had learned about Mahler's death. She tilted her head and listened with an intent look on her face. This time, though, there was no more of that hint of a slip as at the State Dinner, when she had been caught completely off guard.

"I trust that we'll pursue this until we find whoever is responsible," she said.

"Absolutely."

She touched him lightly on his upper arm.

"Thank you, Robert."

"He was a good man, Angela," Hutton said. He believed it to be true, to a certain extent, but he said it mostly because he knew it would please her to hear it. "He deserves every effort we can make to find his killer. And we will. I'll make sure of it."

Chapter 16

I had no idea how long the Field Naturalists meeting would be. As I would have a long walk back home on an unlit road, I decided to take a room for the night just in case the meeting ran late.

Since settling into Syron Lake, I had discovered that the motel belonged to Mayor Demetriou. I wasn't particularly eager to give him my business. But there was no avoiding it. The only other accommodation was at a much more expensive three-story hotel at the far edge of town. It was also owned by the mayor, who held the franchise for the coffee chain and the burger joint, and was also behind Tito's, the only decent restaurant in town.

"I'm sorry but we're all booked up," the young man at the front desk said. "There's a wedding on this weekend and their guests have taken all the rooms."

Change of plans, then. I would go to the Moose Lodge just to find the member who was running for mayor and skip the meeting itself.

By the time I arrived at the squat, brown building, it was well past eight and I was beginning to feel the effects of my lack of sleep over the previous twenty-four hours.

"Are you the young lady that called Gladys, our secretary, earlier today?" the frail, sharp-faced woman who sat at a table near the entrance said. Her hands and head seemed to shake involuntarily.

"Yes. But I'm afraid I won't be able to stay for the meeting."

"I knew it had to be you. We don't get too many people your age coming to our meetings. But, then again, not too many young folks live in this town."

"Your secretary mentioned a board member named Osgood. May I speak with him, please?"

"Would you like to sign up for our club?" the woman said. "It's only twenty dollars for the year. And we have such a good time. It's all nice people. Oh, I'm sure they'll like you. We put on such a nice pot-luck dinner every three months. You should see the feast!"

"Is Osgood here tonight?"

"And they put on really good lectures," the woman said. "Sometimes they get a retired professor or somebody like that from out of town to come speak. Really interesting. But they couldn't get anybody this month. So it's just the police coming in tonight to speak about the citizens on patrol program. Trying to rope more of us old fogies in to help them out, you know."

There was clearly a problem here. My words didn't seem to be getting through.

"Excuse me," I said, louder. "I would—"

"Oh, looks like I don't have any membership forms out here." The woman sifted through the magazines, newsletters, and pamphlets that littered her table. "Silly me. Hold on a while, dear. I'll be right back."

She got up, shuffled down the corridor, opened a door and disappeared behind it.

I stepped away from the table and looked around. I had never been inside this building before. A long hallway with at least a dozen doors extended on either side of me. Behind which door would I find the meeting?

The front door swung open and the dark material of an officer's uniform came into view. I turned so that my back was to him. I wandered off slightly to the right, and pretended to look at the large, framed photographs of past Moose Lodge presidents.

Since I had left behind those unpleasant days as a rookie crime reporter for *The Sentinel*, I had studiously avoided cops. But it was the mayor's virtual threat earlier in the day to see to it that I'd be arrested for trespassing that made me want to be invisible to this badge-wearer now.

"Excuse me." The voice had all the masculinity and confidence I'd found typical in those who carried a gun. "Can you tell where I'll find the Field Naturalists meeting?"

"Sorry, I'm not with the group." I didn't turn around.

"You have any idea, at least, if the meeting is still on in here?"

"Yes."

"Is that 'Yes' as in you do know, or 'Yes' meaning it's still on."

"Both."

I looked at the reflection of his bearded face in the glass of the framed photograph before me. The smile on his lips was matched by the look in his eyes. I was wearing fitted jeans and a black bomber jacket, and his gaze was angled to just below the hem of my jacket, right smack on my derrière. Typical cop, I thought.

He was suddenly beside me.

"You're new in town, aren't you?"

He was tall and muscular. He had a head of luxurious, auburn hair and a short-cropped beard which seemed oddly familiar.

My mind flashed back to the collision earlier in the day. The image of the cell phone crashing to the pavement made me cringe. I made no reply. I shrugged and walked back toward the table.

He followed me.

"Detective Sergeant Paul Parker." He held out his hand. "I think we may have met this morning."

I had already picked up a pamphlet. I stared at it, trying to ignore the extended hand.

The silence was beginning to get awkward when a nearby door swung open.

"I can't find the membersh…. Oh, Sergeant Parker, is it you that's come to speak to us tonight?" The woman from earlier shuffled toward us.

"Hi, Milly." The officer raised his voice several decibels. "The chief asked me to fill in for him at the very last minute. Sorry I'm late."

"Oh don't worry. You won't hear George complaining. He's just been yapping away up there to make up time. Come along now."

The woman turned to me. "And you too, dear. You're welcome to sit in and see what you think about us. And if you like what you see, you can sign up later."

She led us down the corridor toward a double door.

"I didn't get your name, back there," the cop said.

Even if it was now apparent that he hadn't been sent at the mayor's request to arrest me, I was reluctant to say anything.

"Excuse me?" The officer bent his ear toward me.

It was pointless to refuse to answer. It was a such a small town that this cop would have had no trouble finding out my name, and to ignore him further would have unnecessarily deepened the ill-feelings I seemed to have already created with the authorities.

"Stella Jacob," I mumbled.

"Hope we have a chance to meet again, Stella."

As soon as the door opened, the man at the mike called out, "Ah, Detective Sergeant Parker. Not a moment too soon!"

The woman from the front table had already disappeared. Just as well, I thought. I couldn't very well shout a request into her ear for her to point out Osgood to me.

I took a seat at the back and scanned the room, trying to guess who Osgood might be.

Because he was running for mayor, I looked for a jacket, or at least a shirt and tie. Nothing of the sort was in sight. Most men were in sweaters; two or three wore lumber jackets; and some had on thick coats.

I slid across two empty chairs to the man closest to me.

"Can you tell me who Osgood is?" I whispered.

"What?"

"Osgood. He's a director here. Running for mayor."

"Never heard of him. I'm new in town. Just joined the club tonight."

The head with the blue rinse from two rows in front turned around. Severe eyes glared at us. "Do you two mind?" the woman hissed. "People are trying to listen to the speaker."

The man held up his hands in surrender, and I slid back to my original place.

Could I wait out the cop's talk and whatever else was to follow before the meeting ended?

I was about ready to forget about this Osgood character, the breached dam, and this entire business about radioactive pollution. My eyes stung, my head felt light, and all I wanted was to crawl into bed.

Then the figure of a woman slouched into the seat in front of me. I looked two rows ahead at the blue rinse and decided I would take my chances.

"Excuse me," I whispered to the woman who had just sat in front of me. "Do you know who Osgood is?"

"Of course. Everybody knows Osgood." She looked around. "There he is. Leaning against the wall at the side. He's the one in the blue lumber jacket."

I led the way out to the front table, which we found deserted.

He was a small-framed man, bent slightly forward. His salt-and-pepper, shoulder-length mane was tamed somewhat by a terry cloth headband, while his tapering beard reached mid-chest. Wild, shifting eyes peeped out from under all that hair. The air around him carried a slight whiff of stale perspiration.

He stood with a wide stance and folded arms, and nodded in vigorous bursts to my account of the night before and the day's failed efforts to raise an alarm.

"Not surprised at all." His heavily-wrinkled brow creased even further.

"You're not?" I said.

"These greedy bastards in the mining companies only care about satisfying their lust for money. They'll rape and pillage Mother Nature mercilessly and leave her for dead. They couldn't care less what damage they do."

He was right. Of course, he was right. But from the look of him, I was beginning to doubt that he was the one I needed to turn to for advice.

He stuck a bony finger in the air. "Hold on a minute. I think I know what this is all about."

He went through the door the woman who had been at the table had entered earlier. Half a minute later, he wheeled out an ancient-looking bicycle that was covered in rust blisters and fluorescent green and orange paint. He leaned the bike against the wall and dug into a bulging, worn, leather pouch.

He took out a thick stack of papers, letting some of them fall at his feet.

"Here it is," he said after a while. "Read that."

He shoved a wrinkled scrap into my hand, and bent to gather up the mess on the floor.

The clipping from a national newspaper announced that the Canadian Nuclear Regulatory Authority would hold a hearing to review uranium waste management practices in Syron Lake. The CNRA's objective, it said, was to ensure an orderly transfer of responsibilities from the mining companies to the government.

"No surprise that there's a spill right about now." Osgood nodded. "I bet you those greedy bastards didn't want to wait the three to five years remaining before they get to walk away from the toxic dumps they created. They want to leave it all to us taxpayers to take care of. Must of let their facilities rot to hell. Maybe even broke the bloody dam themselves just so that they could duck out early and leave us holding the bag."

He was shaking, as if his body could hardly contain his anger. "And you won't get Mayor Demetriou to say a peep against them. Been in their back pockets for years. How do you think he came to have this hotel, and that motel, and this and that restaurant? All that didn't take chump change to build, I tell you."

"I see," I said.

I knew enough about slander laws not to say anything to encourage him further.

I returned the article to him. He folded it and placed it back in the pouch.

"Why don't you write and try to get in on the hearings to expose this and stop them in their tracks?" Osgood said. "The deadline for applying is long gone at this point. But, with what's happened, there's a chance they could slip you in at the last minute."

I walked briskly back to my house. The quarter moon on a cloudless night was enough to light my way.

My eyelids felt like they were ready to fall off and my head throbbed. But the first thing I did after I got in was switch on my computer.

There was a CNRA hearing that I needed to Google.

Chapter 17

Dromel left the Riverside Drive condo he and Bernice had bought several years before in a show of dedication to the idea that they would stay together forever.

Friends who were on second or third marriages often marveled at how the two had managed to keep the fires burning since they had met as undergrad law students. Bernice often joked that the secret to their success was in not getting married.

Since she had accepted a position with the International Criminal Court just over a year prior, she had been spending most of her time between Europe and Africa. She came back to Ottawa only a few days at a time. Dromel had spent his summer vacation with her in Europe. The arrangement would be temporary, she had said. If all went well with this two-year contract, she could be made permanent, in a higher position. Even on her salary alone, they would be able to relocate to Europe.

Well, the arrangement suited him just fine. While she was off on her high-flying career, he would have his fun.

He took a taxi to a park-and-ride on the western edge of the city. At ten o'clock on a Friday night, the place was deserted, except for three cars. In the far corner of the lot, a figure slouched against a black sedan.

"Hey, Mr D." The figure stood erect as Dromel approached.

The individual lifted his right arm, with his elbow bent and palm showing. Dromel lightly slapped the fellow's palm. He had long ago given up all efforts to make a proper handshake their form of greeting.

"How's it going, man?"

"Fine, fine," Dromel said abruptly. He didn't like that the skinny kid didn't get it that they were not friends.

Dromel took out his cell phone. "Tell me, how easy would it be for you to find this man?"

The two pictures on the phone were terrible. One showed the subject's right shoulder and the right half of his face. The other, more blurred, showed more of the face, but was cut off at the eyelashes.

The second time he had met the stranger who had slipped him the scribbled offer in the bar, Dromel had pretended his phone had vibrated and that he took the call; the shots were the best he'd managed to secretly take.

The skinny kid grabbed the phone.

"From the way he spoke, I have a feeling he's some high-priced lawyer." Dromel folded his arms. "I figure he's from Ottawa. He seems familiar enough with the place as far as I can tell."

The young man squinted as he focused on the tiny screen in the dim glow of the street lamps. "Nice threads."

"Well?" Dromel said.

"I don't know, man. I don't move in those kinds of circles."

Dromel scrunched up his mouth.

"Now, for a price," the fellow said, "maybe I could kick things up higher, up to people who would know people. But, it would come at a cost, you understand."

"The keys," Dromel said curtly, stretching out an upturned palm. He would not be drawn into negotiating with this nineteen-year-old who increasingly seemed to think he'd come across an unending fount of money.

The fellow took the car keys from his pocket and dropped them into Dromel's hand, along with the phone.

"And the stuff?" Dromel said.

"In the glove compartment."

"Okay. I'll call you when and *if* I need you again."

"Chill," the figure said. "Everything's cool, man. Till next time."

The fellow raised his arm and showed his palm again. Dromel raised his hand to meet it with even less enthusiasm than before.

He drove toward Island Park Drive to cross over to the Quebec side of the river, cursing himself for bringing up the subject of the stranger in the expensive suit with the skinny kid. It was a foolish plan to begin with. If by some stroke of luck the kid had found the stranger, what would he, Dromel, do? Call up the stranger and say he wanted more money to get the job done? No, that would only have come off as desperate.

A better plan now came to him. He would give them a surprise. He would send strong signals that he couldn't approve what Syron Lake Resources was asking for. That would surely flush out the stranger with the fancy suits.

They would come to him...begging. Then, he could name his price.

At a stop light, he opened the glove compartment. He took out a small packet. He counted. Two dozen round, white pills. The skinny kid hadn't tried to cheat him this time; not like the last occasion when he was two pills short.

He was growing increasingly disturbed with his majordomo, as he called him. But he couldn't just get rid of the guy. The Ontario car lease and the Hull bachelor pad were under the kid's name. Dromel felt this precaution necessary to ensure there would be no paper trail that would lead to him.

It was also the reason he paid for everything with cash whenever he was with one of his lady friends. If Bernice were to ever suspect anything, there would be no evidence for her to point to.

Guys who got caught and paid for their fun in a painful and expensive split were simply careless or stupid, he thought. He would not be one of them.

He headed to a tiny, out-of-the-way restaurant to meet Cynthia, his latest paramour. He was onto his fourth romance since he had entered this world of intrigue that added excitement and a sense of danger to an otherwise disappointing life.

The first one had been exhilarating. She was whirlwind of pleasure and recklessness. It was she who had introduced him to the OxyContin, and to the weekends of wild escape it brought.

In fact, she was the one who started the whole affair when she ran her shopping cart into his in the frozen dinner aisle and slipped him her cell number after a brief, flirtatious chat.

But as suddenly as she had started it, she had pulled the plug on their dalliance, disappearing without warning out of his life, to return to her husband and children.

He had made the mistake of letting his emotions run away with him that first time. He had sulked for weeks trying to figure out how to find her. Then he realized he was wasting time that he could have been spending with someone new.

He had discovered the deliciousness of married women out for extracurricular fun. They were utterly discreet, totally abandoned, and in no way clingy. He'd come to accept that after what amounted to scratching an itch, they would all eventually retreat back into their anodyne existence of suburban backyard barbecues, SUVs full of kids, and endless trips to swimming pools, hockey rinks, and soccer fields.

Cynthia was nowhere near there yet. He could look forward to a couple of days of fun this weekend, and many more yet to come, whenever she could manage it.

Already, he could feel his pulse increasing at the thought of how she would undo the bun she usually wore and would shake loose her luscious, long, auburn hair that smelled of vanilla and almond.

He suspected Cynthia was not her real name. To her, he was Francis Aube, a government bureaucrat in an unspecified agency.

He had made the mistake during the first adventure of giving his real name, though he had said little about what he did for a living. That first lover had never asked about it; had never seemed interested. When she had broken things off, and he in his crazy despair had gone searching for the street in Fallowfield Village where she had said she lived, he couldn't find it. It didn't exist. That's how he had learned how this game was played.

And, this night, he would dedicate himself to continuing to be a master at it.

Chapter 18

Eric Tremblay saw the bar where he was supposed to meet the Americans, up ahead, on a seedy Ottawa street, between a pawn shop and an adult video store.

He was already nervous about his connection with the two men. Their choice of locale for the rendezvous was not improving matters.

He wasn't familiar with Ottawa. He had been there only once before. It had been just a few weeks prior, when he had come down from Syron Lake with his nephew, Jacques, to help the boy settle in at college.

Tremblay had chosen the city for his meeting with the Americans because Jacques was there, and because it was far from Syron Lake. He was now regretting that he had let the Americans name the exact spot for their encounter.

Tremblay found the capital oddly desolate at eleven o'clock, on a Friday night. Only the occasional car rumbled down the street. But he welcomed the desertedness of this stretch. His near encounters with others along the way had made him jittery. The dimly-lit pavements, the steps of crumbling tenements, and the alleys he had passed had seemed to him to be crawling with human derelicts. He pretended not to see anyone and kept up a brisk pace.

He was of average build and maybe his waistline had expanded a bit too much over the years, but, still, he considered himself a tough guy. He was sixty-seven, had been a miner all his working life, and had witnessed and been part of some crazy things in his day. But that had all been small town stuff. He walked tall, but, inside, he felt no match for the gun-toting dealers or the drugged-up zombies he imagined prowled the mean streets of a big city.

The events of the previous thirty hours had left him on edge. Hell, the events of the past six weeks had turned his world upside down.

Now he wasn't certain he had any hold on reality anymore. He was operating on auto-pilot and he wasn't sure that pilot could be trusted.

He pushed open the door and was immediately hit by a wave of hot air. It was just mid-October, he reminded himself; it was crazy for the place to have the heat on.

He scanned the dimly-lit room. The narrow hall had fewer than a dozen white, melamine tables surrounded by plastic lawn chairs. An elderly man seemed to be asleep as he sat at one table, clutching a beer bottle. The bar was unmanned.

Tremblay recognized the muscular American with the dirty blond flat top haircut and grizzled jaw at the back of the room. A jacket hung from the back of an empty chair opposite him.

Tremblay sighed and walked over to the table.

"Look, if it isn't the man of the hour," said the American, whom Tremblay knew only as Quinn.

The man stood up and noisily dragged a chair out for Tremblay.

He slapped Tremblay on the back and squeezed his shoulder so firmly it hurt.

"Take off your coat and sit down," Quinn said. "Damn, crazy owner has it sweltering in here."

Tremblay didn't have a choice. The American virtually yanked his leather jacket from his shoulders and draped it on the back of the chair before pressing him down into the seat.

"So! Mission accomplished!" Quinn said. "Time to celebrate. I say we get this man a drink." He walked over to the bar. With both hands cupped at his mouth, he shouted, "Hey, we need another beer at the back here."

Quinn returned to his seat.

Almost simultaneously, another man stepped out from behind a nearby door marked "Toilet;" he pulled up a seat to the right of Tremblay.

Quinn jabbed Tremblay's shoulder and nodded in the direction of the other man.

"You remember Young, don't you?"

Tremblay nodded.

He had met both only once before, for a few hours at a casino in Sault St Marie, a town two hours from Syron Lake. That was six weeks ago. He didn't care for Quinn slapping him and punching him on the arm now as if they were fast friends. Heck, he didn't care to even know Quinn, and the same went for his stocky companion with a goatee and plaited ponytail.

The bartender, an aged and slightly-built man, brought a beer, hastily plunked it on the table before Tremblay, and, without a word, disappeared again to wherever he'd been hiding.

Quinn raised his beer and tipped it toward Tremblay. The three men clinked bottles.

"Drink up," Quinn said. "You deserve it."

"You brought the money?" It was the first time Tremblay spoke.

Quinn shot a glance at Young and then looked back at Tremblay.

"Of course we did."

"Well, let's get on with it."

"Not so fast." Quinn clasped Tremblay's shoulder again; the thumb pressed down hard on Tremblay's collar bone. "Enjoy your beer. There's enough time for business."

"I'm not here to hang out," Tremblay said.

He had done what they had asked him to do. Now all he wanted was to get his money and get the hell away from these guys.

"Finish your beer, at least," Quinn said. "You can do that, can't you?"

Despite his urge to get the money and run, and forget he had ever met these Americans, instinctively, Tremblay knew he had better not upset or insult them. He put the beer bottle to his lips.

"This doesn't have to be the end of this road." Quinn leaned in. "The company has need of someone they can rely on, long term. This could, in fact, be only the beginning."

Tremblay pretended to sip his beer in silence. He would not be drinking tonight. Doctor's orders.

Young, the one with the ponytail, leaned in as well toward Tremblay.

"Of course, the company wouldn't be too happy with someone who didn't want to continue to cooperate." Something between a smile and a sneer forced itself across Young's face. "I mean, once you're in on something like this, you're in for good. Otherwise, things could get a little messy. Understood?"

Tremblay's expression remained unchanged. He hadn't heard a word Young had said; he was deaf in his right ear.

"So?" Quinn grabbed Tremblay's upper arm. "We're good for the long haul, then?"

"We'd better be," Young said. He looked Tremblay squarely in the eyes. "Otherwise I've got a buddy named Colt that won't hesitate to spring into action, if you know what I mean."

Tremblay's mind was on the cash that he was yet to collect. It was best to just bear the men out and try to keep his cool.

"We're good," he said.

They finished their drinks without another word.

"Good," Quinn said finally with a nod.

Young stood up. He removed his jacket from the chair and slipped off a black duffel bag that had been under it. He passed it across to Quinn.

"It's all there." Quinn slammed the bag into Tremblay's chest. "And just to show how trustworthy we are, we'll stay right here and let you go in there and count it." He nodded in the direction of the toilet.

Tremblay didn't move. He had dreamed of having the cash — fifty thousand in cold, hard American dollars — in his hands ever since the men had taken him aside in the casino in Sault St Marie. They had given him a small velvet pouch with two thousand worth of chips as a down payment and it had succeeded in convincing him to go along with their plan.

He'd worked for good money in the mines, but money never seemed to last too long in his hands. This was the first time he had such a pile of dough all at once to call his own.

"Go on." Quinn practically pushed Tremblay out of his chair. "Lock the door behind you."

His knees weak and his limbs shaking, Tremblay stumbled into the toilet.

When they heard the click of the door, Quinn nodded to his companion.

Young yanked Tremblay's jacket from the back of his chair. He carefully made a tiny slit in the seam at the base with a penknife. He took a miniature listening device from his pocket. With deft movements, he implanted the device, then replaced the jacket on the back of Tremblay's chair.

The two men continued to wait as if nothing had happened.

The door clicked open.

"All there?" Quinn said.

"Yes." Tremblay immediately picked up his jacket and slipped it on. "Well, so long, I guess."

He had stepped not more than three paces when he heard the voice behind him.

"Hey! Hey!"

He turned around.

"You'd better remember what I told you about my friend, Colt," the man with the ponytail said.

In an alley opposite a parking lot in walking distance from the bar, a third American, Williams, waited for Tremblay to appear.

It was Williams who, in the wee hours of that morning, had smuggled the cash into Canada through Mohawk territory that stretched from New York into Ontario. He had picked up a stolen midnight blue SUV with a false license plate in Cornwall and had made his way to Ottawa.

His job this evening had been to cruise the neighborhood until he had located Tremblay's red pickup. It wasn't too hard to find. The battered Dodge stood by itself in the parking lot.

Williams had passed the last half hour twiddling his thumbs as he watched the dead-quiet scene. Now, he almost burst out in laughter as he saw Tremblay appear, clutching the black duffel bag to his chest and running up the street like a scared rabbit.

Tremblay unlocked the door of his truck and jumped into the driver's seat. He sat behind the wheel, panting. After a short while, he pulled off with a screech.

Williams followed at a discreet distance. The ten-minute pursuit took him up King Edward Avenue, across the Macdonald-Cartier bridge into Quebec, and onto the Autoroute de la Gatineau. The sign above the exit that Tremblay took left no doubt as to his destination: Boulevard du Casino.

Chapter 19

His pants folds tucked into his socks, Marcus Osgood pedaled furiously on his fluorescent green and orange bicycle. His long hair fluttered in the cool, early morning breeze. He sped along the main road that ran through Syron Lake and, after a while, turned down a cul-de-sac.

The gray stucco bungalow at which he stopped was closed. All the blinds were drawn and the garage door was down. The red Dodge he had been expecting to see parked out front was nowhere in sight.

Osgood climbed the steps and banged on the door.

"Eric Tremblay, you dirty dog," he shouted.

The greeting brought no response.

Osgood hopped back on his bicycle.

It was just before seven, Saturday morning. The sun was gentle and a light mist hugged the ground. Osgood didn't feel terribly fatigued by the hour-long ride on the road leading out of town that took him deeper into the forest.

He stopped at a narrow side road, got off the saddle, and wheeled his bicycle along the gravel. He walked for five minutes down the road that cut through the dense stands of pine and cedar. A sharp turn to the right brought him to the shore of a lake. A thin layer of mist hovered over the placid water. He squinted and looked out for a boat with a solitary fisherman.

Nothing.

At the end of the driveway, tucked under a tall cedar was a big, old mobile home with two canoes on a rack at the side. Osgood had been certain he would have seen the red truck here, with a boat trailer hitched to it. But it was not here. And the mobile home was shut tight.

He walked around to the back.

"Eric? Eric!"

The crows in the trees cawed, but there was no human response.

Chapter 20

I thought the figure looked familiar. He slowed down as he approached the house. He got off his bicycle and waited as I climbed down from an old, wooden ladder that I'd found and had been using to get at a leak in the eaves-trough.

Osgood remained at the side of the road and shouted out to me. "You should get Carlton to do that."

"What's that you said?" I walked out to meet him.

"Carlton, you should get Carlton to do that. That's his job."

"Who's Carlton?"

"Carlton, the owner."

I bent my head and chucked.

"A tenant isn't responsible for repairs, you know. That's the landlord's job. Or you should get your husband to do that kind of stuff for you."

I laughed even louder.

Osgood stared at me with eyes that seemed wilder than ever.

"There's no husband here," I said. "And *I* own this place now. Bought it back in August from Carlton. I'm more accustomed to calling him Mr Milken, though."

"You live here all by yourself?"

"Certainly do. And I can handle my own repairs, thank you very much."

"That's not right." He shook his head.

"What's not right?"

"Pretty, young thing like you shouldn't be living on her own out here like this."

I smiled. I hadn't thought of Osgood as a man who would pay attention to a woman's looks, let alone remark on them. I'd never considered myself a beauty in the least, and I certainly didn't think Osgood's opinion on the subject could ever be definitive. Still, his words made my cheeks tingle.

"I can take care of myself," I said with a chuckle.

"Still doesn't make it right."

The night before, my visceral reaction had been to recoil from him. Sure, he looked…different. But now, I found his awkwardness and the gentleness of his demeanor somewhat disarming.

"Nice morning for a ride," I said.

"Didn't plan on it. My fishing buddy bailed on me. He was supposed to come pick me up by five and didn't show up."

"That's a bummer."

"He works up at the old Syron Lake mine. First, I figured he's been run off his feet since the spill and he overslept this morning and forgot to come get me. I kept calling and he wouldn't answer the bloody phone. Finally, I got so fed up, I rode over to his place. No sign of him. Even went over to his camp. Nope. Wasn't there either."

"Maybe he's doing overtime today."

"That's what I ended up thinking. I'm gonna ride up and see if I can get in. See if he can show me how bad things are up there."

I slapped my forehead. "That'll be a long, long ride."

"These old legs can take it." His broad smile creased his already wrinkled cheeks.

He got on the saddle.

"Oh, wait, I wanted to tell you something." I grabbed hold of his shirt sleeve to stop him. "I sent an email this morning to formally request to appear at the hearing."

"Good for you."

"I don't know when I'll find out whether or not they'll let me speak, but I've begun writing up the presentation already."

"Go for it. Get the greedy bastards!"

I watched him ride off, still unable to believe the journey he was about to undertake. There was no way he would use the alternative route to get back after visiting the site. It was too long and too hilly. He had to return the same way.

I was determined to catch him on his return. Hopefully he would meet his fishing buddy. If he did, his report on the damage could make a valuable addition to my presentation.

It was not until dusk that I caught sight of him through the living room window. The thin, white beam of his bicycle light was impossible to miss.

I dashed out the door, just as he passed the house.

"Osgood, wait!"

The bicycle slowed, then stopped. He turned around and pedaled the short distance back to me. We stood in the square of light that shone from my window.

"How was it? What are they doing up there?"

"Didn't get in." He panted.

"Okay, catch your breath."

"Got past the barricade," he continued after a pause. "But they stopped me before I could get anywhere near the tailings pond."

"Oh. That's too bad."

"Some guy acted like a hog. Threatened to have me arrested."

"I'm not surprised to hear that."

"Seems like a lot of activity up there, though. Saw four, five pickups go in and out in the short time I was there. Looks like they brought in outside people to help. I asked for Eric and nobody knew who he was."

"So, you saw nothing that I could add to my presentation?"

He couldn't have missed the disappointment in my voice.

"Well, I'll tell you, I thought of something when those strangers kicked me out." His entire body shook and even in the dim light, the fire in his eyes was unmistakable.

"What did you think of, Osgood?"

"I mean, it's my own damned town and they bring in strangers to run me out of the place and tell me I can't go see what's happening with radioactive waste that could kill me? I tell you, I thought of something. It came to me right then and there."

"What?"

"Sue the bastards!"

He punched the air with his fist.

"What?"

"That's right. Sue the hell out of them."

I stared at him.

"Money! That's the only thing the greedy pigs behind these corporations understand. That's what this is all about in the first place. They rape and pillage Mother Nature and now, when it's time to take care of the mess they created, they want to get out of it. They'll say this clean-up is beyond what one company can be expected to handle. They want taxpayers to pick up the tab for their mess. I say sue them."

"What are you talking about, Osgood?"

"A class action lawsuit."

His words meant nothing to me. I stared blankly.

"File a lawsuit on behalf of every living soul in the town. And maybe the Indian reservation too, I say. God alone knows how bad that spill is. What if it gets into the water table? What if it's letting off gases into the air? I bet that spill's already put all our lives at risk. I say they should be taken to the cleaners for this."

"We can do that?"

"I could get you newspaper clippings about class actions, if that would help. I might have one or two in my bag." He stretched his hand toward the worn pouch on his bike.

"It's okay," I said. "I'll Google it."

Chapter 21

Saturday had been uneventful, as far as they were concerned.

Taking turns tailing him, Williams, later replaced by Quinn and then Young, had observed Eric Tremblay disappear into the Casino de Lac-Leamy after the Friday night meeting.

Just before daybreak, Saturday, Tremblay had left the casino with a buxom, barely-clad woman on his arm and had driven to a nearby motel. The woman had left half an hour later in a cab.

Tremblay had stayed in his room for most of the day, emerging only at five in the afternoon to return to the casino. He'd gone back to his motel just before dawn on Sunday with a different woman, who'd left after forty-five minutes.

Now it was late afternoon, Sunday. All together in the SUV, with Quinn at the wheel, they followed the red Dodge over the bridge as Tremblay crossed back to Ottawa.

"So far so good," Quinn said. "Looks like the gambling loser is staying true to form."

"I'm still worried that we can't understand hardly a word he's saying," Young said. "Williams here speaks French and he can't make head nor tails of it."

"I know just a few words here and there that I picked up from that girl, Monique." The youngest of the three, and out for the first time on such a mission, Williams kept mostly quiet as he rode in the back. "We were together for just about four months; then she had to go back to France. But she spoke proper French, not this pig French they speak over here."

"Not a problem, boys." Quinn pointed to the glove compartment, where he stored bits of his spy equipment. "It's all being recorded. We'll just have to get somebody to translate, if it comes to that. But from the sounds of it, looks like he hasn't had a significant conversation with anybody since he left the bar Friday night. It's just, ordinary, everyday crap."

"That'd be some expensive crap if it had to be translated." Young cackled.

"The boss is good for it." Quinn had not let the others in on exactly who they were working for.

"How much longer you think the battery on that thing will last?" Williams asked.

"Should have enough juice up to Monday morning or so." Quinn answered Williams' reflection in the rear-view mirror. "Gives us plenty of time. It's the first twenty-four to forty-eight hours after an amateur does a job like this that are the most dangerous."

"How so?" Williams said.

Young spat a chewed-up piece of gum out the window. "They get something like buyer's remorse, in reverse."

"Yeah," Quinn said. "Someone not accustomed to this line of work would put down a job and when they get the money in their hands and the reality of what they did hits them, they can start acting crazy, like they want to get out and have no part of it. Except it's too late."

He thrust his chin at the red pickup. "But this one seems like he's good with it. He's enjoying his cash."

"Well on the way to losing it all, more like it," Young said.

"I think our good-cop, bad-cop routine did the trick," Quinn said. "Looked like it sure worked him over good."

Young chortled and stroked his goatee. He had enjoyed that game.

"Where do you think he's headed now?" he said. "That's not the right direction if he's headed home."

"Probably looking for another lay," Quinn said.

Tremblay pulled into the driveway of a rundown house on a street just off North River Road. The neighborhood consisted mostly of single-family bungalows with neat front lawns; but the yard of this two-story was overrun by weeds.

The Americans parked under a tree on the side of the road where parkland bordered the Rideau River. They watched Tremblay enter the house.

They listened.

"Hi, Perry, I came to see Jacques."

"He's in his room. You remember which one?"

"Up the stairs, first door on the right?"

"You've got it."

As plodding footsteps sounded, Young unwrapped a fresh stick of gum and stuffed it into his mouth. "Doesn't sound like he came here for some more action."

"Unless he swings both ways," Williams said.

The three sniggered.

"Allô, Jacques, c'est moi," Tremblay said. *Hello, Jacques. It's me.*

"What the hell?" Young shifted in his seat. "He's back to that bloody pig-French again."

Chapter 22

"Eric? Mais qu'est que tu fais la?" *Eric? What are you doing here?*

Tremblay and his nephew continued to speak French in their thick, Franco-Ontarian accent.

"I need to talk with you."

"And you couldn't just pick up the phone?"

"This is impor—" Tremblay stepped into the room and stood still; his expression hardened as he stared at the open closet. "What the devil is this?"

Jacques sprang off his chair and slid the closet door shut. "What is what?" He folded his arms and planted himself in front of the closet door.

Tremblay pushed him away and reopened the closet. He reached in and pulled a black Harley Davidson leather jacket off a hanger.

He growled, "When and how did this get here?"

The younger man bent his head.

"Look, I specifically told you not to take this," Tremblay shouted. "Didn't I tell you that?"

Jacques pursed his lips. He shifted his weight and stared at the floor.

Perry, the housemate who had opened the door for Tremblay, came up the stairs; he hemmed as he passed the room.

Uncle and nephew stared at each other in silence.

"Listen, Jacques," Tremblay said, still worked up, "God knows I tried to do my best by you since your parents passed. I've raised you like my own son. I will literally give you the shirt off my back. But not *this* jacket. This is the last thing my wife gave me before she died, and you're not having it. Understand?"

Jacques exhaled heavily and nodded.

Tremblay slipped off the coat he had been wearing and tossed it into the closet. He put on the motorcycle jacket.

"Look, allow an old man his sentimental foolishness, okay?" Tremblay said in a calmer voice.

He curved his arm around Jacques' shoulder and shook him.

"Let's get some fresh air."

Chapter 23

Out in the car, the Americans were agitated.

"What the hell's going on?" Young said.

"What was all that noise with the mike? You think they were fighting?" Williams asked.

Quinn, who had been looking in the rear-view mirror, sat up.

"Looks like we've lost audio," he said as Tremblay and his nephew crossed the road some distance behind them. "He changed jackets."

"You think he suspects he was bugged?" Young asked.

"No. I doubt it." Quinn kept his eyes fixed on the two figures as they entered the park. "He isn't even looking around to see if he's being followed."

"Who's this guy he's with?" Young said. "I couldn't understand a word, but, for a minute there, it sure as hell sounded like he was mad enough to kill him."

Quinn turned to face Williams.

"Get out there and tail them as close as you can. See how much you can pick up."

"But I told you, I don't spea—"

"Listen, when you work with me, you just do as I say. Understand?"

Williams blinked.

"I said get your damn ass out there." Quinn bared his teeth and narrowed his eyes.

Williams followed the two men onto the paved path which ran alongside the river. With his head down and his hands in his pockets, he maintained what he figured was a reasonable distance. Quinn was being moron, he thought.

The only words he picked up from the two men were "ecole" and "quitter."

He knew for sure the first word meant school because Monique had taught him that one. He guessed the second word could probably mean what it sounded like in English, but he wasn't sure. Monique had made fun of him, once, calling out French words like raisin, librarie, bras, and préservatif, and laughing when he tripped up by assuming they meant the same as the English words they sounded like.

The young man seemed to be pleading and Tremblay spoke angrily. They stopped and looked back at him. Williams had no choice but to pass them.

Further down the path, he sat on a bench and waited. Jacques stared him down hard as they passed. It would look too suspicious if he tried to follow them again.

He remained on the bench. He felt sure Quinn and Young would not step out of the car and risk Eric Tremblay seeing them. Williams decided to wait there, in the hope that Tremblay and the young man would come back this way to return to the house. Then he would walk back as if he'd trailed them all along.

He would report to Quinn that as far as he could tell, it was a lot of talk about nothing: Tremblay had come to try to convince the younger man not to quit school.

He just hoped he'd got it right.

Chapter 24

Eric Tremblay knew he was a dead man walking.

He had got the death sentence the first week of September, just days before he had driven his nephew to Ottawa to start his electronic engineering technician course at La Cité.

The doctor had been straightforward with him: the tests had come back positive. Stage four non-small cell lung cancer. Prognosis: four months.

His mind was a complete mess. He had come close to breaking down several times as he had helped Jacques pack to move out. But the flurry of activity had been good for him; it had helped push the morbid thoughts to the back of his mind. He was proud to see Jacques become a college man; the first one ever in the family.

When he had got back to Syron Lake and was alone in the house for the first time, it hit him like a thunderbolt that he had messed up; he hadn't lived up to his promise to his brother to do the best he could for Jacques.

For starters, the house and the fishing camp were no longer his. He'd lost both in a poker match to a neighbor, Wilfred Owens. He had transferred the deeds to Owens' name and Owens had been generous enough to say he could continue to use both properties as long as he paid the mortgage. But it meant that when he was gone, Jacques would be left without a home.

Sure he'd leave behind some nice toys: the pickup, the Harley, the boat, the canoes, and the snowmobiles. But he had messed up big time by leaving Jacques without a roof over his head.

Secondly, there were no savings to speak of that could help with any expenses that Jacques' student loan didn't cover.

Tremblay had called around in a panic to see if he could take out a life-insurance policy even after being diagnosed. He got turned down by every company he'd called. Except one. They said they could sign him up and start collecting premiums, no problem; they just wouldn't pay anything if he died before two years were up.

He had driven over to Sault St Marie that weekend, like he did most weekends, to hit the machines. And then, like a miracle, out of the blue two Americans came up to him, offering him money.

He had never seen them before; but they knew a hell of a lot about him.

They knew where he worked and exactly what he did and what his shifts were. They even knew that, several months back, he had reported seeing a small fissure in the bank of the tailings pond. Nothing serious. It could easily be plugged, and even if no repairs had been done on it, the bank would likely hold up for years.

But the Americans were persuasive. They said they were special contractors for the company; the company needed a job done that couldn't be handled under regular, official duties.

The dam's earthen bank had to go.

They said everything had been carefully and meticulously planned. There was an emergency response team in place that would spring into action once the tailings were released. The waste would flow right into Syron Lake, which would act as a larger holding pond. Whatever waste material that didn't drain out of the dam would immediately be hauled into the lake. There would be no danger to anybody or to the environment, they'd said.

All that was required was for Tremblay to wait for the perfect conditions to bust up the bank and make it seem like the spill was an Act of God.

The Americans had pressed a bag of casino chips into his hands. Said it was a down payment. They said he could be holding twenty-five times that, not in chips but in cold, hard cash — US dollars — after the job was done. He carried the bag to the wicket and poured out the chips; the man behind the counter handed him $2,000 back.

Now, the deed was done and his brain felt like it was about to explode.

He had met the Americans again. They had brought the cash, just as they'd said they would. It was after he'd left them that it hit him. The men had reeked of evil; he was appalled by them, scared of them, and ashamed that he'd been seduced by them to do such an insane thing to his own community.

After the whole sordid tale had come gushing out of him, Tremblay fell silent. For a long while, he just stood still with his hands stuffed in his pockets as he stared at the river.

"So, what now, Eric?" Jacques said, finally.

"They said the company might have more jobs for me. But that's it. I'm done with those creeps."

He sighed.

"And there's another thing." He remained silent for a while, took a deep breath, and then continued. "I'm going to confess."

"About the dam?"

"Yes. I did it. I hate myself for it, but I'll man up to it."

"But you've said some pretty harsh things about Father Andre over the years, Eric, and you made sure word of it got back to him. Do you think he'll still agree to see you?"

"I'm not talking about the priest. I'll never go to him."

Tremblay turned to face Jacques.

"I'll do it on *my* terms. And in a way that's best for you. I can't leave you with nothing, Jacques. I know I messed up for myself, and I can go the grave fine with that. But if I leave you with nothing, then I would have failed completely as a man.

"You have to do better than me. I want to go knowing I set you up in life to do better than me. That's why you have to stay in college and get your diploma, so you can get a good job and make good money. You must never be in this position, to feel so desperate that you fall into something like this."

Tremblay rumpled Jacques' hair, as he used to do when his nephew was a boy. Jacques pulled away and smoothed the tuft back into place.

They looked at each other and burst into a laugh.

"So we'll have no more talk about you quitting school, okay?" Tremblay said.

Chapter 25

The email had come long before the press release.

Dromel rapped his fingers on his desk and thought that was a good sign for his purposes.

It was nine o'clock on the Monday morning after the spill. Two hours earlier, at seven a.m., Syron Lake Resources had made its first statement to the general public.

The exceptional event had occurred during the severe weather, the previous Thursday, the company said. The damage was discovered early the following morning and the Canadian Nuclear Regulatory Authority had been immediately alerted, as required.

The spill had been entirely contained within the former mining site, the company assured.

Emergency measures had been taken to relocate all residual material from in the tailings pond to the northwest section of Syron Lake, where most of the spillage had settled.

That section of the lake had been the site of the original waste management operations when the mine was first opened. A submerged berm, a relic from the former operations, had ensured that the solids from the recent spill did not escape into the rest of the lake. That structure was now being elevated to reinforce its resumed work to contain waste material. Tests carried out the waters of Syron Lake beyond this containment area showed readings below the federal standards.

"Syron Lake Resources is confident that the environment will not be impacted as containment systems have operated as designed during this incident," the company press release concluded. "We are focusing on clean-up efforts, and the protection of the environment and the health and safety of our people and the surrounding communities remains paramount."

The email from a concerned resident that had been forwarded to him had arrived in the Inbox of the CNRA's general secretary two days before the press release, on Saturday morning.

Now here was a busybody who apparently was in the know,

and who had nothing better to do on a weekend than hustle off a missive to a regulatory agency, Dromel thought.

The writer stated that she was aware that millions of gallons of radioactive waste had been released into the environment by Syron Lake Resources. Not only did it raise immediate health and safety concerns, but had serious implications for the long term management of uranium waste at that site, she said.

She mentioned her background as a former journalist and environmental activist, and was quite firm in her request to be permitted to address the hearing despite the fact that the deadline for applying to participate had long passed.

She argued that her request should be accepted "in light of this significant development, and in consideration of fairness and the best interests of the public."

Add to that, consideration of the best interests of the chair of the panel, Dromel thought.

An outspoken busybody from the local community would be perfect for putting pressure on the company.

He saw the prospects for his enhanced payday getting better and better.

Chapter 26

Mid-morning on Monday, the Americans criss-crossed the city on the tail of the red pickup. With the young man from the previous day in the passenger seat, Eric Tremblay, cruised around Ottawa's main commercial streets in search of parking. At four stops so far, the two had got out and walked to four different banks.

They spent forty-five minutes on average at each stop.

"Looks like ol' sonny boy here is his partner in crime," Quinn said.

They followed Tremblay down Bank Street, with three cars in between them.

"So what's up with all this movement?" Williams asked.

"Money laundering," Young broke in and answered first. "Looks like the loser is being a little more responsible with the cash after all."

"Must have exchanged the Benjamins for chips at the casino and then converted the chips into Canadian dollars," Quinn said. "Now sonny boy here is running around town, opening accounts at different banks to hide the proceeds. I bet you not one of those accounts will have a dollar over nine thousand. Anything over ten thousand and he'd have to declare how he got the dough."

"So you figure we'll have a problem with this one, or what?" Young asked.

"Mostly, I figure it's favorable," Quinn said. "He hasn't been acting out of the ordinary. And he seemed to not flinch when you threatened him about the Colt, as if he knew he wouldn't have to worry about it, 'cause he wasn't planning to be any trouble."

"So our job here is done then?"

"I wouldn't say so," Quinn said. "I'm thinking I can squeeze about another two, three weeks of retainer out of the boss. Give some kind of bullcrap about the need for extended surveillance with this guy. I'm sure the boss will eat it up. We're in no hurry. I haven't got another job lined up yet, so we might as well ride this gravy train as far as it will run."

Young chortled. Quinn was a business genius, he thought. He was glad to be following him.

Tremblay eased into a parking spot, then he and his companion got out of the truck and walked to a photography store.

"That's more like it," Quinn said. "Knew he couldn't resist plonking down on some flashy, big-ticket junk."

The three cruised behind Tremblay for the next half hour as he drove across the city, heading east. He entered a leafy compound with signs that said "La Cité" and let off the young man. The two shook hands through the window of the pickup. Then the red Dodge reversed course, got onto the Trans-Canada Highway, skirted downtown Ottawa, and then barrelled on, westward.

When they entered the suburbs, Quinn pulled over into a side street. He hopped out with the engine still running.

"Looks like he's headed home now," Quinn said. "You boys follow him and make sure he doesn't do anything crazy. Tail him right to his house. Then get a couple rooms in Sudbury. We'll use there as a base. I'll find me some nice wheels and catch up with you guys tomorrow."

"And where are you going?" Young slid across to the driver's seat.

"I've got to call the boss. And I'll pick up some new equipment. We won't have another chance to plant a bug on him. I know where I can get something that'll work much better."

Chapter 27

I didn't leave the house for five days straight. Ever since Osgood had filled my head with notions of going for the mining company's jugular, I'd sat at my computer day and night, researching.

When sheer fatigue sent me crawling into bed, I could spend no more than three or four hours, tossing and turning under the sheets as the news stories and court judgments of previous class action lawsuits scrolled across my mind.

I thought of Adam Levy and wondered if he had ever heard of class action lawsuits. He'd never mentioned them. But, to me, they seemed the best leash to restrain those rampaging corporate predators.

Class action procedures had been introduced only about two decades earlier in Ontario. They allowed one person to sue a corporation or even the government on behalf of every other person with the same complaint.

Ordinary, everyday folk had gained the power to take on the giants. The numbers were astounding. Corporations and the government had been ordered by the courts to pay $20 million, $100 million, and over a billion, in one case, to the "little guys" they had wronged.

And there it was, the source of the power of class action lawsuits — money. As Osgood had rightly pointed out, it was the language corporations understood. Hitting their coffers was the surest way to get their attention.

I stared out the bay window at the few remaining maple leaves that were being whipped by the wind. Every cell in my body felt just like that — agitated.

We can do this here in Syron Lake, I thought. That company won't be able to ride roughshod over us anymore.

I can do this, I thought. *I* could lead the charge.

My grandfather's saying about there being a reason for everything came back to me and things were beginning to make sense. My whole past struck me as having been an apprenticeship for this moment: my journalism training; the fire Adam Levy had sparked in me to boldly take on corporate predators; all those hours I'd spent researching how corporations were harming the salmon habitat; the strange, new sense of power and possibility that being part of protest rallies had given the meek creature that I'd always been....

Now, it made sense that I'd got lost that fateful night and had witnessed the breaching of the tailings pond. It wasn't that I'd been at the wrong place at the wrong time; just the opposite — I was the right person, in the right place, at the right time.

Even the whole, sorry mess with Peter was beginning to make sense. If I hadn't met him, I wouldn't have heard of Syron Lake. If he hadn't spoken about needing space in our relationship, I wouldn't have ended up in this town. That didn't make things hurt any less, though.

Bang!

The sudden noise at the front door made me jump off the chair, clutching my heart. The momentary panic evaporated when I saw the paperboy pedaling his bicycle further up the road. I made a mental note to tell him to ride into my driveway and deliver the paper in a civilized manner from now on.

I unfurled the tightly rolled copy of the *Syron Lake Beacon.* The front page was all about the municipal elections that were set for the following Monday. Nothing on page three, four or five about the spill. It was only on page six — a lower visibility, left-hand page — that anything appeared.

The story, shorter than five hundred words, filled a thin ribbon of space down the side of a large ad about surplus city land for sale. Most of it quoted the Syron Lake Resources press release that downplayed the incident. It ended with a quote from Mayor Demetriou stating that the city expected the company to comply with all regulations.

The shabby reporting made me even more grateful, now, that Osgood had shown me how we could fight back through a class action lawsuit.

Ah, Osgood. Did I really see his picture in the paper?

I flipped back through the pages. There he was, on the front, in the bank of photos of the three candidates for mayor and the fourteen people fighting for eight council seats.

It was a three-quarter profile of him, with his wild hair hiding much of his unsmiling face; not the most confidence-inducing shot.

"Last chance to see and hear the candidates." the headline read.

The event at the Moose Lodge was sponsored by a new seniors' action group. The meeting was scheduled for that afternoon and was set to start in about an hour. I figured that if I arrived early, I might be able to catch Osgood again.

I had checked the maps and it looked like the Garter Lake First Nation might be even more severely affected than our town by the spill. I knew nothing about the reservation. Perhaps Osgood could help get the tribal band involved in the class action.

The parking lot at the Moose Lodge was packed. Inside, I had to elbow my way though the corridors and into the main hall. Where had all these people been hiding?

Most of the heads were gray, and the waists wide and fleshy; I had come to expect that. But here, too, were dozens and dozens of younger people — mothers struggling to control prancing children; men who looked to be in their thirties, with gold bands on their left ring fingers; other men with no rings, but territorially resting their hands on women's shoulders or lower backs.

I sighed. My single-woman's scan of the room had turned up no prospects.

A commotion erupted over in one corner, and the crowd backed away from a side door.

Above gasps and shrieks, a voice growled, "Get out of here, you old drunk."

After more shifting of bodies, the side door briefly opened and then slammed shut.

"What was that all about?" a woman standing near me said to someone who came from where the disturbance had happened.

"Just old Redmill, drunk as a skunk and misbehaving."

"Again?" The woman who'd asked the question rolled her eyes and shook her head.

Old Redmill?

I'd seen only one "Redmill" in the local phone book. Peter's last name was Redmill. So his father was the town drunk? No wonder he'd never been back to visit. And, perhaps, nothing could induce him to return.

But what was that to me? He was history. Past tense. Never to be remembered.

I pushed my way deeper into the hall. Osgood, unmissable in his blue lumber jacket, stood in front of the raised stage, not far from a group of people whose faces I recognized from the front page. A crowd hovered around each of the candidates and there was a great deal of handshaking and photo-taking in the area.

I walked toward Osgood, but two men reached him before me. The one who shook his hand seemed familiar. Ah, yes, it was the bearded cop from the other night.

He looked less intimidating in khakis and a white, long-sleeved shirt. Still, I didn't care to see or be seen by any cop. I waited until they left.

"So you're up on the big stage tonight," I said when I finally had Osgood to myself.

"Damn rubbish, all this." He shook his head. "Who needs all this show business nonsense?"

"People seem interested. I've never seen so many people in one place since I moved here."

"This is no way to campaign. I bet the mayor's behind this."

"I read it was a new seniors group."

"It wouldn't surprise me that he put people up to form a new group out of the blue to organize this. And why? Because it suits a snake-oil salesman type like him. Just because a man can stand in front of a crowd and wag a silver tongue about doesn't mean that he knows what's best for this town."

He crossed his arms and stuck his hands under his armpits. His chest rapidly heaved and fell with every shallow breath.

I lay a hand on his shoulder. "I'm sure you'll do fine, Osgood."

His eyes were wilder than usual and he didn't seem to notice my gesture. "There's no need for all this, I say. Just walk the street, knock on doors. If people are on your side or at least open to your ideas, they'll invite you in. If not, fine, talk at the door for as long as they'll hear you out, but remain respectful if they disagree with you. Thank them, move on to the next house. That's campaigning. This is show-business."

At the corner of my eye, I noticed someone standing close, waiting to speak with Osgood, the candidate.

"Before the speeches start, I had a quick question about the class action," I said.

"Like what?"

"Garter River runs from Syron Lake and passes through the reservation, then feeds into Garter Lake. I think the Garter Lake First Nation should be involved in something like this. What do you think?"

"They should. Absolutely. No two ways about that. And you can try asking them. But I'm not sure how far you'll get, though."

"Why do you say that?"

"Spot of trouble over there these days. Nasty business. All kinds of accusations flying around about improper spending. But you can still try talking to them."

Someone shoved an arm right in front of me and closed in on Osgood. Now, two others swooped in, blocking my view.

"Thanks, Osgood," I said, and retreated to the back of the room.

The stage was occupied by three rows of metal folding chairs bearing name tags for the candidates. When the master of ceremonies announced the meeting was about to start, the electoral hopefuls climbed the stairs and took their places.

The would-be councilors were trotted out to each deliver a three-minute spiel. Saved for last, the main attraction, the three mayoral candidates, sat among the empty chairs. The candidate, whom I didn't know, wore jeans and a checkered short-sleeved shirt. Mayor Demetriou was the only one in the entire room wearing a suit and tie.

The microphone screeched as the MC adjusted it to Osgood's height.

People whistled and hooted. Others clapped, or snickered, and laughed.

"Osgood's the man!" someone shouted.

The crowd roared with laughter.

Osgood stared out. His wild eyes seemed more spooked than encouraged by the audience's reaction.

"Shhh!" someone said from the back of the hall. The sound was repeated row after row, until the room fell silent.

"I'm no fancy speaker," Osgood said. He cleared his throat.

"But I care about this town. Been here damn near all my life. Was brought here as a baby by my parents and grandfather, who'd been a coal miner in England. Buried all three of them in this town's cemete—"

"We didn't come for a history lesson!" a heckler cried. "Politics! Let's hear about politics!"

Some in the crowd giggled. Mayor Demetriou gave the audience a disapproving frown, even as a faint smile spread across his lips.

The wave of shushing rose again.

Osgood folded his arms and shoved his hands under his armpits.

"As for politics, as mayor of this town, I won't play politics. Not with people's lives at stake. We've had too much of that already over the last dozen years. When you see people with a business, but that business is growing much bigger and faster than there's customers to cause that kind of growth, that's politics. When you see companies easily getting planning permission to do all kinds of things that should first undergo studies and assessments, you know some kind of politics is happening behind the scenes."

The smile was now completely gone from Demetriou's face.

"I'll tell you about politics," Osgood boomed. "This dumping of millions of tons of radioactive waste that happened up at Syron Lake, last week. The mayor knew of it the very morning after. He had a first-hand account."

I bent my head and stared at the floor. This could not be happening. *Please don't let him talk about my trespassing.*

"First thing in the morning last Friday, he knew everything about that radioactive leak," Osgood said. "And what did he do for this town? Squat! There was no warning for you or me. And we are the ones who have to drink this town's water and breathe this air. Which could have been dangerously polluted, mind you. We don't know. All we hear is what the company tells us. And they're not likely to jump up and admit they did anything wrong are they?

"This mayor said not a word to you or me, last Friday. But I will bet you my bottom dollar that after he heard about the leak, he was on the phone to the company.

"And why? Money talks. That's what politics is about. He who pays the piper calls the tunes. This didn't start in this town yesterday. Or last week. It's been going on for years. You all know that."

"Tell it like it is, Osgood!" someone shouted.

Mayor Demetriou folded his arms. His cheeks burned red.

"The current, so-called mayor has done nothing for this town concerning this spill. Well, I may have worked for one of the mining companies when I was younger, but I can tell you, I sure as hell have never pocketed anything under the table from them. As mayor of this town, I wouldn't be beholden to any company. You can bet your life I'd go after them for polluting our environment. And I wouldn't stop fighting for this town until I got some damn good results."

"Give 'em fire, Osgood!" a voice cried.

Osgood's eyes seemed to search the crowd, then they went blank, as if he'd lost his train of thought.

"That's all I have to say," he mumbled.

He bent his head in a stiff, unsure bow. He slouched off the stage, almost as if in a daze, and was lost in the crowd.

Amidst uncertain applause, a few whistles, and the rising din of chatter, the MC called the second contender to the microphone.

The mayor stared blankly at the man's back. By the time he, himself, was on his feet to address the audience, his cheeks had regained their normal color.

"First of all, I want to say that our democracy is such a great thing that it allows anybody a chance to offer themselves to serve in offices like councilor or mayor," Demetriou said. "Unfortunately, that includes people who don't understand anything about running a city. And people who would abuse public platforms like this to descend into defamation."

The mayor nodded as murmurs arose.

"People may say, if there's no truth to a defamatory statement, then the person being slandered would sue," Demetriou said. "Well, my friends, there's a simple reason some people are not sued, even if they are guilty of slander. And the reason is that even if you were to take them to court and win, and they're ordered to pay damages, all they could offer as payment would be, maybe, two pairs of sweaty socks and a beaten up, fluorescent bicycle from the 1970s."

The crowd erupted in laughter.

Fed by the microphone into the speaker boxes, the mayor's guffaw was the loudest of them all.

Chapter 28

After I had voted on the Monday, I rented a car and drove down to Garter Lake First Nation. The band office was deserted except for one secretary who said the chief was away on business. I could leave my name and a message and the chief would call back if he was interested. No, there was no other official that I could see. It was the chief's instructions; all inquiries were to be directed to him and him alone.

On my way back, I stopped at the Garter Lake trading post near the highway. Three women, who sat on the porch embroidering porcupine quills into birch barks, listened to my story about the radioactive spill. They confirmed that children played in the Garter River, and four or five people still went fishing along its banks, even though nobody had heard of anyone reeling in a catch for decades.

The women nodded and agreed something should be done about the mining company polluting the land. But that would have to wait for later, they said. The priority now was for the band to restore peace and harmony. Two factions on the tribal council were fighting; neither would speak to the other, and neither had sufficient numbers to form a quorum, so everything was at a standstill.

Tuesday afternoon, resigned to the reality that I would have to start this battle on my own, I sat where I could be found almost every waking hour; in front of my computer.

Since that night up at Syron Lake, everything I'd researched and written had had to do with the spill. The folder with the incomplete draft of the romance novel had remained unopened on my computer's desktop, and the pile of printed pages had sat on the table, untouched.

Besides fearing the book was gut-wrenchingly bad, I was trying to avoid thinking about romance because doing so inevitably led to having to fight off images of Peter.

I had been steadily plowing through an eight-page judgment when the bold red line at the bottom right corner of my screen indicated an email had just landed in my Inbox.

The sender was "CNRA."

Junk mail, I immediately thought. And then it struck me that that was the acronym for the Canadian Nuclear Regulatory Authority.

My heart pounded against my ribs. My palms itched.

I clicked to open the message.

"Please, please, please," I chanted with closed eyes.

Finally, I looked again at the screen and read aloud.

"We would like to inform you that the Authority has approved your request..."

I sprang to my feet.

"Yes! Yes! Yes!"

I was in! The CNRA hearing and the class action gave us, the little people, a one-two punch against a rampaging corporate predator, or the "greedy bastards" as Osgood called them.

Between the two, there was enough work doing research and writing up papers to occupy an entire small, non-profit. I would be completely buried in this radioactive spill for some time. But that was good because it gave me something to do, something through which I could make a real difference in the world. My time with Adam at the salmon non-profit, and all those rallies he had sent me out to had ignited the passion that now burned inside me to hold corporate raiders to account for harming the environment.

Besides, the romance novel was going nowhere. I needed the break from it and from all the memories of Peter that it inevitably dredged up.

For the sake of my sanity alone, I would have gladly taken on the two projects. With my minuscule house payments and my frugal lifestyle, I could spare a month or two, maybe even as many as four, to dedicate to this battle. After I'd submitted the letter requesting to participate in the hearing, though, I'd learned that I was entitled to apply to the CNRA for compensation for any time I spent to participate in the proceeding. This unexpected good news made me think everything was working in my favor to enable me to get somewhere with this.

Outside, tires rolled over the gravel in the driveway. I could see only a headlamp, so I walked around the table to peer out. A navy blue Mercedes Benz came to a stop. The driver's door swung open and Tito Demetriou stepped out of the vehicle. He took off his shades and walked toward my house with an intent look on his face.

In my rush to get to the door, I knocked over a pile of loose sheets from the table. The pages of my novel cascaded down and scattered all over the floor.

Fine time for this mess to happen.

"Ms Jacob," he said when I opened the door.

"Mayor Demetriou."

Yes, he had been returned for a fourth term. Not with any help from me, though. I had given my vote to guy in the short sleeves.

"May I come in?"

I was tempted to make him stand outside, but found myself opening the door wider and stepping aside to let him in.

"Ms Jacob, how long have you been in this town?"

I noticed him scanning the messy floor. When he looked at me again, his eyes bore a new level of contempt.

"I think I mentioned to you the last time we spoke in your office that I moved here at the end of August."

"So what's that? Less than ninety days?"

"I haven't been keeping count."

"The exact figure doesn't really matter. At any rate, it's a very short time. Almost no time to fully understand this place, its history, and how hard people have worked to make it what it is. Much less what it takes to keep it going."

"I can assure you, Mayor Demetriou, I did my research on Syron Lake before I moved here."

"Research? What? Reading Wikipedia and a bunch of old newspaper articles?"

His tone jarred, and I fought to control my breathing.

"Do you think that qualifies you to say you know better than people who've spent their lives building this town what's right for Syron Lake right now?"

Tito Demetriou may have been the mayor, but he seemed to be forgetting he was standing on my property as he spoke.

"What's your point, Mr Demetriou?"

"I understand you were at the Garter Lake reservation, yesterday."

"And?"

"And you were trying to drum up support for some class action lawsuit you seem to be planning against Syron Lake Resources."

I said nothing.

"Now listen here, miss. Nobody needs you to roll in here to try to play you're some kind of crusader. You're going to do the people in this town more harm than good."

My heart pounded against my ribs, but I folded my arms and cocked my head, and put on my most insolent expression.

Demetriou stood akimbo and sneered.

"Ms Jacob, Syron Lake had an unfortunate accident only because there was a big storm that the dam couldn't handle. But don't you understand that the more you run about making noise about it, the more you damage the image of this community?"

I pursed my lips.

Demetriou jabbed his right index at me.

"With a court case — which you will more than likely lose — you'd be dragging the name of Syron Lake through the mud for years with unfounded accusations about radioactive pollution. Think about what effect that will have on how people from outside will look at Syron Lake. Think about how that will affect property prices."

"You've got to be kidding me." I found myself raising my voice despite my better judgment. "Syron Lake Resources is responsible for leaking millions of gallons of radioactive waste into the environment and *I'm* harming the community if I make efforts to hold them to account?"

"There was no environmental harm. The waste flooded from one containment area into an older containment area that was immediately reinforced. You can't win this lawsuit."

"According to you. But *I* think we have a fighting chance. And we won't find out who's right unless the lawsuit is actually filed, won't we?"

"No environmental class action has been won in Canada, Ms Jacob. This isn't the United States. And you're no Erin Brockovich."

There it was. Another slap in the face from the mayor.

"I think I've heard enough of this," I said.

I walked to the door and swung it open, then folded my arms

and looked Demetriou squarely in the eyes.

He glanced again at the mess on the floor and snorted before walking toward the door. He stopped just before stepping outside.

"You had better put an end to your silly games, for your own good," he said.

The second both his feet were out on the top step, I slammed the door shut.

I found myself trembling from the very core as I knelt to gather up the pages. I let myself fall back on my buttocks as the reality of what had just happened hit me.

I had just had a fight with the most powerful man in Syron Lake. And I had virtually kicked him out the door. Me, the mousy girl who cowered if she heard two people raising their voices at each other.

What did the mayor mean when he said I should stop what I was doing "for my own good"? Was that some kind of threat?

I stared out the bay window that had sold me on the place. *A nice, quiet little town. Fresh air. Closeness to Nature. Perfect place to settle down and get that novel done....*

How could everything have been turned upside down in such a short space of time?

Chapter 29

"I need answers, man. Can't go into the director's office empty-handed the next time he calls me up. I need answers."

Simmons' voice cracked. He leaned against the wall in Sarah Cohen's office with his eyes closed as he rubbed his temples.

The FBI analyst looked up from her computer and chuckled. She tore a sheet from her note pad, crumpled it, and sent it flying straight for Simmons' chest. It met its mark.

Startled, Simmons shook his head and his eyes flung open.

"Get a hold of yourself, Spike," Cohen said.

"It's easy to laugh when it's not your head on the chopping block."

"Why are you beating yourself up over this Mahler case? And you've got so much other work to do."

"The director's breathing down my neck about this."

Simmons felt more than a tinge of pride in saying that. The pressure had robbed him of sleep and, he suspected, was responsible for the persistent headache that hounded him. But its source somehow made it alright; in fact, better than alright. He didn't mind spreading it around that he was taking heat directly from the very top.

He walked over to Cohen's desk and leaned on it, half sitting, half standing. "What more have you got for me?"

"Okay. I'm going to say we should eliminate the theory about some kind of political involvement. I'm just not seeing it."

"Are you sure? The director was pretty worked up about that."

"Throughout the period Magrelma Mines was supposedly some kind of front for the CIA, it operated only in Africa, in five countries. True, three of those countries experienced a regime change. But two of the deposed dictators are long dead, and the third has been in a coma in a Saudi Arabian hospital going on a year now."

"What about rivals at other companies?"

"Nothing's coming up on the radar. No recent aggressive battles for territory; no take-over fights. I'd say, given that the killer had to have gained intimate knowledge of the Mahlers' home and his circumstances on the night of the murder, we should be focusing on suspects that were close to him."

"Well, we have that one partner who fought with him in the bar."

"Yes, Daniel Greene. The argument was about an abandoned uranium mining site in a small town in Canada called Syron Lake. And check this, Spike." Cohen motioned Simmons to come to her side of the desk.

She pulled up the Syron Lake Resources website and clicked through to the press release with the headline, "No environmental impact from breach."

Simmons rested one hand on the back of Cohen's chair and leaned over her shoulder toward the computer. His eyes darted from left to right across the screen. He blinked slowly when he got to the end. He stood up and sighed.

"So, by coincidence, Syron Lake Resources is in the news because a dam burst after a storm, two weeks ago," he said. "What does that have to do with this case?"

"But *was* it a coincidence?"

Simmons jerked back his head. "Come on, Sarah. Really?"

"Look, you asked me to come up with *something*. That's the best I've got so far."

Simmons stared at her.

Cohen shrugged.

"Okay," she said, "I'll admit that speculating that the breach was deliberate doesn't get us anywhere in finding a motive to lay Mahler's murder at Greene's feet. The company is set to give up its license to manage that site. And, besides, Maitland took over control of the company, so I don't see that anything's changed to better Greene's lot since Mahler died."

"No, Maitland's the one who benefited." Simmons recalled what Director Hutton had said about the reins of power and wondered whether "benefited" was the right word in the circumstances.

"That puts him pretty high on the list of suspects," Cohen said. "The name 'Magrelma' is made up of the first two letters of the surnames of the founders, in order of the size of their shares in the company...."

"Mahler, Greene, Ellis, and Maitland," Simmons said, dropping himself onto the chair at the side of Cohen's desk.

"That's right."

"So Maitland has always been the small fry in Magrelma."

"Exactly. But there was a written agreement that if Mahler died, the direction of the company would pass to the next surviving founder in line."

"With Bernard Ellis and Isaac Greene dead and buried years ago..."

"Yes, Maitland stood to directly benefit from Mahler's murder, grabbing control of Magrelma, even though Fran Mahler and the Greene family own more of the company than he does."

"But that won't last for long if Mahler's widow can help it," Simmons said. "The report from the field is that she's moving ahead with a lawsuit so that she can take over."

"The purpose of the lawsuit is to overturn this very agreement we're talking about that gave Maitland control."

"Okay, now I get it." Simmons nodded. "If that's the case, then she probably has a long, drawn-out battle ahead of her."

"What I don't understand," Cohen said, "is if Maitland's struggling in his position as we hear he is, why doesn't he just step aside?"

"Male pride," Simmons said with a shrug.

Cohen threw back her head and laughed.

Simmons shook his head and looked at her. "Seriously, Sarah, the man must have been dreaming of being top dog at that company for the last three decades. Now that he's made it, do you think he'll admit he's not up to scratch, and just give way to a woman?"

"But for the sake of the business...."

Simmons shook his head more vigorously. "A man will hardly admit, even to himself, that he can't handle a job. He'll always tell himself he'll probably learn what's necessary, or that he might get lucky and things will work out by themselves. The last thing he'll ever do is admit to anyone else that he's incompetent; and he'll especially not admit it to a woman gunning for his position."

"So male pride and good sense don't co-exist, then?"

"Sometimes they don't." Simmons shrugged, and then he winked at Cohen. "Just like female intuition and good sense sometimes don't."

Cohen raised her eyebrows.

"Anyway," she said, "as for Fran Mahler, this business with the lawsuit just serves to heighten the focus on her as the main suspect."

"I don't know about that one. I mean, she, herself has raised suspicions that there was something fishy about Mahler's death. Monaco had been portraying it as just an accident, but she came forward and said the nurse couldn't have been smoking because she had never seen him smoke before, and he was well aware that she didn't allow even Mahler to light up in the apartment."

"Well, it could be that she's not involved and genuinely raised that point to help the investigation...."

"But your suspicious mind says it could be otherwise."

"Look, you can't underestimate the tricks a person who commits murder would pull out to cover his or her tracks. She could very well have staged the whole thing and then brought up that little point with investigators to throw suspicion off herself. To make them think exactly what you just said a second ago."

"I suppose."

"Mahler's widow benefited most from his death. She inherited an insane amount. And she's already seeing someone else, less than two months after her husband's gone."

"Not much of a surprise if they were both having affairs." Struck by a thought, Simmons looked up suddenly. "Could it be that one of their lovers was behind this?"

Cohen shook her head. "Don't forget this was a professional hit. Whoever ordered it must have had access to sufficient resources to arrange it. The Mahlers went downmarket for their dalliances. Actresses, models, personal trainers. People who they could use and easily discard, I guess."

"So the wife it is."

Cohen rolled her chair toward her desk and tapped on her keyboard.

"Well, there's also Daniel Greene's mother, Carmela."

"I can't see a motive for that one."

"The latest report is that she's set to join Fran Mahler in the lawsuit."

"I read that in the notes from Paris. But even if those two win their case, it will be Fran Mahler in control, not Carmela Greene. And besides, there's no record of Carmela Greene ever showing any interest in the business."

"True, but it would put Daniel Greene closer to the reins of power at Magrelma. Carmela Greene is quite ambitious when it comes to her son. She boasts about him as being some kind of business hotshot."

Simmons sighed. "Sarah, all this is pure spec—"

"Listen, Spike, there's one other curiosity my research turned up that you might find interesting." Cohen's gaze was steady and her eyes sparkled with excitement.

"Lay it on me."

She placed a printout on the desk, in front of Simmons. "Here's an item in a gossip column from the *New Yorker*, back in the eighties. The writer talks about a friend of hers getting engaged to Mahler the Wednesday before this column was written. Curiously, though, the fiancée mentioned is not Mahler's first wife."

Simmons splayed his hands for the details.

"It was one Angela Woodward."

Simmons heaved his shoulders and scratched his head.

"You don't know who Angela Woodward is?"

"Can't say I've ever heard of her."

"Eight months after this article appeared, she got married to an up-and-coming politician from an old Louisiana family and became Angela Roseau."

"The Secretary of State?"

"Uh-huh."

"Small world."

Cohen nodded. Her eyes darted in the direction of her open door then back to Simmons. She leaned toward him and spoke in a hushed tone.

"Spike, I checked the dates. According to the article, Mahler would have proposed on August 28, all those years ago."

"So?"

"That's the exact date he was killed."

"Huh?"

"You've heard the expression, haven't you?" Cohen raised her hands to the sides of her head and curled her fingers to form quotation marks. "Hell hath no fury like a woman scorned."

Simmons stood up abruptly.

"Now you're really clutching at straws, Sarah. First you try to suggest that that dam in Canada was deliberately busted up, and now you're taking the most tenuous connection and trying to implicate the Secretary of State in Mahler's murder?"

"I'm just trying to—"

"Come up with something better than that before the director calls for me again."

Simmons stomped out the door and banged it shut behind him.

Chapter 30

Towing a fishing boat, the red pickup cut through the low, early morning mist much faster than the posted speed limit.

It was a Saturday morning. Few vehicles were on the road, and the driver probably knew this route, with all its twists and turns, like the back of his hand. Driving like a man should, Williams thought, as he followed at a distance, maintaining the same pace.

This gig had been turning out much better than he'd expected it would when his cousin, Young, had introduced him to Quinn.

Since being kicked out of the Army, he'd been drifting, drinking, and getting into trouble with no clue as to what to do with himself. Except for those delicious few months with that illegal French chamber maid, Monique, it just seemed like his life was on an inevitable spiral downward. He'd been half expecting to soon end up dead or in jail, and wouldn't have been surprised if his undoing came from a brawl over some piffling matter like returning from the john and noticing someone had taken his bar stool.

Now, tagging along with his cousin and Quinn, things were looking up. The last thirteen days had been almost like a holiday. Just rolling around through some nice country, trailing some redneck to work, way up in the bush, following him back home, or when he went fishing, or to the casino.

That Quinn was a real ass sometimes, but he had a head for business, Williams conceded. Quinn had convinced some high-up fool with more money than sense to pay them to hang out like this. They had two motel rooms, and there was plenty of time to enjoy some strong Canadian beer, and some real willing ladies, too. Life was good.

They had one more week of this. Then they'd split up until Quinn called if he needed them for a new job, Young had said. Williams thought he sure as hell would sign up again with Quinn, even if the guy was a jerk, big-time.

The pickup turned off onto a smaller road. The sign read "Seldom Seen Road," and it coursed though a dense conifer forest. Ten minutes in, the Dodge pulled into the driveway of a large sectional mobile home that would have seen better days, maybe a century ago, Williams thought.

He continued past the trailer, then turned around and parked on the shoulder. He peered through binoculars.

He rang Quinn's cell.

"Followed him up a road. Seldom Seen, it's called. Twenty minutes out from the town."

"What's he up to?"

"He just picked up some guy. Nobody I've seen before. Long, gray hair. Long beard."

"Okay. Where's he headed?"

"He's coming back out onto the highway. The guy he picked up dumped fishing gear in the tray. I'm guessing he'll be heading for his camp."

"Okay. We'll pick up his trail once he gets out on the highway. Unless you hear from me again, we'll park at the public boat launch then walk back to his camp, like the last time. Hang back, then do the same."

"Got you."

Another nice, sunny day in the great outdoors, Williams thought.

Quinn would set up that parabolic listening device he'd bought and they would sit around with some cans of Labatt Maximum Ice in a cooler, just like the previous weekend.

Actually, it would be better; the guy had gone solo on his last fishing trip. Now that he had company, this time, there'd be more to hear than just the cawing of crows and the weird cries of loons.

Chapter 31

Eric Tremblay backed the trailer into the lake and tapped his foot on the brake. The boat jerked, then slid off the trailer and into the shallow water. Tremblay jumped out of the truck, unhitched the strap and moored the boat to a large rock without saying a word.

Osgood sat on a stump with his rod leaning against him and his tackle box on his lap. He fiddled aimlessly with spoons and jigs.

Done with launching the boat and parking the truck, Tremblay walked up to Osgood with his hands stuffed in his pockets. "Look, you're just killing the spirit of the day, you know that?"

Osgood kept his gaze fixed on the jiggling plastic worms that he rearranged in a tray.

"You haven't said a word since I picked you up," Tremblay said. "What's up with that?"

"You're who hasn't said a word. You never showed up and you've said squat about it."

"Is this about the elections? About me not turning up for your speech, or to go door-to-door with you, last weekend? I told you I wasn't feeling sociable. Didn't I say I'd call if I felt like it, but if I didn't call, not to expect me?"

"Well that's *two* more things you haven't apologized for."

Tremblay whipped his baseball cap off his head and flung it to the ground near Osgood.

"For Pete's sake, Marcus Osgood! I know you're upset about losing to Mayor Demetriou again, but this is crazy! Why take it out on me? I was one of the seventy-six who voted for you. I must have been the first one. Voted first thing in the morning on my way to work."

"Forget the election," Osgood said. "It's about the Saturday before last week. I waited for you to show up. You never came. You haven't said a thing about it."

"Two Saturdays ago?"

"Yes. The weekend after October 14, the day my grandfather died in 1979. You know he was the most important person to me. You know I always take his favorite fishing rod out on that weekend in honor of him. I had it ready, two Saturdays ago. I waited; you never came."

Tremblay picked up his cap and put it back on his head. He plunked himself down on a pile of leaves, next to Osgood.

"Sorry, buddy," he said. "It completely slipped me. I wasn't even around that weekend. It's been crazy. My mind's been a mess since that day I broke the...."

Tremblay fell silent.

There was a flutter as crows flew into the trees overhead, cawing loudly. The waves lapped softly against the boat.

"Some days, I think my mind is going to explode if I continue to try to hold all of this inside," Tremblay said, staring ahead.

"I wasn't planning on telling you this now," he said after a pause. "Maybe closer to the end. Yeah, I'm sure I would have told you personally before I went. But it's all going to come out anyway, and I might as well tell you now, because it's killing me inside. I was never a saint before, but this was a new low for me."

Tremblay exhaled heavily. "I broke the tailings pond."

"What?" Osgood's eyes burned with the question.

"It wasn't a flood that caused the spill. It wasn't the rain. It was me. *I* did it."

"Madness! What are you saying, Eric?"

Osgood jumped to his feet. He looked down at Tremblay with a scowl.

"Crazy as hell, is right. But, yes, I did it."

Tremblay stood and held onto Osgood's shoulder, as if his legs couldn't support him.

"It was shortly after I got the news from my doctor. I wasn't thinking straight. And then these two Americans came and they offered me fifty thousand dollars. They said the company wanted it done. I've never had that kind of money saved. Never. And, as I told you, I lost the house and the cam—"

Osgood shoved Tremblay, who fell back on his buttocks.

"You're sick!" Osgood shouted. "That's the sickest thing I've ever heard."

He grabbed up his tackle box and rod and stormed off.

Left alone, Tremblay buried his face in his hands and sobbed. He hadn't even got to explain about the cancer that was eating away his life.

Chapter 32

"Well, I'm ready to finish them off," Young said.

He held a Colt .45, M1911 at shoulder height, barrel pointed up.

"Put that away," Quinn growled under his breath.

They were hidden among the trees, just outside Tremblay's fishing camp.

"But he's cracked," Young said. "And that other one sure doesn't look like he'll keep quiet."

"I said put that away!"

Quinn leaned right into Young's face as he stared him down.

Williams stood frozen, watching the two of them.

Young backed off. He cast a defiant glance about him, then looked back at Quinn. Slowly, he returned the gun to its holster under his jacket.

"We don't need to attract attention shooting up the place," Quinn said, in a calmer voice. "The boat launch is just up the road, remember?"

Quinn turned his back to Young and Williams and stepped away a short distance. He stared at the gnarled barks as he tried to organize his thoughts.

"Okay, here's what we're doing," he said, turning to face them, again, after a while.

"You." He pointed at Williams. "Go get your vehicle and pick up that guy who went walking. Bring him back here. And don't accept no for an answer. Got it?"

"Got it." Williams wasted no time in taking off.

Quinn fished out some gloves from the backpack they had on the ground and flung a pair at Young. "You come with me. Leave the other stuff here for the while. But bring the cooler."

At the camp, Tremblay remained as Osgood had left him, sitting on the ground with his head in his hands.

Quinn rested a gloved hand gently on Tremblay's shoulder.

"Hey, buddy, what's up?"

Tremblay recognized the voice. It was one that was imbued with evil. The shock of hearing it at that moment, just after he'd confessed all to Osgood, filled him with an overpowering sense of dread. He could hardly breathe anymore.

He stared at the glove on his shoulder, then slowly looked up with wide eyes.

"We were in the neighborhood," Quinn said with contrived tenderness. "On company business, you know. And we thought we might just look you up."

He sat down beside Tremblay, who was too petrified to say a word.

"Nice day for some sun and fresh air," Quinn said. "And you know what will make it even better?"

He slung his arm around Tremblay's shoulder and shook him.

Tremblay's lips could not move.

"Some nice, cold beer." Quinn laughed.

That evil laugh.

"Get this guy a beer!" Quinn said.

Young opened the cooler. The can hissed as Young pulled back the tab. He pushed the can toward Tremblay, who noticed Young was also wearing black gloves.

"Go on." Quinn shook him by the shoulder. "Take it."

Tremblay's protestations, that he was on medication and that the doctor had ordered him not to drink, had no effect.

Quinn insisted.

Reluctantly, Tremblay complied and downed the first two cans. The final two required further persuasion, amply provided by the .45 which Young pressed against Tremblay's temple.

When he passed out, they dragged him to the boat and dumped him in, along with the empty cans.

Quinn grabbed Tremblay by the hair and slammed his head against the outboard motor.

Thwack!

The impact left a dent in the metal and split Tremblay's scalp in two.

"Quick, get the rope," Quinn said to Young. "I don't want his blood anywhere near the shore."

He started the engine, and Young detached the boat from the rock to which it had been moored.

"Get a canoe." Quinn gave the command with calm authority. "Meet me out there."

He piloted the boat out into the lake and threw down the anchor.

He tumbled Tremblay's limp body over the side and it hit the water with a loud splash. Quinn then pushed his hand into the cold water and held Tremblay's head down until there were no more bubbles.

Young paddled up beside the boat. Quinn wobbled into the canoe and Young paddled them back to the shore.

A short while after, Quinn got behind the wheel of the stolen black truck that served as his ride for this mission. They met Williams on Seldom Seen Road, just down from the mobile home where he had been watching.

Williams had been too late to force the long-haired man into his vehicle. Another driver in a pickup ahead of him had slowed down and the man had got in.

Williams had had a clear view of the driver and passenger from the rear windshield of the truck. As far as he could tell, he said, for the entire drive, not a word was exchanged between them. The man with the long hair had stared out the passenger window the whole time.

The driver had dropped off the long-haired man at the mobile home and had gone on his way.

Quinn ordered Williams to continue to keep watch while he and Young tied up this loose end.

He rolled his truck slowly and almost silently into the driveway. He and Young, still wearing gloves, walked to the door. He turned the handle and found that the door was unlocked.

Inside, the long-haired man stood with his back to them. He held a scrap of paper in his right hand; with the other, he held a phone to his ear.

"Oh come on, pick up the phone this time," the man said into the air.

On Quinn's whispered orders, Young walked stealthily toward the long-haired man. He held the Colt at the ready, arms fully extended, left hand bracing the right, finger on the trigger. He eased himself into the man's view.

Quinn saw the man's body stiffen in surprise and fright; he would add to the man's confusion.

"Put that phone down," Quinn shouted, from behind.

The man immediately dropped everything and raised his hands in the air.

Quinn bent down and picked up the receiver. He placed it back on the cradle.

He surveyed the living room. Boxy, cathode ray tube television; piles of dusty, yellowed newspapers and old magazines sitting on torn and broken furniture; lampshade held together with masking tape....

He caught sight of a tall, wooden cabinet with double glass doors.

Inside were two vintage rifles, standing upright. The slot for a third held an ancient-looking fishing rod with a built-in reel and ornate wooden handle.

Quinn had initially planned to let Young put his beloved Colt to work. But why leave behind their own bullets, or make things so obvious?

He walked over to the cabinet, stooped and swung open a small door at the base. It revealed a keyed drawer, firmly shut.

Ammo, he thought.

Quinn looked over his shoulder. Young appeared to be relishing the chance to display his most ferocious sneer. The ghostly pale geezer with long hair still held his hands up above his shoulders, although no one had ordered him to do so.

Getting him to give up the keys to the cabinet would be easy, Quinn figured.

Chapter 33

"Hey, Paul, can you come pick me up?" the voice said.

"Who is this?" Detective Sergeant Parker lay completely buried under the covers, except for a naked arm and the ear to which he held his cell phone.

"Oh, did I wake you up? Sorry, it's Max."

"It's Sunday, Max."

"I know, bu–"

"It's the only day I get to sleep in."

"I wouldn't have called, except I took my car engine apart and was working on it. Damn near sliced off my left hand and th–"

"Is this Constable Maxwell Kennedy?"

"Yes."

"As in Constable Maxwell Kennedy whose house is a two-minute walk from the hospital?"

"Yes, it is."

"Max, think about it; it takes me seven minutes just to drive over to your place. You need to get–"

"But, Paul, I'm not calling about my hand. Alma bandaged it for me before she left for church. The chief called. I need a ride to the boat launch up at Jay Lake. They found a body floating near there."

"Why didn't you say so in the first place?" Parker flung the covers off and sat up. "I'll be right over."

Nothing ever happened in Syron Lake. The four years he had been on the force, he'd come to expect that. In fact, it was perhaps the main reason he had applied for the job, after the craziness with Sophia. His ex-fiancée had run a tank all over his life, and he had lost steam in what had been a slow but steady climb up through the military police.

Simply walking away from his old life had felt like the right thing to do. But at thirty-nine, and after two decades with the Army, he was not ready to sit around and call himself a retiree. He needed to keep busy — but not *too* busy, his therapist had said. Besides, he felt he needed to get as far away as possible from everybody and everything associated with that wretched history with Sophia.

Syron Lake was perfect. It was a tiny town, way up North, in the middle of the forest. Nothing ever happened in these parts.

He had grown used to dealing with the regular Friday and Saturday bar room brawls; shoplifting by teenagers and the odd pensioner; some vandalism; a car-theft here and there; an occasional break-and-enter; and the encroachment of drug dealers who were trying to gain a foothold in the high school.

A body in the water up at Jay Lake was the biggest thing to have happened in living memory, as far as he knew. The last major investigation had been eight years before his arrival; and that time it turned out that the victim hadn't been attacked as the gossipers had whispered, but had been working on the roof of his house when he slipped and fell backward onto an upturned rake.

Parker felt the blood coursing through his veins as he drove over to Kennedy's house. Maybe he was getting back to his old self. After all, the therapist did say the day would come when he'd look back and the devastation of the break-up with Sophia would seem like a tiny blip in his existence. Maybe that time had come.

By the time he arrived at Kennedy's two-story, his thoughts had swung in another direction. And he was riled.

"Hey thanks, man." Kennedy dropped his large bottom into the passenger seat. He held his bandaged right hand in the air and buckled up with his left.

"You said the chief called you?"

"Yeah. Didn't have time to tell him about my hand before he hung up. He's probably fuming right now that I'm not already there."

Parker clenched his teeth. Kennedy had been with the force for just over a year. Young and carrying a little too much weight for his height, he was eager to work, and intelligent enough. Still, he was a constable, with well below Parker's experience. "So why didn't the chief call me?"

"Don't know," Kennedy said. "But I think he's taking the lead on this."

"Yeah, but–"

"Hey, Paul, I don't want to get all tangled up in whatever *thing* you and the chief have going on, okay?"

"What 'thing' are you talking about? I don't have any 'thing' with Bromley."

Kennedy snorted.

"Honestly, Max, I'm telling you, I don't," Parker said.

"So why is it that you two don't seem to ever get along?"

"*That*, I can't tell you. All I know is, I applied for this job and the police services board seemed pleased with my resume. First two weeks, things were off to a great start. Then Bromley returned to work after an extended leave, and it was like he had it out for me from day one. Even before I introduced myself, he was showing me some attitude. Four years on, it hasn't let up."

"They took you on that time when he was on sick leave?"

"Yeah. What about it?"

"My dad knows someone on the police board. It never came out in public, but around that time there were some real politics happening behind the scenes. Some members were against both the mayor and the chief, and they wanted to get rid of Bromley."

"I'm having a hard time believing a police chief would be so unprofessional as to let small town politics interfere with...but then, again, it's Bromley we're talking about, right?"

"Yeah, it could be that. Or it could be that he just doesn't like your head," Kennedy said, snickering.

They drove to the station, picked up a squad car and headed out of town. A few minutes away from the boat launch, they saw Mayor Demetriou's Benz going in the other direction.

"I'll bet anything he was up there to see the body already," Kennedy said.

"Well, good luck in finding anybody to bet against you."

"Yeah." Kennedy chuckled. "No doubt he was there."

"The man's into everything that goes on in this town."

"Best mayor ever, some say. My folks included."

"Been hearing that since I moved here. I'm yet to see what's so great about that guy."

"The town was as good as dead when the mines closed. People just up and left. My school got closed down because they lost so many students. But then Mayor Demetriou got voted in and he got the retirees to move up here and got this big tourism promotion thing going."

"And turned himself into a fat-cat in the process."

"Yeah. He's done well for himself. But now people have all kinds of jobs, fixing up houses, working in the hotel, the restaurants. Locals and tourist are spending in the shops. Money's flowing again. Not like when the mines were operating, mind you. But at least Mayor Demetriou saved Syron Lake from becoming a ghost town."

"That's exactly what I don't find too healthy."

"What?"

"People in this town talking about this guy as if he's some kind of savior."

Parker slowed down. He eyed a gleaming, beige Ford F-150 parked across a narrow, gravel side road, blocking it off completely.

"Hang on, that's the chief's truck," he said.

He parked behind the pickup, and they followed the road into the woods and down to the lake.

Chief George Bromley wore dirty overalls and a baseball cap. A giant of a man, he didn't need a uniform to look imposing.

He stood watching a small boat anchored a few meters out as it bobbed on the water. Two bright orange kayaks were on the shore.

A middle-aged man with a glum expression leaned against the wall of the camp. Near him, a teenage girl and a young boy sat on the ground, using life-jackets under them as cushions.

"Max, what took you so long?" Bromley turned as he heard the footsteps on the gravel.

"Morning, Chief." Kennedy held up his bandaged hand.

"Morning," Parker said.

"I didn't send for you." Bromley narrowed his eyes and fixed them on Parker.

Kennedy could feel the frostiness in the air as Bromley and Parker locked stares.

"Chief, he's my hands today," Kennedy said quickly. "Can't drive, can't take notes, can't do a lick for myself right now."

Bromley's eyes shifted to Kennedy's injured hand. He looked across at Parker and slowly nodded.

"Fine. But after you're done today, Max, I want you to get to ER and get that properly fixed up. Understand? I don't much care to have invalids on my force."

"Yes, Chief."

"Right." Bromley pointed his chin toward the three solemn figures. "So, this family was out kayaking early this morning and came across this scene. There's a body out in the water. Tangled up in some rope from the boat, it seems. It looks like Eric Tremblay's boat. It's his camp and that there, is his truck. More likely than not, it's him out there in the water.

"The recovery team's on the way to fish out the body. The coroner's been informed. I want you to secure this area and take a statement from these folks."

"Yes, Chief," Kennedy said.

"Remember, if the media asks any questions, I'm the only one that answers. And there's a bullhorn in the backseat of my truck. Take it. If anyone tries to approach the scene by boat, keep them away."

Chapter 34

Parker's eyes were focused on the road as he drove away from Eric Tremblay's camp. But his mind was still back there, in that tiny clearing by the lake. The entrance of the gravel road was now blocked off with yellow police tape strung from trees on either side.

Earlier that morning, it had struck him that he hadn't paid attention to the calendar or the rhythm of life around him.

"Hey, what's the date today, again?" he said to Kennedy.

"Thirty-first."

October 31.

When he had driven over to Kennedy's, Parker had got a kick out of watching the ghoulish decorations that kids, and overgrown kids who called themselves dads, had put out on their front lawns. The town was ariot with plastic headstones; carved pumpkins; scarecrows made of straw; fake cobwebs that tangled hedges; dismembered limbs made of papier–mâché; skeletons that dangled from trees; and all kinds of yellow tape with cheeky wording. He had read one that said: "Polite warning. Keep out, please!"

"In a few hours, the kids will be out trick-or-treating," Parker said. "Lucky thing Tremblay's camp is so far out of town that they won't have to see the real deal."

"I don't know," Kennedy said, "if I was still a kid, I would've found a crime scene exciting, especially on Halloween."

Parker shook his head. Kennedy was still very much a kid, he thought.

"Did you know that guy that owned the camp?" Parker said. "Ever meet him?"

"Don't think so. You?"

"Can't recall ever meeting him. But I've heard of him fairly often. You know Osgood, right?"

"You mean the crazy guy that keeps running for mayor?"

"Hey, I voted for him."

Kennedy burst out in laughter.

"I don't know who's nuttier. Him for going up when he knows

he doesn't stand a snowball's chance in Hell of winning. Or people like you who throw away their vote by supporting him."

Parker kept his peace. There was no need to start an argument over politics.

"Okay, so it's established that you do know Osgood."

"Yeah, everybody knows Osgood."

"Well, he's in my AA meetings and he–"

"You're in AA? Since when?"

"Since two years before I moved here."

"I never knew that."

"I guess it never came up before. But getting back to Tremblay. Osgood and Tremblay are…, well *were* buddies. That's why we're going over to talk with him. He's mentioned his fishing trips with Tremblay loads of times in our AA meetings. In fact, just Thursday he talked about how good it would be to reel in some pike this weekend. To take his mind off the elections."

"So why wasn't he there?"

"Well, that's one thing we're going to try to find out. But what's kind of strange is that Tremblay was drinking at the camp. From what Osgood's said at meetings, I got the impression that Tremblay never brought alcohol up at the camp. *Ever.* It was kinda like a spirits-free zone, on account of Osgood's sobriety."

"Same thing hunting. Back in the day when Osgood used to hunt, Tremblay owned a bush lot. Never took even a single beer there. Then Osgood lost his appetite for shooting four-legged creatures and Tremblay sold the lot or lost it in a poker game or something. I forget how the story went."

"Well, that was just plain stupid." Kennedy snorted.

"What was?"

"Guzzling down four tall ones while out in the water by yourself. That was an accident waiting to happen. What a dumb way to go. Good thing he didn't leave behind any wife or children to mourn over him."

Parker again restrained himself. What compassion, he thought. It took riding with a man at a time like this to really get to know him.

They pulled up at Osgood's place in silence.

Kennedy got out of the car. He approached the door and knocked. Finding it open, he walked in.

Parker took his cool time gathering his pen and notebook. The chief had made it quite clear he hadn't been assigned to the case; that he, Chief Bromley, was in charge; and that Kennedy was conducting the investigation under his, Bromley's, instructions. Okey-dokey. He would hang back a bit and not let Bromley's attitude rile him.

He had just reached the door, when it swung back violently. Kennedy dashed past him, nearly knocking him over.

Kennedy's legs collapsed under him, and he fell onto the squad car's hood. He folded over in two, and his body heaved. Once. Twice. Then all the contents of his stomach emptied out onto the bumper.

"You alright?" Parker called out.

Contorted by spasms, Kennedy was beyond hearing.

Parker took out his revolver and stepped cautiously into the cluttered room.

The smell of death hung in the air.

A large, red splotch stained a wall in the living room, behind a wing chair.

Osgood's body was slumped in the chair. An old rifle lay between his knees. The barrel was pointed upward, toward Osgood's face, only part of which was left intact.

PART II

Chapter 35

I hurried down the corridor of the community center, almost tripping in my high-heels. It was the first time I'd worn them since moving to Syron Lake.

With all other venues being either occupied or too small, the community center ended up serving as the home of the Canadian Nuclear Regulatory Authority for the week.

The hall took on the appearance of an official federal government hearing room as best it could.

Below the basketball hoop at the front of the room stood a slightly raised platform with a table fitted with microphones and three empty chairs. Directly in front of it was another table with more microphones.

To the right of this setting, dour-looking civil servants in two banks of desks flipped through thick files and peered at laptop screens. To the left, the baby-faced radio reporter sat fiddling with large, ancient-looking recorder, and a journalist from the newspaper scribbled notes on a pad.

Two unmanned television cameras bearing C-PAC logos stood on tripods, one at the center of the room, trained on the panel's table; the other at the side, was pointed at the presenter's table.

The rest of the hall, which on most days served as an indoor walking circuit for seniors in the morning and a basketball court for teens on afternoons, was taken up by rows of chairs, most of which were occupied.

It was easy to tell the ordinary townsfolk from the town officials and the strangers.

The locals, sprinkled across the hall, but mostly in the back rows, were in sweaters, flannel shirts, jeans, and sweatpants; the majority of them were regulars who attended every Council meeting or political event and whose faces often showed up in the background of photos in the newspaper. Mayor Demetriou, a few councilors, and some City staff sat together in various degrees of business casual.

The strangers wore suits, the cuts and material of which made it obvious that they were way beyond the average Syron Laker's budget. Both men and women sported sleek, coiffed hair. Their watches, bangles, necklaces, and earrings shone and sparkled with the brilliance of real gold, silver, and diamonds. Apparently the mining business was doing well, very, very well.

I took one of the empty seats at the front, aware that my best wardrobe on a non-profit editor's salary had never been spectacular to being with. I was glad, though, that I had at least thought to change out of my grubby walking shoes and into the high-heels for the occasion.

The door at the far end of the room swung open. Three men entered the hall and approached the panel table. More suits.

The C-PAC cameramen, sporting oversize headphones, dashed to their equipment, and the public servants sat up with more alert expressions.

Murmurs in the hall had died down but not completely, and when a bald-headed man took the seat at the center of the panel, he tapped his gavel three times.

"Order. Order, please."

A hush fell over the room. Even Mayor Demetriou, who'd been chatting with a councilor behind him, abruptly ended his conversation and turned to face the panel.

"Bonjour et bienvenue." The bald-headed man adjusted his microphone. "Good morning and welcome. We are here this week to consider plans that will affect the long term future of this community...."

I felt a slight tremor course through my body. The battle had begun!

As an administrative tribunal, the CNRA functioned somewhat like a court, in that the panel was to hear evidence and arguments and make a decision that would be legally enforceable. It was no surprise, then, that the majority of the strangers representing Syron Lake Resources and the other mining companies were lawyers.

Seeing them in the flesh in their expensive suits, I began to wonder at my sanity in going up against them. I had no legal training whatsoever and had known nothing about uranium mining prior to moving to this town.

But events had landed me right smack in the middle of all this, and turning back out now was out of the question.

Since Osgood had suggested that I apply to be a participant, speaking at the hearing had been only a remote possibility. Now, with reporters' recorders and television cameras rolling, and a roomful of strangers watching and listening, it was all too frighteningly real for someone more comfortable tapping away at a keyboard in obscurity.

In three short days, I, just an ordinary resident, would have to occupy the presenter's table. I'd come here to take a swipe at a powerful company on a subject I didn't feel I understood fully. And I hadn't even finished writing my presentation yet.

Could I really do this? Could I get those "greedy bastards" as Osgood had urged?

I looked around the room, searching the faces of the enemy; searching, too, for a friendly face.

Where was Osgood, anyway?

Chapter 36

From his desk, Parker watched a young man push open the glass door of the station and walk toward the reception counter.

The detective craned his neck to listen.

"I'm Jacques Tremblay."

"Oh, yes. Eric's nephew." Zoe, the receptionist spoke unhurriedly. "I'm so sorry about Eric. You must be devastated."

"I just got back in town. I was told someone by the name of Kennedy, Constable Kennedy, wanted to speak to me."

"Come, I'll take you to where you two can talk."

Parker knew she would lead him to the interview room. He hurried down the corridor, in the opposite direction, but didn't find Kennedy at his desk.

The men's room was two doors down. Parker poked his head in. Kennedy stood over a urinal.

"Eric Tremblay's nephew just walked in."

"Thanks. He got here quick enough."

"I think one of the things we should ask him about is the beer. That keeps bugging me."

"Sorry, Paul, 'we' are not asking him anything." Kennedy zipped up his fly. "You're not on this case. That's the chief talking, not me."

"But your hand–"

"I tried to tell him the same thing. You know what he told me? Write with my left hand. Or my toes, if I had to. He means it, Paul. It's his case; I do the dog's work for him; you're out of the picture. End of story."

"Look, I won't say anything. I'll just sit there, silently taking your notes."

"Zoe got me a tape recorder. Gave me fresh batteries, too. I'm good."

Back at his desk, Parker sifted through reports and papers. He found it difficult to concentrate.

That part of him which once throbbed with curiosity, that well, which had once flooded his every molecule with energy — which he had thought had dried up completely when his life came crashing down — was beginning to spring anew.

He'd been very good at his job — once.

Back in the day, when he'd been fully engaged in his job with the military police, he had cracked several cases that had started off as impossible conundrums. Uncovering hidden secrets and bringing perpetrators to justice and, in doing so, avenging victims who'd been dealt a cruel hand — that's what had once propelled him.

It irritated him that instead of being able make use of his skills and experience, he was running into a brick wall erected by Chief Bromley.

The hinge of the glass door creaked and pulled him out of his thoughts.

A short man carrying an indecent amount of weight, which he supported with a walking stick, pushed past the door and stood in the corridor.

"Can I help you?" Zoe was apparently back at the reception counter.

"I heard on the radio–" the man managed to say before breaking into a coughing fit. "I heard that the police wanted to hear if anyone saw anything suspicious concerning Marcus Osgood's death."

"That's right."

"Well, I might know something. I don't know if it's anything. But it might be of interest."

"Constable Kennedy is the one you'd want to see. But he's busy now. If you'll have a seat, I'll let him know you're here when he's available."

Parker was on his feet and out in the waiting area in an instant.

The visitor sat with his elbows on his knees, while his fingers toyed with some red object.

Parker decided he couldn't talk to the man there; nor would his office work. Zoe was in a corner going through a filing cabinet, but she would hear everything. And that would mean the chief would surely get the full lowdown.

The man squeezed on whatever he hand in his hand, aimed for the bin in the corner, and missed. The object landed on the floor. Parker smiled; it was a crumpled cigarette pack.

He hurried out the door. When he returned, two minutes

later, the visitor still sat in the same position.

With his back to Zoe, Parker cleared his throat. The man looked up.

Parker held a fresh packet of cigarettes. The same brand as the discarded ball near the bin. He slowly peeled the plastic away, then flipped open the top. His eyes met the visitor's. All it took was a twist of the wrist toward the man and a slight tilt of the head toward the door.

"So, you're a new cop in town?"

They leaned against a rail at the back of the station. Thin plumes of smoke — from one cigarette hanging from the stranger's lips and a second in between Parker's fingers — wafted upward in the still, mid-morning air.

"Been here four years now."

"Never seen you before. But that's not saying much. So many new faces around here these last few years, I can't hardly keep up."

Parker didn't want to push — he had to be careful that this did not appear to be an interview — but he didn't have time for small talk either.

"So, what part of town do you live?" Parker said.

"Don't actually live in the town itself. Got a place up at Tooley Lake. Know where that is?"

"Can't say that I do."

"Up past Jay Lake, about two miles from the boat launch. Nice and peaceful up there. Even this town's too crowded for me."

"Wasn't too peaceful up there last weekend."

"That's just too bad about Eric. Nice guy that was. Young, too."

Parker was getting impatient. He scoped out either end of the building. No threat, so far, of anyone bounding around the corner.

"Yeah. And it's so sad about his fishing buddy, Osgood," Parker said.

"That's what I came to see you guys about. I think I may have seen something. But maybe it was nothing."

Parker looked at the man and raised his eyebrows to prompt him to continue.

"See, I gave Osgood a lift from, I don't know, maybe half a

mile or so from the boat launch, last Saturday morning. He was heading toward town. Had a fishing rod and a tackle box. I figured he must of been at Eric's camp and decided to walk home. Which is crazy. Would have taken him all day, practically, on foot."

Parker nodded.

"See, I was going for fresh eggs. You know old man Victor Hartford who keeps bees and sells fresh eggs way up on Seldom Seen Road? The wife sent me up there last Saturday for eggs. We always get a dozen or so every weekend, but she wasn't up to going with me, that day. So it was no problem for me to give Osgood a ride home.

"The thing is, when I turned off on Seldom Seen, there was this SUV behind us. I noticed it because there's usually no traffic on that road unless it's someone who has business there. Between Osgood's place and Victor Hartford's there's maybe two, three houses. But that's it. Nothing to see or do up there.

"Well, see, the SUV just disappeared somewhere before I let Osgood off. When I was headed back home and I passed Osgood, I saw the SUV parked on the shoulder.

"The driver was some young fella with a big, ugly red spot on the back of his hand, maybe a scar or something. Can't really describe him, otherwise. Didn't get too good a look at his face as he had the brim of his cap pulled down low. It didn't look like he was stalled. He didn't have the hood up or nothing. He was just sitting there with binoculars.

"To me, it looked like he was looking at Osgood's place. That's what I first thought. Then I thought that's stupid; he must of been a birdwatcher or something. But since I heard on the radio that anyone who saw anything should come in, I thought I would mention it."

"Well, you're a good neighbor and good citizen to do so."

"Maybe, but I'm almost afraid to say the last bit about what I seen, as I'm not too sure of this. My memory ain't all that good nowadays, as the wife always reminds me."

"What did you see?"

"Well, I can't say for sure, but looking back at it, I think I passed that same vehicle up at the boat launch before I picked up Osgood. That and another one, a black truck, I think.

"It just struck me as strange, those two vehicles just parked up there at that hour of the morning. Neither had a boat trailer or a rack for canoes or kayaks. Nobody was around fishing from the launch. Just two abandoned vehicles way out there at that hour of the morning. Don't know if any of that'll do any good. Seeing as I didn't get no license plate or nothing."

Parker dropped his cigarette and squished it with the heel of his boot. He handed the rest of the packet to the man.

"No, you've done the right thing to come down to the station," he said. "I'm sure Constable Kennedy will want to hear everything you have to say."

Chapter 37

After the lunch break, Benoit Dromel set a laptop on the table, slightly to his left.

The morning session had held some entertainment; he had read a long introductory speech for the audience and the cameras. He was most pleased about the cameras. That was his doing; the result of repeated calls and emails to the CNRA's communications director to impress upon her the need to lobby for coverage by at least the cable channel that carried live Parliamentary debates and select government-related events.

Now, however, the hearing was plunging into interminable blather from the presentation table.

There would be company reports, and proposals, and requests, all delivered in arcane jargon and burdened with diagrams and calculations. There would be some opposition, with conflicting reports, condemnations of the previously articulated proposals, and requests for denials of requests, all wrapped up in the same technical argot, with more diagrams and calculations that attempted to show how the previously outlined figures were convoluted and just, plain wrong.

The laptop was his antidote to the lethal boredom that threatened to ensue.

It could be placed strategically so that if he bent his head at a certain angle and peered over his glasses, no one — except, perhaps, the target — could tell that he was actually looking over the top or slightly to the side of the screen at some interesting face in the audience, or on the staff table.

A pretty face was always welcome; and when a certain redhead with freckles from the legal department was on duty, he was guaranteed an enjoyable hearing. But at most proceedings, which were heavy on the testosterone, just a pleasant to interesting female face would provide enough inspiration for a romp into fantasyland.

There'd been a couple of occasions when the pickings had been dire and he'd had to fall back on recollections of evenings with his latest inamorata to help him while away the hours. He feared that would be the case for the rest of the week in this backwater town.

He scanned the women in his line of vision, from the rear of the room to the front. Rather boring regulatory types, and lots of gray hair. Too much gray hair.

Later, Dromel shifted the laptop to his right and picked up his survey, from the back of the room, all the way to the front.

Well, this was unexpected.

She was young, maybe mid-twenties. And yes, attractive — rather pretty, in fact.

Those high cheek bones. Those dark eyes that focused on the presenter, totally engrossed in his speech. Jet-black hair that fell to her shoulders. Nice, full lips. A cute, straight, little nose.

Dromel smiled. If she stuck around for the rest of the week, this would turn out to be a rather enjoyable proceeding.

Chapter 38

As the afternoon session wore on, I began to get the distinct impression that I was being watched. I looked up from the notebook in which I scribbled points I thought I might add to my presentation.

At the staff desk, no one appeared to pay any particular attention to the audience. On the other side of the hall, the baby-faced radio reporter was gone. The newspaper reporter's eyes remained permanently down in his note pad.

I shifted and looked at the rest of the audience. Still no Osgood. But I now saw some faces that were familiar from the Field Naturalists Club.

Turning forward again, I caught the panel chairman's eyes looking directly into mine. My gaze drifted upward, to his shining pate. Was he the one whose eyes I'd felt upon me?

The speaker at the presentation table, who was not from Syron Lake Resources but represented one of the biggest mining conglomerates in the world, began to talk about financial provisions to deal with cleanups in case of an accident.

This was good stuff, and my gaze fell back to my notebook as I jotted down his words.

After the hearing was adjourned for the day, I made my way over to group from the Field Naturalists. A small woman with thinning, white hair and a severely arched back stepped forward and introduced herself as Dorothy, the secretary with whom I'd spoken when I first called the club.

"I was looking out for Osgood," I said. "I thought for sure he would have been here for this."

"Oh my!" Dorothy took both of my hands into her own small, trembling hands. "Didn't you hear?"

"Hear what?"

"Osgood's gone."

"What? Where to?"

"It was on the radio. I didn't hear it myself. Someone told me."

"What was on the radio?"

"Happened just this Saturday. Gunshot wound to the head.

People are saying it must have been suicide."

I changed shoes, again. I didn't even bother to put the heels away neatly in my handbag; I held them by their straps, and they swung limply in my hands on the walk back home.

I found myself biting my lower lip all along the way as hot tears rolled down my cheeks.

How could he be gone?

Unwashed, hairy, and wild-eyed, he'd been rough-mannered, but gentle in spirit, and so full of passion. He'd seemed a presence that would be around forever. How could he be gone?

I'd only just begun to know him. And yet I'd already come to lean heavily on him; up till that moment, I hadn't realized just how much so. He'd been my only true ally in this crazy fight I'd let myself get drawn into. Now, the world suddenly felt like it had a great big hole in it, and I felt small and so very alone.

They're saying it was suicide.

I wished, now, that I had voted for him.

Osgood was not mayor material; my rational mind had not even entertained the idea of giving him my vote. But if I had done so, and if he'd had that one extra vote, perhaps the loss to Mayor Demetriou might not have stung so much and, maybe, he would still have been around and would have been pedalling all over town on his fluorescent green and orange bicycle and raising hell about Demetriou for many more years.

Back at home, I switched on the computer and opened the document with my presentation for the hearing. At the top, I typed: "Dedicated to the memory of Marcus Osgood."

I had failed him as a friend while he was alive. I could not fail him now. He had been as eager as I was to see Syron Lake Resources held to account for "raping and pillaging Mother Nature." I owed it to him to get those greedy bastards.

Chapter 39

Parker stood on the top step of the gray stucco bungalow. It was just past five on Tuesday afternoon. He was off duty and wore jeans and a sweater. His jeep was parked in the driveway, alongside the red Dodge.

He was sure he had seen the blinds move when he got out of his vehicle. He rang the doorbell and waited. No answer. He rang twice again. Nothing.

On the third ring, he was sure he heard shuffling noises. Still, the door remained shut.

"Hey, Jacques. I know you're in there," he said.

Silence.

"My name is Paul. I'm sorry about your uncle." Parker paused for a response. "I just want to share my condolences."

A chain rattled; the knob clicked. The door swung open. Jacques stood as if guarding the entrance, his arms folded in front of him. "Listen, I've seen you around town before. I know who you are; you're a *cop*." He almost spat out the word.

Jacques had had a run-in with the police seven years before. His mind carried him back to that time, a week after his thirteenth birthday. He had been hanging out with Zack, an older boy from down the street, who borrowed a car one night and took it for a joyride. They were stopped by the police. Jacques escaped and hid in the bushes. He saw the officers drag Zack out of the car; he saw the batons rain down on Zack. The newspaper reported that the police said the suspect sustained injuries "while trying to escape." So, no, he wasn't eager to have any more dealings with the cops than was absolutely necessary.

"I know this must be a difficult time for you," Parker said.

"I got that talk already. I was down at the station this morning. You guys wanted to see me and I showed up. So will you keep out of my face now?"

Jacques backed inside and slammed the door. His entire body trembled. He bent his head and ran his fingers through his hair.

Not only did he not trust cops because of what happened

to Zack. Sitting in four different bank accounts in Ottawa were thirty thousand reasons why he wasn't eager to talk with the police.

Parker sighed and walked briskly back to his jeep. He had struck out with the kid. Now, he would have to take the riskier step of broadening his inquiries.

It was a long shot, but he knew some people tended to be chatty when getting their alcohol; maybe someone out there who knew Eric Tremblay could confirm his belief that Tremblay would never drink at the camp, at least not when Osgood was supposed to be there with him.

The LCBO liquor store was almost empty. Parker milled about, picked up a wine carrier, and waited till he was the last in line.

"That would be four-twenty please." The cashier looked harried and in no mood to chit chat.

"Lots of bad news around town this weekend, eh?" Parker rifled through his wallet.

"Uh huh."

"That guy who drowned, Eric Tremblay, you knew him?"

"Tremblay, you say?"

"That's right."

"Hmmm.... Nope. Don't think I know any Eric Tremblay."

Parker slapped down a five-dollar bill on the counter. "Don't worry about the change," he said.

Strike two. Yeah, it was a long shot.

He made it into The Beer Store just before closing. This time, a baseball cap served as his prop.

"Lots of bad news around town this weekend, eh?"

"You're telling me!" The man behind the counter shook his head while scratching his stubbly cheek. "Who'd think Osgood would of done himself in like that? And for Eric to up and drown the same day? Man, that's some kind of weird."

"You knew Eric?" Parker patted his body as if searching for his wallet, buying himself some talk time.

"Sure. He was in here all the time."

"Really?"

"Sure. He'd come in on a Friday night, pick up a six-pack of Canadian and he was good to go."

"Canadian, huh? And what about Labatt?"

"Not a chance." The man laughed. "It was Molson Canadian for him all the way. Used to say Labatt sold water, not beer."

"Hey, Labatt's got Maximum Ice. That's pretty strong."

"Nah, he never went for that stuff. Eric was one of those guys who'd settled the Molson versus Labatt debate in his mind long ago. Beer for him was a bottle of Canadian. Now, mind you, if somebody offered him something else, he wouldn't refuse. But when *he* was buying, it was one thing and one thing alone."

"Sold any of that Maximum Ice this past weekend?"

It was a dumb question. He knew it from the moment it left his lips, and he wished he could have taken it back.

"I'm sure we must have," the man said slowly. His eyes passed over every inch of Parker's face, now, as if studying him. "What's with all the questions?"

Parker shrugged. "Just curious."

He paid for the cap and left quickly.

After he had a light dinner at Tito's, he pulled up at the graffiti-covered payphone at the entrance to the parkette in the middle of town. It would be his last effort. He didn't want to use his cell, or his home phone; and he certainly couldn't place the call from the station.

The morning they had discovered Osgood's body, the first thing he had searched for was a suicide note. Kennedy, when he had recovered his composure, insisted on helping with this task. They had come up empty-handed.

Parker had shown Kennedy a scrap of paper he had found on the floor. It had four numbers scribbled on it. He had no idea what Kennedy made of it.

He, however, had memorized the numbers. Since he had found the scrap near the phone, he had a hunch they were the last four digits of a phone number.

There were just five prefixes used for phone numbers in Syron Lake. Parker had jotted down all five possibilities.

A reverse lookup search on the Internet had given him a name for only one number. But that didn't mean the four didn't exist.

He could be wrong about it being a phone number. Or if he was right, it could be an out-of-town number, not a local one. And even if it was a local number, it may not lead anywhere. But he had nothing else to go on.

Something, no matter how remote, was better than nothing.

The first number returned the screeches and whistles of a fax machine.

He scratched that off. On to the second.

"Hello, Stella Jacob here."

The sound of her voice sent a jolt to his chest.

"Sorry, wrong number." He quickly hung up.

His heart pounded and the middle of his palms suddenly itched and felt clammy. He shook his head at his reaction.

He looked around at the empty streets and felt somewhat sleazy, speaking to her while standing in the graffiti-riddled booth, under a pool of light from the nearby streetlamp, with the stench of urine in the air.

Two more numbers to go. He would regain his professional demeanor and carry on, even if what he was doing was sneaking around his boss.

The third and fourth numbers were not in service.

Now he tried the last number, the one for the person whose name he had found through the reverse lookup.

"Gerry Wayman speaking."

"Hi, Gerry. My name is Paul. Marcus Osgood was a friend of mine. I just–"

"Sorry, you're a friend of who?"

"Marcus Osgood."

"Osgood, you say."

"Yes, Marcus Osgood, who ran for mayor."

"And what of it? What's this all about?"

"I'm calling because I understand you might have known him."

"I know *of* him. Or *knew* of him, I should say. Heard he shot himself in the head the other day, God rest his soul. What did you say your name was again?"

"Sorry, looks like I mixed you up with somebody else. Sorry to bother you."

As Parker hung up, it dawned on him that it made sense that it was Stella Jacob's number on that paper. He had seen her approach Osgood at the meeting of the Field Naturalists Club. And, again, at the mayor's debate, the Friday night before the election.

He knew where she lived; she walked everywhere, and, the other day, it had been no problem to cruise along in his jeep to see where she would end up. He'd been curious, that's all.

Well, after work the next day, he'd just have to swing by and knock on her door....

Chapter 40

Dromel's eyes followed the movement of her hair as it brushed against her shoulders. He was surprised to see that his "face" was the busybody who had written in at the last minute, demanding to be allowed to speak at the hearing.

She took a seat in the middle of the long, empty presentation table. Behind her, the lawyers, low-level executives and experts from mining companies, one or two of whom he knew well from other hearings, looked on with varying degrees of dismissive expressions, or occupied themselves with their laptops or files from their briefcases. The Syron Lake Resources contingent whispered among themselves and threw contemptuous glances her way.

Brave girl, Dromel thought.

Chapter 41

I pulled the microphone closer and drew my chair up, so my ribs pressed against the table. That gave me a connection to at least one thing that felt stable, because no part of me felt that way.

The pages of my speech shook visibly in my hands; I lay the sheets flat and pressed my palms over them. That helped somewhat with the trembling.

"Good-morning, Mr Chairman, members of the panel." My mouth was dry; my tongue, heavy. I could almost hear every beat of my overactive heart.

"I'm not an expert on uranium mining. If you asked me three weeks ago about uranium tailings management, I probably wouldn't have been able to string together a full sentence.

"But I don't think you need any university degree or depth of experience in this field to come to the conclusion that the system is failing the people of this community who live in the shadow of all this radioactive waste.

"Our sense of well being — and, if we can get unbiased test results they may even show that our physical well being, itself — has been dealt a blow by the recent release of millions of gallons of toxic waste within a few miles of where we're now gathered.

"The system is failing taxpayers of this generation and of generations to come.

"It's riddled with loopholes that lead to *us* being forced, in perpetuity, to bear the financial burden of trying to keep these toxic garbage heaps safe. Meanwhile, shareholders of the mining companies who created this mess, get to ride off in the sunset and enjoy the enormous profits that the mines generated.

"And the system is failing the planet.

"Even if the recent spill was contained at the mining site and didn't encroach on Crown land or the private property of others, it posed a danger to animals that roam these forests; to birds that are oblivious to Man's artificial boundaries; to plants and trees; and to fish and other aquatic life in the lakes...."

I made it through one page, then another, and another. The

trembling subsided; my breathing returned to something near normal.

My presentation conjured up the horror of the prospect that, ironically, a company could be rewarded for its poor performance because it could claim that cleanup costs were beyond it, prompting an early transfer of responsibilities to the authorities.

"Common sense and basic human decency would dictate that those who reaped enormous profits from mining endeavors would directly contribute to fixing the problems they created, even if that meant they had to put every penny back in. But the system has been woefully short of both common sense and decency.

"Look at what's happened, for example, on Navajo lands in the US – in Arizona, Utah, and New Mexico. Over five hundred uranium mines were exploited and then abandoned. Those mines made money. But the US government can only find owners for a few dozen of them. Where the owner can't be found, it's taxpayers who have to pick up the tab for any cleanup costs.

"Three years ago, a hearing, something like this one, resulted in the US Government coming up with a five-year cleanup plan to spend $110 million in federal funds. And how much did the mining companies have to pay toward the cleanup costs? A measly $17 million.

"Think that kind of craziness happens only in the States? Think again.

"Over here in Canada, we have the Gunnar Uranium Mine in Saskatchewan. In that debacle, the private company that made millions of dollars also made itself disappear. And since the corporation has ceased to exist, it has escaped all of its responsibilities.

"That has forced the government to shell out $20 million to clean up the radioactive waste that the company left behind.

"And that's just to *start* the process. Cleanup costs are likely to run into hundreds of millions of dollars – taxpayers' dollars.

"That's money that should have gone, instead, to fund schools, and hospitals, and social programs."

My pulse raced, partly out of the terror of speaking in public, but mostly because I was getting worked up about the unfairness of the situation.

I was breathing too hard and reading too fast. I paused,

swallowed slowly, then tried again, at a calmer pace.

"We can't let that, or anything similar, happen here. Syron Lake Resources shouldn't be allowed to simply pass on the burden to taxpayers.

"We don't want to see them give up their license and escape responsibility to reverse the damage they've caused by claiming this cleanup is beyond their means.

"That would only result in the government taking over and using our tax dollars to do the company's job.

"And we don't want to hear, that like Gunnar, Syron Lake Resources ceases to exist, meaning we, the taxpayers, have to bear the costs of cleaning up this spill.

"This panel has the obligation to ensure no such outrage occurs with Syron Lake Resources, or any of the mining companies that have left their toxic waste behind in this area. All loopholes must be closed.

"This community and taxpayers across this province and all across this country are looking to the Canadian Nuclear Regulatory Authority to protect us today, and to save our children and their children from burdens that should rightly fall on the shoulders of those in the mining companies who exploited these lands. Thank you."

It was over!

I sat back and my lungs collapsed in an involuntary sigh. I was startled to hear the sound amplified over the speakers.

"Thank you, Ms Jacob." The chairman smiled. "I don't have any questions for you. But perhaps one of my colleagues on the panel might."

Reading the written presentation had been hard enough; now I had to answer questions?

My armpits itched and I felt a lump in my throat.

"I followed what you were saying with great interest." The panelist sitting behind a nameplate that read "Victor Rigby" played with a paperclip as he glowered at me. "What I haven't heard is what, specifically, you believe is the harm that's been done that you think we should take into consideration."

"That goes to the heart of the problem, Commissioner." I bent forward to the microphone, again. "We don't know exactly what happened during that spill. We don't know how bad that spill was for the environment or for us, in the short or the long term. And we don't have any means of finding out, either. We have no access to the site.

"All the information we have is what's being fed to us by Syron Lake Resources.

"The company is telling us to trust them when they say the spill was nothing serious. Well, all this time they were saying we should trust that they were competently managing this toxic waste, and look how that's turned out."

Some snickering rose from the audience. The chairman looked up and frowned.

Rigby continued. "Yes, but in your presentation you called on the CNRA to impose, and I'm quoting here, 'any and all punitive measures available,' in addition to holding Syron Lake Resources to its financial responsibility for management of the tailings. Certainly you must realize that if there is to be punishment, there first has to be a crime identified, so to speak."

I shook my head. "That's what I'm trying to point out is wrong with the system. We — the people whose health and wellbeing may be affected by this — we don't have any means to arrange the kind of independent testing that would uncover the crime, to use your term."

"The CNRA is doing its own investigations and tests in addition to the company, Ms Jacob," Rigby said.

I shook my head again. "In an ideal world, we, the people who are affected, would be able to send in our own investigators who we could be sure would be looking out for *our* interests, and whom we could rely on to look under every last rock to find every danger that might be lurking."

Rigby bristled. "You can rest assured that the CNRA's investigative staff are competent and thorough."

"It's all well and good to say the CNRA is doing its own testing," I said. "But people are aware of a thing called 'regulatory capture,' where regulatory bodies, these so-called watchdogs, end up in the back pockets of corporations. And so, they turn out skewed reports and issue lopsided decisions, and end up protecting the very entities they were set up to police."

Murmuring broke out in the room.

I pursed my lips and cringed. I had unintentionally insulted the very people whose help I had come here to seek.

All through this question period, words had been tumbling out of my mouth without first being processed by my brain. And now, this.

I had a sensation of sinking deeper and deeper in quicksand as the seconds ticked on.

Rigby cleared his throat. "Mr Chairman, I have no further questions."

"Thank you, Ms Jacob." The panel chairman gave a shallow nod. "That brings the morning session to a close. After lunch, Syron Lake Resources will have the floor."

I kept my head bent as I gathered up my papers slowly, delaying as much as I could at that lonely table. I felt too embarrassed about my performance to speak with anyone.

I hadn't been confident that my presentation would have been all that convincing in the first place. But if I'd made even a little headway with the panel, surely it had been undone by my hasty responses to Victor Rigby.

I had let down Osgood; I had let down myself; and I had let down anyone else who had wanted to see Syron Lake Resources get its comeuppance.

When I finally left the hall, I walked down the empty corridor toward the washrooms with the hope that splashing cool water on my face would revive my spirits.

As I passed the men's room, the door swung open. The panel chairman appeared. Six feet tall. Dark, elegant suit. A shinning pate.

Our eyes met.

He smiled.

He winked at me.

Then, he walked away.

Chapter 42

The Syron Lake Resources team was led by a paunchy lawyer with salt-and-pepper hair and a matching beard, who went by the name of Goran Stanko. The fourteen men and one woman with him filled the presentation table and occupied most of the chairs in the front row.

They had upset the seating arrangements, and I was forced to shift from my usual place.

They came armed with reports, and slides, and maps, and historical test results. Final findings on the recent spill were still to be prepared, Stanko said, but preliminary indications showed that there had been no environmental impact and no danger to the community or to employees.

It was the company's press release ad nauseam, I thought.

Then Stanko coughed and said, "Mr Chairman, at this juncture, I have an important update to provide."

He remained quiet until the chairman stopped reading from the laptop that was before him and Victor Rigby set aside a thick folder he'd been thumbing through. With the eyes of all three panelists now focused on him, Stanko resumed.

"Syron Lake Resources had previously sought to hand back its tailings management license in the coming years," he said. "But, today, I would like to make it absolutely clear that the company is officially withdrawing its request to hand back its license."

The hall erupted in gasps and whispers.

The chairman banged his gavel. "Order. Order."

My jaw dropped.

Had I heard right? They were *not* trying to pass the burden of this mining waste site and the cleanup operation onto the government?

Had we really just got the victory that Osgood had suggested we would have had to fight tooth and nail for?

Stanko continued: "Given the unfortunate and unforeseen developments due to adverse weather, as a responsible corporate citizen dedicated to protecting the health and safety of the community and to protecting the environment, we are committed to holding on to our waste management license indefinitely. We will continue to take full responsibility for this former mining property."

He took up another thirty minutes congratulating himself and Syron Lake Resources on the civic-mindedness of the altered request.

"Thank you, Mr Stanko," the chairman said after the lawyer closed his presentation. "There are a couple of things I'd like go over with you."

The chairman, whose nameplate indicated he was called Benoit Dromel, had appeared unfazed throughout Stanko's presentation. Now, he wore a stern expression, like that of a principal facing down a truant in his office.

"You've presented us with reports on your past performance, and projections for this cleanup, and for the long term," Dromel said. "But we've heard little about how you plan to address the concerns in this community that your company's waste management practices may be so deficient as to pose a possible threat to the environment and to this community's well-being."

Even from looking at his back, I could tell that Stanko bristled at the question. He threw back his shoulders and sat up.

"Well, Mr Chairman, I think you should keep in mind that you've had people come up here making unfounded accusations about Syron Lake Resources.

"For instance, there was the insinuation that the unfortunate spill of three weeks ago would kill fish in Syron Lake. But the fact is, there's no way that spill could have had that effect, because if you look at page five of the 1998 report I've submitted, you'll see that Syron Lake was historically used as a tailings containment area and no live fish have been recorded in Syron Lake for the last thirty years."

"That's hardly something to boast about, Mr Stanko," Dromel said.

"It's not a boast," Stanko boomed. "It's a fact, plain and simple. And I raise it simply to highlight the point that uninformed members of the public may come before this panel to make appeals based on nothing but emotions and conjecture. However, it's the duty of the CNRA as an evidence-based decision-maker to ignore such baseless utterings and concern itself only with the concrete facts before it."

"That may be so, Mr Stanko. But, even if this panel does find that the evidence you've provided is persuasive, you may want to consider that you might have a public relations problem that needs addressing."

"Thank you, Mr Chairman. I'll see that your advice is passed on to the relevant department in the company." Stanko looked around at his colleagues and snorted.

The chairman continued on, picking at the Syron Lake Resources presentation. Members of company's team went digging into their binders to pull out answers to his long and detailed questions.

By the time half an hour had passed, Goran Stanko's voice had lost all the buoyancy that had been present when he had made his announcement. At one point, his sigh was audible over the speakers. I imagined that he was startled by that as much I had been when it had happened to me.

"Just a couple more points, Mr Stanko, and I'll turn things over to my colleagues, if they have any further questions," Dromel said. "We heard mention of 'regulatory capture' earlier today. We'll not go into whether such a notion is relevant to this Authority. But as a regulatory body, the CNRA must be mindful of public perception, wouldn't you agree, Mr Stanko?"

"Of course." The lawyer shifted in his seat. "Justice must be seen to be done, and all of that."

"Precisely. So, I find that I must come back to the question that was raised earlier about the level of competence your company displayed prior to the recent incident.

"The CNRA has a responsibility, Mr Stanko, to assure the community that acceding to a company's request isn't taking some kind of shortcut that could jeopardize the community's interests, even if that request involves the company paying all costs for a cleanup and continued maintenance at its waste management site. If a company...."

I scribbled feverishly, as I had been doing all afternoon. The notes were for the written reply I would have to submit to the CNRA to complete my participation in the hearing. They might be also useful for the class action lawsuit, I thought.

But my mind was floating in a mist of euphoria and confusion.

I had come with my pebble and sling shot, only to discover Goliath waving a white flag.

Victory had come easily. Too easily, perhaps. Should I rejoice, or be wary? Was there some kind of trick behind Syron Lake Resources' decision to hold on to that toxic dump for all eternity?

And then there was the panel chairman.

Silently, I cheered all of his questions. Here was one government official who understood, who seemed to be on our side as the affected community. And particularly on *my* side. He was jabbing Goran Stanko with arguments from my presentation.

Able to relax now that my speech-making was behind me, I found myself paying attention to the chairman each time I lifted my eyes from my notes.

I had not noticed before what an intelligent face his was.

And at first, I had found the shaved head somewhat disconcerting. Now, the self-assurance that it hinted at, along with his firm, yet urbane manner, added up to a magnetism emanating from that middle seat on the panel — a magnetism which I made no effort to resist.

Chapter 43

His Russian business partners were late, and Daniel Greene hated waiting.

He sat in a booth at the far end of the Huxton pub with his back to the trendy Londoners. He was stoked for this meeting. He had taken a hit of pure white dust before leaving his flat and he would not be drinking this night.

He had much to tell about Syron Lake.

He tapped his fingers on the table and looked across at Nadia, his personal assistant, bookkeeper, cook, sometimes bedmate, and procurer of all his pleasures, whether in powder form or of the feminine kind. At least she amused him while he waited, rattling on about inconsequential matters and stroking her long, brown hair which fell on an almost flat chest that was plainly visible under a fitted, bra-less top.

He liked their arrangement. No promise of permanence; no demand for exclusiveness. She was loyal and reliable. There was none of those unworkable romantic expectations that poisoned relationships and destroyed the families that were built on them.

No, he arranged his affairs so he would not be sucked into anything like that insane, three-decades-long ride through Hell he had witnessed his mother endure with the man known to the world as his father.

Isaac Greene was *not* his father. The man had said so himself, a long time ago, when the family still lived on Fifth Avenue in New York. Even as Nadia spoke, Greene's mind replayed the memory as vividly as it had done countless times over the years.

He was nine, at the time. His mother and Isaac Greene were in their bedroom, arguing as usual; they didn't know he was listening at the door.

"I can't continue like this," his mother had said through sobs. "You're abroad all the time now, we never see each other, and God knows who you've been with...."

"How dare you?" the gruff male voice had said. "I am out there busting my tail to build this business so you can enjoy living in style, and this is the thanks I get?"

"What's the use of all of this if you're never around for me or your son?"

"Don't get me started on that, Carmela. I looked into that. There's never been anyone in my family with a cleft lip."

"What are you trying to imply?"

"Ten years ago, I was almost full-time on the road, criss-crossing Africa, remember? I was back only a handful of days that year. You were still working at Braun Jewellers, remember? Well, I looked into it, Carmela. And guess whose great-grandfather had a cleft lip?"

"That's totally out of line, Isaac. You know Daniel's condition is not necessarily genetic. It could have been caused by all the stress I was under with you being away all the time."

"Don't try to give me that. I know you and Alfred Braun had eyes for each other. That imp you gave birth to is *his*, not mine."

The slap came first. Then came the crashing sounds, and the muffled cries.

Little Daniel flung open the door; next to a broken lamp, Isaac Greene was entangled on the floor with his mother, each of them grabbing the other by the throat.

Later that night, when his mother had tucked him in bed, she had asked about what he'd heard. He lied and said he had been in the bathroom and had come running to their bedroom only after he'd heard the crash of the lamp. The incident was never brought up again.

But the fights never stopped. Decades later, Isaac Greene and his co-founders had done extremely well with Magrelma Mines, extracting wealth from the bowels of three continents. The man no longer needed to work hard; still, he was never long in the same place with his wife. What was different was that her competition had become young enough to be her daughters, and she had become almost completely worn down.

It couldn't go on like that indefinitely. Nor could Daniel Greene wait indefinitely in the shadow of a man who pledged to die with his jackboots on.

It was the only such business Daniel Greene had personally taken care of. Isaac Greene was home alone at the family's Grosvenor Square flat. Daniel had used his mother's keys to sneak in by the back door, away from the prying eyes of neighbors or their servants. He saw the surprise in Isaac's eyes, and the relief when Isaac heard Daniel's reconciliatory words and plea for fatherly advice concerning some business matter.

They had never really got along over the years, but, now, as two mature adults, they could have a long heart-to-heart over a few drinks, Daniel had said. The old man had several glasses of Scotch; Daniel matched him, except much of his drinks disappeared into a wide-mouthed flask when Isaac wasn't looking.

Daniel needed as much lucidity as he could hold on to in order to complete his task.

After some time, he had excused himself to go to the bathroom. Isaac's medicine cabinet was a veritable cache of lethal weapons. The oxymorphone prescribed for Isaac Greene's chronic back problems would do the job.

Crushed and stirred into the next drink, which Daniel, with all humility and kindness, offered to pour, it brought a permanent end to the pain — for all three members of the family.

Nadia, of course, had backed up his story that he had been with her the whole night.

The autopsy concluded that Isaac Greene's demise was one of a growing number accidental deaths from overdoses of prescription drugs, the consumption of alcohol serving to double the effects of the medication to a lethal level.

That was almost two years ago.

Daniel Greene looked at Nadia's small, simple face in the amber glow of the dim lights at the Huxton pub. She smiled at him and toyed with the diamond-encrusted bracelet he had given her for her birthday, the week before. Yes, this was the better way to arrange things, Greene thought. No complications.

"They're here." Nadia gazed beyond his shoulder, then slinked away to another table.

Two smartly dressed men in their late thirties took the seats opposite Greene.

"You're late; I don't do late," Greene said.

"Accept our apologies," Boris Nazarov, the more muscular of the two, said in a thick Russian accent. "Dr Laschenko, here, thought he saw someone staking out his apartment. We had to take evasive measures."

"Listen, if *his* problems are going to get in the way of *my* business, then maybe he shouldn't be involved in this."

Anton Laschenko, Greene had been told, was a hunted man.

When he had been a PhD candidate at the St Petersburg State Mining Institute in the mid-nineties, he and a fellow student supplemented their meagre scholarship funds by writing dissertations for older, mid-career candidates who didn't care to open a book, but lusted for the framed bits of paper in order to catapult up the ranks.

When his colleague had fallen ill, Laschenko had to take over the job for one particular individual whose thesis was on an area of economics which Laschenko knew nothing about. He copied large sections of an old American textbook, and cobbled together bits of obscure research papers. All three men got their degrees. Laschenko became an academic with the Institute and his friend went on to work in the privatized mining sector. The mid-career official rose high, very, very high, Greene had been told.

Four years ago, Laschenko's friend had called out of the blue; he had sounded scared and had wanted to know whether it was true that the dissertation for the official had been plagiarized; strange-looking men had been asking about it, he'd said. A few days later, the friend was shot dead. When he heard that Russian secret service agents had been to the Institute asking for him, Laschenko lost no time in fleeing the country.

"This won't be a problem," Nazarov said as he stared at Greene. "Laschenko knows how to live on the run. Besides, the Syron Lake project can't go anywhere without him."

Greene knew Nazarov was right.

Laschenko was the man holding the files.

The academic, Greene had been told, had come across the files in a vault in the basement of the St Petersburg State Mining Institute, which was more than two-centuries-old. The Institute's Museum had close to a quarter of a million exhibits collected from more than eighty countries around the world. The vault had not been opened for almost half a century, Nazarov had said, and the files had probably not been seen since they had been mysteriously deposited there.

Partly in English but mostly in Hungarian, the documents revealed the betrayal and greed that had accompanied the very birth of Syron Lake Resources.

Greene knew the company had been established by four Eastern European immigrants to Canada — a Hungarian engineer and three Polish backers. What Nazarov and Laschenko revealed was that the company had been plagued with in-fighting and intrigue even before the first samples had been bored.

The engineer, disgruntled at what was to be his share, falsified reports that went to his partners, and hid certain drilling samples. He secreted away the true findings about the Syron Lake stake to a contact in Hungary, where he had hoped to get his own backers and buy out his partners, Greene had been told.

The engineer never got to carry out his plan. Greene knew that the Hungarian went down in a plane crash shortly after the mine opened.

Somehow, after the engineer's death, the secret files and samples that he'd sent to Europe made their way into the vast collection of the Institute's mining Museum, Nazarov had said.

Now the documents were in Laschenko's possession; they were all the academic had taken with him when he had fled Russia.

They held the secret of the Syron Lake mine's true potential — potential that Greene suspected Mahler had refused to acknowledge because he instinctively knew that the rejuvenated mine's stratospheric earnings would cause Greene to supplant Mahler in importance at Magrelma.

The biggest irony was that when operations shut down in the nineties, as far as Greene could make out, the waste from the Syron Lake Resources uranium mine had been dumped in the tailings pond somewhere in the region where any new operation would need to be centered.

Greene did not speak Hungarian. Nadia, who was half-Hungarian, had been with him the afternoon Nazarov and Laschenko had shown him the files. She had said that what the men had said corresponded with the few pages she had been allowed to read.

But Greene wasn't born yesterday. He had demanded that the papers in the file be verified by an expert.

After much wrangling, the Russians had agreed to hand the stolen documents over for authentication — but to one man alone who could be trusted, an early Russian émigré who'd had a long and distinguished career as an Imperial College London mining history professor. Greene knew of the man, had heard of his recent retirement. He had not flinched at the hefty fee for the retired professor's confidential services.

Now, six months after everything had checked out, Greene felt well on his way.

Fate had dropped into his lap the opportunity to make his first billion. And it would come long before he turned fifty-two, the age Isaac Greene had been when Magrelma's worth had hit that mark.

Greene drew in a breath with more than a hint of satisfaction. "Just so that you know," he said, "the tailings pond has been drained. It's been all taken care of."

The Russians exchanged glances.

"What is this?" Nazarov's forehead folded in deep waves. "This was never in the plans."

"I don't gave a damn about your plans. This is my company; we'll do things my way."

"This project was supposed to be handled discreetly."

"And it is. Mahler is the only other person who knew about it. And he's no longer a problem."

"But Magrelma is not your company. You don't run it."

"Don't have to. I haven't said anything to Maitland, although he's supposedly in charge now. All I had to say to him was that I would be focusing on our Syron Lake assets. The drunkard was happy as hell to have one less thing to think about."

"But, draining toxic waste from a dam, just like that...this is not done."

"Ah, it *has* been done. The dam was breached. What didn't spill out is now being carted away."

"But the authorities...."

"Relax. It's all taken care of."

Nazarov's jaws pulsated.

"Do you think I'd try to handle this on my own?" Greene snorted. "There's nothing to be concerned about. There are some very high up individuals taking care of things. All will be well."

Nazarov stared Greene with hard eyes. Laschenko remained silent, as he'd always done at these meetings.

"Look, it had to be done." Greene leaned forward and continued in a lower voice. "Right now there's a hearing to review plans for all the mining companies in Syron Lake. They're supposed to hand back their licenses and turn the properties over to the government to maintain the waste sites. All the companies had confirmed they wanted to bail out in the next three to five years. Syron Lake Resources included. Mahler had ordered the company to file documents saying that.

"But with the dam now busted, it would be political suicide for the government to take back the Syron Lake Resources license because they would be saddled with the cleanup bill. Taxpayers wouldn't be too happy about that.

"So, that's where we've jumped in and said — out of the goodness of our hearts as responsible corporate citizens, of course — we'll hang on to our license, bear the cost of the cleanup and hold on to the property for the long term."

Nazarov's face remained taut.

"See, it all works out." Greene leaned back and smiled. "In this way, we're already clearing the ground in preparation for our new operations. It's being done right under their noses and nobody knows it."

Nazarov shook his head.

Greene narrowed his eyes at the gesture; he felt irritation rising in his breast that his cleverness seemed not to impress the Russians. "Look, if we'd gone the official route, applying for permission to relocate the tailings pond, that could have meant years of bureaucratic red tape and, in the end, we still might not have gotten the go-ahead."

"This is too risky. It could jeopardize everything," Nazarov said.

"That risk has been taken care of." Greene nodded with an air of triumph. "The official chairing the review panel is our man. That's been doubly assured. There's no way we're losing that property."

"Getting this project off the ground was supposed to be left to *us*," Nazarov said through clenched teeth. "That's what we discussed."

Greene's nostrils flared and turned bright red.

Nazarov sensed that he had let too much of his anger show.

He swallowed hard and switched to a calmer voice. "We already have a company set up to do all the preliminary work. You don't have to get involved in this manner. All you need to do is provide the equity. Really, you should not worry yourself with all these complications. Let us handle the details. Just–"

"No!" Greene slammed his palm down on the table. "This has to be done right. *I'm* leading this project and we'll do it *my* way. Understood?"

Chapter 44

He had been eager to finish work all day. When he arrived home, he showered to go over to Stella Jacob's place for what he planned as a casual conversation about her connection with Osgood.

As he pulled on a crisp, white shirt, he caught sight of his face in the mirror. He frowned.

He had not always looked like this.

This face had manifested itself on him in the days that followed Sophia's abrupt exit from his life.

They'd dated for three years. She'd become friends with his friends and had spent time with his parents and his sisters. She'd even attended his father's funeral and had held his hand before and after he'd given the eulogy.

Three years, and she'd waited until the last day before their wedding to leave a note saying that she couldn't go through with it, that she couldn't continue to live a lie, and that she was taking off with the person she really loved.

He had let her ghost beat him down for long enough now. That was the past. History. He was ready to crawl out from that dank, windowless dungeon or wherever the hell it was that he had been trapped these past seven years.

He scanned his face in the mirror. The beard had to go.

Chapter 45

I tapped intermittently on the keyboard in a vain attempt to type up the day's notes. Every so often, though, my mind wandered to the parts of the day's events that would not leave me. The reminiscing was aided by Jan Arden's *Could I Be Your Girl?* which I had set to repeat on my computer's CD player.

That smile.

Those hazel eyes.

That wink.

It had lasted mere seconds, yet it had spawned hours of daydreams.

I had scrambled home to Google him. But all I could find on Benoit Dromel was the bio that accompanied his appointment to the CNRA, a couple of years before.

Born in New Brunswick. A double major in engineering and law at the University of Toronto; so, obviously ambitious, with a brilliant mind. Admitted to the bar some twenty years ago. A brief stint in the private sector and a steady climb through the public service, culminating with the post of Director at the Canadian Boundary Waters Commission, before being selected by the prime minister — Prime Minister Peabody's predecessor, that is — to serve a five-year term.

No mention about a wife or family.

I, of course, had taken notice of his left hand. *No ring.*

The website didn't give a date of birth, and without hair of a color that could give away his age, his wrinkle-free face suggested he was in his early forties. His CV, though, pegged him at a decade older.

His image — both the picture on his web profile, and the intelligent features I'd begun to pay attention to since the afternoon session — was now burned into my mind. That smile....

Somewhere in my reverie, I was aware of car lights turning into my driveway. Still, I was startled to hear the knock.

"Ms Jacob." The man at the door dipped his chin in a somewhat shy bow. "I'm Detect– I'm Paul Parker. We met at the Field Naturalists meeting the other night."

At first I didn't recognize him. Then I noticed the freshness of his clean jaw. *So there'd been a more than decent-looking man hidden under the beard, after all.*

No ring, here, either.

Still, he was a Syron Lake cop. The panel chairman may have been supportive of me, but I figured that Mayor Demetriou may not have been as pleased with my presentation.

Demetriou had left for an out-of-town conference after the first day of the hearing, but city staff had been there earlier in the day and surely would have relayed my harsh words about the company and the authorities back to him.

This cop was employed by the town, so, ultimately, Demetriou was his boss.

"What do you want, Detective?"

He widened his eyes and pulled his head back, as if he was surprised at my tone.

"It's about Osgood. I have just a few questions. May I come in?"

I stepped aside and he entered, fidgeting with the leather jacket in his hands.

The chair scraped the floor in an ugly screech when I pulled it from in front of the computer and offered it to him. I would have preferred to have set him down at the other end of the table, far away from my computer. But that other chair was pilled high with copies of reports that I had collected from the CNRA hearing.

I leaned against the table and folded my arms. For some reason, unlike with the mayor, I was not at all bothered as this cop scanned the almost bare room, which was still littered with unpacked boxes.

"You, of course, heard the news," he said.

"Yes. Still can't believe it. Someone from the Field Naturalists said he committed suicide."

"Actually, there was no suicide note. But he did have your number jotted down."

"Well, we exchanged numbers the night we met at the Field Naturalists meeting."

"You were at the Moose Lodge the Friday night of the speeches, right?"

"Yes."

Parker shifted forward and perched himself at the edge of the chair. "Osgood didn't make too many friends in high places on that occasion, did he?"

What kind of trap was the mayor trying to lay for me, here? My body stiffened and my tone grew colder.

"What are you on about, Detective?"

"I'm just trying — as a friend, you understand — just trying to get a sense of what was happening with Osgood just before he died."

"But you seem to be suggesting his death wasn't a suicide."

"I'm not suggesting anything."

"So what is this inquiry all about then?"

"Look, I'm not here on duty, okay?" He smiled sheepishly. "This isn't anything official."

"If it isn't, why are you here, then?"

"Osgood had his eccentricities and, sure, he was a joke to some and a nuisance to others. But he was a good guy. I knew him fairly well. Well enough to think he deserves to have questions about how he died thoroughly checked out."

I remembered how this cop had shaken Osgood's hand the night of the political meeting; yes, it had seemed warm and sincere. And now, too, he sounded earnest. Perhaps he wasn't here at Mayor Demetriou's behest after all.

I stood up straight and faced him. "Osgood was advising me on how to deal with the spill. He was the one who suggested I apply to speak about it at the federal government hearing, which I had the chance to do, today. He also encouraged me to launch a class action lawsuit."

"Did anyone else know about this?"

"Mayor Demetriou found out about the lawsuit."

"Did he know Osgood was advising you?"

"I've no clue. I'd gone to the reservation to try to get them involved and I think Demetriou found out because someone from the reservation told him about my visit. He came to see me about it."

"And?"

"Let's just say he wasn't too pleased. He warned me not to go ahead with the class action."

"When was that?"

"It was the Monday or Tuesday after the election."

I felt my throat tightening. The memory of my encounters with the mayor rattled me. Perhaps I'd already said too much to this cop. I was still too new to this town. I didn't fully understand the dynamics of this place. The pendulum of uncertainty had sung again, making me wary about saying anything further to Detective Sergeant Paul Parker.

"Look, I've got a lot of work to do," I said. "Are we finished here?"

Parker seemed to hesitate. "Yes. Thanks. I appreciate your time."

He stood up. As he did, the CD kicked in a repeat of *Could I Be Your Girl?*. The song had been playing quietly in the background all this time.

Parker's eyes darted toward the computer and rested on the pile of Jan Arden CDs that sat on top of the tower.

"My elder sister's a big fan of hers, too." He smiled.

The Web browser on my computer was open and showed a page with Benoit Dromel's picture — enlarged to fill up the screen. I didn't have a screensaver running. My heart pounded at the thought of the cop's eyes gliding from the pile of CDs across to the screen. I feared that with that particular song repeating, the frenzy of emotions which now possessed me concerning Benoit Dromel would be laid bare.

"Well, thank you for stopping by." I took a step closer to the door and extended my hand toward it.

Parker seemed taken aback by the abrupt gesture, but proceeded to leave.

I followed him to the door. Through the thin material of his white shirt, I observed the taut muscles of his back. He smelled of sandalwood and cedar. Nice aftershave, I thought.

He stepped across the threshold, then turned around sharply. He stood there, hesitating.

"Look, I'm not sure what happened to Osgood." he said, "but, yes, I have my doubts about the suicide theory. I don't mean to frighten you. But if what happened to Osgood had something to do with what he was talking to you about, there may be a possibility you could be in danger too."

So were we back to this cop being the mayor's messenger out

to scare me off this battle with the mining company? My eyes narrowed to a stern stare.

The detective pulled out a pen and a small notebook from the pocket of the leather jacket and scribbled.

"Look, if you ever need help, give me a call."

He tore off the page and extended it to me.

I shrugged and took it, telling myself that there wasn't any circumstance under which I'd feel the need to use it. Little did I know how wrong I was about that.

Chapter 46

The last day of the hearing, I arrived early to reclaim a seat at the front. I hadn't enjoyed having to peer over heads, nine rows deep, as I'd been forced to do the previous afternoon when the Syron Lake Resources team swiped the seat I'd had the entire week.

From my position, I had a clear view of the panel chairman — and he of me. He called the session to order. Three minutes into the presenter's speech, he flipped open his laptop.

I looked directly into his eyes — and he into mine.

A surge of warmth flooded every inch of my body. I bent my head and bit my lip to restrain the giddy grin that threatened to break out on my face.

"Does this have potential?" I wrote in my notebook.

Throughout the rest of the session, practically every time I looked up, I met his gaze. No, I was not mistaken about his interest.

Embarrassed at where I had allowed my thoughts to wander, I looked away almost immediately every time our eyes met. Except on two occasions; at those moments, I saw the sides of his lips curve slightly upward. A knowing grin. An alluring grin.

The hearing ran right through lunch without a break and wrapped up at half past one.

As Benoit Dromel delivered his closing remarks, I scribbled a couple of words, and drew a line down the left side of the question mark I had written earlier. I smiled giddily and filled it in.

The note now read, "Oh boy! Does this have potential!"

Chapter 47

With a rolled-up twenty-dollar bill held to his right nostril, he inhaled sharply, drawing up the last remnants of the crushed OxyContin pill. He checked his face in the mirror. He brushed away what looked to be specks of the powder, dusted down the dresser, and began to pack his suitcase.

He had hoped to adjourn the hearing at noon to give himself enough time that he wouldn't have to rush. No such luck. The last presenter was so long-winded, and Rigby just kept firing off questions, as if any of it really mattered. Two or three more proceedings, and Rigby would learn, Dromel thought to himself.

A three-hour drive to the Sudbury airport lay ahead of him. He would have twenty minutes to catch his flight to Ottawa.

Bernice would be back that weekend, well, for a few hours anyway.

She was in the air already, on her way from Paris. She was scheduled to be in some African nation or the other the following Monday. She had planned things so that they'd meet at the Ottawa airport, spend the night at a nearby hotel, and then she'd catch an onward flight, early the next morning.

He could not afford to miss his plane.

The knock on the door startled him.

He had already checked on the staff and delegated the work of ensuring the orderly return of equipment to the CNRA headquarters; he wasn't expecting anyone.

Through the peephole, he saw a young man who nervously looked about him. The stranger knocked again.

Dromel flung open the door.

"What do you want?"

"Are you the nuclear hearing chairman? My buddy from high school works at the front desk. He said this was your room number."

So much for professionalism and concern about the safety of guests at this hotel, Dromel thought.

"Well, are you the chairman? Are you Mr Dromel?"

"Yes."

"Can I come in?"

"What for?"

"I need to speak to you about something important. In private."

The young man took to the captain's chair in the corner of the tiny room. Dromel shifted the clothes that lay on the bed and sat beside the open suitcase.

"I read about you in today's papers," the young man said. "I don't know if you read the local paper?"

"I glanced at it."

"Well, my uncle is the one who drowned last weekend at his fishing camp. Eric Tremblay. The story was on page three."

Dromel looked at his watch.

"My uncle worked for Syron Lake Resources. They mentioned that in the article."

"What does this have to do with me?"

Jacques Tremblay bent his head and looked at the floor. After a while, he propped his elbows on his knees and clasped his hands over his face. His shoulders shook.

Dromel remained silent as he listened to the sniffles and sobs. He checked his watch again. "Look, kid, I hav–"

"Sorry, sorry. I didn't mean to...." Jacques wiped his eyes with the cuffs of his sweater. He sniffled. He took a big breath, then continued.

"I'll get straight to the point. About two weeks ago, my uncle came to see me in Ottawa. I'm in college down there. So he came down and he said he needed to get something off his chest. He'd done something bad. He wasn't thinking straight when he did it, because he'd been to the doctor and they'd told him he had cancer really bad and he had four months to live."

Dromel looked at the open suitcase. He was tempted to start packing and tune the kid out. But the young man's agitation caused him, instead, to merely shift his weight on the bed.

"And?" he said.

"Well, shortly after he got that diagnosis, some people approached him. Said they were from the company. They knew all about his work, his shifts and everything. They said the company wanted the tailings pond breached. But it had to look like an accident. So he waited until there was a big storm and then...he broke the dam."

"What?" Dromel stood up.

"He was ashamed of himself afterward. He told me that he planned to let it out in public, like, you know, like a deathbed confession, just before the cancer took him. But then the accident happened. He never got the chance...."

Jacques bent his head again and sobbed.

Dromel rested his hand on the young man's shoulder.

"Thanks for coming to me with this. Does anybody else know?"

"As far as I know, no." Jacques wiped his eyes. "I'm his only family and he didn't have a girlfriend. His best buddy committed suicide this weekend, too. I don't know if my uncle may have told him. He was supposed to be out fishing with him that day. He wasn't too right in the head, that guy. Something like that could have sent him off his rocker; or he could have found out my uncle had drowned and then decided to do himself off."

Dromel paced in front of the bed.

"I came to you because my uncle had made me swear that if the cancer took him before he could make the video public that I would do it for him. We'd spoken about me anonymously passing it to the police. But I don't trust the cops. Don't want to have anything to do with them."

Dromel continued to pace in silence.

Jacques watched him, his head moving left to right, like a spectator at a tennis match.

"I don't know if I'm doing the right thing." Jacques propped his elbows on his knees and cupped his chin with his hands. "I'm feeling kinda zoned out right now. Got no family left now. Don't even know if I should go back to school or not."

Dromel stood directly in front of Jacques.

"Look at me, kid," the panel chairman said sternly.

Like a child, Jacques obeyed and lifted his eyes to meet Dromel's.

"Give me a straight answer," Dromel said. "How much was he paid?"

Jacques looked away.

"What? Did you think the cops would ask and I wouldn't? Talk to me. How much?"

Jacques bit his lip.

"Speak up!" Even Dromel was startled by the ferocity with

which the command came out.

"Fifty grand," Jacques said under his breath.

Fifty grand, Dromel repeated in his mind. And they had offered him only six times that much for his part in whatever grand scheme Syron Lake Resources was up to. He began to feel insulted.

"What happened to the cash?"

Silence.

Dromel checked his watch.

"Where is it?"

"I don't know what he did with the rest, but he gave me thirty grand. We spread the money in four different banks in Ottawa, under my name. None has more than eight thousand."

Wise, Dromel thought. Unlikely to raise suspicions. This situation should not be a problem.

Dromel tried on a tone of sagacious authority. "What your uncle did is a very delicate matter. It has to be handled with the utmost discretion. Do you understand?"

Jacques nodded.

"Leave this with me," Dromel said. "I'll consult with the relevant individuals at the CNRA in order to ensure the matter is dealt with effectively."

Jacques smiled uncertainly. "I was thinking I should maybe, you know, make myself scarce for a little while. Go somewhere where I can chill out and clear my head."

Dromel immediately understood the kid's convoluted manner of communicating. He was really asking whether he could consider the cash his to keep.

This naive pup had put himself in a totally vulnerable position. If he, Dromel, had been wicked in nature he could have easily frightened this yokel into emptying the bank accounts and handing all the money over to him.

But the kid was now alone in the world. What was he, eighteen, nineteen? At any rate, he was a few years younger than Dromel had been when he'd lost his father, a hardy lobster fisherman, who was the last of the elders in his family. Dromel remembered the confusion and the sense of being adrift that he'd felt, and which the kid had just seemed to have described. Unlike the kid, Dromel had been lucky; he'd been well into his studies and he'd begun a serious relationship, and that had kept him grounded.

The money seemed to be all that this kid had. Dromel didn't need it; he was going after a much larger paycheck.

He caught sight of the clock on the bedside table. He had to get going in the next few minutes, otherwise his brief reunion with Bernice would be in jeopardy.

He walked to the door.

"Good idea," Dromel said. "Go away, somewhere. But don't go living high on the hog, calling attention to yourself. Understand?"

"I'm not like that." Jacques got up and walked toward the door, grinning for the first time. "I'm actually really responsible."

"Remember: absolute discretion." Dromel wagged his index finger. "Don't talk about this with anyone."

Jacques reached for the door knob, then spun around.

"Oh, wait. I almost forgot. What should I do about the video?"

"The video?"

"When he was down to see me, my uncle got this fancy camcorder that he couldn't make head nor tails of. So he asked me to help him tape his confession. I figured out how to work the thing and we did the recording in his truck as he gave me a lift to my school. It's all still on there."

"Do you have the camcorder?"

"Not on me. I saw it up at my uncle's camp. I could go get it."

"Not enough time."

Dromel walked over to the bedside table and scribbled on the hotel stationery.

"Here's my address in Hull." He handed Jacques the paper and opened the door. "Copy the video on a stick and mail it to me. Don't use my name; just put the address on the envelope."

"Sure, no problem." Jacques slipped the scrap into his pocket.

"I mean it, kid," Dromel said. "Keep in touch. I need to know where to find you, if I have to."

Chapter 48

My feet took me down Ontario road. Destination: Syron Lake Inn. *He* was staying there.

I had remained behind after he had adjourned the hearing; I had stood at a window in a quiet corner of the community center and had watched for him to enter the parking lot.

The first three letters on the plate of the green Prius he drove was all I'd managed to get. I'd watched him turn onto Ontario Road, which would have taken him to the Inn, the crown jewel in Mayor Demetriou's empire.

I had remained at the window of the community center for what felt like an eternity, nibbling at an egg sandwich and looking out for the Prius. He would have had to pass this way to get out of town and I had been glued to my vantage point so that I could get that last glimpse of him.

But now, my feet were taking me toward the Inn.

My mind was blank. I had no clue what I would do or say when I got there. All I knew was that I felt a compulsion to once again see those hazel eyes, that square jaw, and that now seductive, bald pate.

Somewhere inside, I felt my entire future was wrapped up in those hazel eyes.

A swift movement caught my attention. A green car came flying around the bend, a few meters ahead. *It was him.*

His eyes were fixed on the road. He zoomed past in an instant. He didn't even see me.

I stood and watched the car grow smaller in the distance, until it disappeared behind an outcrop of rocks.

No, I thought; this could not be how the story would end. It could not be that he had come all the way to this town, had come into my life at this moment, and had ignited something deep and primal inside of me, only to slip out of my life forever, just like that.

Chapter 49

Chief Bromley slammed down the phone. He walked to the window behind his desk and leaned against the frame. He tapped his fingers slowly, letting each one hit the glass separately.

Parker, who had been on the other end of the line, entered.

"Sit down, Parker."

The chief took a deep breath, which expanded his already enormous chest. He walked over to his chair, but remained on his feet.

"An eyewitness told Kennedy that the other day you went out back for a smoke and offered him a cigarette. Said you were a real friendly guy. Kind, even. That you gave him almost a whole pack. Now, tell me Parker, since when did you start smoking?"

"I started when I was nine or ten," Parker said matter-of-factly. "Nasty habit, I know."

It was true. He *had* started at a young age. He was just leaving out the part that he'd quit in his mid-twenties after one of his early girlfriends had insisted she would not kiss a smoker. He had completely lost the craving for nicotine, and hadn't lit up until that morning when he needed to ease some information out of the eyewitness whom he had lured behind the station.

"Right," the chief said. "Another thing. Word got back to me that a neighbor on Eric Tremblay's street saw you banging on the door of his house. Said you left his grieving nephew very upset."

"I never banged on Eric Tremblay's door. That's simply not true."

"And the next thing. You've been asking questions around town about Eric Tremblay's drinking habits."

Parker said nothing.

"What does this add up to, Detective Sergeant?"

Getting no reply, the chief continued. "I'll tell what it adds up to: insubordination."

Parker's jaw moved up and down as he ground his teeth.

The chief narrowed his eyes and drew himself up. "I believe I made it clear to you the other day that you're not assigned to this case."

"I was only trying to help Max. He's a good cop, but, let's face it, he's very green."

"Parker, how many civilian cases of possible drowning and suicide have you investigated? Answer me that."

"None, but—"

"But nothing. This is not the military. This is a small town. With small-town folks. As far as dealing with civilian cases in a place like this is concerned, you're on par with Kennedy. So don't think you can waltz in here flashing your military experience as if that'll make you some kind of hotshot cop in Syron Lake."

His so-called superior was not covering himself in glory with his logic, Parker thought. He battled with his facial muscles to prevent the contempt he felt from leaking out in his expression.

"Perhaps it has escaped your notice, Parker, but *I'm* the one in charge around here," Bromley said. "And I am giving you a final and very clear warning. If I ever catch you covertly investigating this or any other case that I've not assigned you, I am going to haul your sorry tail before the disciplinary committee so fast, your head will be spinning. Now get out of my office and get to work on the cases I've assigned you."

"And a good-day to you, too, Chief," Parker said as he walked out the door.

Chapter 50

Director Hutton walked with leaden feet down a corridor at the White House. Two minutes before, he had been in the Situation Room in the basement taking a beating.

It was late November and the president was not a happy man. The opposing party was gloating at its gains in the mid-term Congressional elections a few weeks earlier. Meanwhile, the Administration was not looking good at all in the news.

Hutton knew the latter all came down to him.

Earlier in the week, a terrorist attack on a Bangkok disco packed with American tourists had left five dead. Among them were a Florida cheerleader who was celebrating her twenty-first birthday, and an otherwise ordinary Houston medical student who had walked in with three pounds of plastic explosives strapped to his waist. The morning's Washington Post had led with a damning leak: the FBI had had the bomber on its radar eighteen months before, yet was unable to prevent the tragedy.

When he'd received the summons to attend the National Security Council meeting, Hutton had fully expected to have his head chewed off. He'd been in the business long enough to have developed a thick skin. But the ferocity of the pummeling from a president who'd always seemed completely unflappable had left him reeling.

Maybe you're getting too old for this, he told himself.

He suddenly found a hand rubbing his back, making wide circles from one shoulder blade to the other.

"So you got his full nuclear blast."

Her voice bore sympathy with a touch of amusement. Secretary of State Angela Roseau finished by patting Hutton's lower back, then walked side by side with him.

His dressing down had been all that much worse because *she* had been there to witness it. He hadn't been able to turn his head in her direction during the entire meeting. And he could hardly find his voice now.

"Don't worry," she said. "That wasn't about you. I don't think he's recovered from the mid-term elections. We lost the House, and our majority in the Senate slipped quite a bit. He's going to have a rough time getting anything done from now on, and he knows it."

"Umm," was all Hutton could muster.

"He's been raging at everyone lately. He's even going ballistic about this softwood lumber dispute with Canada. Ordered me off to see Peabody in Ottawa, next week. I'm not looking forward to that at all.

"I've tried every strategy in the book with Shirtsleeves and so far nothing's worked. So I'm not sure what I can accomplish with this visit. If it was his deputy, Danforth, that I was dealing with, I'm sure there'd be progress. Danforth is a reasonable man. But Peabody seems to take more pride in flaunting his pig-headedness than in trying to prove himself a wise leader of a major nation."

Roseau sighed.

"The president has me under his thumb because he needs this softwood lumber trade deal. It's his last term and it's supposed to be part of his legacy.

"And the party is getting antsy, too. We'll hurt badly if we don't stitch this thing up. It could lose us a lot of financial support from the lumber industry, not to mention cost us a chunk of union votes.

"If we get this trade deal done, we'll be sitting pretty, but failure would make life difficult for whoever the party nominates to run in the next election. So you can imagine how the president is getting an earful these days from everyone around him who could be in line to take up his place when he vacates the Oval Office."

"Okay, I see the big picture," Hutton said, finally; he hadn't realized before how much he would enjoy having her try to perk up his spirits. "But I don't know, Angela. Maybe I'm getting too old for this business."

"Nonsense," she said. "You've got years and years of service to this great nation ahead of you yet."

She stopped and faced him. She smiled, and as he observed the way her blue eyes sparkled, Hutton wished there were some way to capture and contain their brilliance that he could bask in it whenever he wanted.

"So no more foolishness about bowing out, okay, Robert?

Even if he wouldn't admit it in that meeting, the president needs you, and this nation needs you."

"Thank you for that, Angela."

"Oh, there's nothing to thank me for." She chuckled. "I'm just speaking the truth."

At the far end of the hall, Kathy Wang walked out of a door and stood waiting. She clutched her notebook computer, as usual, and her face bore a harried expression as always.

Hutton and Roseau resumed walking.

"How's that investigation into Bill's death going?" Roseau said.

The subject had become inescapable with them. Since the State Department hosted the FBI's legal attachés at embassies around the world, Hutton had always been aware that their respective offices linked him and Roseau professionally. But the Mahler case was different. This one touched her on a deep and very personal level, and must have reminded her, as it did him, that their personal connection stretched back a quarter of a century. The Mahler case was a thread that now interwove their lives and seemed to be irresistibly drawing them closer together. At least Hutton hoped so.

"Nothing conclusive yet," Hutton said. "Of course, as the primary benefactor, Fran–"

"Yes, of course." Roseau nodded. "The surviving spouse is usually the prime suspect."

"We're also paying closer attention to the remaining partners."

"So, Maitland, then."

"And there's also Daniel Greene."

"Isaac's son?"

"Yes, he's been active in the company two years now, since his father died."

"Well, if it turns out he's responsible, how tragic that'd be, all round."

"Do you know him?"

"Not personally." They stopped just before reaching Wang. "But if I remember correctly, that boy was left behind at a boarding school in Dobbs Ferry when the parents moved to Monaco.

"He had some kind of condition and needed surgery every so often. They said he had to remain in the States so he could be under his long-time surgeon's care."

Roseau shook her head. "Imagine going through that all alone as a child. I heard Carmela came back once or twice when he was in the hospital, but I always thought that whole situation was unhealthy for the boy's emotional development."

"Thousands of kids get shipped out to boarding schools every year, Angela, and they don't grow up to kill their business partner. It may make for a lonely upbringing, but it's no excuse for murder."

"Oh, I agree with you." Roseau touched Hutton lightly on the forearm. "No matter what anybody goes through as a child, he's totally responsible for his choices as an adult. So I expect Daniel Greene to face the full force of justice, if you find that he's behind what happened to Bill."

"I assure you he will." Hutton nodded. "He absolutely will."

Chapter 51

The dark, frigid waters of the Rideau Canal swirled directly below him. Another night of waiting; another night of disappointment. He shelled out two tens on the table to cover his drinks and a generous tip. He left sober, too sober, searching every face, hoping for the encounter that would mark the start of the rest of his life.

For the moment, that life was feeling rather crummy. Because he felt he needed to be alert when next he conferred with the stranger who had never bothered to give him a name, he had curtailed his imbibing, even though he now appeared almost nightly at his customary watering hole.

He had scheduled no wild nights at the house in Hull since he had returned from the hearing in Syron Lake; it would have been too much of a distraction.

It was now the first week of December and no one from the company had shown up.

He wondered whether his trip to the UN Headquarters to represent the CNRA the week after the hearing had caused him to miss a possible contact.

His mind latched on to this notion; he pictured the stranger in an expensive suit walking into the bar and looking about for him, then turning around and leaving, never to return.

This sequence rolled incessantly before his eyes. It tortured him to think that while he had milled around the fringes of a terminally boring conference in New York on a $200 per diem, his one chance to make his fortune could so easily have slipped out of his hands.

The night air was chilly. The ground had turned white with a light dusting of snow. He took out his keys, folded his arms tightly in front of him for extra warmth, and walked around to the back of the building where he was parked.

He stood in the dim light, fumbling to find the keyhole.

"Dromel," a voice said in a firm whisper. The figure emerged from the shadows.

It was him.

Dromel leaned against the car. He slid his freezing hands under his jacket. He tried on a stony face to hide his excitement and the vague sense of fear that suddenly descended upon him.

The stranger, gloved and wearing a dark coat, approached.

"I thought I told you no surprises, Dromel."

"I figured you might show up one day."

"People aren't happy with how you conducted that hearing. I hope what transpired is not an indication of what will be in the decision."

Dromel remained quiet. He would play it cool. For whatever reason, they wanted that property badly, and he was the only one who could deliver. He could call the shots.

"When is that decision going to come anyway?"

"Four months, approximately."

The stranger nodded.

Relishing the upper hand, Dromel decided to turn the screw.

"But that's just an estimate. Could take twice that, according to the complexities we run into."

The stranger lit a cigarette and drew on it. "The time it takes isn't an issue, as long as it's reasonable. It's the result that matters. And that's where there's some cause for concern. What was that song and dance about at the hearing?"

Up to this point, the stranger had never stated the company whose bidding he was supposed to do, but Dromel was quite sure of who he was dealing with. "Syron Lake Resources released millions of gallons of toxic waste that was under its management. That could not go unaddressed."

"Fine, just as long as we understand what you said was all for show."

"Well, actually, this spill wasn't in the picture when we last spoke." Dromel tried to keep his tone steady, but wasn't sure he was succeeding. "It's one hell of a complication. I'd say it pretty much killed any chance that I could maintain the guarantees given before the incident."

"What are you getting at, Dromel?"

"The stakes have gone up."

"Get to the point. I don't have time to play games."

Dromel looked around. No one else was in sight.

With his index finger, he wrote out his price in the snow on the hood of his car. His hand trembled; perhaps the stranger would think it was only because of the cold.

"You're asking for a million dollars?"

"Half now; half when you've got your decision."

The payment schedule was utterly reasonable, Dromel thought. He rubbed out his writing from the snow and folded his arms again. The company he was dealing with was so desperate that it would deliberately break a dam containing radioactive waste to achieve whatever ends it was after. He could afford to name his price and hang back.

He knew the stranger was thrown by his demand. The man likely had no power to negotiate.

The stranger took a long drag on his cigarette, then flicked it away. He tilted his head back and exhaled. A thick jet of smoke and condensation shot up from his lips.

"The people I deal with don't play games," he said slowly. "We had a deal. If you plan to break it, you'd better be sure you're prepared for the consequences."

With the man's very deliberate delivery of those words, the apprehension of fear crystallized; Dromel felt as if icicles pierced his heart. He swallowed the hard ball that was now lodged in his throat and tried to maintain a steely expression. He would say no more.

"Have it your way, Dromel," the stranger said. "You will have an answer."

The man walked off briskly and disappeared around the side of the building.

When the key found the keyhole, Dromel flung open the door and collapsed into the driver's seat.

His entire body shook uncontrollably. He started the engine, opened the air vents and turned the temperature knob to the highest it could go. The night was just too bloody cold, he thought.

Chapter 52

Carmichael house, the venerable private member's club on Bank Street, was a hive of activity, as it usually was on a Friday evening. Ottawa's business mandarins and political elite sauntered through its portico and thronged its plush, red-carpeted corridors, as had generations before them.

Upstairs, in a private room, far from the din and laughter of the wood-paneled restaurant, Prime Minister John J. Peabody sat in an ancient wing chair, watching the lights of cars streaming by on the road below.

"Angela Roseau is an absolute bitch," he said. He took a sip of wine, then leaned his head back and closed his eyes.

Firestone, who sat in a matching chair directly facing his boss, kept quiet. He had been with him nearly two decades now, and knew when he was needed only as a prop so Peabody could listen to himself rant.

"She tried to strong-arm me." Peabody looked again at the traffic. "I mean she actually said she was putting it bluntly that America was losing patience with *me*. She didn't say Canada, or our negotiation team, but me. It was almost as if she was treating me like a schoolboy. Can you imagine? As if she was some sort of school madam running a play and I was a two-bit player she wanted to shoo away so the president could take center stage. Damn those Americans!"

He finished his drink and slammed the glass down on the table beside him.

"Well, I'm even more determined not to give an inch on this softwood lumber business. They're going to have to refund every last penny of import duties they imposed in the last three years and that's non-negotiable."

He adjusted his tie, yanking it roughly in either direction, and choked himself in the process. He leaned forward in a coughing fit.

Firestone smiled. It was a little reward for enduring this particular tirade.

Peabody leaned toward his chief of staff and spoke in an almost conspiratorial tone. "I've been thinking…"

Those were words Firestone had grown over the years to dread.

More often than not, they were followed by a suggestion so outlandish or so petty that it was either impractical to pursue, or unworthy of being acted upon. He wished Peabody would get it through his head that his job was to pose during photo ops and to read speeches written for him, and that he should leave the strategizing to those around him who actually had a mind for the business of running the country.

"That invitation that I got the other day to open a refurbished pulp and paper mill in Northern Ontario that I turned down, I think I'll accept it after all," Peabody said. "I'll use it as a backdrop to launch some zingers on Madame Roseau. I'll show her that she can't intimidate me. I want you to arrange this. And work the media so that they'll have the cameras rolling to catch every word."

Peabody nodded to himself. He smiled, already relishing his triumph in his mind.

Firestone kept his head down and scribbled notes in silence. There was no point in advising the prime minister at this time that antagonizing the Americans on this already touchy issue was not the smartest move.

"John," a voice said.

Kees Verhoeven approached with an extended hand.

Firestone knew to make himself scarce. He stood, bowed and left.

The prime minister stood. The men shook hands and Verhoeven took the seat vacated by Firestone.

"Can I get you anything?" Peabody looked around for a waiter.

"No. I'm fine. I have only a few minutes. Thank you for seeing me, tonight."

"Any time, Kees. Any time."

"So, Dromel's in charge of the Syron Lake panel after all."

"Quite. Funny how things worked out with his chairman. It was such a shock to hear about his accident. But my chief of staff was brilliant at ensuring Dromel got that file. You know how he did it?"

A twitch of Verhoeven's lower lip was all the prompting Peabody needed.

"All he did was tell the deputy chairman that I wanted to see him, and that the only time I had space in my calendar for that was the first week of November — which just so happened to be the week of the Syron Lake hearing.

"Of course, the deputy chair is hoping to get the nod to take over when the chairman retires in eighteen months, so there was no way in hell he was going to pass up a meeting with me. Dromel's fate was sealed, and no one was the wiser."

"Yes, well, unfortunately, I understand that he's not quite cooperating."

"How so?"

Kees looked around the room, although it was empty except for the two of them and Verhoeven's muscle-bound son, who leaned against the door frame.

Verhoeven spoke almost in a whisper. "Syron Lake Resources wants to hold on to its license. A couple of months ago, there was an accident, a little bit of a spill of its waste material. But I understand that's all been cleaned up. Dromel, however, has the power to revoke the license because of that mishap, and the company's getting a bit worried because he's been making some hostile noises."

"So it's Syron Lake Resources we've been talking about, is it?" Peabody raised his eyebrows. "I was figuring it was one of the larger public companies."

"What difference does it make?"

Peabody thought it over for a moment, then shrugged. "None really. Truth is, though, I had Firestone talk with Dromel before the hearing to smooth the way. But to be fair, Kees, that was before the spill. An accident like that does change the picture."

"Yes, well, that may be so. But what are you going to do about it?"Verhoeven let the question hang in the air; it was a challenge that carried the weight of the entire future between them.

Peabody's son's career with Verhoeven's company in Hong Kong was at stake. More importantly, Peabody knew how deeply connected this old university mate of his was on both sides of the Atlantic. An "in" with him would open up the doors to boardrooms in every desirable city in North America and Europe; ahead lay the possibility of a lifetime of private jets and year-round international hobnobbing once the prime ministerial gig was up.

"Dromel won't be a problem," Peabody said. "Leave it to me."

Chapter 53

The freezing rain from the night before made the roads slick and dangerous, and drivers had been warned not to venture out unless absolutely necessary. But it had dressed the naked branches of the trees in a thick coat of ice, transforming the forest into a magical, hoary landscape.

For a hiker like me, it was perfect.

I drew in the crisp, early morning air in short breaths, and listened to the crust of ice crack under my feet along the ungroomed snowmobile trail. The steady, serene sound provided a rhythmic counterpoint to wild, giddy thoughts, which focused on one subject: Benoit T. Dromel.

If Fate had intended us to meet, then Fate was cruel.

Dromel was different to Peter, my two other so-called boyfriends, and every other romantic prospect I'd worked up the courage to actually speak to. All those connections had brought me so much pain and had dealt such a blow to my self-esteem that I wished I'd never met any of those guys.

And here, finally, was a man who seemed deeply interested in me, perhaps as much as I now was in him. But there seemed to be an unbreachable gulf between us.

The age difference, my twenty-six to his early fifties, was not a problem; my own mother had been two decades younger than my father. From the few times he'd spoken to me about her, it sounded like they'd been happy together; and while the Trinidad woman whom he later married had been closer to his age, his second pairing had been fraught with bitterness, turmoil, and pain. So, to me, age didn't matter when it came to love.

The problem was more insidious.

Not only did geography separate us, but his job and my role in his world seemed to be conspiring to make it impossible for us to be together.

On my part, there was no problem. I was just an ordinary citizen, free to give my heart wherever I wanted.

But the nuclear authority was a quasi-judicial body and he was presiding over a matter in which I was a participant.

Anything between us would be a clear conflict of interest for him.

Every time I let myself be taken on a wild, imaginary romp between us, I would be yanked back to reality by the thought of our names appearing in the national newspapers under big, bold headlines that included the word "scandal."

I was nobody's daughter; my mother had been just one year out of university when she died giving birth to me, and my father had left this life as a penniless architect in Trinidad. Yet I considered my name — my good name — my most valuable possession.

I had built a life for myself as a single woman through honest, hard work; it mortified me to think that wanting to follow my heart could lead to public disgrace.

Good sense told me this possibility, alone, should have made me forget about Benoit Dromel. But how much happiness as a woman had restraint and good sense brought me so far? I was so unacquainted with words like "love" and "passion" that I struggled to make any headway with my romance novel.

My conservative self had battled with my desire ever since the moment Benoit Dromel had winked at me. The previous night, as the temperature outside had warmed and the rain had come down like shards violently pelted from the sky, I had sat at my computer with a firm resolve to settle the matter. And I had determined to do so in the same way that I had got ahead in my career: by copious research.

I read scores of blogs and agony aunt columns at the websites of traditional newspapers; I tapped the wisdom of relationship gurus hocking their latest tomes, and scrolled through hundreds of forum entries from ordinary women — and men.

The hands on my watch had ticked well past midnight when I had finally shutdown the computer.

No one out there had the answers as to how to deal with my exact situation.

But in a few intense hours, I had run through the gamut of human romantic relationships and the challenges they faced, from a lack of money to too much of it, from drug addiction to terminal diseases, from orbiting former flames to partners with roving eyes, from confusion over sexuality to reluctance to reproduce, and a whole lot more.

Those who had things easy — the fortunate ones who had met their sweetheart in high school and from there, sailed on smoothly to marriage, raising a family, and growing old together — were few and far between. For most of us, this thing called love was a messy business, and if you wanted it, you had to take a chance...and fight for it.

The sun had risen to an angle at which it pierced the ice encasing the branches in such a way that the rays split into the colors of the rainbow. All around me, the scene shimmered with a fragile beauty. I drew in a deep, cold breath that gave me a twinge as it coursed its way down into my lungs.

I made up my mind then and there.

I had a meeting with a class action lawyer in Ottawa the following week; it would provide the perfect "I was just in your area" cover if — *when* — I happened to run into Benoit Dromel.

Chapter 54

The knob clicked once, twice; Dromel followed the movement of the door as it creaked slightly ajar.

"You there, Mr D?" The voice was hesitant.

"Of course," Dromel snapped.

"You left that door open, man?" The skinny kid entered, closed the door, turned the lock, and swaggered over to the sofa where Dromel sat.

An enthusiastic hand raised for a hi-five made contact with a reluctantly-offered palm. The skinny kid didn't seem bothered by this. He pointed at the door.

"That's not wise, man. Not wise at all. This is a nice neighborhood and all that, but if I was you, I wouldn't go leaving my door unlocked."

"I left it open because I was expecting you," Dromel said sharply.

He shook his head and wondered how he found himself now having to explain himself to this guy. The dynamics of this connection were changing in a direction he wasn't liking. He wanted to rid himself of this uncouth, over-familiar lout; but he knew his supplier knew too much about him to be simply discarded. Besides, he needed him now more than ever.

The business with the payout of a lifetime in exchange for his approval of the Syron Lake Resources license ate away at his mind. All through the day until he hit the pillows, staring at the ceiling at night, he swung between delirious fantasies about spending his new-found riches and terror that he might end up garroted and left for dead in some abandoned mine site where his body would never be discovered.

He needed something to steady him through these uncharted waters.

"You got the stuff as usual?"

"What do you mean if I've got the stuff? Have I ever let you down?"

The young man bent over Dromel and grabbed his right hand. He reached into his jacket pocket, then slapped a small plastic bag of white pills into Dromel's open palm. He stood up and grinned.

Dromel exhaled loudly and pursed his lips. He could do without the dramatics from this fellow. He made a quick count, then slipped the packet into his pocket.

"And what about the recorder?"

"Got it right here." The young man took a slim box from a pocket deep inside his puffy winter jacket. He flicked open the lid and shook out a matte, black pen with silver finishing.

"See, you get it going by twisting the top section here. Then to start recording, press down the clip. Piece of cake."

Dromel reached for the pen.

The skinny kid made as if handing it over; but as Dromel attempted to close his fingers around the instrument, the young man whipped it up higher. Dromel reached out again, only to have the prize pulled away at the last moment.

"Just give me the damn pen," Dromel shouted. The indignities he had to put up with!

The younger man threw his head back and cackled.

"Ease up, man." Sill laughing, he dropped the pen into Dromel's hand.

He walked toward the door, then stopped and turned around.

"Next month, you can just double up on what you usually give me for the rent. That'll cover everything."

Dromel turned the pen around, examining every inch of it.

"You hear me?"

"Yes. Sure," Dromel mumbled.

The cost was outrageous. Some majordomo, he thought. Robbing his employer like a highway bandit. But the meeting at which he would put this to use was in less than two hours; he was in no mood to fight over a few hundred dollars when so much more was at stake.

"So what's that for anyway?" The young man opened the door and hesitated. "You turning undercover cop or something?"

"Just mind your own damn business." Dromel didn't look up.

The skinny kid shook his head.

"Hey, man, whatever crap you get yourself into, just watch out for yourself, you hear?"

Dromel finally looked up at the skinny kid. He thought he'd

heard real concern in the guy's voice.

"I don't want to see you get hurt or killed, okay? You're my best customer. Peace."

With that, the majordomo was out the door.

Dromel was already on edge about the mission the pen would help him accomplish; the kid's words hadn't helped to calm his nerves.

Chapter 55

He sat in a quiet corner of the room at the Chateau Laurier. It was minutes to midnight and he had been waiting for five hours. He had missed dinner and was not in a good mood.

He leaned forward and scribbled on the pocket-sized note pad on the table: "Patience is a virtue!!!"

Those were not the words running through his mind. No, that piece of real estate was currently occupied by very colorful language. But he had to exercise restraint, in case the security detail scrutinized his notes.

A soft click came from the other side of the room. He looked up. The door opened and Firestone strode in. "Good, you're here."

"Yes," Dromel said coldly. "I arrived at seven, actually. Thought I'd do the polite thing and show up half an hour early."

The sarcasm flew right past Firestone.

"He's not going to be able to come up." Firestone walked over to the door and opened it fully, motioning an unseen person to enter. "Something's come up and his whole schedule's gone haywire. You'll have to talk to him in the car. He's got a flight to catch."

A young man with cropped hair, who wore a dark, cheap-looking suit, entered.

Firestone looked at his watch.

"Make it quick; we're running late," he said.

The young man approached Dromel with both arms stretched out in front of him, palms up. He waved his hands upward; Dromel rested his pen on the table and got to his feet. As the man patted him down from the front, Dromel noted the officer's red, droopy eyes.

"Let's go; let's go," Firestone said impatiently.

Dromel turned around and the young man hurriedly patted him from behind.

"Let's make a move," Firestone shouted, then disappeared out the door.

Dromel bent and whisked up his pen and notepad and walked

briskly toward the door. The young man followed, shuffling his feet.

Poor sod, Dromel thought, having to work like a dog for long hours to protect that hideous man.

Outside, Firestone opened the rear door of the Chevrolet Suburban, then trotted to the black sedan parked in front of the SUV. Dromel climbed in and the young man with the cheap suit got into the front passenger seat.

"Benoit Dromel!" Prime Minister Peabody said with a wide grin. He sat in the far corner of the backseat with his arms folded as he watched Dromel strap on his seatbelt. "I believe we were at U of T around the same time."

The tone of mock friendliness mixed with dominance grated.

The man could not have got off to a worse start, Dromel thought. Given their history, bringing up their university days was bad enough, but the callousness of suggesting he was so insignificant as to not have staked a place in Peabody's memory just riled Dromel.

He swallowed hard and focused on fastening the buckle.

When Firestone had called the day before and said the prime minister needed to speak with him, Dromel was quite sure he knew what the subject would be. Now, he kept quiet and braced himself for what was to come.

The four-car prime ministerial convoy snaked unhurriedly along in the streets that were almost empty at that hour.

"Okay, Dromel, I'll get straight to the point." Peabody shifted to face him directly. "One of the companies in the Syron Lake hearing you've chaired has offered to continue to take full responsibility for operations at its site indefinitely."

"Yes."

"Well, you have to see that that's a good thing for the public purse. It's not every day the private sector shows such sterling corporate citizenship and makes such a generous gesture. Think about it; approving their retention of their license will in all likelihood save the taxpayer millions of dollars."

"Actually," Dromel said, "if you look at it from a broad perspective, it may not be an 'either,' 'or' situation."

"What do you mean by that?"

"For instance, we've had a concerned citizen suggesting that the license for that company, Syron Lake Resources, should be revoked and that on top of that, they be made to bear the financial responsibilities."

The prime minister snorted.

Dromel ignored the sound. "In such a scenario, the day-to-day management of the tailings would fall to others, such as a government agency or even an NGO. So the taxpayers are relieved of the burden, while the surrounding communities have peace of mind that the waste is being managed by an agency that has a vested interest in their safety, rather than in keeping costs down for a private company."

Dromel saw Peabody's face twitch. The prime minister's grin was gone.

He would rub it in a bit more.

"The idea is worth exploring," Dromel said, "especially since, as that intervener put it, the recent spill makes one question the company's competence to manage such dangerous waste."

"Let's not play games, here, Dromel. I think you know what's expected."

"Prime Minister, I was appointed to the CNRA to ensure the safe handling of all nuclear material. Our mandate is to safeguard human health and to protect the environment, and I hold that as a solemn duty."

"You're aware your appointment is revocable, aren't you?"

Dromel looked out the window.

"You worked in the private sector for just three years, didn't you?" Peabody said, breaking the silence. "Other than that, you've spent your entire working life as a public servant, haven't you? You've got, what: ten, twelve years before retirement? What's your next move after your term on the CNRA ends? Hoping for the security of the public purse, no doubt, eh?"

Dromel turned to face Peabody; their eyes locked in a cold stare.

The prime minister sneered. "I can make it so that you never again work in any federal capacity while I'm in office."

"Is that a threat?"

"Take it however you will."

"As an arm's-length body, the CNRA is supposed to be free of political influence. So if you're threatening me, I think I should inform you, Prime Minister, you're totally out of line."

Peabody's nostrils flared. He glanced quickly at the driver and the security officer in the front passenger seat. Transparent wires ran from their ears, down into their collars; their heads were stiffly facing the windshield. They apparently had not heard that affront. They couldn't have, not with the soundproof barrier up.

Peabody's cheeks burned as if he had been slapped. And by whom? Some obscure, low-level public official only temporarily given a taste of power because his superior was in the hospital. He wasn't going to let this little runt jeopardize his post-prime ministerial plans.

"I'm not trying to influence you, Dromel," Peabody said through clenched teeth. "I'm *ordering* you. Let Syron Lake Resources keep its license, otherwise your sorry ass will be out in the rain for as long as I can manage it."

The prime minister pressed a button on the armrest of his door. A red light flashed on the dashboard. The SUV slowed down and pulled onto the shoulder.

"Now, get out of my sight," Peabody said.

Dromel hopped out of the vehicle and stood at the side of the road. Firestone emerged from the car ahead, which had also stopped, and brushed past him to take the seat he had just vacated. Three cars from the convoy continued on.

The fourth, which had been at the rear, pulled up beside Dromel. The window wound down.

"Want to get back to the hotel?" the driver asked.

Back in his own car in the garage at the Chateau Laurier, Dromel grasped the steering wheel to steady his trembling hands. He bent his head forward; his breath exploded past his lips as he exhaled.

His shaking right hand dipped into his pocket. He pulled out the pen. He manipulated it, held his breath, and listened.

"I'm not trying to influence you, Dromel. I'm *ordering* you..."

The pen recorder had worked, just as the skinny kid had promised it would.

Chapter 56

Peabody had ridden in complete silence for twenty minutes. Now, words tumbled off his lips as he stared out the window.

"First thing when we get back, I want you to arrange with CSIS to put Dromel under surveillance. I want any dirt we can find on him."

He was giving instructions to Firestone, but mostly thinking aloud.

He knew, for all his bluster, his threats had been largely empty. He couldn't just yank Dromel's position away from him. It would cause bad publicity and who knows what the snooping media hounds would find.

No, in order to ensure cooperation from Dromel, he needed leverage.

Everybody had secrets, those proverbial skeletons in the closet. He would unleash the national intelligence apparatus to ferret out Dromel's skeletons. He would use the agency to bring Dromel to his knees.

He wanted to send CSIS after the insolent cur, just because he could. He would relish stripping the mangy mongrel of any right to privacy he may have imagined himself entitled to. What was the use of being prime minister if he didn't take advantage of such power that was at his disposal?

"Did you get that Firestone?" Peabody said. He turned to face his chief of staff, whom he had found unusually quiet.

"John, it doesn't work like–"

"Is every bloody person I talk to tonight going to defy me?"

"I'm just saying–"

"Just get it done."

Chapter 57

Nadia's bare knees clutched him from behind, at the hips, as he sat at the edge of the bed. She pressed her body against his back. Her fingers kneaded into his shoulder muscles, through his shirt, bruising yet soothing the flesh there. She timed her breathing to match his. As their bodies heaved and fell in unison with every breath, he felt himself yielding to her touch.

Yet, Daniel Greene didn't want to be soothed; he didn't want to yield. She had teased him all night about being grumpy. What did her attempt to pacify him mean? That he wasn't entitled to his anger?

He shoved her back on the bed, and got to his feet.

"What?" Nadia lay on her back, her skirt hiked up, her blouse undone. "I don't please you anymore?"

"You're beginning to make this complicated." He lit a cigarette, took a puff then held it between his fingers as he poured himself a shot of whiskey. "And you know what? If it get's complicated, it's over and done with, and you're out that damn door."

Some of the liquid sloshed out of the glass as he pointed to the tall, gilded door.

Nadia slid back on the bed and leaned her head against the padded, satin-covered bedhead. Her eyes followed the sweep of his gesture, taking in the silk curtains, the antique furniture, the original art hanging on the walls, and the artifacts from archaeological digs that he collected as a hobby and stashed throughout the Chelsea loft.

He knew the world she had been born into was far removed from this and that she had been aspiring to it when they had met by chance, twice in one week, five years prior, as she hung around the lounges of ritzy London hotels hoping to snag some rich old fool. He had rescued her from having to offer up herself nightly to some disgusting, wrinkled geriatric with no redeeming qualities other than a big bank account. No, she wasn't going to risk this life slipping out of her hands so easily.

His words had been cruel, and they both knew it.

He had intended them to sting. Women made much of mere words and he wanted to put her in her place. He would not let her tell him what to feel or how to behave. He was in control here, not her.

And yet, the last thing he wanted right now was to see her walk out that door. He needed her; that he knew all too well. She had always been evasive about her background, but he knew enough about her absent father, and drug-addicted whore of a mother, and numerous half-siblings to understand how desperately she clung to his world. She was efficient and willing to do anything he required. And when he had studied it in the past, he had realized how cheaply her services had come. Like a typical dumb broad, she hadn't even considered negotiating a price for anything, and seemed to be content just with living in the style he offered and receiving occasional baubles as gifts.

"Look, it's not you, okay?" He puffed and quaffed and paced the room. "Things are just screwed up at the moment."

Nadia unfolded her arms. Her face relaxed.

"Anything to do with that deal with Nazarov and Laschenko?"

He finished his drink, then poured himself another.

"They're being downright asses, for sure. Trying to pressure me to fund a shell company they've set up. But that's not the problem. I can handle them, just fine. They know even if they hold those files, it's worthless in their hands without me. I'm the only one who can start this new Syron Lake operation."

He paced in front of the bed, drawing on his cigarette, unconcerned about the ashes that dropped onto the Persian carpet. If it got ruined, he could always order another one.

"It's some bloody official in Canada. Some low-life loser who thinks he can double-cross me.

"First he agreed to a price to secure the license. Then he turned everything upside down, making damaging public statements about the company. Turns out he wants ten times what he originally agreed to."

Greene threw his head back and gulped down his drink. He shook his head as the liquid raged like fire at the back of his throat. He put the glass down and filled it again.

"I don't give a damn about the amount. That's peanuts compared to what this project will yield."

Greene walked to the side of the bed and sat. He spoke without looking at Nadia.

"What concerns me is that he made a deal and broke it. Who's to say he won't come back asking for more after this payoff? Let's say, three, four years down the road, when the mine's ready to produce, he could try to claw his way back into the picture, threatening to tell all if he doesn't get another million or two."

He felt irritation gush up inside of him, like steam popping the lid on a kettle. Suddenly, he flung the glass across the room. With a crash, it exploded into splinters; the wall darkened where the liquid splashed against it.

"Damn!" Green yelled.

He just wanted to just get on with his business. There was a hell of a rough road ahead of him as it was with all the straightforward planning and execution required by a mega mining operation. He didn't need all of this...this nefarious complication.

Who did this greedy Canadian loser think he was, throwing up roadblocks in his way? Perhaps the man was contemplating trying to put a stranglehold on him and his company for life.

Well, he wouldn't allow that.

If a heavy hand was what was required, he would apply a heavy hand. He could keep up with the pace of these developments. Despite what Isaac Greene had thought of him, he was up to this task.

He bent his head and ran his fingers thorough his thick hair. Elbows propped on his knees, he clutched either side of his skull and closed his eyes to focus his thoughts.

Nadia, who had gasped and cringed when the glass smashed into the wall, now pressed one shoulder against the bedhead and pivoted off it. She walked on her knees over to Greene and pressed herself against his back. She slipped her hand down his shirt, and onto his chest, lingering there to caress the mat of hair.

Greene leaned toward the bedside table to stub out the cigarette in an ashtray. His motion sent Nadia tumbling to her back onto the bed. He looked at her wide-open eyes, defiant yet inviting.

The outburst had left him with a racing pulse. But it had allowed him to let off some steam, and he felt much better for it.

He stroked the bare leg that Nadia extended toward him.

This time, he would yield.

Chapter 58

Sarah Cohen heard a familiar, high-spirited laugh as she walked to her office. The sound came from beyond the corridor, and she stood with her key in the doorknob, waiting for the owner of the voice to appear around the corner.

"Hey, Spike! Got a moment?"

Simmons turned away from the two other agents with whom he had been walking. He smiled at Cohen. "For you? Always."

The computer beeped and its fan kicked into a soft whir as Simmons entered the room.

"Can you shut the door behind you," Cohen said, her face taut.

Simmons raised his eyebrows as he complied. That was unusual, he thought. He couldn't recall any time before that he'd been in Cohen's office when the door was not open.

"What you got for me?" He sank into the chair at the side of her desk.

"First, remember that hearing that Magrelma's Canadian subsidiary was supposed to be involved in?"

"The one about the spill?"

"Yes, that one. It's turned out to be about the breached dam. But, originally, it was just about whether the company would hand back its license and turn over the property to the authorities."

"What about it?"

"When Mahler was alive, the company had instructions to give up the site. At the hearing, though...."

"They changed course?"

"One hundred and eighty degrees. Surprised everybody it seems." Cohen handed Simmons printed sheets. "These are from the local newspaper's website. They went big with the story."

Simmons stroked his chin as his eyes scanned the sheets. "Hmmm. So the argument in the Monte Carlo bar takes on a new significance."

Cohen tapped the point of a pen on her note pad and stared at Simmons.

He looked up from the printouts. "So you're thinking Mahler didn't support Greene's plan to hold on to the property, so Greene got rid of him."

"Seems plausible."

"But I don't get it," Simmons said. "Why would Greene kill Mahler just so they could continue to maintain a toxic dump?"

"No, it doesn't make much sense, does it."

"There has to be more to this. Something we can't see."

"Maybe there isn't."

"What do you mean?"

"What if it's just pure coincidence that the two men had this argument just before Mahler's death?"

"Coincidence?"

"Yes. What if someone else was responsible for taking Mahler out, and Greene just got lucky; he no longer had an obstacle blocking his plans for the property, whatever those plans might be."

Simmons scratched his head. "I don't know, Sarah. I don't like it when you fall back on coincidence as the basis for your theories. Labeling something as a coincidence is such a cop out."

Cohen tilted her head and let her jaw hang as she narrowed her eyes.

Simmons didn't like the look. It usually meant she was hopping mad. He hunched his shoulders. "What?"

"Spike Simmons, I seem to recall that someone — who will go unnamed — shot down the notion that the Syron Lake dam might have been deliberately breached by referring to the incident as a coincidence."

"That was completely different."

"How so?"

"There was bad weather. Nobody has control over that. A storm blowing through in the midst of our murder investigation, now that's what you call a coincidence."

"You should look up the word in the dictionary sometime, buddy. It's not as limited as you seem to think."

"I know what the word means."

"But you just–"

Simmons raised his hand to stop Cohen. "Look, let's just face it, Sarah. We're flopping around here with this case like fish out of water. We're coming up empty and it's driving both of us crazy, and we're just getting on each other's nerves at this point."

They both sighed.

"I guess you're right." Cohen folded her arms. "It's pretty frustrating to have not cracked this thing already."

"What are the guys on the ground saying these days? Have we got anything more solid on Fran Mahler?"

Cohen shook her head.

Simmons thought he saw her body stiffen. Her eyes glanced up at the closed door, then met his.

"Talk to me, Sarah. What's on your mind?"

Cohen took a deep breath.

"Everything related to the suspects tied to Magrelma has been leading nowhere. So I did some further digging, Spike."

Simmons leaned forward in his chair in response to Cohen's lowered voice.

"Angela Roseau–"

Simmons sat back up again. "Don't go there, Sarah."

"Will you at least hear me out?"

Cohen's eyes shone with determination, and Simmons sighed.

"I got bits of info from obituaries of Mahler's first wife and of his father-in-law; of Roseau's people, too; plus, wedding announcements; society page stuff from New York and Louisiana; profiles of all these people; news stories.... I checked it all. I think I pretty much know what went on there."

Simmons leaned back and folded his arms.

"At the time she and Mahler got engaged," Cohen said, "Roseau was an articling student at one of the most prestigious New York law firms. Got in on her own brilliance it seems, because she had no ties in New York, so, likely, no strings to pull. Back then, her stepfather was just an assistant to the Louisiana governor. This was a couple of years before he ran and himself became the governor.

"Mahler, on the other hand was an up-and-coming business hotshot. Magrelma already had some success under its belt, and looked poised to prosper. Mahler proposed to Roseau on August 28, 1985, and from what I can make out, they remained engaged for under two months."

"Any idea why?"

"Money."

Simmons splayed his hands for an explanation.

"Mahler's eventual father-in-law was a very wealthy industrialist. He was an ailing widower who had one surviving child, a daughter who'd taken care of him for years. Late thirties. Older than Mahler. They were married before the year was out. The father-in-law invested a pile of money into Magrelma. Died about ten months later, a couple of weeks after Mahler's first child was born."

"So, something of an old-fashioned, arranged marriage then."

Cohen nodded. "Looks so. And Mahler dumped Angela Roseau when this deal came along."

Simmons stared at Cohen.

"It must have been devastating for her," she said.

Simmons shook his head. "Who says she didn't dump him? Or that something else wasn't the cause of the break-up?"

Cohen stared back. She formed her lips as if to say something, but paused.

"Well," she said, eventually, "probably only the two of them will ever know what went on, exactly. But backing out of an engagement is not something a woman would normally do. Women are socialized to see marriage as their crowning achievement, as the apex of their existence."

"You don't believe that crap do you?"

"As a modern woman, of course I don't. But Angela Roseau is from a time when that kind of thinking was more prevalent. With that kind of social pressure, a broken engagement would have been a devastating slight, especially in the social circles that Roseau and Mahler ran in, back then in New York."

"No doubt it would have been embarrassing."

"Spike, you're probably underestimating Angela Roseau. Women are not all sugar and spice, you know. There's something to be said about that old line that hell hath no fury–"

"Like a woman scorned." Simmons shook his head. "You keep harping on that. But if you're going with that theory — and I'm certainly not encouraging you in that — why now? Why after all these years would Angela Roseau take revenge on her ex-fiancé?"

"Could be that she never had the means to before." Cohen shrugged. "This is what, her second year as Secretary of State?

Sure her husband is from old money, and, sure he was a congressman for one term. And, yes, she's been working her way up as a State legislator and then congresswoman for the last two decades. But that doesn't mean she had ready cash lying around to pay for this kind of hit all those years."

Simmons tapped his shoes on the floor and stared at them.

"Listen, Spike, as Secretary of State, she's now in a position of immense power. She has access to information and resources that few can even dream of."

Simmons stood up. "She's also in a position to have both our heads."

Cohen's eyes followed him, back and forth, as he paced her office, his face taut.

"I'm not much into politics," Simmons said, "but even I have heard that she's not one that you mess with lightly. Our entire–"

"Which just strengthens my point."

"Yes, but *my* point is that just one word from Angela Roseau could be all it takes to put an end to both our careers."

"Look, it's our job to explore every plausible theory, no matter who it points to." Cohen made imaginary quote marks above her head. "You know, 'without fear or favor.' Right?"

"Yes, but I can't go to Director Hutton with this, Sarah." Simmons let out a burst of air, which rumbled past his lips. "I can't go dragging the name of one of the top members of the Administration into this murder investigation. Not based on a few old newspaper clippings that you've cobbled together."

Cohen raised her eyebrows and shrugged.

"No," Simmons said, dropping back into the chair with a sigh. "We've got to come better than this."

Chapter 59

It was early afternoon and the tall buildings of Bank Street channeled a bitter Arctic blast straight down Ottawa's main thoroughfare. It felt like the wind jabbed a thousand needles into my face. I was relieved to push past the revolving door and step into the warmth of the building where I would find the offices of Kobec, Crayton & Vohles.

But I was also nervous. This was the eight law firm that I would be approaching to ask if they would launch a class action lawsuit on behalf of the residents of Syron Lake.

The seven others I had tried before had courteously taken my phone calls and had asked me to send further information by email. Then they had all written me back saying the law firm would not take on the file, but that they encouraged me to seek legal representation as soon as possible, if I intended to pursue the matter. No explanation given.

Unlike those previous others, when he first called after hearing my voicemail asking if his firm would look at our case, Randy Vohles had requested to meet me in person. He had even offered to reimburse my "reasonable travel cost" to Ottawa as he couldn't make it up to Syron Lake to see me.

Perhaps it was because my approach to him had been different to the one I had tried with the others.

I had prepared a thirty-five-page backgrounder on the Syron Lake Resources spill, including the history and geography of the town and the company's mining operations, as well as all the information I could get my hands on about the spill itself and the dangers of radioactive material to human health.

This had gone out to all the previous lawyers; but I guessed at the weakness of the case from their perspective. How could they prove that the health of the surrounding communities had indeed been imperiled by this specific release of contaminants?

It was, again, that lack of resources to make scientific arguments that undermined the little guy. The corporate titans could then say if you can't prove there's been harm, then we're not liable and don't have to compensate you.

This time, when I wrote to Kobec, Crayton & Vohles, I added the suggestion that the class seek compensation for harm done to property values.

Contamination of the environment, or just the mere possibility of it, would certainly make a house or commercial building less valuable. This was the fear that had stirred up Mayor Demetriou enough to send him flying to my door the day after the elections.

Dollars and cents. It was language lawyers would understand, I thought.

Randy Vohles nearly crushed my fingers with his handshake. He had a powerfully-built upper body, as a result of having to propel himself around in a wheelchair.

"When I was in high school, a drunk driver ran head-on into the car my buddies and I were driving in on our way home from a baseball game," he said. "I was lucky. My best friend, who was at the wheel, and his brother, who was in the front passenger seat, died on the spot."

He listened, and fired off questions, and scribbled notes furiously as I told him about my background, about how I had ended up in Syron Lake (leaving out my hopes concerning Peter, of course), about how I came to witness the spill, about the unenthusiastic response of the town's mayor and my run-ins with him, and about the CNRA hearing and the panel chair's reaction to my speech (leaving out anything of a personal nature, of course).

Almost every sentence Vohles uttered during our two-hour conversation included some variant of the word "interesting."

"I'm very interested in considering this further," he said when we shook hands again at his door. "It looks to be an uphill battle, but challenges don't faze me."

Still, like the seven other lawyers I had consulted before him, he said, "I'll get back to you after we've reviewed this and made a decision on whether to take the case."

So far, from Vohles' reaction, my new approach seemed to be doing the trick.

I hoped it would work. Now that the CNRA hearing was over, I'd vowed to put every effort toward getting the class action started

— in Osgood's memory. It was the only way I could rid myself of the guilt I felt at not voting for him, and of the uncomfortable feeling that I was partly responsible for his suicide.

If we could only get Vohles' firm to champion our cause, we – the ordinary folk, the little guys – would finally have a chance of bringing at least one corporate predator to its knees. As the elevator took me to the ground floor, I began planning to scour the Internet for any new or remotely related information that I could email to Vohles as a follow-up in order to keep Syron Lake at the front of his mind.

I pushed my way through the revolving door and re-emerged on Bank. It was three o'clock and the wind was blowing as hard as ever.

I hugged myself and maneuvered around other pedestrians battling for the narrow strip of sanded pavement. A couple of blocks past Somerset Street, I came to Peppard Street.

His street.

I bolted into a coffee shop and claimed a place where I could look out, yet remain hidden by the dingy curtains. Opposite was a car park adjoining Peppard Place, a massive government complex in steel and glass that took up an entire block.

I could relax now. The Greyhound bus back up to Syron Lake was not until midnight. I could take my time with a bowl of minestrone and crackers; after that, I would stretch out a tall latte for the hour or two I imagined it would take to see him appear. If he did appear.

By the time my watch said it was half past five, the second hope I had for this Ottawa trip had all but faded.

During the CNRA hearing, the panel chairman had never been without a cup of coffee; he would either come into the hall with a cup in hand, or, before his arrival, one would be placed at his spot on the panel table by some underling.

Apart from giving a view of the car park adjacent to his building, the coffee shop was the only one on this stretch of Peppard Street. I had figured this would have doubled the chances that I would catch a glimpse of him, caffeine addict that he seemed to be.

But the hours had worn on and he hadn't appeared in the almost steady line-up for coffee and donuts.

He didn't show up, either, in the car park, which had quickly emptied just past four o'clock and now had only a few vehicles left.

In the corner of the lot closest to me, a gloveless driver wiped snow from his windshield. He alternated between using his right and left hand to hold the brush, and shoving frozen fingers under the armpits of his coat.

As I watched the hapless creature, it finally dawned on me that it was hardly likely that Dromel would have been parked there.

He sat almost at the top of one of the major agencies that occupied Peppard Place. A complex of that size was certain to have underground parking. And he, more than likely, would be among those privileged to have a reserved spot, protected from the rain and snow.

I sighed, feeling my spirit deflate along with my lungs.

I had traveled hundreds of miles to this city with a hope of... of what? I wasn't sure, exactly. All I knew was that I craved to see him again. I longed to look into his hazel eyes again. I needed to see if those eyes would still lay on me with the fierce intensity that had stirred up a hope of...yes, a hope of love.

Now that hope seemed illusory, like all the times love had been teasingly dangled in my face before.

I had come to accept that there would be no reconciliation with Peter. Where that relationship was concerned, I had put one foot in front of the other and was marching on to better things. Or so I'd thought.

I wasn't so naive as to believe that Benoit Dromel was in love with me.

No, I had read enough in the online forums and agony aunt columns to understand that for men, desire, or to put it plainly, lust came first. But, what I'd understood from what I'd read was that men come around eventually, and begin to love the object of their desire.

After my online research, it had dawned on me that, in all my weak attempts at romance so far, my mistake had been that I'd set out expecting men to think and act like I, and perhaps every other woman, did when we entered into relationships. We put love first because we start out with the expectation that a relationship should be founded on love.

All during that week of the hearing, Dromel had laid bare what *he* wanted. Surely a desire of such intensity could be watered and nurtured by the love I could offer so that love would eventually bloom in its place, or alongside it.

The memory of the way he had looked at me was intoxicating; to have been wanted like that by someone....

I'd never felt as if I had been fully loved, or even quite belonged anywhere.

At home, my dad's and his second wife's drinking meant neither of them was ever really available to have an intelligent conversation, let alone a relationship with me. I loved my grandparents — two gentle, old people who'd shown me the most embracing love I'd ever known; but they were of a different generation, which left miles of distance between us.

At the convent school in Trinidad, there were a handful of girls with whom I spent some of my free time, but we weren't very close, partly because my dad's problem with the bottle made me afraid to open up to anyone, and partly because the meagre finances of my home created a stark contrast with my classmates' middle and upper class backgrounds.

For most of college and my early working days the sense of isolation had lingered on. I'd thrown myself so fully into trying to get ahead, I'd had little chance to open up to anyone. And when I did try, well, all my attempts at romance just petered out and died.

This is my fate, I thought, to always be alone.

I pursed my lips, as if doing so could hold back the tears that began to well in my eyes.

A waitress appeared in the far corner of the empty cafe and began wiping down the tables and noisily adjusting chairs around them. It was now a quarter to six. I took the hint, slipped on my coat and exited into the frigid street.

Two doors down, the lights inside a bookstore glowed invitingly. The sign on the door said they closed at ten. Through the large shop window, I could see a couple of chairs among the clutter of shelves and display tables. Perfect.

It didn't matter that it was a French bookstore and I couldn't read French. Just to appease the sullen, elderly woman who sat at the cash register, I bought a celebrity magazine. Between that and the novels I'd brought with me, I would kill four hours before heading to the Greyhound station.

I found a chair in a private spot, in the furthest corner at the back of the store, and settled down. The place was quiet, except to for the radio going on the cashier's desk, which was near the door and out of sight.

I had been the only customer in the store for a while, and then the bell at the entrance sounded.

After a brief, muffled conversation, footsteps approached my way. I looked up and saw a man in a back toque and a long, black leather coat moving down the aisle, his face turned toward the shelf as he seemed to be reading the titles of the books.

My heart suddenly jack-hammered against my rib cage. I could hardly breathe.

It was Benoit Dromel.

Feeling panicked, I got up. I wanted desperately to see him. And I also wanted to flee. But there was only one way out, and he was blocking it.

Dromel came halfway up the aisle and I froze.

He pulled a book from the shelf, and, as if suddenly becoming aware of being watched, he turned to face me. He tilted his head and scanned my face, as if searching his memory.

"Ms Jacob?"

A warm sensation rushed through my body. The soles of my feet and my palms itched maddeningly.

He strode closer, his teeth glistening in a broad smile.

I cleared my throat. "Mr Dromel."

"Visiting Ottawa?"

"Had some business to take care of."

Ottawa was not a large city. Yet still, it must have seemed to him quite a coincidence that I'd ended up right in the vicinity of his office.

"Working late?" I blurted.

He nodded and stopped just a couple of feet from me. Those eyes. Yes, those hazel eyes were on me as intensely as ever.

"I heard this was a very good book store." The lie fell uneasily from my lips. "Best place for French Canadian literature."

"It is." He held up the book he'd chosen. "Came to get this. It's just out. By a former teacher of mine."

The sign above the aisle said "Littérature acadienne." I knew just enough about Canadian culture to understand that referred to books from the Atlantic provinces. He was from New Brunswick, so, yes, his presence here made sense.

He bent his head and flipped through the pages. He hadn't worn a ring during the Syron Lake hearing, but I wanted to make doubly sure. My eyes followed his left hand, but he turned it before I could glimpse his ring finger.

He looked at his watch. "I've got a business dinner in about an hour. Are you driving? Or can I give you a lift anywhere?"

His dilated eyes penetrated mine. They made me quiver. The way he said it, a "lift" sounded like it meant more than just a ride. I bit my lower lip and drew a deep breath. Involuntarily, my eyes darted to his left hand again.

When I looked up at him again, it was obvious that he had followed my searching glance. He seemed amused.

We were both on the same wavelength. I might as well be direct.

"Not married?" I said.

His smile widened. "No, I'm not married."

"In a committed relationship?"

He threw his head back slightly; he chuckled. "No, again. Not in a committed relationship."

He moved closer and gently curled his left hand around my upper arm. My heart pounded so hard, I was sure he could hear it. He bent his face toward mine.

I wanted more that anything for our lips to merge, to be wrapped up in his arms, and to let myself be swept away by the tidal wave of emotions and sensations that seemed on the brink of overwhelming me. But I raised my hand and held back his shoulder.

I stepped back.

He straightened himself. The smile was replaced by a look of confusion.

"Look," I said, "I know your position with the CNRA and my participation in the hearing makes things complicated."

He said nothing.

"Not so?" I continued.

"I guess it does."

He bent his arm and checked his watch again.

"Well," I said, "I've read up on conflict of interest. And, well, if you were to recuse yourself from the part of the panel decision involving Syron Lake Resources, then there shouldn't be a problem."

He shifted his weight.

"I mean," I said, "you can still decide on the licenses of the other companies. I didn't speak about them. But if there's to be anything between us, I think it could only happen if you didn't take part in the Syron Lake Resources decision."

He looked past my shoulder.

I had an unbearable sensation of drowning, and felt compelled to continue trying to persuade him. "I mean, the company's already agreed to do what I always thought was right. They're saying they'll bear all costs. As for my further suggestion that they be made to pay the bill and still lose their license, I know that's maybe a long shot. But I'm sure the other two panel members can be trusted to make the right decision."

Dromel still said nothing.

I bent my head. I had made an utter fool of myself, and the heavy lump in my throat was my only reward.

"That's a pretty major decision." Dromel spoke softly, and I thought I heard kindness in his tone.

"Well, if you went to the Ethics Commissioner about it...."

He held me by my left elbow, and I looked up at him.

"Okay, leave it with me," he said.

I swallowed hard and nodded.

He released his hold on my elbow, turned, and walked away. After a few steps, he turned around and came back. He took out a pen and a business card from his pocket, scribbled something, then handed the card to me.

He winked, then left.

I watched until he disappeared around the corner. I stood motionless, unable to draw normal breaths as I listened to the cash register being rung up. The bell tinkled as Dromel left.

I raced to the front of the store and peered out the display window. Dromel opened the door of a beige Audi, got into the driver's seat, and took off.

The cashier had her eyes fixed on a thick novel that she held up close to her face. A deep-voiced French crooner softly belted out an oldie over the radio.

I glanced down at the back of business card Dromel had given me. It had a handwritten phone number on it.

I took two paces to a nearby chair and dropped down into it; my legs were too weak to support me.

"What have I done?" I whispered.

Chapter 60

The black SUV pulled up in front of the hotel near the Ottawa airport. The driver swung the front passenger door open and stared at the man who stood outside hugging himself as he hopped from one foot to the next in the ankle-deep snow.

"Get in," the driver shouted.

"Oh man! What the devil is this? Damn near froze my tail off, standing out there just two minutes."

"Welcome to the Great White North, Simmons." The driver chuckled.

Spike Simmons heaved himself into the seat. As soon as he buckled up, he rubbed his hands together and blew on them.

"For heaven's sake, Pablo, how do you people live in this place? Damn, that's cold!"

"Just dress for it. It's not that bad."

"Look here, I'm wearing my best winter coat and still that bloody cold shot right through my bones. You must really hate me to make me wait outside that place."

"Sorry, bro, but I probably shouldn't even be meeting you, in the first place. I'm kinda suspecting I'll regret agreeing to see you."

Pablo Rojas turned onto Lester Road, welcoming its lack of traffic and the long, desolate stretch lined with trees and brushes that lay ahead. It meant few or, hopefully, no eyes would fall on them.

The agent with the Canadian Security Intelligence Service had often told Spike Simmons that he loved him like a brother. It was because he owed his life to him, literally.

Five years earlier, they had been at a meeting of international intelligence officers in Atlanta. At lunch, Rojas had an overenthusiastic conversation with his mouth full, and before he knew it, the world was going black before his eyes and he was gasping for breath. Someone grabbed him in a bear hug from behind and slammed clasped hands into his torso. The blow was so hard, it cracked two ribs; but it freed his windpipe and he crumbled to the floor gasping what he would forever think of as the sweetest breaths he'd ever taken.

His savior was now sitting beside him, splaying his palms before the vent that spewed heat from the engine.

"So what's this about Simmons?" Rojas said. "You call me up out of the blue, second day of the year, and say meet you at the airport in three days. What's up?"

"I should have stuck to my guns and insisted you meet me inside the airport, where it's nice and toasty." Simmons shook his head. "Instead I had to taxi it over to this hotel and stand in the bloody snow. That's cruel, man. Just cruel."

"Come with it, Simmons. Why are you here?"

"I need your help with this case I'm–"

"I knew it! I knew you didn't want to come up here just to wish me happy New Year."

"Look Pablo, Director Hutton himself is breathing fire down my neck on this one. But I'm stuck. We're at an absolute dead end with this thing. I need anything, and I mean every bloody scrap that can be scrounged up."

Rojas groaned softly.

Simmons continued as if he hadn't heard that. "A couple of good ol' American entrepreneurs are among our prime suspects in a murder we think might be linked to a former mining operation here in Ontario."

"Geez, Simmons, haven't you heard of official channels?"

"Look, trying to go through official channels would take time and would get me only so far; I need to go as deep as this can go, and then some. And like yesterday, too. I'm tapping all my contacts where these people do business."

Simmons was silent for a while. "I'm desperate, man." His voice was raw. "Director Hutton asked me to keep on top of this case. Seems he's taken some kind of personal interest in it. I'm directly in his sights with this one and I feel this could either make or break me."

Rojas glanced across at Simmons. Even from the side, he could see the wild look in Simmons' eyes as he stared out at the desolate road.

"I don't know if I can help you," Rojas said after a while. "But

I'll see what I can dig up."

"Thanks, man."

"Don't go thanking me just yet. We don't know if I'll find anything useful, or at all. But, tell me about your globe-trotting, American entrepreneurs...."

Chapter 61

By force of habit, he stopped at the convenience store five streets down from his Riverside Drive condo. He bought a packet of mint chewing gum and walked toward the washrooms, next to which was a payphone.

This place served his purpose well; there were no security cameras anywhere, and the manager — whoever he or she was — seemed incapable of keeping counter staff around for more than three months. It was from here that he checked his voicemail at the Hull house, and once or twice had called to arrange a rendezvous with a paramour. The chances of Bernice ever cluing into what he was up to were almost nil.

Bernice — now, there was a scab on his existence.

He had just dropped her off at the airport. She had come home for Christmas and their two weeks together had been anything but joyous.

He had first noticed a subtle change in her attitude toward him the previous time she had been back, when they met for one night after the Syron Lake hearing. What was this new element that tainted all their interactions now?

Was it contempt? She was beginning to feel surer now of securing her permanent position and spoke incessantly about flying all over the place, meeting important figures on the world stage. She had barely remarked on his first appointment as chair of a hearing.

He doubted it could have been suspicion about his activities at the Hull house; he had taken all the precautions he could think of to conceal this part of his life.

Could it be that she was seeing someone else? Every time the possibility tried to enter his mind, he blocked it out immediately. That was unthinkable.

She'd said it was just stress from such a demanding job. But whatever it was, it had driven a wedge between them. The holidays had been spent with long periods of silence with each retreating to their own corner to sort out bills, read novels, or catch up on office paperwork. When they did speak, the exchanges rang hollow, and more often than not, ended in fault-finding, angry words, and cold stares.

Things would work themselves out soon, he thought. She would get her permanent post, and he would retire with a nice, fat balance in the account of his Belize offshore company. He would join her in Europe and her big salary would provide the perfect cover. He would take life easy, enjoy all the pleasures money could buy; and if their relationship continued to fray, well, he could just install himself with his million dollars on the Cote d'Azur and he'd have women half her age throwing themselves at him.

He picked up the receiver and dialed. He wasn't expecting to hear anything in particular; he thought maybe one or two of his ladies might have remembered him and left a holiday greeting in between trimming the tree and preparing the turkey dinner for their family.

He listened to his voice prompt and pressed the numbers to playback the messages.

"Hi, it's Stella, um, Stella Jacob," the voice said. "Just called to wish you a happy new year, and also happy anniversary. You can call me back at...."

He grinned broadly as he jotted down the number on the packet of gum.

Usually, he would not drive to Hull in his own car. Anytime he went to his love shack, he would arrange for the skinny kid to drop off the leased car for him somewhere in Ottawa. But it was the first week of January and the streets were mostly empty, and besides, he was not eager to encounter the guy that early in the year. He parked his car a few streets down, then walked to the place.

He plopped down on the sofa, took out the packet of gum and began to dial.

He was a little uncertain about this one. Was she for real, or was that girlish naiveté just an act? His Hull ladies had become his paramours because they had caught his fancy with their sexual assurance, their complete abandonment to what they fully understood to be naughty, forbidden.

But this one had sought to make him confirm, first up, that he was not married and not in a committed relationship.

He felt comfortable that he had answered her truthfully. No, he and Bernice had not exchanged vows, so he definitely was not married. And neither was he in a committed relationship; he no longer felt committed to Bernice, and theirs had ceased to be a mutually exclusive relationship since the day he'd got under the sheets with his first lover.

Well, he would run with this, see how far it would go. She was young, slim, attractive, and did seem quite taken with him. He smiled at the memory of their encounter in the bookstore; her wide, frightened, yet eager eyes, and that pair of luscious, willing lips that he had been sorely tempted to devour.

She picked up after only two rings. "Hello, Stella Jacob here."

"Hi, Stella. It's Ben. Happy New Year to you."

Silence.

"Hello? Stella? What anniversary were you referring to in your message on my voicemail?"

"Hi, Ben." She sounded flustered, he thought. "Your appointment."

"What?"

"Your appointment. I read in your bio on the website that your appointment to the CNRA took effect on January the eighth, four years ago."

"Wow," he said with a chuckle. "Thank you for noting that. I think you're probably the only person in all of Canada who did."

There was silence on the line again.

Perhaps he shouldn't have laughed. He had been charmed and that had been his spontaneous reaction. But maybe his laughter had made her feel foolish. She seemed like the sensitive sort.

"Um, Ben? We discussed certain things the last time. I was just wondering, did you...did you see the Ethics Commissioner?"

"Yes," he said.

Okay, it may have been the case that he had neither spoken to the Ethics Commissioner nor laid eyes on that gentleman's person since he and Stella Jacob had run across each other in the bookstore. But he did see that particular official at conference for members of regulatory bodies the previous May. So, yes, he did see the Ethics Commissioner.

"And?" she said.

He was amused by the excitement, the suspense in her voice.

"Well, you were absolutely right, Stella. Recusal would be necessary. And, like you said, I'm sure my colleagues on the panel can look at the public record and come to the right decision about Syron Lake Resources, even if I'm not part of the process."

"Yes. And, like I said, you wouldn't have to recuse yourself from the other four decisions, and those involve bigger operations."

"Absolutely." He was positively enjoying himself.

"I'm really glad to hear you're comfortable with that, Ben."

"Oh, I can go with the flow."

He was on a roll. "Now, the advice I've received is that even if I'm off the Syron Lake Resources matter, things would have to be discreet. I mean, it won't do to go flaunting a connection like this. Otherwise you might get some horrid media types sniffing around and looking to sensationalize the situation, just to get a big headline, when there's no story there."

She laughed. "Hey, I used to be one of those media types, remember?"

"Were you? Oh, yes; that's right. You mentioned it in your email requesting to be a presenter at the hearing. A newspaper out West, right?"

"Yes, *The Sentinel*, out in Vancouver."

"Well, then you should know better than me how something innocent can get twisted by a newshound desperate to get his byline in the papers. Next thing you know, the important work of the panel gets buried and all you have is a crazy media stampede to see who can get the biggest scoop on some imagined scandal."

She laughed again. This time she sounded somewhat uncomfortable, he thought.

"I'd really like to see you, Stella." He went for a mellow, earnest tone. "But if we see each other, we'd need to be very, very discreet."

Silence.

"Okay," she said, finally. "We'll be discreet."

Chapter 62

Prime Minister Peabody closed the wooden shutters behind his desk, blocking off the only source of natural light. The resulting dimness better matched his less than jovial mood.

It was a Monday, the last day of January. More importantly, it was the first day back out to work for Angus Firestone. He had taken the previous three weeks off to spend time with his twin preschoolers, whom his ex-wife had carried , out West when she'd moved back in with her parents in Victoria.

Peabody had a long list of matters he needed Firestone to put his devious mind to. And first, he wanted to talk about Benoit T. Dromel.

"I bumped into that cur, Dromel, last night." Peabody leaned against the oak-panelled wall. "It was at the opening of some play by my wife's niece. Gloria dragged me there, of course."

"You said you bumped into him?"

"Not literally. When we arrived, he was in the foyer. Our eyes met. He pretended not to see me. I think he turned away with a sneer. In fact, I'm sure that was the expression on his face."

"Probably it was best you two didn't get close enough to exchange words, then." Firestone had an idea where the conversation might go, and he was hoping to avoid it.

"Insolent cur." Almost two months on, Peabody felt his cheeks go flush at the memory of their conversation in the backseat of his Suburban. "So what dirt has CISIS found so far on him?"

Firestone coughed.

Peabody stared at him.

"Well, they haven't actually been digging," Firestone said, finally.

"What do you mean by that?"

"They haven't been watching him."

"And why not? I specifically told you I wanted him under surveillance."

"Actually, it's all my fault, John. It just completely slipped me." Firestone lied. He hadn't forgotten. He had doubted he could get anywhere with an arbitrary request like that. Even a cursory inquiry with an official in the CISIS Director's office had elicited guffaws. He had dropped the matter and hoped his boss would forget about it too.

"That's a big slip, Angus. I don't expect that from you."

"Sorry about that. But, you know, it's not so easy to make someone a surveillance target. There's a whole process. It has to go before a committee for approval."

"And just who's on that committee?"

"The Director, the Deputy Minister of Public Safety, senior CSIS officers, and representatives from the Department of Justice. The Solicitor General must be consulted, too."

"These are all our people, or they should be. I can't see why you think this would be a problem."

Firestone bent his head and pinched that area of his nose where it met his forehead. His boss seemed to forget that he had occupied this wood-panelled office for less than two years and that his party had been in opposition for a dozen years before the last election. He may have been the most important official in Canada now, but his sphere of influence was not as wide as he seemed to think.

Firestone sighed. "There has to be proper justification for targeting citizens, John. There has to be a threat to the nation."

"Damn it, I'm the prime minister of this nation and I'm saying Benoit Dromel is a threat. Tell them that. The prime minister's word must count for something."

"I'll see what I can do."

"No! You will *see to it*. No 'ifs' or 'buts.' When I ask for something to be done, I expect you to get it done."

Peabody pulled his chair out. He sat and leaned back as far as the chair could go. He spoke more to himself than to his chief of staff.

"I mean, you've come through brilliantly for me for so long. It still boggles my mind how you pulled off my victory at the polls that last round. Twenty points behind with one week before the election. Then you came up with the cancer leak. That was pure genius."

Peabody stared at the white molding of the ceiling as his mind wandered back to that watershed moment. The Cancer Leak. It was the last act of desperation of a campaign that faced certain doom. He had been reviled in his riding because he had done nothing to support a protest against the closure of a ketchup factory in his constituency. The hundred or so affected workers had managed to sour his relationship with Ian Brunton, the biggest union boss in his mostly blue-collar riding. Without Brunton's endorsement, Peabody was certain to lose his seat.

The stakes had become higher than ever because he had only months before got the job as leader of his party. Winning meant he would get to be prime minister; and losing when that plum prize was within reach would have increased the sting and shame tenfold.

For weeks he'd made desperate overtures to the union boss and had got nowhere. Peabody had almost resigned to being drummed out of office when Firestone, acting then as his campaign manager, had burst into the campaign office with a plan. He had learned from a friend of a friend who worked at the hospital that Brunton had been diagnosed with prostate cancer.

Before the end of the day, Peabody had fainted at a campaign event — of course one where lots of cameras were rolling — and had to be rushed to the hospital. Word somehow got out that there were worries that Peabody's cancer had returned, after several years in remission. He spent the night in the hospital, during which time further details emerged of the previously unknown radiation therapy Peabody had undergone; local radio talk show hosts speculated that that could have explained how pale and listless the MP and newly-minted Opposition Leader had seemed the previous winter.

He was thronged by reporters upon his release from the hospital the next day as he walked hand in hand with a reticent Gloria Peabody. He refused to answer any questions about his medical condition.

But he made one statement: "My doctors gave me a clean bill of health, today. I will not go into my medical history. Everybody has their ups and downs with their health. We all have battles that we must face with courage. I'm not going to talk about myself to get sympathy votes. I've been dedicated to my constituency for eight years and, I want to say I am here to continue to give it my all, and to fight for my constituents for years to come."

He had delivered the lines with a mix of hesitation, humility, and self-assurance, just as Firestone had coached him.

The clip played over and over on the radio and made the weekend news, even showing up on a Monday morning television talk show.

His next appeal for a meeting with Brunton met with enthusiasm. The reconciliation resulted in a suddenly strong bond between the two of them and led to a hastily arranged workers' rally, at which Peabody received Brunton's endorsement, four days before the polls. His numbers ticked up and up. At his victory party on elections night, he hugged Firestone almost as long as he had embraced his wife.

"You're capable of such brilliance, Firestone." Peabody sat up and looked at his chief of staff. "Once, you were fearless, invincible even."

Firestone pretended to scribble into his daybook.

"I don't know what's got into to you in the last year or so," Peabody said. "Is it the divorce?"

Firestone shot his boss a wounded glance.

"Look, I already said I would take care of the Dromel surveillance, didn't I?"

Chapter 63

Just over one month after his first ever visit to Ottawa, Spike Simmons was there again. This time, he came better prepared, with a puffy down coat that swallowed up his slender frame.

Thankfully, Pablo Rojas had been a bit more considerate in his arrangements. He had instructed him to go to a roadside steakhouse that was less than ten minutes from the airport. Simmons slipped a couple of twenties into the bill folder for what had been a hearty dinner of Alberta sirloin and PEI potato skins.

He went outside and headed around to the back.

A red hatchback with dark, tinted windows flashed its lights as soon as he turned the corner.

"I liked your other wheels better," Simmons said as he settled himself into the passenger seat.

"We're acting — *I'm* acting — outside protocol; it ain't wise to use the same vehicle twice."

"So, what've you got for me, bro?"

"I still can't believe I'm doing this." Rojas pulled a manila envelope from the side of his seat and slapped it onto Simmons' thighs. "That's everything I could scrounge up related to this."

Simmons grinned. He made a fist and gave Rojas a friendly jab.

The smile disappeared as he flipped through the papers and pictures in his lap.

"What is this crap, man? I don't see anything on Daniel Greene or Henry Maitland."

"That's just it. They're not in our sights. We have zilch on those men. And I could get only some crumbs of info on that mining firm."

"This hearing that they were involved in, we already know about that," Simmons protested.

"I'm telling you that's as much as I could get," Rojas said through clenched teeth.

Simmons looked out the window and shook his head.

Rojas broke the silence, in a calmer voice. "Listen, you said Greene had a fight with Mahler about pulling a fast one on the regulatory authority, right?"

"Yes, that's the main reason Greene's a suspect."

"Well, check this out. Before the murder, the company, Syron Lake Resources, was asking to give up its license for the property where it manages a pond that holds mining waste. Shortly after your Mahler guy croaks, bam! This pond breaks. Next thing you know, the company is doing a complete about-face and asks a panel hearing the matter to let it keep its license indefinitely. If the Greene guy is calling the shots now, that looks like a motive to me."

"But it was 'An Act of God,' Pablo. You're forgetting there was a massive storm on the day of the flood."

"Yeah, but I don't put anything past the types that run these corporations. Where money is involved — and, believe me, they can sniff the dough in places where we ordinary folks have no clue about — where there's money to be had, they'll stop at nothing."

"So you think there's a possibility the spill was deliberate?"

"It's a hunch."

Simmons sighed as Cohen's image flashed through his mind.

"I checked with the local police in Syron Lake," Rojas said. "Spoke with some detective up there to see if there had been any reports of vandalism or break-ins at the mine site around the time of the accident. There was none.

"But the officer was happy to talk. Spent maybe half an hour with me on the phone, and something more interesting turned up. I may be completely off my rocker here, but look at those guys in the pictures there. The local police are calling it an accidental drowning and a suicide. I managed to get a copy of their files. And where does it turn out the one who drowned used to work?"

"Let me guess: Syron Lake Resources."

"Bingo. He used to do maintenance work on the pond that broke. Conveniently, he took off and went to visit an out-of-town relative the day before the spill. Who's to say that after he was seen leaving town he didn't circle back to the mine site? When I checked the map, there's a road further down on the highway that you can take to get to the mine."

"So Greene and/or Maitland may have sent down the command and got this employee to do the dirty work, and then bumped him off?"

"It's a theory."

"And how does this other one.... Good grief, this photo is gruesome. How does this one figure into all of this?"

"The suicide victim? Not too sure. Could be suicide...or something else. He was this first guy's fishing buddy. He was in the same place where his friend drowned that fateful morning.

"An eyewitness reported suspicious vehicles near the scene of the drowning and also at this guy's home, where he was found with his head blown off. Now, if one or both of your all-American, globe-trotting entrepreneurs could liquidate their own business partner to get their way, what's two redneck nobodies to them?"

Simmons nodded. "Sounds interesting."

"Best I can do for you, bro."

"Yeah, thanks, man. I appreciate it. Really." Simmons grabbed the seat belt and drew it across his chest. "So you're taking me back to the airport?"

Rojas pulled a small rectangle of paper from his pocket and waved it in front of Simmons' eyes. "There's a stop just down the street. A bus comes every fifteen minutes. One should be here soon."

"Oh, come on, man!"

"If you came by taxi and want to take one back, I'm sure the restaurant will let you use their phone. But dropping you off at the airport would be too much visibility for me. I love my job, Simmons. I want to keep it."

Simmons let the seat belt slip out of his hand and recoil. He stuffed the papers and pictures into the envelope and curled his fingers around the door handle.

"Oh, there's one other thing," Rojas said. "I don't know if it's related or not. But you know that hearing to decide whether or not to let the company keep its license?"

"Yes?"

"Well, turns out that the chairman of the hearing panel is now under surveillance by our guys, as of a few days ago. Word is that there was some kind of wrangling about it, but, in the end, the higher ups agreed to put two of the greenest agents on the case."

"Might not be related," Simmons said. "But it's *something*, and right about now, I'm so desperate I'll take anything. If you guys are following him, maybe we should be taking a closer look at this chairman too."

Chapter 64

I drove the rental hard along the Trans-Canada Highway, whizzing past the snow-laden trees and outcrops of rocks that reminded me I was still very much in Northern Ontario, and a long way from my destination.

It was just past ten on a Friday morning, with a cloudless, pale blue sky overhead. The weather would be on my side all that weekend.

Sure it was a bone-chilling minus-twenty degrees Celsius, with the mercury predicted to dip further over the next few days. But since the white stuff came down only when temperatures were around zero, my mind was at ease that I would not have to drive through any snowfall either on the seven-hour journey from Syron Lake to Hull, or on the way back on the Sunday afternoon.

The cold weather also meant we would spend the entire weekend indoors, cozily wrapped up in each other's arms.

It would be our first time laying eyes on each other since that evening in the bookstore. In a million calls, and voice mail messages, and emails exchanged between us, Benoit Dromel had grown more charming to me. No, not just charming; irresistible.

He had traveled across Europe, and was able to regale me with tales of taking in the fjord view from on high at the scary Pulpit Rock in Norway; passing through the Blue Grotto in Capri; sailing down the Volga; walking around Hohensalzburg Castle in Salzburg while listening to the music of a local boy by the name of Wolfgang Mozart on his Walkman; seeing the anatomically correct proportions of Michelangelo's David up close....

He would relate personal memories of events I had only read about in books and old magazine articles. He laughed easily, and often, and never failed at the end of our bedtime talks to let me know how much he longed to have me in his arms.

And now, he had invited me to spend the weekend at his place – the weekend just before Valentine's Day.

We would not be together on the big day itself; that fell on the Monday and he would have to be at work. Besides, I would have to leave the Sunday afternoon so I could return the rental on Monday morning. But still, I didn't miss the significance of us being together for the first time, this weekend of all weekends.

I had packed only a tiny overnight bag. I wouldn't be needing too much in the way of clothes over the next forty-eight hours. Those had been his words, uttered with a deliciously devilish laugh. I smiled and gripped the steering wheel more firmly as I heard the sound of his voice in my mind, and imagined the glint in his eyes.

I was doing 115 kilometers an hour in a ninety zone on a deserted stretch of the highway. If I kept this up, I could arrive early in the afternoon. He had told me I would find the keys at the side of his house, on a hook about waist-height behind a trellis arbor.

"If you arrive early, relax; make yourself comfortable," he had said. "I love the idea of coming home and seeing you in a bubble bath."

I was excited by the idea of having the run of his place.

That, more than anything, made me feel sure that this was real, that he was The One; he trusted me and had nothing to hide from me.

That wild, intoxicating, all-encompassing thing called love had finally brought me together with the man whom I was destined to be with.

Being with him that day didn't come as soon as I'd expected, however.

An eight-car pile-up on the highway had delayed me by a couple of hours. Darkness had fallen by the time I turned onto his street. Now, my nervousness about night-time driving, along with my unfamiliarity with the place, and my rising excitement caused my entire body to tremble.

His street was a cul-de-sac. It ended at a river, which ran perpendicular to it. Up ahead, I could see the band of dark, shimmering water, and the squares of light emanating from the apartment buildings and houses on the bank on the other side.

I inched along, looking at all of the houses on the left side to ensure I didn't miss his. That was not really necessary because he had said his was the last on the left.

I was somewhat surprised that a man of his stature lived on this street. All the houses I passed were about half the size of mine, with tiny front yards, and no garage. Still, they were neat, and I had no doubt were more than triple the value of mine, being located so near to the nation's capital.

As the last house on the left came into view, I felt disoriented and almost sure I had mistaken the directions. I had been looking out for the beige Audi in which I had last seen him drive off, but only a black sedan sat in the short driveway of the last house. My eyes scanned the cars parked along the street to see if the Audi was among them, but there was no sign of it.

Feeling unsure of myself, I pulled up alongside the sedan. I couldn't stop my fingers from trembling as I pressed the doorbell. My heart pounded hard and fast as I heard footsteps approaching.

The handle clicked, and the door slowly swung open with a soft creak.

Benoit Dromel stood in the doorway. Light from a chandelier reflected off his bald pate. His eyes twinkled with obvious delight. He smiled, then bit his lip.

Without saying a word, he slipped his hand around my waist. A warm sensation surged through me. My knees turned to jelly, and I felt light-headed.

He drew me gently toward him, pulling me into the house, and then he closed the door behind us.

Chapter 65

From the SUV with dark-tinted windows parked higher up the street, the CISIS rookie watched it all.

Unknown to him, another pair of eyes had also taken in the scene.

Lurking in the darkness of an apartment on the other bank of the river, an ex-NYPD officer, who took off-the-book contracts with the FBI whenever he could get them, peered through a high power telescope.

"Looks like Old Baldy's gonna have an early Valentine's, while we have to sit here and watch," he whispered to no one. His teeth ripped away at a slice of cold, rubbery pizza. Some guys just seem to have all the luck, he thought to himself.

Chapter 66

"And just who is this Dawit Bekele character that the house in Hull and the car belong to?" Peabody sat in his office, leaning back in his chair with his eyes closed. The grin stretched from ear to ear.

"Someone who no one in Dromel's position should be associated with."

Firestone was nearly as pleased with the developments as Peabody was. "No convictions, but known to law enforcement. He hangs out with drug dealers and the like. Suspected of peddling, even. But he actually comes from a fairly respectable background. No parents in this country; they're possibly dead. He was raised in Gatineau by an uncle who runs a small mechanic shop."

"And the floozy?"

"Stella Jacob. Here's the best part. She is an intervener in the Syron Lake hearing."

The prime minister opened his eyes and sat up. "What?"

He cackled.

He got to his feet and walked to the front of his desk, then sat at the edge of it. "That's very interesting news."

He began to pace the room, cracking his knuckles. "Call up over at the CNRA and at the Ethics Commissioner's office. Make inquiries. Quietly, though. See if he's declared any connection like this and recused himself. I'm guessing, not. But let's confirm. Discreetly."

"So can CISIS call off the surveillance now?"

"Absolutely not."

"They won't be pleased."

"That's not my problem, Angus."

Firestone pursed his lips and sighed quietly.

Peabody opened the shutters behind his desk, flooding the room with light. "Isn't he married?"

"Dromel? No. But he has a common-law wife he's been with since law school. I understand she's hardly around these days. Works in Europe."

"Sun of a gun. Well, his glory days are about to come to an end." Peabody returned to his chair and leaned back. "When we've heard from the CNRA and the Ethics Commissioner's office, I think I'll want to have another word with Mr Benoit T. Dromel."

Chapter 67

A week after our magical weekend, I lay in the bath, back home in Syron Lake, under a sheet of white suds, luxuriating in the aroma of rose oil and rose-scented candles.

I paid no attention to the chipped enamel of the tub, or the ceiling stained by condensation as a result of a faulty fan that I'd not yet got around to replacing. The warmth of the water caressed every inch of my body, relaxing all my muscles.

Yet my heart raced. The cause was both excitement and nervousness.

I looked at the too-silent phone, which I'd dragged into the bathroom and placed on the floor within arm's length. Then I glanced at the clock that I'd placed beside it. Quarter past six. I closed my eyes and leaned my head against the rim of the tub. It was still not time for him to call.

I tossed the romance novel that I'd been trying to read onto the rickety shelf above my head. It took its place alongside the latest local newspaper and another novel, both of which had been equally incapable of holding my attention.

My nervousness didn't stem from wondering whether there would be a call. Either he or I had rung the other up every day since I'd returned from that fantastical weekend in Hull. It was a given that we'd be in contact.

No, the butterflies gathered in my stomach because of what I wanted to ask on this particular occasion.

An unexpected friend request on Facebook earlier in the day had ushered me into this state.

Aileen Castillano had been an acquaintance at the girl's convent school I had attended in Trinidad. Aileen came from old money, one of the richest families on the island. She had a life outside of school (outside of the island even, as she hopped onto planes as easily as ordinary folk would jump into a taxi), and so she was never fast friends with anyone in the class. But as our desks were side by side in home class and Aileen realized she could always catch up on her incomplete homework by borrowing mine, the two of us spoke often. The bond, however, was not so strong that either of us thought to keep in touch after I moved to Vancouver.

Recently divorced, a childless Aileen discovered Facebook and began feverishly building a circle of friends. It didn't take too long for the Facebook chat to lead to an invitation to visit Trinidad for Carnival, which was three weeks away.

She had said we could have the guest house that overlooked the swimming pool on her family's property.

Yes, "we."

I had mentioned — vaguely — that there was someone in my life and Aileen was clear that I was welcome to bring a partner along.

Dromel had once told me that he had long wanted to experience Trinidad's Carnival, on account of an old friend who worked in Grenada as an engineer and would regale him with adventures involving sailing over to Trinidad for the festival.

This would be the perfect opportunity for us to grow closer as a couple.

It was not until six-thirty that he rang; I figured he would have just walked in the door at his house in Hull after a long day at the office on Peppard Street.

The warmth of the water made every inch of my body tingle, but it was the sound of Benoit Dromel's voice that sent waves of pleasure from my head to my toes.

"I'm blowing those bubbles away," he said. "Blowing them left, and right, and before long, those suds won't be hiding any part of you."

"Naughty man!" I giggled. "Allow a lady a bit of decency, will you?"

"A lady? Come, come, now; you were anything but a lady when you were here with me."

"Don't make me blush, now."

"What was it that you said an old woman told you was the rule for the perfect relationship? Something about being a lady in the parlor and a whore in the bedroom?"

"Bite your tongue, Mr Dromel. I'm not in your bedroom now, so, yes, a lady."

"Okay, Miss Lady. You may be able to control what I say, but you can't control my imagination. I'm not going to tell you what I'm picturing right now, but it looks damned fine to me."

"Naughty, naughty man." I giggled much more.

Suddenly I shrieked and dropped the phone. After scrambling about, I finally regained my composure and picked back up the handset.

"Sorry about that," I said.

"What was that all about?"

"My bathroom shelf fell over. Came down right down on my head along with the newspaper and a couple of books that were on it. I built it myself, last month. Guess I'm not that good as a handy-woman."

"Sounds like you need a man around the house. If you weren't so far, I'd probably come right over."

His words lit up my mind. The idea of him being in my house, helping me to make it more of a home, excited me even more than the thought of what might follow between us after the repair job.

Benoit T. Dromel. My man!

Finally, a good man to call my own.

I was a little embarrassed at my eagerness and didn't want to betray how my heart grasped at the idea. An over-eager woman could send a man running for the hills.

I changed the subject, blabbering anything that fell from my lips.

"Oh boy, now I'll have to get another copy of the latest local paper — if I can find one. Everybody's talking about it. Plastered with pictures of the prime minister. He was up here to open a refurbished mill in a nearby town, and he gave a speech about some quarrel over lumber Canada has with America. A few big wigs from Syron Lake, including the mayor, of course, went for the opening and the local editor went crazy with the photos of the PM shaking hands with everybody."

Dromel had remained silent while I had prattled away, and now he sighed.

"Oh, Stella, now you've gone and killed the mood."

"What did I say wrong?"

"Why did you have to bring up that jerk?"

"Mayor Demetriou?"

"John 'Jackass' Peabody."

I chuckled. "Sounds like you're not the biggest fan of our illustrious prime minister."

There was silence on the line.

"He came off well on this visit," I said. "Seemed down-to-earth and likable; at least from the photos he seems that way."

"He can't ever be trusted." Dromel's voice had an edge to it I'd not heard before. "He's devious and conniving. He's a total slimeball."

"Are you saying that just because he's a politician?"

"I know from personal experience."

"You know the prime minister personally?"

"Yes."

It sounded as if he had hissed through clenched teeth. I bit my lip at the thought that I'd seemed overly impressed about his knowing Peabody. He breathed heavily into the phone and it dawned on me that I had somehow touched a nerve.

"So what has he done to make you so mad at him?"

"Apart from more recent sins, which I can't get into, I got to see what a lowdown scoundrel he is when we were at U of T together."

"Tell me."

"It may seem like nothing to you."

"Tell me, Ben. I want to hear it."

"When I joined the debate club, he was the president and he ran it like a fiefdom. It was as if he felt the whole set-up was there for his benefit and that of his clique. They seemed to think themselves some kind of blue-bloods. I believe his father was a bank executive or something like that. Anyway, there was lots that went on that wasn't as it was supposed to be. But one incident in particular I'll never forget."

"I'm listening."

"The club was invited to send a delegation of four to Ottawa for a three-day visit on Parliament Hill. The club had a general meeting, and it was decided that two spots would be for the president and vice president, and the other two would be for members who won a couple of special debates.

"Well, I won one of those spots. That didn't seem to please Peabody because I beat one of his buddies to get there.

"I worked as a waiter at a campus coffee shop to help pay my way through university. And I had the early morning shift the day we were supposed to leave for Ottawa. I finished up early and rushed to the appointed spot where I'd been told we were to meet to be picked up by the van that would take us to Ottawa. And guess what?"

"They didn't pick you up?"

"The bloody van never came to pick me up."

"That's a bummer."

"When I got back to my room, I found a handwritten note that had been slipped under my door. It was from Peabrain saying there was a last-minute change and everybody had to wait for the van somewhere that was a million miles from where I had originally been told to catch the ride to Ottawa.

"The thing is, he knew my shift. He used to come in for breakfast almost every day, and I had taken his order at the till loads of times before. He knew I would be at work all morning and that I'd never see that note until it was too late."

"Sorry to hear that he did that to you."

"My whole life would've been totally different if I hadn't been tricked out of my place by Peabody."

"How so, Ben?"

He sighed, then he continued. "The four who did go to Ottawa, their fortunes were made on that visit. They were hosted by Thomas Schuckler. You're familiar with that name?"

"It vaguely rings a bell."

"Well, he's a little before your time. He's dead now. Was a stalwart in Canadian politics. He took those four under his wings. Groomed them. All became MPs and three of them left politics and went on to claim spots on various boards. And, of course, Peabrain, who just barely passed to get his degree, is now prime minister of the second largest country in the world."

He exhaled a long, sorrowful breath.

"It kills me to think of what I could have been if I hadn't been robbed of my place on that trip."

After a pause, he almost whispered, "I haven't ever really told anyone about this."

"Peabody acted like a total scoundrel," I said. "But, Ben, why should you be upset about how things turned out for you?"

He said nothing.

I continued, "I mean, look at where you are – commissioner at one of the most important agencies in the nation, doing important work to keep Canadians and this land safe. And you're taking over duties for your chairman these days. Seems to me like you've done pretty well for yourself."

"I suppose." There was little conviction in his voice.

He could do with a bit of cheering up. This was as good an opening as any. I took a deep breath.

"How about forgetting about that unhappy trip that never was by joining me on a trip to somewhere warm and sunny."

He seemed to catch his breath, but didn't say anything.

"Ben, are you there?"

"Yes. What are you talking about?"

"Trinidad. I told you I grew up there, remember? Well, one of my old school friends found me on Facebook, today. Her family's one of the richest on the island. They own a hotel and other businesses. Well, she's invited me to come for the Carnival."

I paused and thought carefully how to phrase the next bit. "She said it would be okay to bring someone along."

There, I'd got the proposition out. Tried to sound casual. But the tremble in my voice betrayed that I knew it was a big deal. I had not used the word "boyfriend" or "partner." But it hung in the air.

Traveling together would be a declaration of our status as a couple.

"I don't know, Stella–"

"You don't have to answer right now." I cut him off before he could commit himself verbally to a "no".

There was silence on both ends.

"I mean, we have a few days to play with," I said. "Carnival is not for another couple of weeks or so. You could give it some thought. I mean, she said we could stay in the pool house. It's a little, one-bedroom guest-house. It's got its own kitchen and everything. Totally separate from the main house. So we'd be on our own."

"I'll give it some thought, Stella. That's all I can promise."

I stifled a sigh. It was not the response I'd hoped for. But at least he had given me reason to hang on to my hopes.

Chapter 68

Dromel stroked his beer bottle until the beads of condensation flowed down in streams formed by his finger. It was Monday night. The dimly lit bar was empty, except for one other lonely sap who walked around the billiards table, cue in hand, looking for the best angle to shoot the next ball in a game against himself.

Eyes fixed on the player, who bent to assess the situation from the level of the table, Dromel shook his head at the thought that, to the waitress who sat picking her nails behind the counter, he, too, must have seemed as much a loser as the guy with the cue stick.

He looked at his watch: ten pm. Another night of waiting in vain for the stranger in the expensive suit to turn up.

Had he played it too hard? Did the Syron Lake bosses decide to back off because he'd got too greedy? Or were they playing mind games with him, calculating that he'd begin to second-guess his strategy, just as had done a second ago? Or that he would start looking over his shoulder for some ominous figure in a trench coat?

Whatever, he thought.

The stranger's veiled threats would not sway him. He would double his resolve.

In two months, he would turn fifty-three. No other chance like this would ever come around again. He would let nothing pry his million dollars from his hands.

Dromel threw his head back and finished his beer. He slammed the bottle back down on the table, surprising himself with the loudness of the thud. The waitress jumped off her stool and looked in his direction. He pretended he didn't see her, stood up, fished some bills from his pocket and slapped them on the table.

As he wound his way aimlessly through the rough, unplowed streets, he was glad for the utter desolation of Ottawa at that hour. He inched through the snow, grasping the steering wheel and listening to the tires groan.

He let his mind go blank, focusing only on the moment and navigating the ruts. He was glad for this mental reprieve. Thinking had become too much of a burden because his thoughts would only slip back into the merry-go-round of wondering when, or where, or whether he would see the well-dressed stranger again.

At a quarter past eleven, just as he pulled into his spot in the parking lot at the Riverside Drive condo, his cell phone rang. A long distance number showed up on the screen.

"Hi, Berni–"

The voice on the line was sharp and short. "I thought you would've called today."

"What's that, darling?"

"Actually, I mean yesterday. What was yesterday for me. But it's still today for you."

"Slow down, Bernice. You're not making any sense."

"*I'm* not making any sense? Just how disconnected are you from this relationship, Ben? Do you mean to say that you haven't even realized that you had to call me today?"

The shrillness of her voice sent his pulse racing and left him disoriented. He didn't have a response.

"What's the date today, Ben?"

"Today? Today is the– Oh, sorry! Sorry! Sorry, Bernice. Happy birthday."

He sat in the car, unwilling to get out and face the frigid air.

"Ben, that sounds so hollow because I had to practically drag that out of you."

"Look, I'm sorry. I'm really sorry I forgot. I've had so much on my mind lately. There's this big project and it's kind of stalled and that's killing me."

"Oh please, Ben. Enough with the excuses. After more than two decades together, you'd think I could count on you to do something as simple as remember my birthday."

"I said I was sorry."

"I try so hard to keep things going between us, to make this work even though we're on two different continents. But when you're so tuned out from me like this...it...it just makes me wonder."

"Wonder what?"

"Wonder whether it's worth it to continue."

"Whoa there, Bernice. Sounds to me like you're overreacting over this."

"I'm over–" She sighed heavily. "Look, I'm so angry and disappointed right now, it's best that we hang up before I say something we might regret."

"As you wish, Bernice. But, I'm really sorry. Okay?"

The line went dead.

He hugged himself against the cold and dashed to the door. As the elevator took him up to his floor, the conversation rang in his ears. It occurred to him that Bernice was spoiling for a fight. Maybe she was just really upset. But could it be that she was fishing for a reason to call things off?

That nagging thought came to him again, that maybe she had found someone over there in Paris. Maybe some smooth-taking Frenchman had wined and dined her for her birthday and had got her thinking she didn't need ole Ben back in Ottawa anymore.

His blood raced; he could feel it pulsating in the veins and arteries of his neck.

At his door, his fingers fumbled with the keys; when he entered, he slammed the door shut, not caring that the sound echoed down the corridor.

He flung the keys on the table and patted himself down, reaching into every pocket in his coat, jacket, shirt and trousers. He knew the stash of little white pills were not on him; they were in Hull, in a box hidden in the floor below the fridge, where he always left them. But the craving he felt now drove him to make what he knew would be a futile search of his pockets for the fix.

He walked immediately to the fridge, pulled out a beer, twisted off the cap and paced the living room. He stopped at the window and looked down at the blanket of white, where the blue waters of the Rideau River would normally be shimmering.

It was bloody cold out there. The prediction was for Arctic air to drift down over the next week, plunging temperatures even further to record lows.

Damned, crazy weather.

With the million dollars, he could be permanently free of this frozen hell.

In the meantime, he'd take whatever relief was coming his way.

He dialed and waited.

The voice that answered the phone was bright, if a little uncertain.

Dromel cleared his throat. "Sorry to call you so late. You weren't asleep were you?"

"No. I've been fighting to get my novel going again."

"Listen, Stella, I've decided I will join you for Carnival after all."

"Really, Ben? That's the best news ever!"

"But, and listen to me carefully, Stella, we still have to be discreet. Even there."

He heard what sounded like a grumble.

"We can't travel down together," he continued, "and I can't stay with you at your friend's either."

"Oh?"

"But I do want to see you again. I long to be with you again."

"Me, too. I long to be with you, Ben."

"I'll take this as a opportunity to kill two birds with one stone. I'll travel to Grenada and then sail over to Trinidad for the Carnival. I've always wanted to do that. I'll call you when I get there. We'll have a great time, just the two of us."

He paused and listened to the silence on the line. "Still there, Stella?"

"Yes." Her voice was subdued. "That's not really how I'd pictured this trip would be, you know."

"I know, but the world's a small place. Your friends might take pictures and plaster them all over the Internet, and that won't do us any good, would it?"

"I guess not."

"Trust me on this, okay? It's better this way."

"I suppose."

Chapter 69

The pounding grew louder and more incessant. Williams rolled over in his bed and scrunched into a fetal ball.

This must be the granddaddy of hangovers, he thought. He'd had too much to drink the night before and had dragged himself to the nearest motel.

Where was he? Somewhere in North Carolina. Or was it South Carolina? He couldn't remember.

All he knew was that he and Young were on the road, living it up on their share from the Canadian gig. Young had got lucky with a shapely, young blonde the night before, and he wasn't willing to share. So, he, Williams, had stayed behind and drank until the bartender threw him out in order to close up the place.

Now he was paying for downing all that booze.

The pounding grew louder and more urgent, until he realized it was not coming from inside his head. He flung the covers off and sat up, and immediately paid for the sudden movement as a throbbing pain seized his brain.

The sound was coming from the door.

"Wake up, you lazy bastard," a voice growled above the banging. Young's voice.

Williams staggered out of bed, in nothing but his jockey shorts, and flung the door open.

"Grab your things. We're heading North again." Young pushed his way into the room.

Williams bent his head and raised his arm to shield his eyes from the light that flooded in.

"Damn, what time is it?"

"Who cares? We're pushing out."

"What's up?"

"Quinn called this morning. The boss from the last job has something else he wants done."

Williams grabbed his jeans off the chair and struggled into them.

Young took out a cigarette from his pocket and lit up.

"So, what's this job like?" Williams pulled a t-shirt over his head and grabbed his coat. He picked up his duffel bag and followed Young out the door.

"Well?" Williams said.

"Some bastard needs some sense knocked into him." Young fished keys from his jeans pocket as they approached the car. "Some high-up paper pusher. Name of Dromel."

Chapter 70

The elevator was empty when Simmons stepped in. It was two-thirty in the afternoon and the grumbling in his stomach finally drove him to leave his office in search of lunch.

He pressed the button for the ground floor and pulled out his mobile. His thumb scrolled through pictures of his son, which he'd taken at the Hirshorn Museum the previous weekend. The kid had enjoyed the cultural experience; well, had mostly enjoyed turning up his eyes and laughing at the modern art. Simmons stroked his chin as he scanned the pictures and congratulated himself on having scored some points as a dad.

The elevator doors opened.

It wasn't the ground floor. Simmons looked up just in time to see five men, who had been waiting in the corridor, turn around and head toward the elevator. In the midst of them was Director Hutton, gesticulating as he spoke.

His heart suddenly pounding violently, Simmons stabbed the button to close the doors.

"Hold that elevator!" one of the men shouted.

Just before the doors shut, Simmons' eyes met Director Hutton's. He was sure the director made him out.

The tiny box continued its downward cruise, and Simmons slammed his palm against the wall.

"Damn, that was not cool," he shouted.

The Mahler investigation was still scrappy and Simmons didn't feel confident enough to see the director just yet. Now his sophomoric reaction in the elevator was sure to make Hutton get down on his case. He was certain there'd be a call ordering him into a meeting before the week was over.

He took the stairs to Sarah Cohen's floor. Lunch would have to wait.

Her door was open and he strode right in.

"So, how's this Mahler picture shaping up?"

Cohen narrowed her eyes and stared at him. "Haven't you ever heard of calling ahead, or knocking before entering?"

"Has anyone ever told you that you look cute when you're annoyed?"

"Spike Simmons, you could get into trouble for going around making comments like that."

"Hey, I don't 'go around' making such comments; I don't tell anybody else I work with that they're cute." He pulled up a chair at the side of her desk and sat. "Well, that may be because everyone else I work with is a hairy, male agent."

He laughed. She didn't.

Cohen shook her shoulders and drew her chair closer to her desk. She tapped on the keyboard to call up the Mahler file.

"We've got no new leads."

"Why am I not surprised?"

"The latest news, though, is that the wife is now dating a much younger man. A different one from the guy she was with shortly after the funeral. This one's moved in with her. Has the title of business affairs manager, apparently."

Simmons rolled his eyes.

"She's trying to install him at Magrelma, it seems, even as pre-action protocol letters for the lawsuit are flying about."

"Business affairs manager, huh?"

"And as for the other partner, Maitland, well he's practically drinking himself under the table these days. Who knows how long that situation can last."

Cohen lowered her voice. "And as for Angela Roseau, I'm not sure how we can get anything more on her."

Simmons shook his head. "Don't take me there."

His stomach growled. Cohen widened her eyes.

"Haven't had lunch," he said.

Cohen nodded. "Pushing yourself too hard on this Mahler case?"

Simmons hardly heard the question. "Look, maybe this Dromel guy in Canada can turn up some answers. There's something fishy going on there. I can just smell it. Whatever Greene had in mind, Dromel has the power to make it happen or to kill it. I mean, has Dromel been in cahoots with Greene all along?"

"Well, we've been looking into all Dromel's relationships and activities going back to when Greene took over from his father to see whether they intertwine. Nothing much there. But Dromel did spend all of last summer in Europe. Mind you, he was mostly in Paris with his common-law wife and they traveled around together a bit. Then, late last year, he took a quick trip to Belize, by himself."

"Belize?" Simmons perked up. "What do we know about his time there?"

"Nothing. We just know what flights he took."

"I have a contact there who I can tap. Something tells me Dromel didn't fly down the Belize just to go snorkeling. That's one of those sunny places for shady people; major tax haven right there."

"His fooling around with this girl from the hearing is just bizarre. He must know this could cost him his job. And he's got a partner he's cheating on too, to boot."

"Come on, Sarah, it's really not that hard to understand."

"No?"

"Well, from the picture in the local paper, she's not bad looking. Young. Nice body. Once he realized all that was available to him — bam! He was a goner. Don't matter what hell may break loose."

"Men are that stupid?"

"Some men are that simple. If it's there for the taking, they take, no matter what the consequences."

Simmons chuckled as he saw how Cohen narrowed her eyes and scrunched up her nose. "And then you have guys like me," he said, "the more evolved type. My lady will know she can count on me to not be distracted, no matter what's dangled before my eyes."

Cohen loudly cleared her throat.

"Coming back to the case," she said, "well, maybe it's more than simple lust. Maybe the girl's somehow tied up in Dromel's entanglement with Greene. The operative who's been keeping tabs on them says that from what he's heard using a laser microphone, it looks like Dromel and the girl are heading down to the Caribbean."

Simmons threw his head back and chuckled. "Well, what'd ya know? That bastard made out as if I was the Devil himself to make him go up to frigid Canada to tail Dromel. And now he's gonna get a trip to the sunny Caribbean out of the gig. Ain't life sweet sometimes?"

An hour later, Simmons settled back at his desk and licked his lips to savor the grease that lingered from his late lunch of barbecued pork ribs.

The blinking light on his phone indicated a message on his voicemail.

"Hi, Spike. It's Meryl from the director's office. Call me back as soon as you get a chance."

Damn, that was faster than he'd expected.

He dialed the number.

"Hi, Meryl. I got your message." He tried to sound as cheerful as he could.

"Spike, the director wants to see you. He said he wants an update on that Mahler file."

"What mood's he in?"

"Crabby as hell. Truth be told, he's got the whole floor feeling tense."

"He couldn't be that upset about a missed elevator."

"What are you talking about? Haven't you been reading the papers?"

"Not really. Been buried in this case."

"Well, the director's all over the news with this bombing by the Texas student. They're blaming the Bureau for letting the guy slip through the cracks and the director's getting it from all sides."

With the phone cradled between his ear and shoulder, Simmons typed in Hutton's name in Google and did a news search. The media smelled blood and were hounding him. Story after story threw up questions about the competence of the Bureau; some called for the resignation of the director. Congress was set to haul him over the coals in a hearing over the next few days.

This was not looking good.

The big fish were eating up the little fish, and he was the lowest on the food chain. He couldn't show up in the director's office with just a pile of conjecture.

He slipped into his most sultry voice. "Meryl, we both know that as the director's scheduling secretary, you're the most powerful person in the building. Hell, you've got control over the director himself. And you're the only one who can save my skin this afternoon, because there's no way I'm going to make it out alive if I step into his office right now."

She erupted in giggles. He waited for them to subside.

"Don't worry, Spike. There are only two spots left in his schedule this afternoon. I'll put Peter Aker from the Latin American section ahead of you. There's no way he'll finish in time for the director to see you before he has to leave for a meeting outside. After that, the next I can fit you in would be for Monday, at three in the afternoon. How does that sound?"

"If I was right there in front of you, I would drop to my knees and kiss your feet. You're a goddess."

More giggling.

As soon as he was off the call, he rang up Bruce "The Bruiser" Coswell in Belize. Coswell was a CIA agent whom he'd met years ago at a joint CIA-FBI training exercise in Quantico. A good agent. Really intelligent. But lacking a certain finesse in his investigative techniques.

They exchanged pleasantries. Although the voice was familiar, Coswell spoke at a more sluggish pace than Simmons remembered. Probably the result of the years catching up on the old rogue, or more likely, it was due to some strong Caribbean rum, Simmons thought.

"So what can I do you for?" Coswell said.

"There's a Canadian regulator I need to check up on. Guy by the name of Benoit T. Dromel. Came down your way recently. I'll have a file sent over to you on him."

"Why's he on your radar?"

"We have reason to suspect he may have come into some moolah that he doesn't want to have to explain anything about."

"So a bribe-taker, then."

"Yeah, we think so. I need to know everything about his little jaunt. If he slept somewhere, I need to know the thread count of his sheets. If he met somebody, I need to get their present and three last known addresses. If he's hiding money in a secret account there, I need to know how much, down to the last penny."

"You're asking a lot, there."

"The heat's coming direct from the top."

"You mean Hutton?"

"Yeah. This Dromel guy's mixed up in a matter that the director's keeping close tabs on. He's breathing down my neck and it ain't funny. So, I don't care what your boss thinks. If you have to crack a few skulls to get the dirt on Dromel, I'd greatly appreciate it."

Chapter 71

Thursday, March 03

I packed a small suitcase then sat at my table, with the phone by my side, waiting.

It was six-thirty in the evening, the Thursday before Trinidad's Carnival. I stared out at the snow-laden trees, and thought that, instead of soaring as it should have on the eve of a trip like this, my heart felt as weighed down as the branches bowing under their cold burdens.

Half an hour later, the shrill ringing pierced the silence.

"All set?" Dromel said.

"I guess. I'm taking the bus tonight to Sudbury. I'll catch a flight from there to Toronto and then it's straight on to Trinidad. So what's the plan? When will you arrive?"

"I'm heading down to Grenada tomorrow afternoon. I know somebody there with a yacht. We'll sail over and I can meet up with you first thing Monday morning, for the opening of the Carnival."

"For J'ouvert, you mean?"

"That's the part where they bathe in mud and wear face masks, right?"

"Well, um, yes, kinda. Some people wear masks."

"So, we'll meet for J'ouvert, then. You've got a number I can reach you on the island?"

"I'll email it to you."

"Okay. Have a safe flight and I'll see you Monday."

"Have a safe trip, Ben."

I replaced the handset and sighed. In spite of our previous conversation, I'd hoped – yes, against reason, I know – that planning our first trip would have felt like marking a significant step in our status as a couple. But it felt like nothing more than scheduling any ordinary rendezvous, except this one required hopping on a plane.

There was no togetherness in the arrangements. He wouldn't meet my friends. And my blood ran cold at the thought that he might be planning to wear a mask when meeting me, in order to avoid being seen with me.

And then there was the class action lawsuit.

I'd thought that after recusing himself, he could become my confidante and adviser as I pressed on with trying to hold the mining company to account for the spill. I missed Osgood in that role and longed to turn to Dromel to take up his place.

I'd been bursting all day to share the news that Kobec, Crayton & Vohles had filed the lawsuit that morning. But I couldn't see how I could get in a word edgewise about it.

This relationship was beginning to feel like a raw deal, and some part of me wanted to protest.

But he was older, wiser, more worldly. Hadn't he explained why things had to be the way they were? He'd probably think me a spoiled brat if I protested.

So far, I'd known only immature boys and had been left reeling by those experiences. I'd never had a man as good as Benoit Dromel in my life before. I wanted to be with him...so I would play by his rules.

Chapter 72

Early on Friday morning, he called in a personal emergency. Said he would be unable to make it to work for a couple of days. The deputy chairman was in Japan attending a conference, so there was no one to question him.

Cynthia had somehow remembered he existed and had rung him up. Her husband was out of town. Dromel saw no reason to blow her off. In fact, her call had made him begin to feel like his luck was looking up.

He had a flight to catch in the late afternoon, he'd told her, so they could meet at his place mid-morning. She was fine with that as she would be free after she dropped her kids off to school.

He figured it was a waste of time trying to get his majordomo to bring around the leased car at such short notice. He caught a taxi over the bridge, then switched to another one, arriving at his Hull bachelor pad with enough time to prepare to receive his auburn inamorata.

Fueled by a couple of little white pills, the morning rushed past in a heady romp that left him exhausted. When Cynthia left, he slept a couple of hours. It was not till two in the afternoon that he taxied back to his condo to get his passport and bag.

The phone was ringing when he opened the door. Was it Stella? Bernice? The office? He hesitated, but eventually gave in to the shrill cry of the phone that had rung well over a dozen times.

"Well, finally," the voice said. "I've left five messages since this morning. Don't bother to listen to them."

"Who is this?"

"Firestone. I called for you at the office. They said you weren't going to be in. So I got your home number. The prime minister is leaving tomorrow for a two-week tour of Asia but he wants to see you before he goes. There's a driver in a car outside your building. He'll take you to meet the PM's car and bring you back."

"Who the hell does he think he is that I should agree to see him at the last minute like that?"

"Well, if you were at the office where you were supposed to be, then you would have got the call this morning and it wouldn't have been so last minute."

There was silence on either end.

"Well, Dromel, so what do you want me to tell the prime minister?"

He had a few choice words. But if he sent them in a message through Firestone, then he wouldn't have the pleasure of seeing Peabody's reaction himself.

"You're in contact with that driver?" Dromel asked, finally.

"Yes."

"Tell him to meet me right outside the front door. I'll be downstairs in two minutes."

Chapter 73

The prime minister's SUV stopped in a leafy Ottawa suburb. Dromel got out of the car that pulled up behind it. A security officer, wearing dark shades and an ear piece with a white cord that ran down his collar, jumped out of the front seat.

He frisked Dromel — this one did a thorough job, this time. Dromel didn't care. He wasn't wearing his pen recorder. That was safely hidden away in the Hull apartment. All he wore now was a deep resentment of John J. Peabody, which the prime minister's security detail had no way of knowing was more dangerous than any weapon he could tuck away on his person.

He climbed into the back seat and was greeted by Peabody's sneer. The officer slammed the door shut on Dromel, then hopped back into the front passenger seat.

"How have you been since our little chat?" Peabody's voice was shot through with glee.

"What's it to you?"

"Oh, are we a little hostile this afternoon?"

"I have things to do. I don't have time for games. If you want to talk about something, let's talk." Dromel glared at Peabody. He didn't even shift his eyes to the officers in the front seat to see how or if they reacted to his steely tone.

Peabody snorted. He looked away and straightened his tie.

"I understand you have a wife, a common-law wife, who's off in Europe." He fell silent to let his opening take effect. He sniffed the air and continued. "And I understand you've been quite a busy boy since she's been away."

Dromel's heart pounded against his ribs. His mind immediately flashed to Cynthia and the morning's abandonment. He clenched his teeth and glowered at Peabody.

The prime minister leaned over slightly toward him and said in a mock conspiratorial whisper, "Been mixing it up with the ladies, haven't we?"

Dromel turned the word over in his mind. Ladies. Plural. So this was not just about this morning. What exactly did Peabody know? He flinched; he was sure Peabody saw it. And that enraged him.

"Who I sleep with is my own affair," he said. "Keep the hell out of my private life."

Peabody looked out the window. He slowly turned again to Dromel, as if wanting to stretch out and savor this moment for as long as he could.

"Ah," he said, "but when the chairman of a CNRA panel starts sleeping with a party in a hearing over which he's presiding, we then have a public matter, wouldn't you say?"

So, that was that. Totally exposed.

He watched the grin broaden on Peabody's face.

Dromel felt every muscle in his body tighten. It took every effort to restrain his right hand from flying up and smashing Peabody's jaw.

"Couldn't resist temptation couldn't you?" the prime minister said. "Who could really blame you? What is she? Twenty-five, twenty-six? Must be a real rush to be with someone half your age. So you're the type of man who likes a bit of variety, eh?"

Dromel could no longer bear to look at that face. He turned his head and stared blankly ahead.

"Problem with giving in to that sort of pleasure is that it almost always ends badly," Peabody continued dryly. "Always leads to all sorts of trouble for those involved."

They rode in silence. Peabody watched Dromel's clenched jaw and smiled to himself.

"Of course, these things can always be swept under the carpet," Peabody continued. "If everybody cooperates, do as they're supposed to, then these sorts of problems can easily fade away, as if they never existed."

This irritated Dromel. He narrowed his eyes and drew in a deep breath. So this was how they were trying to squeeze him out of his million dollars?

He could just imagine Peabody eagerly agreeing to be the company's errand boy for such a task. Dromel would not allow Peabody to snatch his future right out of his hands this time.

With a sharp turn of the head, he faced Peabody.

"You want to make this public? Well go right ahead. Because the moment you do, I'm going to release a recording, made in this very vehicle not so long ago, of a prime minister threatening a commissioner of what's supposed to be an independent agency to do the bidding of a private company whose fate the commissioner is deciding."

Peabody's face went a shade lighter.

"Oh, two can play at the spy game, you know." Dromel didn't know whether it was his anger or the lingering effects of the morning's white pills that drove him, but he could not hold himself back. "That's right. I got it all. I was wired and your guys didn't catch it. If you don't believe me, just go ahead and try calling my bluff. I think Canadians will be very interested in hearing how their prime minister acts as a lap dog for private companies.

"And oh, by the way, make that a private company that resorts to deliberately breaking tailings ponds and even to murder to get its business done."

The blood drained away completely from Peabody's face.

Dromel relished seeing how easily he caved. He felt wild enough to say anything to crush him further.

"That's right, Prime Minister. That's the kind of company you're keeping these days. That dam that spilled the radioactive waste? Deliberately breached. By an employee of the mining company. For fifty grand.

The man confessed all to his nephew. And it's all on video too, which he wisely had the boy film. Because you know what? After the company's goons showed up to keep him in line, the man ends up dead. Thank goodness for cheap video cameras, though. Because they mean dead men do tell tales."

Peabody reached up to his necktie and loosened it. He swallowed hard, as if gasping for air.

"So, go ahead, Prime Minister. Do whatever the hell you want with your info. Because if and when you do, you can be damn sure I'll be more than happy to share mine with the world."

Peabody turned away and stared wide-eyed without looking at anything in particular.

His hand slid alongside the armrest and felt for the button to communicate with his driver. His trembling fingers found it; it took all the energy he could muster just to press down.

The SUV slowed and stopped. He expected Dromel to know the drill. There was nothing more to be said. He heard the door open and, at the side of his eyes, he saw Dromel hop out.

As the vehicle moved off again, his shaking hand reached into his jacket pocket and pulled out a Blackberry. He scanned the list for Verhoeven's number. He wrenched his tie completely loose, blew out a sharp breath and dialed.

Chapter 74

Firestone and Peabody sat alone in the prime minister's office. The mood was as heavy as the thick, ancient wood paneling that enclosed them.

Peabody leaned his head back and closed his eyes. He scrapped the leather armrests with his fingernails. It was the only sound in the room.

"Do you believe these recordings really exist?" Firestone said eventually.

"I don't think he's bluffing." Peabody didn't open his eyes, nor did he move an inch. His head was throbbing and each breath seemed to lack sufficient oxygen.

"CISIS said he got on a flight to Grenada after speaking with you. Should they send someone down there?"

"Oh God, no." Peabody opened his eyes and sat up. "They must pull back immediately. Call off the surveillance."

"You want to call them off now? John, this is when you need them the most."

"No." Peabody slapped the armrest. "I want them to back off now. And all traces of the operation must be erased. There must be no hint that I was in any way even remotely linked to any of this."

He stood up and walked to the shuttered window. He stared blankly ahead. "I spoke to Verhoeven. I called at a bad time. He was in London attending some function so we couldn't talk for long. I'm going to have to call him back. But he was furious. He was quite clear that I should wash my hands of the whole thing."

He turned to Firestone. "I only got involved as a favor to him. I hold no candle for this Syron Lake company." He shrugged.

Firestone knitted his brows. "But if any of Dromel's recordings leak out, or if he decides to go to the press with this...."

"Well, it hasn't and he hasn't so far. I mean, he's had this material for a while now, and it only came out because...well, because I pushed him."

Peabody walked over to his seat and sat again, noisily rocking back and forth. "I think Verhoeven's right. I need to back off. Get myself out of this. Make as if I was never involved."

"Easier said than done, John," Firestone said. The creaking of Peabody's chair irritated him.

Peabody planted his feet and came to a stop. His face was drawn. "This is serious, Angus. I must be shielded completely from this. I don't want to go down in history as another Nixon."

Chapter 75

Surrounded by three bodyguards, Hans Verhoeven marched through the packed, cavernous hall. Blinding strobe lights flashed in unison with techno music turned up to a deafening volume.

The small phalanx forced a path through the gyrating mass of bodies pressed close together. They entered a long passageway that was lit by dim floor lights and lined with clubbers in various stages of stupor induced by alcohol and God only knew what else.

The bodyguards led the way up three flights of stairs. They stopped at the door marked "Passion's Gate." This was the room where the girl at Greene's apartment said he would be found. A fourth heavy was still with her at Greene's place to ensure she didn't call him to warn him.

One of the bodyguards tried the knob. It didn't budge. He looked at Verhoeven, who nodded. Two of the men, who were built like oxen, slammed their shoulders against the door. It yielded with a terrific crash.

"Daniel Greene," Verhoeven roared as he entered.

Two barely-clad women ran past him, screaming.

Greene, wearing just a tie and boxers, rolled over on the bed and sat up, stunned. In the midst of his disorientation, he recognized the leader of the men who invaded his room as Kees Verhoeven's youngest son.

Verhoeven kicked past empty wine bottles on the floor and grabbed hold of Greene's tie. He yanked him off the bed and slammed him against the wall.

Greene doubled over, holding his throat and gasping for breath as he crumpled to the ground.

"You punk!" Verhoeven shouted. He turned to the bodyguards and nodded.

Two of them lifted Greene by either arm and dragged him back to the bed. The third man rammed his fists into Greene's ribs over and over again.

Greene fell back onto the mattress, howling in pain.

The men backed off.

Verhoeven paced in front of the bed.

"You bastard!" he said. "What the hell do you think you've you been doing?"

Greene curled into a ball and clutched his ribs. But he was done with letting Verhoeven see him cower. He clenched his jaw and breathed fiercely to get past the pain.

"How dare you get my father mixed up in your crazy, messed-up business?" the Dutchman yelled. "Breaking a dam and releasing radioactive waste? In Canada? Seriously? What makes you think you're so smart that you could get away with that? And then committing murder to cover it up?"

Greene mustered all his strength to sit up.

"Where are you getting all this?"

Verhoeven paced back and forth in front of Greene, recounting everything Peabody had related. Without warning, he swung at Greene.

Crack!

The back of Verhoeven's hand smacked Greene's jaw. Greene felt his head fly in the opposite direction, as if it would detach from his neck. With his eyes closed, he swallowed the pain.

Verhoeven grabbed Greene's tie and yanked him forward. He spoke so close to Greene's face he could feel his own breath ricochet off Greene's cheek.

"If those tapes get out and sully my father's name, you're a dead man. I swear, I'll kill you with my own bare hands."

Verhoeven rammed a fist into Greene's nose and watched him topple off the bed and crash onto the floor.

Chapter 76

They spared no expense to follow him. They were not spending their own money after all; and they expected to be handsomely rewarded for stalking their prey.

The boss had not flinched when told they'd need to charter a plane to catch up with Dromel's flight to the Caribbean. When he landed and promptly headed for the marina to set sail for who knew where, they were thrown into a mad scramble and only scored a vessel by getting the captain of an already booked yacht to bail on his passengers for three times his regular fee.

In the darkness of an insanely early hour of the morning, they had landed into another scramble, this time for a taxi to track him down. Now they found themselves in the midst of some kind of wild, manic revelry, as Dromel and his sole companion from the yacht plowed through a crowd and into a bar.

From a distance, they followed, jostling with crowds, making sure he never slipped from their sight.

Chapter 77

Dromel leaned against a wall of the jam-packed bar to steady himself. His head was throbbing, and it was not just from the heart-racing calypso music that blasted from the dozens of speaker boxes stacked to shoulder-height outside the front door.

He'd got no sleep on the cramped, red eye flight to Grenada. The turbulence the aircraft met could hardly compare with the torture he endured as the memory of his last exchange with Peabody played over and over again on the screen of his mind.

Setting sail for Trinidad so soon after he'd landed had not been such a good idea. The first whiff of the bracing, salty air had revived him somewhat, but what little benefit it brought was quickly eroded as the small yacht was tossed about by choppy seas.

Jet lag, lack of sleep, missed meals, too-strong rum, and now strange music turned up at a level beyond deafening, all should have made him miserable. But he leaned against the wall, groggy with tiredness, and delirious, despite himself.

He was intoxicated with the infectious abandon around him.

Inside the bar, hundreds of locals and a sprinkling of what looked to him to be foreigners, like himself, milled about, drinks in hand. Men and women connected in sultry gyrations, at random, it seemed. Everywhere, faces were smiling or laughing; bodies pressed close. People hugged, with gaiety and such ease. The whole mass of humans seemed out to enjoy the moment, without even the slightest hint of inhibition.

The captain of the yacht, a grizzled old Brit with skin wrinkled and reddened by too much sun exposure, huddled nearby with a group of locals who had greeted the old seaman with much back slapping and play-fighting.

Dromel could hardly understand a word any of the locals spoke, so he remained out of the circle. Yet he stuck close and shuffled behind them as the sway and rhythm of the crowd caused the group to shift as one mass. Before they landed, the captain had laughed and warned him of how easy it was to get separated and swept away in a Carnival crowd.

His head was spinning at the abundant feast before him. Everywhere he turned, exotic, nubile beauties writhed seductively. He even allowed himself to believe some of them, by their glances in his direction and their suggestive laughter, were extending an open invitation to him to join them in this sultry ritual that eliminated the boundaries of personal space between absolute strangers.

The idea excited and frightened him. He shrugged off the temptation and waited for a lull in the captain's conversation.

"Got to call my friend," Dromel shouted in the captain's ear.

The seaman pulled out a cell phone and handed it over. He nodded toward a dingy, black door. "The loo," he shouted. "Quieter there. Not much, though."

Dromel elbowed his way through the crowd and slid into the toilet. All the stalls, and urinals, and sinks were in use. He was overwhelmed by the stench of urine, and by the wet, muddy floor.

It was hardly romantic.

He pulled out the piece of paper from his wallet on which he'd scribbled the phone number she had given him.

Someone, whose voice he didn't recognize, answered and said she was handing the cell over to Stella.

"Hello?" Her voice was shot through with excitement.

"Hey, Stella. I made it."

"Where are you?"

"Some bar called Tall Boy's, I think."

"Great. I know it. I'm actually not far. I'm at a party with friends at the Hilton."

"So you can meet me here? I'll be at the back, near the washrooms."

"Be there in fifteen, twenty minutes."

He thought it sounded as if she was about to hang up. He shouted quickly into the phone as he left the washroom, "It'll be just you, right? No friends?"

"Yes, just me."

Her parting words had been significantly less enthusiastic than the greeting. But he would not relent on the point.

He jostled his way out of the bathroom. As he slipped the

phone back to the captain and returned to his place against the wall, it occurred to him that Stella had invited him to Trinidad, not so much for the Carnival, but to introduce him to her friends; to take whatever connection she thought they had to a deeper level.

That was definitely not in the cards.

In fact, he was questioning his sanity in even going through with the plans to be there.

Why had he rushed to the airport after that meeting in the prime minister's SUV? Oh, yes, the trip had already been bought and paid for. And he was so pissed at Peabody, he needed to get away.

After the encounter, there was no way he would return to his condo to look out at the bleak wintry scene and mope or cringe in fear as he imagined the weasel might have expected him to. He was sure Peabody knew about the trip, and if he didn't go, he would come off as the weaker one in this game of dare.

Something else he was sure of was that that fateful ride had cut a dividing "before" and "after" line in his life. A gauntlet had been thrown down. The resentment against Peabody that had been seething in his breast for years had now erupted into what felt like open warfare. When he returned, he would have to face up to his new reality.

And what he was also certain of was that Stella Jacob would not be part of it.

For now, though, he was eager to throw himself into this infectious revelry with someone he knew and felt safe with. He would enjoy himself as much as he could; enjoy the sweetness she would offer, for what would be the very last time.

"Thirsty?" The captain shouted in Dromel's ear and brought his hand up to his mouth as if holding an imaginary drink.

Dromel nodded. Now that he'd made the call and he knew Stella was on her way, he felt more at ease, more connected to this strange ritual in full play around him. He watched as the captain slipped away through the crowd in search of libations.

Dromel wandered off to what looked like a quieter corner, to ease the throbbing in his head. The nook offered little relief. When he turned around to return to his original spot, he found two strangers in his way.

They were tall, beefy, and definitely not locals. He stepped aside to get around the one with long, straggly hair. But the man would not let him pass.

He felt the man's left hand grip his arm. Suddenly he felt himself being thrust toward the men by the shifting of the crowd. He crashed against the long-haired man's right arm, which was covered with a cloth, under which he could feel something hard press against his ribs.

Panic surged through him. His body went cold, from the sole of his feet right up his spine as he caught the menacing look in the man's eyes.

The other man squeezed his right shoulder and leaned into his ear.

"Those tapes...."

Suddenly, they released their grips and turned. They walked off and disappeared into the crowd.

Before he could steady himself, he felt a slap on his back. He turned around. The captain was right behind him, holding two bottles of beer aloft in one hand.

"Local stuff," the old Brit said. "Very good."

In a daze, Dromel grabbed the drink and gulped. He was shaking.

"Those your friends?" the captain asked.

Dromel shook his head. He was too stunned to even utter a word.

He could hardly process what had just happened. Surely he hadn't heard right. Those strangers could not possibly have known anything about his conversation with Peabody.

Surely it was just his mind playing tricks on him. He'd been thinking too much about those damned tapes that he was now hearing things.

Those men must have bumped into him by purely accident. It was a wild, crowded bar, after all.

Dromel sucked on the beer bottle and scanned the dark room. There was no sight of the men.

The captain's group had dispersed and now the old Brit had his hands full with two local girls. Literally. His arms draped around the shoulders of one and the waist of the other as they bounced hips and swayed to the music.

With a racing heart, Dromel swiveled his head, scanning the room for the strangers and eyeing the door to catch a glimpse of Stella.

He was desperate to tell the captain that he wanted to go back to the boat immediately and head back to Grenada. And he would, as soon as he saw Stella.

He would tell her something came up and he had to rush back Canada. It was totally the truth, but he could give her no details. He could picture her protesting. Things would probably deteriorate into an argument. He dreaded it, but welcomed it, too.

It would mark the beginning of the end. A messy, but necessary end.

He looked around for the captain and suddenly realized he was no longer there. Deep in the crowd, Dromel thought he could make out a figure that he thought was the captain. He started out toward the guy but, as he looked toward the door, he saw a silhouette he recognized.

His heart leaped.

Stella had arrived.

Despite the let down he was about to deliver, he was relieved and excited to see her.

He jostled his way through the crowd and headed for the door. Their eyes met across the room and they began moving toward each other.

Suddenly, Dromel found his way blocked.

His eyes drifted up from the men's chest to their faces. It was the two strangers from before.

He stepped back.

They drew nearer.

His heart banged against his ribs and he felt a cold tremor run down his spine.

Just past the shoulder of the man with long hair, he saw Stella approaching. She was smiling broadly, looking directly at him as she squeezed her way through the gyrating bodies.

Dromel saw the man with the long hair thrust his arm toward him, the arm still draped with a shirt.

He heard Stella call out. "Ben."

The men lurched forward. Dromel panicked and swung at

the man's covered arm. The other stranger struck him on the shoulder. He lost his balance and felt himself tumbling toward the long-haired attacker.

His reflexes kicked in and he grabbed the man's covered arm. He felt the hard object again. The three men jostled as Dromel tried to wrestle away the object.

Stella was right upon them.

"Ben, what's going?"

Bang!

The sound was deafening. The entire bar erupted in screams. The music stopped. People began stampeding for the exit, and in the confusion, Dromel fell into Stella's arms.

"I'm hit."

"Oh my God!" Stella screamed.

"Get me out of here."

Chapter 78

I tightened my grip on his arm. There was no power in his legs and I knew I would have to do the running for both of us.

Going with the crowd in either direction down the street would not do. We would quickly get trampled in the stampede. I drew in a deep breath and rounded the side of the bar, carrying Dromel's weight. We jostled through a narrow alley, which ended at a concrete canal. I stepped down into the drain and let Dromel fall onto me. The deadweight of his body almost dragged both of us down.

"I've got you," I whispered.

I righted myself and we continued up the canal, away from the bar and the screams of the panicked crowd.

Struggling on, not knowing where we were heading, I heard Dromel's gasps and groans, and felt the side of my blouse that was pressed against his side become sticky and wet. Suddenly, I felt his weight pulling me down as he stumbled and tumbled to the mossy, concrete bed of the canal.

"Can't go any farther." He slid back, and propped himself up against the stone wall.

"Ben, this is crazy. What's going on?"

Now that we weren't running anymore, the shock of our predicament slammed in on me.

In the dim light of a quarter moon, I looked down at my blouse. A large, dark blotch stuck to my flesh. An overpowering sense of fear, the fresh scent of blood, and the stench of the mossy channel made me want to wretch.

"You're bleeding. We need to get to the hospital," I said.

"No."

"Oh God, we need an ambulance."

I started to climb out of the canal to go find help.

"No, no," Dromel said.

"Why not? Why did we run?"

"Listen, Stella." Dromel waved me down, sighing weakly with the effort. "You've got to listen to me. Don't worry. The police will get to the bar. They'll find me soon enough. I'm sure they'll follow the trail of blood."

"But will it be soon enough, Ben? Oh, God, look at the state you're in!"

With his eyes closed, he breathed with difficulty.

I sobbed out of fear and frustration. "I don't understand. Why don't you want me to get help?"

"Stella! Listen! Will you just listen?"

The ferocity of his tone startled me.

He doubled over and groaned, as if the last words had drained the life out of him. I knelt by his side.

"I'm useless, Ben. I don't know first aid. I don't know what to do to help you."

"I'll be alright. Don't worry about this. They'll find me. But we can't let them find you with me."

I rocked back onto my bottom and stared at him.

"I've something to confess." Wincing, he leaned to his side and clutched his ribs where the blood on his shirt was freshest. "I didn't recuse myself from the Syron Lake matter."

I shook my head, and tried to make sense of his words.

"Yes, I lied to you about that, okay? I'm sorry. The hearing is the highest point in my career so far, and I couldn't back out of it. But I also wanted badly to be with you. So I thought I could have both."

"What are you saying? I can't believe this."

"Scold me later, okay? But you can't be found with me."

A dog barked, and in the distance, sirens blared. I had the odd sensation of floating above my body, watching myself live through a nightmare too horrible to even imagine.

"Listen, Stella. There's something important I need for you to do." Dromel's weak voice was down to a whisper. "I think I know why I was shot. It has to do with Syron Lake."

"What?" My brain was pulsating, and his words kept pushing any sense of reality further and further out of my grasp.

I'd assumed that he'd been the victim of some kind of random Carnival violence, or of a robbery gone horribly wrong. It was too shocking and bizarre to think, now, that it was all linked to the hearing that had brought us together.

"The men who shot me...they were after the tapes. Stella, you've got to protect those tapes."

"What are you talking about, Ben?"

I looked helplessly at the widening red patch on his shirt. He was losing a lot of blood and was becoming delirious, I thought.

"They'll most likely go looking for the tapes."

"What tapes?"

"One is at my place. In Hull. You've got to get it before they get to it. It's hidden under the fridge. There's a false tile; you pry it up and there's a box. It has a pen that's really a mini tape recorder. On it, there's a conversation between me and someone who was trying to influence my decision on Syron Lake."

I stared at him.

"The other tape, I don't have. It's a video. You've got to find the kid who has it. He's in Florida but I don't know his new address. It should be in a letter from him in the box under the fridge. It was in the mail Friday, but I didn't have a chance to open it."

Trembling with fear, confusion and anger, I shook my head. "Why should I do anything for you? You lied to me. I trusted you that you'd do the right thing to make our relationship legitimate. But you lied to me, Ben."

I stood up as I heard the sirens come closer.

"I said I'm sorry about that, Stella. But I can't undo that, now, okay? Right now, you've got to listen to me and do as I say. Please."

He groaned and I knelt by his side again. I was almost blinded by the tears that filled my eyes.

"The man who's on the tape in Hull is the prime minister, Stella. The prime minister of Canada. Who would take my word against the prime minister that he was trying to influence my decision? Nobody. But if the tape is safe, they can't deny what he did."

"Peabody?"

"And the tape the kid has, it's of his uncle confessing to busting the dam. The uncle's now dead, so it's the only proof left that he did it."

"Oh my God." I slapped the side of my jaw in disbelief. My heart was pounding. My head spun. I could hardly take all of this in.

"Yes. It was done deliberately by the company. You get that video and the company is done, finished. But you've got to get to the kid before they do. His life may be in danger. If they did this to me, they could go after him, if they get his address from my place."

Dromel doubled over and moaned. My body went weak at the sound of his cry. I bent over him and draped myself over his shoulders.

"Ben, Ben. I hate seeing you in pain like this. Oh God, I wish I could help you."

Tires screeched and the blaring sirens stopped traveling.

"Sounds like the police are here." Dromel leaned back against the wall of the canal. "The only way you can help me now, Stella, is to get those tapes before anybody else does. Without that evidence, I may as well be dead."

"I can't leave you here like this. What if they don't find you? I have to at least to see that you've got help."

"They'll find me. Please, Stella. If they see you, you'll have to be questioned and that'll mean we'll lose any hope of getting to the tapes first. Go, go now, please."

He raised his hand and pushed me weakly.

The sound of voices and commotion broke the silence of the early morning. Dogs began a chorus of barking.

I held Dromel's hand in mine. I bent over him and lightly pressed my lips against his.

The voices grew louder.

I kept my face close to his. "I lo–"

He raised his hand to silence me. The smell of blood on his fingers filled my nostrils and, involuntarily, my head jerked back. I felt sick to my stomach.

"Please go, now," he whispered.

I stood up. Without looking back, I crossed the canal and got to the rock wall opposite Dromel. I mounted it and ran down a dark, narrow lane, my cheeks streaming with tears.

PART III

Chapter 79

I ran up the hill, through the narrow lanes and passageways between ramshackle houses. I ran for fifteen or twenty minutes, going wherever the openings took me.

Once or twice, I thought I'd looped back to where I'd been before, but I wasn't sure. In the darkness and in my state of panic and confusion, one rundown hovel looked like any other.

Dogs barked and rushed at me, but no one poured out of the houses I passed. Once or twice, lights suddenly flicked on at the sound of my footsteps under a window. But most people must have been out somewhere having a good time at the Carnival celebrations.

I ran until my lungs gave out and I dropped to my knees gasping for air. Hugging myself, I rocked back and forth, hoping to shake myself out of the nightmare I was experiencing.

It could not be true that I'd just left Dromel, faint and bleeding, in a foul and wretched canal. And what he'd said to me about how this all came about couldn't be real.

He'd been shot? The prime minister of Canada was somehow involved? The men who shot him were after some tapes.... And he wanted me — no, not just wanted, he'd begged me — to find the tape hidden in his house, and to possibly save the life of some kid who had the other?

"No, no, no." I buried my face in my hands.

The dampness of the red stain on my blouse and the sickening, fresh smell that filled my nostrils reminded me that it was all too true.

My panicked, aimless flight had cost too much time already. I needed to pull myself together and get moving with this.

I was high on a hill. Down below, the lights of houses and buildings abruptly gave way to a massive, dark expanse which I knew to be Queen's Park, the sprawling savanna at the northern edge of the island's capital.

Now that I had my bearings, I knew I needed to go down the hill and around to the right in order to get to the Hilton Hotel, where I'd been when Dromel had called.

Halfway there, I came across a yard with a line on which clothes billowed in the breeze. The holes in the decorative bricks of the wall gave a clear view of the yard. There was no visible sign of a dog. I clambered over the wall and dropped down into the yard.

The choice on the line was not appealing. A boy's school shorts that was much too small for me; a pleated school skirt; school shirts with monograms on the pockets; and a negligee so large that three people my size could fit into it and there'd still be room left. I plucked the school skirt and a shirt that I imagined could probably fit.

I unzipped the fanny pack in which I kept all the cash I'd traveled with and clipped three US twenty-dollar bills onto the negligee with a clothes pin. That ought to make up for the stolen uniform.

Once back over the wall, I ran down the street, rousing more dogs as I hurtled toward the main road that encircled the savanna.

Almost to the bottom of the hill, opposite houses in total darkness, I came across a standpipe. I shed my bloodied clothes, and washed my face and body. The water was cool, refreshing, even; but my stomach felt hollow at the thought that it was Dromel's blood that I washed away.

When I had patted myself dry with the parts of my own clothes that were not bloodstained, I forced myself into the school uniform. The zipper of the skirt could not go all the way to the top, and I lost the last two buttons on the shirt. But it would have to do.

I was sure I looked silly, a grown woman in this get-up. But, on this day, out of all days in the year, it would hardly cause an eyelid to flutter. I could easily be mistaken for someone in a J'ouvert costume. The whole point of the first hours of Trinidad's Carnival was to dress up in a ridiculous manner, in something old and ugly which you didn't mind being smeared with mud, which was likely to happen if you came across revelers carrying pails of the stuff in the streets.

Once I'd made it to the road that ringed Queen's Park, it took me no time to sprint across to the path that would take me up to the Hilton.

The sound of calypso music booming from the hotel reminded me of the excited and relatively carefree girl I'd been a short time ago while partying with Aileen.

I imagined she was still in there, worried half to death that I hadn't called her from my friend's cell, as I'd promised I would. Who was I kidding? We hadn't clicked and the reunion had fallen flat. I guess it had failed to soothe whatever wounds of rejection the new divorcée had invited me over to help her heal. More than likely, she was still in there, completely wasted and draped over some man, or maybe two or three men, as she had shown herself to have fully embraced the Carnival spirit earlier in the evening.

I headed straight for the row of taxis outside the hotel entrance.

"I need to get to the airport, fast," I said to the driver standing at the head of the line. "I mean real fast."

"Fast?" The man looked me up and down. "Is Carnival. It have plenty traffic on the roads."

"How much is it usually to get to the airport?"

"Eighty US."

At any other time, the drive to Piarco International took about an hour.

"Get me there in under two hours and I'll pay you double." His shifting eyes had a scampish look, and I silently prayed he was the kind who knew all the back roads and wouldn't think twice about taking shortcuts going the wrong direction on one-way streets.

"Get in," the driver said.

Chapter 80

The entrance to the airport was quiet at four in the morning. For all the crazy twists and turns we'd made, and the curses and blaring horns the taxi had encountered along the way, we'd arrived with bad timing. Two planes had left within the past hour, and the departures board showed nothing leaving until hours later.

A few people loaded with luggage milled about. I rushed past them and headed for the deserted Caribbean Airlines ticket counter.

Nothing happened when I called out.

"Hello," I yelled again. "Excuse me! Hello!"

After ten more minutes of staring at the door behind the counter and praying someone would emerge, I left in search of a payphone.

Dromel had sent me on an impossible mission. I would have to get to his house in Hull and then down to the kid in Florida before unknown forces that were somehow connected with the prime minister could manage to.

I wasn't even certain I wanted to risk setting foot back in Canada with all of this hanging in the air. The clock was ticking, and the only thing I was sure of was that I couldn't do this on my own.

I inserted my credit card, then pulled out a scrap of paper from my wallet and dialed the number scribbled on it.

With the handset pressed to my ear, I swiveled my head, scanning the cavernous and almost empty lounge. Down at the back, a man came from behind a corner and our eyes met across the distance.

My blood went cold.

There was no mistaking him. It was the long-haired man whom I'd seen jostling with Dromel just before the shot had rung out.

He came charging up the hall, right at me.

I dropped the receiver and dashed toward the main exit.

My feet weren't moving fast enough. The squeaks of sneakers

on the polished concrete floor coming from behind told me the man was gaining on me.

Breathing hard, I charged past a row of seats. Up ahead, a sleeping man lay on his back on three chairs with his feet on a trolley loaded with large suitcases. When I reached him, I yanked the trolley away, and sent it hurtling toward the man pursuing me. It wobbled and toppled over, spilling the luggage in the long-haired man's path. He tripped and crashed to the floor, face first.

That bought me precious time and my feet made the most of it. Out the main entrance, I glanced right and left and realized there was no place to hide. The building was also too long; I didn't have it in me to run to its length and around the corner before the long-haired man emerged.

Two men with keys in their hands, whom I took to be taxi drivers, stood chatting in the cool, morning air. They faced away from me and stared in the direction in which one of them pointed. Their cabs were the only vehicles nearby.

I didn't have time to explain anything. I ran past them, grabbed the handle of the closest door, and threw myself onto the floor of the backseat.

"What the hell?" one of the drivers said.

I spun around and wedged myself into the tight space between the back of the driver's seat and the edge of the back seat. My pleading eyes met the drivers' eyes for a split second, just before I drew the door toward me and quietly pulled it until it clicked shut. I pressed the lock and crouched into a ball.

Oh God, save me!

Almost immediately, I heard hasty footsteps approaching, only to stop suddenly near the car.

I was sure the thumping of my heart was loud enough to give me away.

"Where'd the girl go?" The voice was gruff; the accent, American.

The question went unanswered.

"See a chick run past here?"

No reply.

"You guys deaf or something?"

Still silence.

"Dumb natives."

Grumbled curses and angry footsteps rounded the vehicle.

A few moments later, I worked up the courage to peer through the back window and saw the sole moving figure grow smaller. The long-haired man crossed the largely empty car park, his mane visible under the dull, amber lights.

The engine of a waiting car rumbled. The man got in and the car took off with a screech toward the exit.

I got out of the taxi with the drivers watching my every move.

"You okay, there, miss?"

"You need the police or something?"

I shook my head. I bowed in thanks, but also to hide my terrified face from the drivers. Then I ran back into the building.

With tears streaming down my cheeks, I made it to the washroom. Trembling so violently, I could hardly stand, I bent over the sink and splashed cool water onto my face. Breathing hard, I looked at the wild-eyed, ashen creature staring back at me.

You must remain calm, Stella. You have to find the strength to get through this.

At the payphone, my credit card was still in the slot. I picked up the scrap of paper from off the floor, where I'd dropped it.

After about the eight rings, a groggy male voice answered.

"Detective Parker, sorry to wake you. But I need your help. I think I'm in big trouble."

It was a long shot, an act of sheer desperation.

Since he'd visited my house to ask about Osgood, I had seen the cop a few times around town: in the grocery; on the streets while we were both on foot; in his squad car while I walked home. It was always from a distance, but he'd always flashed a friendly smile at me.

At Christmas, when the town had gathered in the Moose Lodge after the Santa Claus parade, I'd observed Parker's interaction with Mayor Demetriou. Off duty and mingling with the crowd, the detective had showed no particular warmth toward the mayor when Demetriou had approached him to shake hands.

I had to believe, now, that things stood as he had hinted — that his loyalty lay with Osgood and, that, far from being the mayor's stooge, he distrusted Demetriou just as much as I did.

"Who's this?"

"Sorry. I forgot to say. I'm just so scared and confused right now. But it's Stella. Stella Jacob."

"Stella?" Parker sounded more alert. "Where are you?"

"In Trinidad."

"Where?"

"I'm back home, in Trinidad…on the island. I was supposed to meet up with the chairman of the panel from the Syron Lake hearing, but he got shot and now I have to save this kid from?"

"Wait. Slow down, Stella."

"Sorry, Detective. It's confusing, I know. But I'm confused. And scared. I don't have time to explain everything. But I desperately need your help. You said you thought there might be danger because of this Syron Lake business. I didn't really believe that, but now I've just seen someone shot because of that spill."

"Are you alright?"

"I'm shaking like a leaf, but I'm still in one piece."

"Okay, good. Is there any immediate danger?"

"Someone who was there when Ben…when the panel chairman got shot chased me down here at the airport. But I got away from him. I just saw him take off in a car."

"Listen, Stella, be very careful. You're in a dangerous situation. You need to stay calm and remain on the lookout. I'll do everything I can for you. How can I help you?"

"I need to locate someone else who might be in danger. Ben said a man who worked at Syron Lake confessed that he broke the dam. The man videotaped himself before he died. His nephew has a copy of the tape, and the people who shot Ben know about it."

"You mean Eric Tremblay broke the dam?"

"I didn't get a name. But if they get hold of that kid, that evidence is as good as gone."

"It could only be Eric. He's the only Syron Lake employee who's died recently. Okay. Where do we find Jacques, his nephew?"

"In Florida, but I don't know where exactly. Ben said he had the nephew's address written down in a box hidden at his house in Hull. And, Detective, this is the scariest part. The prime minister is tied up in all of this."

"What? You mean Peabody?"

"Yes. Ben said Peabody was trying to pressure him to do what the company wanted. There's a pen in that box. It's actually a tape recorder that Ben used to secretly record their conversation."

I ran out of breath and Parker seemed to be holding his.

"Where's the panel chair now?" Parker said eventually.

"I'm praying to God that the police found him and took him to the hospital. I left him in a terrible state in a ditch in Port of Spain. I didn't want to. But he begged me to leave so I could get the tapes."

"So you want me to break into his house?"

"There's a key to the front door hidden in the trellis to the side of the house. I'm going to try to catch the earliest flight I can to Miami or Fort Lauderdale, whatever I get. I'll call you again, later, to get Jacques' address."

"No way, Stella. If people are running around with guns looking for this evidence, you can't go searching for Jacques alone."

"I have no choice."

"I'll come down there to help you."

Had I heard right?

"What did you say?"

"I'll come meet you."

"In Florida?"

"Yes."

I felt as if ten thousand tons of weight had been yanked off my shoulders.

"Oh my God. Thank you, Detective. That's the only good thing I've heard since this craziness began. I didn't know who to call for help. With Peabody being tied up in this, I don't know if I can trust the authorities."

"I couldn't do otherwise, Stella. I'll leave for Hull right now. Keep in touch, okay? This is my cell so you can call me whenever you need to."

Chapter 81

Aileen didn't answer her cell when I called, so I left a message saying there was an emergency back home and I had to fly out immediately. I imagined that even in a million years, she'd never guess at the nature of the emergency.

Our connection was so fickle I figured that after hearing the message, she probably wouldn't even try to contact me to find out how things went until after the Carnival festivities were over, in another couple of days. Her maid would probably toss my suitcase in the trash or swipe whatever she liked, and my visit would be quickly forgotten.

The Caribbean Airlines ticket office still showed no sign of life.

I banged my knuckles on the counter.

"Hello! Anyone there? Hello!"

After a while, the door toward which I'd projected my voice slowly swung open. A plump woman with tired eyes approached the counter. She seemed none too pleased to have been roused from whatever she'd been doing.

"Yes? Can I help you?" The expression on her face was entirely contrary to her words.

"I need to get on the next flight to Florida, please."

"You serious?"

"Yes. I'll take Fort Lauderdale or Miami, any flight I can get."

The woman snorted. "You feel you could really just waltz in here and get a flight just so?"

"This is urgent."

"Well, this is Carnival, dearie. Busiest time of the year. Everything's overbooked, coming and going. It ain't have nothing available."

My throat tightened. "Will you please check? Maybe somebody canceled."

We locked eyes, and after what seemed an interminable showdown, the ticket agent snorted again. She stepped toward the computer, tapped noisily on the keyboard, and scanned the screen.

"Exactly what I said. Nothing available for Fort Lauderdale. Nothing for Miami."

With an exaggerated swing of her arm, she pressed a button to shut down the computer, and, without saying anything further, she turned and slipped behind the open door.

I heard a long, loud "steups," a familiar sound made by Trinidadians by sucking wind through clenched teeth to express annoyance.

"But where these people does come out from?" The woman's voice had gone up a pitch. "This girl barge in here at this hour of the morning and feel she could demand a ticket dry so? And you should see how she dress too. Wearing she top tight, tight, tight, as if she chest is everybody's business. Lord have mercy. The people you does have to put up with on this job, eh!"

My thoughts wandered to a young man somewhere in Florida with his uncle's video confession. Was the uncle Osgood's fishing buddy? The man he'd cycled out to meet the Saturday after the flood?

As I strained to make the link, I had an eerie notion that somewhere Osgood was rooting me on. "Get it, Stella. Get that evidence and nail the corporate bastards!"

The kid was a sitting duck, unaware of the danger that Ben had said was likely to descend upon him. And I was stuck here on this island, helpless and unable to do anything about it.

Approaching footsteps made me look up. A thin, frail-looking man with a head of gray emerged from the door behind which the woman had disappeared. He looked me up and down; then his eyes rested on my bosom as he stepped toward the computer.

"Where you going, miss?" His eyes darted between the computer and my chest.

"Fort Lauderdale, or Miami, or anywhere in North America at this point."

He scanned the screen, then he shook his head. "Sorry. No opening on anything."

I sighed.

The man gave me a sympathetic smile. "You could try your luck with Liat, but you might have to do some island hopping before you get to the States. They open in a couple of hours."

He sneaked a final peek at my overly small top, then shut down the computer and shuffled back behind the door.

The stragglers with luggage from earlier had thinned out. A couple of drowsy security guards milled about, and a cleaning lady pushed a cart loaded with rolls of toilet tissue and two long, filthy-looking mops.

At a bank of seats, the hapless passenger whose luggage I'd scattered earlier had recovered the trolley and his suitcases. Now he lay stretched out on four adjacent chairs; a handkerchief tied to his wrist was also attached to the handle of a dingy, leatherette suitcase wedged among the others on the trolley. I envied him his sleep.

My head throbbed and all I wanted to do was lie down, close my eyes and melt into that world of oblivion where nothing mattered.

I couldn't risk dozing in the middle of the airport lounge. What if the long-haired man came back? Was he here before to look for me? Or had he been trying to secure a flight out of the island, himself? If he had, again, there was a danger that he might return as there was no other airport on the island.

I wandered the corridors until I came to a washroom. The only sound was the hiss of a faucet that wouldn't shut off fully. I doubled over and peered down the row of stalls. No sign of feet.

I had the entire fetid place to myself.

The tenth stall, the one furthest from the door, would do. If anything, it would give me the most time to react if someone entered the washroom.

I put down the toilet bowl lid, unrolled three layers of tissue paper over it, as well as across the tank. I sat on the tissue-covered seat, leaned back against the tissue-covered tank, and folded my arms. My eyelids easily folded down and brought the darkness I craved.

Twenty-four hours ago, I'd had a luxurious, little pool house in the poshest neighborhood on the island all to myself as I awaited the arrival of the man with whom I'd meekly begun to hope I'd spend the rest of my life. We were to while away a glorious two days together and I'd made plans to show him the wild, joyous party thrown by the island on which I'd grown up.

Twenty-four hours ago, I'd been quietly giggling to myself, half asleep, half awake, as I imagined how Dromel would try to dance to the fast-paced calypso music, missing the rhythm entirely. I'd planned to grab hold of his hips in order to train him to dance like an islander, gyrating in a slow, sensuous motion.

How could it be that now I was sitting on a germ-laden public toilet, scared for my life as I hid from God alone knew who, after I'd left Dromel bleeding in a lonely, cold, smelly canal?

My head fell forward then snapped back in a reflex motion. The hiss of the faucet filled my ears, and I suddenly realized I had dozed off. I checked my watch. Only half an hour had passed. This was interminable. I covered my nose with both hands to block out the awful odors.

I was to blame for this horrible mess. Dromel would have been safe and happy in Canada if I hadn't tempted him to come down here.

Ah, but he'd confessed that he'd lied to me. He hadn't recused himself as he'd promised he would have.

The thing I'd most feared, the scandal I'd tried to avoid, was sure to come now.

Or maybe not. Maybe if he said nothing about meeting me to the police or anyone else, our relationship would never come up.

He was a man who had his wits about him. Perhaps he would make up some story that locals shot him while trying to steal his wallet.

Yes, it would be bad for the island's reputation, but a story like that would be perfect for covering up the truth. Robberies happened all the time during Carnival; people would buy that story.

Bang!

The noise made me jump. I'd fallen asleep again. Now my eyes were wide open and my heart raced. A squeaking sound filled my ears, and then came the voice, humming a tune. Through the crack in the door of the stall, I saw the cleaning lady wheel her cart into the bathroom.

Still humming, the woman bent down and pulled a bottle from the cart. She held it to her ear and shook it.

"You mean to say this finish already?" She left the cart and exited the restroom.

So much for my refuge. There was still an hour to go before the other ticket counter opened.

I abandoned the stall and poked my head out the washroom door. Apart from the guards and one or two new local stragglers who chatted standing close to a huge pile of luggage, the place looked empty.

The cleaning lady emerged from a black door a few feet away and passed me on her way into the washroom. She had left door slightly ajar.

There was keyed lock on the outside, but a simple knob on the inside. I slipped into the tiny supply room, curled up on the floor behind a stack of boxes and soon went dead to this world.

When I awoke again, the room was in total darkness; the door was closed shut. Apparently the cleaning lady had been back and hadn't noticed me.

The reflectors on my watch told me that in a few minutes, the Liat ticket counter would open.

The airline had two cancellations on the next flight out to Grenada, where I could catch a plane to St Vincent, and then fly on to Antigua. From there, I needed to switch airlines but should have no problem getting a flight to Jamaica and then to Florida, the ticket agent said. It was unlikely, though, that I'd set foot in the States anytime before the next morning.

"I'll take anything you've got."

The flight was not scheduled to leave for another three hours.

My head was spinning at the amount I had to shell out for the ticket. But, in the situation, I couldn't quibble about cost.

The airport was somewhat busier. At the Caribbean Air counter, the brusk woman now glowed as she chatted with what looked like a foreigner in a white short-sleeved shirt, who sported a dark buzz cut.

The door to the supply room was just slightly open as I'd left it, and I slipped in to try to catch a bit more sleep. Twenty minutes before my flight, I re-emerged, groggy and bleary-eyed.

Sprinting for the customs area, I remembered Parker. I'd have to tell him where to meet me the next morning. I walked briskly to the bank of telephones with my head down.

I'd punched the first few numbers when I had a strong sensation that I was being watched. I turned around and saw a man walking with an air of determination. He seemed to be walking directly toward me. My mind clicked with a sense of recognition; and then I realized it was the man who'd been chatting with the brusk ticket agent from earlier.

I dropped the receiver and sprinted toward security. The man didn't continue on toward the phones. He swerved toward security, too.

I picked up the pace. The man doubled his steps. With his long legs, he was quickly gaining on me.

I burst into a full, panicked dash, almost tripping as my feet tried to move faster than humanly possible. The security gate was just ahead. Panting hard, I gave it my all to make it.

As I neared the glass doors to the security area, I slowed down a trifle and waved my ticket at the female airport officer who stood at the entrance chatting with a guard.

"No luggage?" she said.

I shook my head, exaggerating the look of desperation on my face.

"Hold on a minute!" She grabbed my ticket, eyed it, then stuffed it back into my hands.

"Your flight leaving right now, girl. Hurry, hurry, hurry!" The woman laughed. "Run, run, run."

I blasted through the doors. But my feet couldn't keep up and I went crashing to the floor.

On the other side of the glass doors, I saw the man in white short-sleeves come pelting toward to security entrance. The guard who'd been chatting with the female officer flung out his arm, forcing my pursuer to stop dead in his tracks. I scrambled to my feet and shot down the corridor toward the scanning machines.

Chapter 82

"Where's your ticket, sir?"

The female official had been amused by the oddly dressed young woman who'd come waving her ticket in a mad rush to catch her flight. She'd been lenient on the girl and had allowed her to hustle the ticket check. Now, she suspected this thick-necked foreigner had seen the whole thing and was looking to pull a stunt by trying to dash past her without a ticket.

She would have none of it.

"Your ticket, sir." She raised her voice. "I need to see your ticket."

The man doubled over, catching his breath. He stood up, pulled out a badge holder, and splayed it open.

The security guard, who was at least five inches taller than the foreigner, stooped and squinted as he inspected the credentials.

"FBI? Is that for real?" the guard said.

The man slapped the flaps of the badge holder back together. "I need to speak with someone before she gets on a plane."

He threw back his shoulders and stepped toward the entrance to security.

The guard immediately shifted to place himself between the foreigner and the doors. He was no fool. Sure he'd failed the written police entrance exam, but he had loads of friends who were policemen and he discussed law enforcement with them whenever they met up at the rumshop, which was almost every weekend. He would show this foreigner he knew how things really worked.

"Listen here, man, even if that badge's not fake, this is Trinidad, not the US. The FBI have no jurisdiction here."

The foreigner glowered.

The guard stuck out his chest and snorted. "You hear what the lady say? She say she want to see a ticket. If you have no ticket, you not going nowhere."

The foreigner stared daggers at the guard.

Finally, he shoved the badge back into his pocket, grunted, and walked away.

Chapter 83

The small, turboprop plane landed in Antigua, and I disembarked with my head bent as I followed closely behind a middle-aged couple who fussed over an elderly woman. Occasionally, the couple threw frowning glances at me, but I kept up the pretense of being part of their group all the way across the tarmac until they entered the terminal building and arrived at the ticketing area. They proceeded toward the exit with suspicious backward glances at me, and I slipped behind a tall, potted palm to scan the scene.

The man with the long hair was nowhere in sight. Nor was the one in short-sleeves. But being chased up to the security gate in Trinidad had left me spooked. I decided to ditch my flight plans just in case either of them had talked to the Liat attendant at the Trinidad airport.

"There's no direct flight to Florida," the young woman at the Caribbean Air counter said, "but you can go up the islands to Jamaica and get a connecting flight there."

"No, I can't go that way," I leaned in toward her and whispered. I sensed a line forming behind me and I swung my head around to scope out the newcomers.

The ticket agent narrowed her eyes and studied my clothes and then my face. The shake of her head and the shrug were subtle. Some crazy woman, she must have thought.

"Well, you could go across to Barbados and get a direct flight from there to the States, and that would actually get you into Ft Lauderdale early in the evening. But you'd have to hurry to catch the plane to Barbados. It leaves in twenty minutes."

Ticket in hand, I headed for the phone booth. After one ring, he picked up.

"Parker here."

"Detective, it's me, Stella Jacob."

"Where are you?"

"Antigua."

"You're alright?"

"No, I'm not sure I'm alright. Somebody else came after me in Trinidad."

"Who?"

"I don't know. Maybe an agent sent by the prime minister. I don't know. I'm scared out of my mind now."

"This is sounding even more serious than I thought."

"It's serious, alright."

"But, listen, you've got to stay calm, okay?"

"I'm trying."

"You've got to keep your wits about you."

"I just dropped all the travel plans a ticket agent worked out for me in Trinidad, just in case she snitches on me."

"So what are you doing now?"

"It works out better, actually. I'm going to Barbados to get a direct flight to Ft Lauderdale. I should land around six this evening."

"Okay. I'm heading into Ottawa as we speak. As soon as I pick up that tape and the address for Jacques, I'll fly down there to meet you."

On the plane, I squeezed past two long legs encased in a hideous checkered fabric and settled into my window seat. Beside me, a deeply tanned man with a sharp, rat-like face smiled broadly.

"Beautiful island, just beautiful," he said.

I gave a slight nod and looked out at the tarmac.

"My first time down here," the man continued. "The golfing was incredible. Four days on the most immaculate course. Unbelievable. And you know the best part of it?"

He leaned over to me and whispered, even though I continued to face out the window.

"Here's the best part: It cost me nothing. Not a cent!"

He slapped his knee and cackled.

Good grief. I'd been placed next to one of those overly friendly travelers.

"The whole shindig was sponsored by the company," the man said. "They called it employee development or some kind of corporate mumbo jumbo. I figure it was really an excuse for the big wigs to live it up large. They stayed at the top hotel on the island, but the rest of us didn't have it too shabby, mind you. We had a couple of hours of seminars and stuff every day, but mostly, we had a free pass for the links. Best job I've ever had. Started with them five months ago and I still can't believe my luck."

The flight attendant began her safety spiel. I pointed my chin toward her to shut the man up.

I was not in the mood to chit-chat. I wanted to think only about getting Jacques Tremblay to entrust Parker and me with the video his uncle had made. And I wanted to figure out just what we would do once we had all the evidence and had ensured Jacques was safe.

Perhaps by then Dromel would have recovered sufficiently and I'd be able to get back in touch with him. Would he remain in the hospital on the island? Or would he try to get himself airlifted out of there? Where would he go? I didn't imagine that he would want to return to Canada, not in the vulnerable condition he was in.

The plane rumbled down the runway and I felt my body slam into the back of the seat with the thrust of the take-off.

I squeezed my eyes shut.

Get better quickly, Ben. God, keep him safe.

"And you know what?" The man at my side started up, again, as if there had been no break in his monologue. "The wife can't believe our luck either. I'm headed over to Barbados where I told her to come meet me. Twenty-three years together and it's the first time we're having a getaway outside the States since our honeymoon."

"Good for you." My tone didn't match my words. I made sure my expression didn't either.

The man stared back, apparently surprised. He looked about at the passengers in the other aisle, then stared straight ahead. In silence.

After a while, he leaned forward and pulled a duffel bag from under the seat in front of him. He searched through the bag, which was emblazoned with a logo of an anchor. Some of the garments spilled out onto my lap. I felt my annoyance rising as the man continued his search, unconcerned about the invasion of my personal space. Then I realize the clothes also bore the anchor logo, and a thought struck me.

The man pulled out a thick book from the bottom of the bag and began stuffing the garments back in.

"Swag from the trip?" I tried to inject sweetness into my voice.

"Uh huh." My seatmate had crawled into himself and had closed up now, it seemed.

"I don't imagine you're too particularly attached to that stuff, huh?"

"Not particularly." Glancing from the corner of his eyes, he surveyed me from head to toe, taking in the too-tight, monogrammed shirt and the bareness of my legs beyond the short, pleated school skirt. Then, as if something clicked inside him, he added, "But, maybe, somewhat attached. It's from my first big trip with the company, you know. The stuff kinda has sentimental value."

The shark! He had caught on that his trash would be my treasure.

I turned to my side and shifted my weight as I zipped open the fanny pack to see what I had left. I flipped through the bills. Just one hundred and seventy. I would offer forty...sixty tops. It was a lot for some stranger's probably unwashed duds, but it would be worth it to change my appearance.

"But I suppose you could be persuaded to part ways with at least a t-shirt and a pair of pants, right?"

"Well, I'm not really interested in pulling out a shirt here and some pants there. But for, maybe...for two hundred I could just get rid of the entire lot and be done with it."

The rat! He must have peered over and seen me count my money.

We stared at each other in silence. Then he leaned over as if to place the bag back under the seat.

"I have one-seventy," I said.

"Sold!"

The man plopped the bag into my lap.

I pulled out the last of my holiday money and placed it into his grubby hands.

"Thank you very much." Smiling broadly, he shoved the cash into his shirt pocket, then opened his book and acted as if I wasn't there.

It was merely paper, I told to myself. What was mere paper when lives were at stake, my own included.

Chapter 84

Parker drove slowly down the snow-covered Hull street on which he expected to find Benoit Dromel's house. He glanced at the address that he'd scribbled into his notebook, then checked the street signs again.

Yes, he was on the correct road, but Dromel's house didn't appear as he had expected.

First, it seemed too tiny to be the abode of such a high official. Second, the front door was slightly ajar. And third, on the street, right in front of the house, sat a brown sedan with a thick-set driver at the wheel who kept a close eye on the door.

Parker pulled into a driveway, a couple of doors down, on the opposite side of the street. Before he had finished adjusting his mirrors to survey the scene, a figure appeared in Dromel's doorway.

This second, burly man, who looked very similar to the driver of the sedan, stepped out onto the small porch and pulled the door shut behind him. Metal creaked as the man raised the lid on the mailbox. He then walked briskly to the waiting car, stuffing a handful of envelopes into his jacket pocket. He got in and the car took off, slipping and sliding through ruts in the snow.

"Great." Parker slapped his steering wheel. "Someone's got there before me."

Stella's story had sounded bizarre when he'd heard it after being jolted out of sleep by his ringing phone at four in the morning. Now things had just gotten much worse.

People were following her, and one had chased her as far as the entrance to security. Now someone was snooping around the house of a high government official, stealing his mail, while the man lay wounded and bleeding in a far-off country.

Parker backed out of the driveway and edged closer to Dromel's house. The key was where Stella had said it would be, but it was not needed. The door yielded to a slight push. Parker looked at the lock; it had been crudely broken. Brazen, he thought.

Inside looked like a tornado had landed. Books, CDs, magazines and newspapers were scattered across the room.

Shelves and chairs lay overturned. The sofa had been shredded.

In the kitchen, all cabinet doors were open; all drawers had been pulled out and dumped on the floor, along with their contents.

Parker stepped cautiously among broken cups, glasses and plates and stood in front of the tall, solid refrigerator. Its doors were left open, and its shelves were bare with a mound of food at its base.

Thankfully, though, it appeared not to have been shifted out of place.

Parker kicked aside the rubble in front of the fridge. He rocked the massive box from side to side and pulled it forward, out of its slot between the wall and a cabinet.

He knelt on the floor and began to wonder if Stella had got her information wrong. All the laminate stone tiles seemed normal.

He picked up one of the knives from under an upturned drawer and ran it along the grooves. At last, one tile shifted. He stuck the knife further in and prised up the laminate square.

The cigar box he found held a packet of small white pills, a bunch of photos, some banking information, a couple of envelopes with foreign stamps, and a pen. No ordinary pen, this, according to Stella. On its tiny internal circuitry was a conversation so dangerous, it got its owner shot.

The first envelope he picked up was postmarked Sanibel Island, Florida. Parker pulled out the one-page letter, which was little more than a hastily-scribbled note. It was dated early December.

"Can't survive here," it said. "Too expensive for me. I'll be heading to the mainland soon. I'm going by the name of Josh Taylor these days."

The letters "JT" were printed below.

Parker snatched up the second, unopened letter, which had another Florida stamp. He tore it open and unfolded the small sheet of paper, which looked like a page that had been ripped out of a ring binder notebook. The letter started off with apologies for the delay in writing.

"Not settled yet and I don't have a phone over here," it ended. "Planning to move around the middle of next month to a cheaper place in Daytona Beach, if I can get it. I should be able to copy the video and mail it when I settle in."

This note also carried the initials "JT" and was dated late January, but the postmark showed that it had been actually mailed only about nine days after it had been written.

Parker frowned. Based on the timing, it was more than likely that the goon from earlier had pocketed a letter from JT. Maybe even one that contained a copy of the recording he was after.

Just as he stuffed the items back into the cigar box, he heard the sound of creaking metal outside the front door.

He shot to his feet and his entire body snapped erect. His gears shifted into fight mode. He would not wait inside like a sitting duck to see if the goons were back to further their search.

He picked up a knife and stole through the rubble toward the front door.

He pressed his body against the wall in position to pounce on anyone who entered.

The seconds ticked away, and no one came. No further sound came from outside either.

With the knife concealed behind the length of his hand, he eased open the door and stepped out on the snow-covered porch.

The brown sedan was not there. The street was empty, except for the figure of a postman, laden with two carrier bags, sliding along the sidewalk, a couple of doors down.

Parker dipped his free hand into the mailbox. He dashed back inside with a half dozen envelopes.

He tossed the bills and the junk mail onto the ripped-up sofa. The last envelope bore a Florida postmark.

He ripped it open. One page again. Signed "JT."

"Scrap the Daytona Beach address I sent the other day," it said. "I couldn't last even a week in that hellhole. The landlord was a psycho. This new place is much better. Hoping this is the last move so I can finally settle down."

Parker collected the cigar box and stuffed the new letter into it. He stuck the box under his coat, slipped out the door, and headed for his car.

"Destination, Ft Lauderdale," he said to himself as he turned the ignition.

Chapter 85

Spike Simmons entered Sarah Cohen's office carefully balancing a large plastic tray in each hand.

"Your sushi's here."

"Thanks, Spike." Cohen spun around in her chair and reached for a handbag atop a cabinet behind her. "How much do I owe you?"

Simmons laid the platters on the desk and waved off the question. "Got some news about a big break in the case. Turns out that our Canadian–"

He stopped mid-sentence and craned his neck to read the webpage on Cohen's computer screen.

"You're hooked on the director's big day before the cameras, too, aren't you?" He dropped into a chair and shoved a seaweed-wrapped roll of rice and avocado into his mouth.

"I watched the live feed online this morning," Cohen said in between nibbles on raw salmon.

"I caught it on television, upstairs, with a couple of guys from the office."

"Can't say how many times I've replayed that clip of the clash of the century. I've never seen a senator behave like that new guy did. What's his name?"

"Lovell. Or, maybe, Lovelace. Something like that."

"Well, that one. He was all over Hutton this morning about that Texas student bomber thing. It was brutal."

"He's just a loudmouth, no-name rookie trying to get attention at the director's expense. Very un-statesmanlike."

"I thought Hutton handled himself well, though; took the blows to the chin, but remained on his feet. Still, I don't envy you having to face him after that. When's your meeting?"

Simmons dropped his chopsticks on the desk. He pulled up his sleeve and looked at his watch.

"In one hour, twenty-two minutes."

"Good luck."

"Sarah, I need more than luck. Did you get the goods on that company I asked you to look into this morning?"

"Yeah. What's the deal with that?"

"That's my good friend Bruce Coswell's little find in Belize. Seems that Canadian official, Dromel, skipped the snorkeling and went and opened himself a secret bank account under some business name. Unluckily for him, but lucky for us, he chose to open it with Vincent Gratino."

"Who's that?"

"A shyster from New York who was within a hairline of being indicted for racketeering and mail fraud some years back. Can't remember what exactly happened, but Gratino quietly disappeared off the scene after a while.

"Needless to say, Coswell couldn't have been happier to have a reason to come down heavy on Gratino. Threatened to haul his tail stateside to make those old charges stick if Gratino didn't cough up some info. Turns out Dromel netted a tidy sum from that company I asked you about."

Cohen shrugged. "It's a three-year-old shipping outfit owned by another company out of Kazakhstan."

"It's not a Magrelma entity?"

Cohen heard the disappointment in Simmons' voice. "Sorry, but no. The directors are all from former Soviet Union republics. There's nobody there that's remotely on our radar."

Simmons put down the chopsticks and sighed.

"But hang on, let me check something." Cohen tapped on her keyboard.

Simmons looked at his watch again and thought of Hutton. He pushed the sushi tray away. His appetite was gone.

"Check this, Spike," Cohen said after a while. "I think you'll find this interesting. That company ships ores out of the former Soviet republics into China. From their manifests, it looks like sixty to seventy percent of all of their shipments have been for Magrelma subsidiaries."

"That's some strong Magrelma ties."

Cohen nodded. "So those directors could very well be cronies of the Magrelma guys."

"That's a good enough link." Simmons' voice was brighter. "They thought they hid that payment, but they didn't hide it well enough to fool *us*."

His mobile vibrated and he jumped to his feet to fish the

phone out of his pants pocket.

"Simmons," he said into the cellphone.

Cohen watched as Simmons listened to the voice on the other end. The hint of a smile that had been on his face vanished completely.

"What? Damn!" He kicked the chair. "Damn! Damn! And where's the girl now? Okay. Call me as soon as you have an update."

He slipped the phone into his jacket pocket and slammed his right fist into his left palm.

"Damn!"

"What's up, Spike?"

"It's Dromel. He'd been taken to hospital earlier this morning in Trinidad, after the police found him with a gunshot wound."

Cohen raised her eyebrows.

"That's the news I had to share with you. When our guy down there first called me about it, earlier today, I thought, 'Great! Finally we've got a break in this case.' I figured we could use Dromel's weakened state to pump him for information. Find out what's his connection exactly with Syron Lake Resources, and, hopefully, get some answers on how Mahler's death figures into all of this."

Simmons fell silent.

"And?" Cohen said.

"He's dead, Sarah."

"No!"

"Died not too long ago on the operating table."

Chapter 86

The bedroom door of the private suite at the Huxton nightclub flung open and two buxom, young blondes spilled out into the anteroom. Nadia put down the *Hello* magazine she'd been reading, and pulled two thick rolls of fifty-pound notes from her purse. She walked over to the women and shoved the money toward them.

"That bloke's a bloody, rough bastard," the older of the two said.

"But you're well paid for your services," Nadia said dryly.

The older girl snatched the money with a grunt and led her companion toward the door. Nadia marched ahead of them, opened the door and let them out. They walked past two men who stood in the corridor. Nadia nodded to the men and closed the door again.

She found Greene in the bedroom, shirtless and bent over a side table with a straw to his nose. Bruised and still aching from his encounter with Hans Verhoeven, Greene had been in a permanently foul mood. Nadia waited until he had done the line, then approached him, holding out his shirt for him to slip into.

"Nazarov and Lashenko are outside. Said they need to see you urgently."

"Well, tell them to buzz off. I'll see them when I need to speak to them, not the other way around."

"Already told them as much. Nazarov said they're not leaving until they see you."

He yanked the shirt out of her hands and shoved his arms down the sleeves, holding his breath to stifle a groan of pain. Not bothering to button up, he marched to the door and flung it open.

Nazarov, who'd been leaning against the wall, stood upright and pushed past Greene into the room. "It's about time," he said. "We need to talk."

Lashenko followed. Greene glowered in silence.

"We've heard nothing from you, lately." Nazarov's jaw muscles moved up and down as if in a spasm.

Greene said nothing.

"We won't sit around waiting," Nazarov said. "It's time to act. Either you release the funds to our company to get this project going, or–"

"Or what?" Greene snorted.

"Or you can forget about ever touching the files again."

The Russian's mouth snapped shut and his entire body stiffened.

Greene walked around Nazarov toward a decanter that sat on a table, and poured himself a drink.

"I wouldn't be too quick to make threats like that if I were you." Drink in hand, Greene walked back to face Nazarov.

"See, knowing that your friend over there," Greene said, tilting his head toward Lashenko, "knowing he's on the run is very useful to me. If anything happens to that Syron Lake file, I'm going to make damn sure that I find out who's pursuing your friend and give them every scrap of info I have on you. No doubt you two will either be found and strung up in no time, or you'll have to crawl into the ground and remain deep in hiding for the rest of your sorry lives."

Greene stood erect. "I'm in charge here and we'll do this on my terms and on my timetable. Now get the hell out of here."

Greene and Nazarov faced off like two bull moose about to butt heads.

The shrill cry of a ringing phone cut through the chilly air.

Nadia rushed to the sofa and grabbed up the phone from where it lay, then walked to Greene and handed it to him.

He would take this call: the ringtone had been assigned to the Iraq vet he had hired to get that Canadian official under control.

"Yes," Greene snapped. He walked toward the bedroom, then stopped. "He's what? How the hell did that happen? Wait a minute. Just hold on a minute."

Greene spun around and hurled the glass he'd been holding in the direction of the Russians. It whizzed within an inch of Lashenko's face.

"What the hell are you two still doing here? I said get the hell out!"

Nazarov clenched his teeth and stared Greene in a way that made it clear he had murder on his mind. He exhaled heavily, then slowly turned to Lashenko and nodded slightly. The two exited quietly.

Greene kicked over a coffee table on his way to the bedroom, then slammed door behind him.

Nadia heard his muffled shouts as she went about picking up broken glass and straightening the room. The fragments she heard told her all was not well.

Someone who was only supposed to have been threatened had ended up being killed. Some girl saw it, and had been tracked down at an airport, but then lost. A car had been stopped at the Canada/US border and the men in it couldn't complete their mission. Someone else had to take up the slack.

"Get your asses to Florida right now and get that tape, even if you have to kill the guy to get it," Nadia heard Greene say. "And find back that girl and get rid of her. I don't care how you do it. Just do it."

The sound of more crashing glass erupted from behind the door. Nadia sank down onto the plush, leather sofa, picked up the *Hello* magazine again, and flipped through the pages to find where she'd left off reading.

Chapter 87

Robert Hutton stabbed a button on his computer keyboard with his index finger. A darkened screen replaced the CNN website and the director let his head fall back onto the headrest of his chair. He rocked back and forth with his eyes closed.

He thought of the unimaginative sameness of all the news websites. They all ran virtually the identical clip of the morning's Congressional hearing: an angry exchange between him and a first-term senator who'd got under his skin. The Bureau had lost focus and discipline, and perhaps it was time for a change at the top, Senator James B. Lowell had suggested. Perhaps what was needed was new blood that better understood the challenges of the heightened threats faced today in a world overrun by terrorists, Lowell had said.

The young runt was running around in diapers when Hutton had taken up his first diplomatic appointment and began on the long road into the corridors of power. Lowell was just a whippersnapper blowing hot air in order to make the headlines. And yet, the pipsqueak had got to him.

Hutton wasn't thinking of the blow-up in front of the cameras. His thoughts were of the walk away from the hearing room.

He'd felt all eyes on him in the hallway just outside the chamber and he had walked with the erectness his military training had ingrained in him. But further on, away from the busyness and clatter of the hearing room, he'd felt a tightening in his chest, as if a cold hand had gripped his heart and had begun squeezing the dear life out of him.

His attendant, who carried his briefcase, had been too far ahead to hear him gasp for breath. Hutton had staggered past an open door into an empty room. Alone, unseen, he'd allowed himself to groan as he'd clutched his chest and doubled over as searing pain overtook all his senses. He'd sucked in air slowly and, after about a minute, when he'd gotten his breathing under control, he'd stood up again.

The worst had passed. A sharp sensation had lingered in his

chest, but if he walked at the right pace and held himself slightly forward, he could ignore it.

He contemplated revealing all of this to Valerie and was recoiling at the domestic commotion it would stir up when his secretary buzzed him.

Simmons was outside for his appointment.

"Send him in."

As soon as Simmons' foot entered the door, the director started on him.

"Why the devil is this Mahler case not wrapped up yet?"

Simmons walked to the front of the director's desk and looked at the empty chair but was not sure he should sit. "I'm sorry, sir, but–"

"Hold the excuses, Simmons. Excuses just make a man look like he's not up to the job."

Hutton saw Simmons' head snap back as if he'd taken a blow under the chin; but he also saw the defiance in the agent's eyes. He liked that.

He stretched out his hand toward the chair. Simmons sat and the director leaned forward on his desk with clasped hands.

"So where's this investigation at?"

"We have a developing situation, sir. Someone who we thought could maybe help us link Greene or, perhaps, Maitland to William Mahler's killing has himself been killed."

The director pursed his lips, but said nothing.

"He was Canadian. The head of a regulatory panel looking into whether Syron Lake Resources, a company owned by Magrelma, should keep its license to manage a former uranium mine site. The last time Mahler and Greene were in contact, they argued about this. Greene wanted to keep the license, but Mahler wanted to give it up.

"We've discovered the deceased had a secret bank account in Belize, into which he received a suspiciously large payment from a company linked to Magrelma, only a few months ago."

"So he was taking a bribe?"

"Looks very much like it."

"But why would he be killed if he was key to Greene getting his way with the regulators?"

"We have no information as to who killed the official or why."

"So where does that leave you, Simmons? Right back to zero? Is that what you've come into my office to report to me?"

Simmons tugged at his tie.

"There's what seems to be a pattern here," he said. "People associated with Syron Lake are dropping dead or disappearing.

"There's also the case of the site maintenance worker who was responsible for the area where the tailings dam broke, late last year, causing the spill."

"What spill? What does this have to do with your murder in Monaco?"

"This spill gave Magrelma's Canadian subsidiary the pretext for asking that they not give up their license to the site, contrary to Mahler's plans. That worker, who by all accounts was an experienced fisherman, suddenly turned up dead. Drowned while drinking excessively alone in his boat, something no serious fisherman would do.

"We wanted to speak with his nephew, whom he supposedly told his employers he visited the night the dam broke. But that nephew has dropped out of college and, apparently, off the planet. Nobody has any clue as to his whereabouts."

"So, like I said, you're telling me you have nothing."

"Not quite, sir." Simmons eased forward and sat at the edge of the chair.

"That Canadian regulator who was killed had gone down to the Caribbean for a rendezvous with someone from the town of Syron Lake. Someone who had appeared before his panel; a girl he was having an affair with. An operative who had been following the official said the girl was there when he was shot. It's possible she saw the killers."

"And?"

"She's on the run. The operative says she's spooked. He tracked her down at the airport in Trinidad and tried to approach her, but she fled like a scared rabbit."

"So this girl slipped out of our hands, just like that?"

"We believe she's headed for Miami or Ft Lauderdale, but have no clue what route she's taking to get there or when she'll arrive. We had information that she was supposed to have gone through Jamaica, but our later checks revealed she didn't board any Jamaica-bound flights."

Simmons fell silent, then cleared his throat. "We'll need a fair amount of resources to be on the lookout at both airports if we are to pick up her tracks again."

The director took in a deep breath. It momentarily eased that lingering sensation in his chest. He thought about the impertinent senator from that morning, chiding him for running a Bureau with no focus that had lost its way.

He knew deep down that this whole investigation was personal, more than anything.

Yes, William Mahler had been an important, even if undisclosed, conduit for promoting US policy abroad, something he, Hutton, had had some hand in engineering during his days as ambassador to Cairo. And, yes, at the time of his death, Mahler had been an American businessman heading a powerful mining company with operations across the globe. Both of those facts would have been justification to pay attention to his untimely death.

But Hutton knew those reasons had never been part of his consideration of the matter.

This had always been about him and Angela Woodward.

Twenty-five years earlier, he had walked into his New York law office and had heard a woman's laugh outside his door. It had sent a curious, warm sensation right through his body. He'd rested down his briefcase and gone in search of her. He'd heard the laugh again, and when he'd turned a corner, he'd come face to face with her at the photocopying machine, that ethereal creature with sparkling, blue eyes, who, at that moment, had unknowingly taken over possession of some deep, secret corner of his being.

He wasn't a poet, or an artist, or a philosopher. He didn't examine or analyze the thing. All he knew was that he was drawn to this sprite whose eyes were animated by what he came to recognize as an ever upward-moving force within her.

She was an articling student assigned to a rather senior partner, which meant their interactions were minimal. As a new partner who was buried in work and trying to prove his worth to the firm, he could only watch her from a distance. He and Valerie had already had their two boys and were approaching their seventh anniversary. There had been every reason for whatever sentiment that had lodged itself in his being to have dissolved into nothing. And, besides, before she even finished her time at the firm, Angela Woodward had become Angela Roseau.

And yet *something* had lingered there for all these years, despite his efforts to ignore it, or to tell himself, later in life, that a man in his line of business had no space for such whimsical nonsense.

When he had first got wind of the developments in Monaco, his first impulse had been to get all the facts so that he'd be the one to break the news to her. He'd been possessed by the notion that the blow would have been somehow softened for her if word of Mahler's death came from his lips.

And then he'd begun to relish the deepening connection with her that the case had finally brought him. But to what end? Angela hadn't changed and he was still hanging on to unfulfilled desires that stretched back decades.

If Valerie were to learn any of this, she would say he was being just an old, sentimental fool. A fool who'd regressed to the antics and emotions of a lovesick high school teenager.

Maybe he had regressed. What was the saying? Once a man and twice a child? Generations before him had recognized the march that signaled the coming final exit, he thought.

The shortness of breath and the new aches and pains he'd begun to experience since the last summer gave him a chilling reminder of his own mortality. And that made unfulfilled desires take on an importance and urgency that he could not brush aside.

Hutton felt the rookie senator's finger wagging at him.

He looked at Simmons staring at him, waiting for a response.

To hell with it, Hutton thought. He would not let a guy who was in diapers when he was off shaping his country's image abroad browbeat him into submission.

"Simmons," he said, "deploy as many agents as you need. Find that girl, find out what she knows, wrap up this case, and let's look as if we know how to do our damned jobs."

Chapter 88

My flight arrived fifteen minutes early. I jostled my way through a rowdy clutch of teenagers who had been on the plane with me and were now hanging around, waiting for their friends to also disembark.

Parker was just outside the arrivals area. He was easy to spot as his well-toned form stood head and shoulders above almost everyone else. His eyes scanned the scores of people who streamed out the doors.

I walked within inches of him and passed him completely. Then I circled back and tugged on his sleeve.

He spun sharply and his eyes fell first on my pants — hideous golf checks in canary yellow, overlaid with fire-engine red, forest green, and turquoise. Then his gaze moved up to my oversized turquoise blazer with an embroidered, navy blue anchor on the breast pocket. And, finally, he scrutinized the turquoise cap, which also bore the anchor logo and was pulled low on my brow.

"Detective, it's me," I whispered.

"Stella?"

"Yes, still in one piece."

He ran a hand through his hair and laughed. "Where did you find that get-up? Those pants are so ugly, it's scary."

"It did the trick didn't it?" I pushed the cap up a little so we could see each other better. "I walked right in front of you and you had no clue."

"None whatsoever."

"If anyone followed me..."

"Don't worry." He clasped my shoulders and I felt as if electricity shot through my body. "You're with me now. You're safe."

The jolt took me by surprise and made me suddenly confused. Or more confused than I already was.

"I sure hope you're right."

"Besides," Parker said, looking around at the throngs of passengers and those awaiting them, "this is a busy, public place. Nobody would be crazy enough to try anything here."

I shook my head. "Detective, we were in a Carnival party when they shot Ben. You can't get more crowded and public than that. Maybe the people we're dealing with *are* crazy."

He nodded.

"So, you got the box?" I said.

"Yes."

"And the pen with the recording?"

"Yes."

I exhaled in relief. "So where do we find this kid?"

"A trailer park. It'll take two or three hours to get there, according to the traffic. I've rented a car."

"Well, let's get going, then." With my head still bent, I headed in the direction of the exit.

"We need to make a couple of stops," Parker said. "I need to pick up something downtown."

"Can't we just go straight to the trailer park?"

"This is important, Stella."

I pursed my lips.

"It'll only be quick stops, I promise."

I shrugged.

"The first thing I need to get is some summer threads," Parker said. "I'd die outside in these winter clothes." He glanced at my outfit. "And we need to get you into something decent."

His tone of good-natured mockery made me smile. It was the first time I'd experienced anything approaching mirth in what felt like ages.

The smile was short-lived, though.

First, I heard a great deal of commotion — male voices shouting out names and the command "Catch!" and female voices screaming "No."

Then I felt a powerful blow to my back. It knocked the wind out of me and sent me catapulting to the floor.

My cap flew off my head and my hair came cascading down. The world went black and the next thing I knew was that two muscular teenagers were piled on top of me and I was kissing a tan-colored, leather football.

Parker yanked the teens off me and shoved them aside.

"Idiots," he shouted.

"Sorry." Three other teens came and huddled over me. "We were just foolin' around. You alright?"

Parker picked up the football and slammed it into the chest of one of the teens. "Get out of here," he shouted. They wasted no time obeying.

Parker helped me to my feet.

"You okay?"

I nodded, although I felt groggy from the impact.

As I bent over to retrieve the cap, I had a sensation of being watched. Looking up, I noticed two men in suits staring directly at me.

Probably just curious about the commotion, I told myself. Then I saw them walking briskly toward me.

"Detective, I think I might have a tail."

"Where?"

I pulled the cap down on my head and turned my back to the men.

"Directly behind me. Two suits headed this way."

"Recognize any of them?"

"Never seen them before. They're dressed neater than the men who shot Ben."

"So you're thinking they're with some kind of service, then?"

I nodded. "Sent by Peabody. Are they still coming this way?"

I didn't have to wait for an answer. Parker grabbed me by the arm and started toward the exit.

We picked up the pace and I looked behind; I caught the men matching our trot.

"They're catching up to us," I said.

Parker curled his arm around my waist.

"Okay, run," he said.

We elbowed through the crowds, knocking over luggage and hearing more than a few curses hurled our way. Backward glances told me the suits were gaining on us.

Once we hit outside, the air felt as if an oven blast after the air conditioned airport. Parker grabbed my hand.

"This way."

We darted across the road, bringing a taxi to a screeching, honking halt.

We had barely crossed to the pavement on the other side when the men came out the door after us.

I held on to Parker's hand for dear life and ran as fast as I could. My lungs felt as if they were ready to fall out, and I had to give it my all to keep up with his long, powerful legs.

We hurtled past acres of cars with the suits bearing down on us.

Just when I felt my legs would give out, Parker let go of my hand.

"Get in," he shouted as we neared a white sedan.

The doors unlocked with a click and the lights blinked as Parker pressed the remote.

I tugged at the handle and flung myself into the seat, slamming the door shut.

Within a second, Parker was in the driver's seat. He turned the key in the ignition.

Nothing.

I saw the men just a few cars away, racing toward us.

Parker pounded his fist on the steering wheel.

"Come on!" he shouted.

He turned the ignition again. The engine, whimpered, then rumbled. Parker slammed down on the gas pedal and the engine roared as we screeched off, just as the men in suits arrived. They could only thump their fists on the trunk of the car as Parker and I sped away.

Chapter 89

We stopped at a small tourist shop that was chock-full of trinkets which had the word "Florida" emblazoned on them, but carried labels in fine print that read "Made in China." Parker led the way to the back, where there were t-shirts and bikinis and the sort of brightly-colored clothes that only tourists who were giddy with the heat and the excitement of being on holiday could possibly deem fit to adorn their bodies.

He emerged from the changing room in jeans and a flaming orange short-sleeved shirt festooned with blue palm fronds.

I'd ditched the corporate swag and appeared in khaki shorts and a white, long-sleeved, muslin bodice.

Parker's eyes started from my ankles and slowly worked their way up, until they met my eyes. He smiled and nodded approvingly. I bristled at the inspection.

"Get a couple of changes of clothes," he said. "Hopefully we can find the kid tonight and we won't have to be here longer than a day. But you never know."

He paid and we were on our way.

"How much do I owe you?" I said as I buckled up.

"Don't even think about that."

"No, really. I'll pay you back for the clothes."

"Forget about it. It's nothing."

As he checked his mirrors and turned on the indicator, I realized he didn't give it a second thought.

I had not a cent in my fanny pack, but I still had my credit card. He didn't have to pay for my new clothes. It was a nice gesture. But no man had ever bought me clothes apart from my father and grandfather, and even they hadn't done so after I'd hit my teens. So the cop's gesture left me feeling a little uneasy.

I wanted to be able to simply accept his kindness. But I was still on edge and a little voice in my head warned me not to be too easily won over and be lulled into what could possibly be a false sense of security.

That niggling concern remained that if Parker was tied in with Demetriou, and if the mayor was hooked up with the mining company responsible for the spill, then I would have only jumped out of the frying pan and right into the fire.

Everything he'd done so far made me feel I should trust this cop. And I hoped that *I*, and not the suspicious little voice in my head, was right.

"Can I ask you something?" I said after a while.

"Sure."

"Why are you here?"

"Come again?"

"Why are you doing this?"

He turned his head and eyed me for a while, then focused on the road again. "Well, I was minding my own business, enjoying my sleep when, in the wee hours of the morning, I got a call asking me to get involved. Anything about this sound vaguely familiar?"

"I know I asked for your help. But why did you respond?"

"My vacation starts in a couple of days. Didn't have anything planned, except for some fishing and then heading back down to Toronto to visit family. I figured I might as well call in sick and start my vacation early, 'cause this would be a whole lot more exciting than hearing about Aunt Bertha's bunions."

He chuckled.

I frowned.

"Okay, let's try this one," he said. "I'm a sucker for a damsel in distress."

I pursed my lips and turned away from him.

"Hey, you need to loosen up, lady," he said as he gunned through an intersection on amber.

"Detective, this may be fun and games for you; but while you're getting your jollies off this, I think it's deadly serious. And I'm scared. A few hours ago, I saw someone I love get shot, and I left him bleeding in a ravine."

"Fun and games for me?" Parker huffed. "I think I know even better than you how dangerous this situation is."

After racing on in silence for a while, he spoke in a softer voice. "The trick is, though, that you can't let any of this get to you. If you fall into the trap where all you can think about is how nervous and scared you are, then whoever you're up against is controlling your head. And all you'll be doing is reacting when they push your buttons.

"You need to lighten up, loosen up. Stay in control of your own mind. That way you'll remain alert enough to stay one step ahead, always planning your next move."

He was probably right. No, he was right.

But I hadn't been angling for a lecture on crisis thinking. I'd been trying to weasel out of him whether he had agreed to help me find Jacques out of genuine concern over my and the kid's predicament. Or whether he was here doing Mayor Demetriou's — and ultimately Syron Lake Resources' — bidding.

I decided to let the matter rest there. I was tired, and hungry, and still shaken, and there was no way I could have handled this search for Jacques Tremblay on my own.

Even if this cop was tied in with the enemy, I needed him at this moment. I would just have to remain wary and alert and be prepared to fight or flee if or when he dropped his hero act.

Parker drove down a litter-strewn street in a rough section of Fort Lauderdale. Stores were shuttered and graffiti was scrawled all over the walls. Derelicts shuffled along aimlessly as darkness fell.

He drove to the back of a bar where the neon sign was missing several letters and the exterior paint was peeling. Although the sun had disappeared, Parker unfolded a sunshade across the windscreen. After he got out of the car, he whipped around to my side and opened my door. Without saying a word, he led the way in by the back door.

The bartender, who wore a wife-beater, sauntered over to us. Every visible part of his upper body, except for his face, was festooned with tattoos.

"Want anything?" Parker said.

I shook my head. The bartender shrugged and walked away.

"Okay, stay here," Parker said. "I need to go to the men's room."

Before I could say anything, he disappeared around a corner.

The small barroom was dimly lit. Three shirtless men bearing a general look of stupor sat at a table cluttered with about a dozen beer bottles. In the middle of the room, an elderly man kept his head bent and his eyes closed; his long white beard rested on his ample stomach, heaving and falling with his every breath.

A few feet from me, a grizzled figure in shorts and an unbuttoned shirt leaned against the bar counter. Suddenly, he raised his right hand and waved a finger in the air. "The government!" he shouted.

The bartender, who now had his back to the counter as he watched a ball game on a large screen, paid no attention. The grizzled figure let his hand fall back to the counter with a thud and curled his fingers around the beer bottle before him.

My immediate impulse was to dash back out the door. I peered in the direction where Parker had disappeared. From the opposite corner, a sunburned woman with unkempt, dirty-blonde hair came swaggering into the room as she whistled a tune. She wore a bikini top and denim shorts that covered very little. Her eyes widened as she saw me.

"What's the matter sweetie?" She stopped and stood before me with her hands on her hips. "You look like you're lost or something."

"I'm fine, thanks."

"You sure? Larry's not ignoring you now, is he?" Without waiting for a reply, she shouted to the bartender, "Hey, Larry, get this girl a drink!"

Larry seemed too engrossed in his game to hear anything.

With sudden ferocity, the woman screamed, "Hey, Larry! Larry!"

"It's okay," I said. "I really don't want anything. I'm just waiting on someone."

The woman shrugged. "Well, if you change your mind and Larry's ignoring you, just let me know. It's not such a bad place. You just have to know how to demand some respect around here."

She strode over to the shirtless men and shoved one of them on the shoulder. He caught her around the waist and she fell into his lap, cackling.

The grizzled man at the counter shot his arm into the air again and yelled, "The government!"

I turned to look at the back door again, and as I did, I felt someone touch my arm. I jumped.

"Okay, let's get out of here," Parker said as he walked at a clip toward the door.

He didn't let up his pace, and jumped into the driver's seat as soon as he reached the car. By the time I got to it, he was leaning over on the passenger side. He popped open the door for me.

"Hop in." He wore a satisfied smile.

I watched him nonchalantly fold away the sun visor and toss it in the back.

"You sure know how to pick your pit stops," I said as we turned the corner and the worn-out front of the bar came into view.

"What? You didn't like the joint?" He laughed.

"Are you just trying to get on my nerves? Because if you are, you're doing a great job."

"There's method to my madness," he said. He pointed his chin toward the glove compartment. "Open it."

I squeezed the latch and pulled down the tray. The matte, black handle and the long, silver barrel looked dangerous even just sitting there. A chill went down my spine and I slammed the compartment shut.

"Do you have a license for that?"

"No."

"But you're a cop. I mean, come on, Detective, how could you have that in here?"

"Well, let's get a couple of things straight. First, cut it with the 'detective,' okay? My name is Paul. If that's too personal for you, then call me Parker.

"And second, as I told you before, I think I understand better than you do what level of danger we might be in for. I got that piece *because* I'm a cop. I've spent my whole life dealing with bad guys, both military and civilian, and believe me, you don't want to mess with them unless you make damn sure you can protect yourself."

We rode in silence. I guess he saw my pursed lips and squinted eyes.

"Listen, Stella. I haven't had a chance to tell you yet, but when I went to Dromel's house, I was not the only one there looking for the tape and Jacques' address. Someone beat me to it."

"But I thought you said you got the cigar box."

"I did. But two men got to the house before me. I think only one of them went inside. A hulk of a guy. Trashed the place completely. It looked like a tornado passed through there."

"Someone was inside Ben's house?"

"The goon ripped everything apart. Never thought to move the fridge, though. Clever hiding place. I'll give Dromel that."

I exhaled. "Good, so if they never got to the box with Jacques' address, at least he's safe for the moment."

"Yes. But there's a problem. I believe those guys got a letter with Jacques' last address."

"Not the one he's at now, that we're going to?"

"No. But neighbors know far more about you than you could ever imagine. And they talk. If those men make a few inquiries here and there at Jacques' former address, it's quite possible they'll end up exactly where we're headed."

"So where exactly are we headed, Detec–"

Parker hemmed and cast a sideways glance at me.

"I mean, where are we headed, Paul?"

"Campground, a good few miles south. Jacques' a big boy out on his own. I doubt he'll be in bed by the time we arrive."

I nodded. "So what's the plan when we find him? How do we get him to hand over the video?"

"We'll figure that out when we get there. Let's find him first."

We rode on in silence, leaving behind the office buildings, hotels and shops of the downtown area. Now, way past a string of strip malls and innumerable motels, the highway was lined on either side only by dark bushes.

"So, what exactly is on that recording with Ben and the prime minister?" I said after some time.

I'd been waiting for him to volunteer the information; to even place the box he'd retrieved from under Dromel's fridge into my hands. I wavered between feeling brave and being sassy with this cop, and feeling my old mousey self, uncertain about how far I could push. I was also still coming up somewhat short when it came to trust, but at this point, what choice did I have but to rely on him?

"An argument over Syron Lake. Peabody was–" Parker pumped the brakes and the car jerked before slowing down. "What's this?"

Blue and red lights flashed up ahead.

"Looks like we have a road block," he said.

He stopped about five cars behind a line of three squad cars parked across the road. Half a dozen uniformed cops stood talking to each other or into their walkie-talkies.

"Stay here." Parker flung open the door and walked over to the officers.

After a lot of nodding and pointing, he returned and dropped himself back into the driver's seat.

"Nasty crash further down this way," he said. "Teens drinking and drag-racing, apparently."

He turned the ignition and put the car into reverse.

"There's no way this road's going to be cleared anytime soon."

"So will the detour cost us a lot of time?"

"There isn't one. What should have been it is closed for repairs. This is the only route, at least it used to be until half an hour ago."

"So what now?"

"We have to turn back, spend the night in a motel and try again first thing in the morning. And hope those guys from the airport don't catch up to us."

"Or beat us to Jacques. What do you think they'd do to him if they found him first?"

"Let's not even contemplate that," Parker said.

I thought of Dromel, and of what Parker said the men had done to his place. I cast my eyes on the glove compartment, and I felt a sense of relief knowing what lay in there.

Chapter 90

Parker rolled into the parking lot of the first motel we came to and killed the engine.

"Home for the night," he said.

"Kinda rough isn't it?"

"It's either this or we drive another hour or more in search of something fancier for you."

He was smiling but the comment riled me. "Are you trying to suggest I'm some kind of prima donna?"

"I'm not trying to suggest anything. I was just saying–"

"Well *I* was simply stating a fact. This place is a dump. But if it's where we have to stay so we don't lose any time in the morning, then so be it."

Parker leaned over and stretched his hand toward the glove compartment. I didn't want to see or know what he was going to do with what he had hidden in there. I jumped out of the car and headed toward the door with the small, neon "Office" sign.

As darkness had descended, I had found myself growing more and more uneasy about being confined in the car all alone with Detective Sergeant Paul Parker.

It was not that he had done anything to make me felt unsafe. It was just the opposite, actually.

He had been a perfect gentleman. And he fit the role of hero completely, what with his imposing physique and his decisive actions, like pulling those rowdy teenage boys off me at the airport.

The trouble was that I had found my eyes returning to that physique altogether too frequently. They wandered to his muscular chest; scanned the length of his strong, aquiline nose; and lingered far too long on the short, dark, silky hairs on his arms.

My response to Parker shocked and embarrassed me. Every time my glance strayed over to the man at the wheel beside me, I would feel a guilty twinge at being disloyal to Dromel.

And then I would remember that Dromel had betrayed me by not recusing himself and lying to me about it. Everything he had said and done in our relationship had been illegal and our entire connection stank of scandal.

And then I would get the faint whiff of blood, Dromel's blood on his fingers, and I would see his form in the darkness, leaning weakly against the rock wall of the canal, groaning in pain as he clutched his side, and it was all I could do to hold back the tears.

To put it plainly, I was a complete and total mess, and I was grateful that Parker had shown not much inclination to talk for most of the drive.

Ray's Roadside Haven was a narrow, tumbledown building that seemed to stretch as far as the eye could see. A sad collection of rusting and dented clunkers sat in the parking lot, which was bordered on one side by a row of huge metal bins. The air smelled of rotting garbage.

The scrolling LED sign at the entrance of the compound said "Free Internet in Rooms, Free Computer for Guest Use." I'd been disappointed to discover that Parker's cell phone was a simple clamshell that was useless for getting online. Even if our haven for the night was a fleapit, I was glad that at least I would finally be able to do a search for news about Dromel here.

Just as I reached the door, Parker, whose long stride had apparently allowed him to catch up with me, pulled it open and waited for me to enter.

He tapped the domed bell on the empty counter, but nothing happened after the ring echoed in the dingy room. He rang three more times and we waited in silence.

Finally, a rotund man in pajama bottoms and a thin, white vest that covered only two-thirds of his stomach, shuffled out from behind a door. He yawned and scratched his gray stubble. A tiny woman with a shock of white hair followed him into the office, leaning heavily on a cane. With much effort, she placed herself on a chair and propped both hands atop the cane.

"Yes?" the man said, rubbing his eyes.

"A room with two single beds," Parker said.

I saw the man crane his neck to look past Parker and directly at me. The man sighed and shook his head as he looked across at the old woman, as if to say, "Yeah right. Who do they think they're fooling?"

He ran a fat thumb down the motel's register.

"You can have Room 19," he said.

I turned away and tuned out as Parker checked us in. We hadn't discussed this, but, yes, it would be best for us to take one room. The motel was creepy enough for me to feel uncomfortable in a room by myself. But we also had the men at the airport to worry about. What if they had picked back up our trail?

Yes, it was better to spend the night in the same room with this detective whom I hardly knew — with him and that thing from the glove compartment that I didn't want to know too much about.

Parker finished checking us in and passed me on the way to the door. I turned back to the man behind the counter.

"There's a computer hooked up to the Internet in the room, right?" I said.

"This ain't the Hilton, lady."

"But that's what your sign promises."

"What sign?"

"At the entrance."

"You misread, lady. Ain't no sign that says you get a computer in your room with Internet. Bring your own computer; you can use WiFi in your room. Otherwise, there's a computer over there."

Barely lifting his arm, he pointed to a table in the corner. The dust-encrusted, gray box, which looked like a relic from the eighties, was plugged in, but the screen was blank. I moved the mouse, hit some keys, and reached back to fiddle with the power switch.

"This doesn't work," I said.

The man shrugged. "Like I said, this ain't the Hilton."

He turned and walked away and I felt all hope of getting online to search for news about Dromel being yanked away from me.

"Well, if you can't provide the amenities you promise, then you can't be charging the full price," I said, hardly knowing what words escaped my lips.

The man spun around and glowered at me. He jabbed a stubby finger in my direction and shouted, "Don't you come here telling me how to run–"

Parker was back at the counter in a flash. "Hey, buddy, don't talk to this lady like that."

The old woman whacked the man in the leg with her cane.

"Perry, how many times do I have to tell you not to lose your temper with the guests?"

"But she's–"

"But me no buts." The old woman pounded on the floor with her cane. "Do I have to knock this into your thick skull every day? The customer is king. They could be pigs and all, but you have to treat the customers like kings. Let her have Ray's old laptop for the night."

The man disappeared through the door and returned with a clunky device and a power cord. He faced Parker, ignoring me.

"Here," he said. "Make sure you return it when you check out, otherwise you'll have to pay for it."

In the room, I sat at the tiny, rickety table beside what we'd agreed would be Parker's bed. The dinosaur of a laptop took forever to show the websites for the Trinidad newspapers. All I wanted to do was check whether there was anything about Dromel, before letting my exhausted, jet-lagged body collapse in my bed for the night.

Parker had disappeared into the bathroom to shave, much to my relief. The room was so small, two people could hardly move an inch without bumping into each other.

When the pages finally loaded, my eyes caught the headlines and my heart slammed against my ribs. My jaw dropped, and, in reflex, my hand flew up and covered my mouth.

Parker entered the room. "I'm thinking we can leave around four, maybe four-thirty."

I turned and saw him standing just outside the bathroom, shirtless, holding a razor in one hand and lathering his cheeks with the other hand.

Rage swelled within me. I had no control over myself. My hand grabbed the nearest pillow and flung it, missing Parker by an inch.

"Put your clothes on," I yelled.

Parker reeled back with wide eyes. "What's up with you?"

I stood up, and the chair tumbled over. I said nothing, but began pacing the tiny space between the bed and the wall, my arms folded as I bit my lip.

Parker disappeared into the bathroom, then re-emerged, buttoning up his shirt.

"What's the matter?"

I stared at the dingy carpet. My face was wet and I could see the drops of tears forming a dark spot at my feet. My entire body trembled.

"Ben's dead."

I buried my face in my hands. The noise that rose from my throat was like the wail of a wounded animal.

Parker was suddenly at my side. His arm curled around my back. I let myself collapse into his chest as I sobbed.

We stood like that for some time, Parker saying nothing, just keeping his hand lightly on my back and bearing my weight.

Eventually, I found my legs again and eased away.

"You okay?" Parker held me by the shoulders.

I nodded.

He took my hands and led me to the foot of my bed and sat me down. He sat on his bed, with my hands in his.

"Look," he said softly, "I'm sorry he's dead. I realize he meant a lot to you."

I exhaled and chewed back a new flood of tears.

Parker held my hands more firmly. "You have to understand, though, that Dromel's death makes the situation more dangerous. This has turned into a homicide and the stakes are higher now for those behind it. They'll probably stop at nothing to get any evidence that would incriminate them."

I nodded.

Parker got up and peeled back the cover of my bed. "You need to get some rest. We'll leave as early as possible in the morning."

I felt numb, dead inside. I didn't resist as Parker slipped off my shoes, led me by the hand, and tucked me in bed.

Chapter 91

It was still dark when Parker loaded up the car with our belongings and checked out while I waited in the passenger seat.

Between tortured memories of my last moments with Benoit Dromel and a rock hard, musty mattress, I'd hardly got any sleep.

After hours of tossing and turning, and shifting my face to avoid the damp spots on the pillow formed by my tears, I'd actually been relieved when I'd felt Parker's warm hand cup my shoulder and shake me gently.

I got out of bed in a rage. Those scum had killed Dromel. They had done so to keep a company's misdeeds in Syron Lake secret. I was determined to get the evidence that would bury them.

Every time the image of Dromel's ashen face flashed across my mind, I felt as if I would collapse. But we had a job to do. I needed to pull myself together; I didn't need Parker to tell me that. I breathed deeply, slowly, and pursed my lips to keep my emotions sealed inside. By the time he settled into the driver's seat, I would have everything under control, I told myself.

Silhouetted by the rectangular glow of the office door, Parker walked briskly toward the car, scanning the car park.

He rested the motel bill and some papers between the driver and passenger seats and inserted the key. He turned to face me. I turned away and stared out the window. The corners of my mouth were tense and contorted.

"You alright?" he said as the engine rumbled to life.

I nodded slightly.

Out on the flat, empty highway, Parker floored the brakes and we drove in silence for about ten minutes.

"So when are we going to talk about the recording?" I managed to say, finally.

I wanted to make up for letting myself down a few minutes earlier, by letting him see how much I was still affected by news of Dromel's death. How could I not be? Despite the anger that burned inside me at his betrayal in not recusing himself from the Syron Lake file as he'd promised, he was still the man who, up until the events of the previous morning, I'd hoped I would grow old with.

Parker kept his eyes fixed on the road as he sped along at almost double the limit.

"Did you hear me?" I said.

"What?"

"The recording that you found at Ben's place. When were you planning to tell me what's on it?"

He raised his eyebrows, as if surprised at the sudden harshness in my voice.

"Under your seat," he said.

I switched on the overhead light, then felt under my seat and pulled out a cigar box. Inside, a slim pen and a small tape recorder sat on a pile of papers.

"The pen is what he used to make the recording," Parker said. "Didn't know how to operate it until I searched online at a kiosk at the airport. I bought a microcassette recorder and transferred the conversation onto it so we wouldn't have to fiddle too much with the pen."

Holding the recorder to my ear, I cranked up the volume.

"There's airport noise in the background," Parker said. "Couldn't avoid that. But the conversation's clear enough."

I closed my eyes and concentrated on the voices on the recording.

"Wow!" I hit the rewind button. "Doesn't sound good for the prime minister."

"It's pure BS."

"What?"

"Sure, Peabody made a complete ass of himself," Parker said, "and that could do serious damage to him if it gets out. But Dromel was just blowing hot air."

"Excuse me?"

"It was all just an act on Dromel's part, Stella. This business about resisting Peabody's request on behalf of the company was just for show."

"You don't understand what you're talking about, Detective. Ben was prepared to stand up against that company. He spoke out publicly at the hearing about how they mishandled the spill."

"Listen, the name's 'Paul,' okay? Believe me, it looks to me like both Peabody and Dromel were batting for this Syron Lake company. Except Dromel wouldn't let on, even when confronted by the prime minister."

"You really don't know what you're talking about."

"Have a look at that bankbook and those papers."

The small, brown bankbook had one entry — a deposit with lots of zeros. The papers revealed the account belonged to an offshore company registered in Belize.

"I checked the dates while I was at the airport," Parker said. "The company was formed and the money deposited shortly after the spill in Syron Lake. Shortly after Dromel would have been appointed to head up this panel to decide on the company's fate."

"Could be pure coincidence."

"Don't be blind, Stella. This is how things are done. What other plausible explanation would there be for a commissioner of a nuclear regulatory body in Ottawa to suddenly establish an offshore company and be paid one hundred and fifty thousand dollars by someone or some company that provides only an account number and no name on the wire transfer?"

"International consultancy work. For which he didn't want to pay tax."

"You're clutching at straws. Benoit Dromel was not the knight in shinning armor that you thought him to be. No wonder he went to lengths to hide that little cigar box. It's a testament to his total lack of integrity."

Parker shook his head.

"See those pills?" he said.

I fished out the small, clear plastic packet.

"OxyContin," he said. "Very addictive. If he got it with a legit prescription, there'd be no need to stuff it under a fridge would there?"

I couldn't say a word.

I took a photo out of the box. It was one of Dromel and me, cheek to cheek. He'd snapped it himself in his living room by setting the timer on his digital camera shortly after I'd arrived for the weekend. He'd printed it out and stuck it to his fridge with a magnet, telling me it would allow him to have me with him on Valentine's Day, even if I had to return home a day early.

"Know where I found that?" Parker said.

"On the fridge at his place. He took this picture of us when–"

"Sorry, Stella. Your picture was in that box, *under* the fridge."

My jaw dropped.

Parker shook his head. "A different photo was on the fridge, held there by a magnet. I put it in the box. It's the one with Dromel and the woman with long, auburn hair. Not the other one, mind you, of him with the older woman sporting the blonde bob."

I lifted some papers and stared at the two photos lying face up at the bottom of the box. I could feel anger rising as blood rushed to my brain.

"Look," Parker said, "I pass no judgment on your involvement with Dromel, but he was a bad character."

He picked up printed sheets that he'd placed between our seats earlier. "I'm sorry, but you need to read the latest updates from the Trinidad newspapers. I got the manager to print them off for me this morning."

Rage rattled around inside me, but I managed to keep my hand steady as I took the pages from him.

Parker spoke as my eyes ran across the sheets. "One paper describes the woman who flew in from Paris to collect the body as his wife. The other calls her his common-law partner. Either way, same thing. This guy didn't seem to have one drop of morality in his body."

I tossed the pages over my shoulder.

"Will you just shut up," I shouted.

"Huh?"

"Have you no decency?"

"What?"

"Didn't your mother teach you not to speak ill of the dead?"

I dumped the bankbook, papers, and the recording equipment back into the cigar box and snapped the lid shut. I bent forward and shoved the box back under my seat.

Parker looked down at me with confusion written all over his face. "I was simply trying to show that the scumbag was not worth your tears, and that makes me a louse?"

I sat back up, folded my arms and tuned my head away from him.

Under his breath, he mumbled, "How irrational can a woman be?"

The dark forms of trees and bushes rushed by in a blur as we continued on like this for several minutes. Apparently irritated by the icy silence, Parker noisily turned a knob on the radio. He settled on a rock station, catching the tail end of screeching electric guitars. An announcer's deep-bass voice warned of inclement weather later in the day, and then segued into a stream of commercials.

Parker grumbled and attacked the radio again. He switched through several channels, then stopped when a familiar refrain came through the speakers. Jan Arden's unmistakable voice cried out, "*Could I be your girl?*"

My heart flipped.

The man at the wheel beside me knew only that I liked Arden's music. He had no idea what that particular song meant in relation to the man about whom we'd just fought.

This was *our* song.

Or, at least, it was the soundtrack to which I'd fallen completely under Benoit Dromel's spell.

My mind traveled back to late autumn. The air had grown chilly and the trees outside my window had turned into barren trunks and branches. Yet, inside, with the volume of the computer turned up, I'd danced to this song, warmed by the hope of love that blossomed in my heart.

Those eyes. Hazel and sparkling. The intensity of the desire they had communicated. That smile. His quiet, yet unquestionable control of the hearing. He had come to my town and had taken charge to such an extent that even Mayor Demetriou had to shut up and pay attention when Dromel banged his gavel. The hero that he had been, taking down company lawyers and speaking up for us, the community — speaking up for me.

And then there were those long walks I'd taken through the woods, bundled up against the approaching winter, remembering his wink, and wondering if it would ever be possible to be with him....

It all came rushing back, flooding my heart and my eyes.

When we'd finally gotten together at his place, he had abandoned all urbanity, and surrendered himself totally to the sensuous journey on which his eyes had beckoned me, long before, in the Syron Lake community center. He'd been sensuous yet gentle, and as I had lain in his arms, sweaty and exhausted, our heads sharing the same pillow, I had dreamed that it could all last forever.

Hot tears poured down my cheeks, and I shifted my body away from Parker, as far as the seatbelt allowed.

It could not be possible that the man from these memories was the scoundrel Parker had described.

It could not.

And those other women whose pictures were in the cigar box.... Surely they were from his past. He could not have been with them at the same time that he had been with me.

The thought that it was otherwise made my blood curdle — then boil. I was thankful that concerns about pregnancy had led to us being triply cautious, which would have protected me in this scenario. But, yuck!

I could have strangled Benoit T. Dromel if he had appeared in front of me just then.

But he was gone.

I would never, ever see him again. That realization, the finality of it all, felt like a stab to the heart.

A jingle for a furniture store broke in even before the last strains of Arden's song played. It jolted me out of my thoughts. And it irritated Parker, apparently.

He switched off the radio with a loud click.

We drove the rest of the way in silence.

Chapter 92

It was four in the morning and nothing stirred in this stretch of Daytona Beach. It was on the mangy side of town where weeds were more common than front lawns, and termites staked their claim as the true owners of almost all man-made structures.

Williams sat in the stolen black sedan parked at the edge of the gravel road with the engine idling quietly. He kept a tight grip on the steering wheel, ready for any orders to make a quick getaway.

The lights were off in the closest house, which was set back deep in the overgrown yard. A nearer building, a small garage converted into a studio apartment, was also in darkness.

Williams squinted and tried to follow Quinn's and Young's movements as they walked briskly to the garage. He smiled at the thought that the little twerp who had given him a hard stare when he'd trailed him along the river path in Ottawa would soon get a rude awakening.

At the garage, Quinn clasped the knob of the steel door as Young stood erect, holding his Colt pointed skyward. The handle didn't budge.

There was no window at the front of the structure. Quinn motioned Young to follow, and they crouched around to the side, and then to the back.

They mashed down wild shrubs, and Young cursed under his breath when he stumbled on a pile of discarded cans.

They came upon a wooden door at the back, which gave a little as Quinn pulled on it. He motioned Young to return to the front to guard the entrance. Then he whipped out his Glock.

With one powerful blow of his shoulder, he broke the door open.

He pelted into the room, and steadied himself into a squat. Swinging left, then right, he trained the muzzle on all corners of the dark room as his eyes searched for a stirring figure.

All he could make out was a rumpled bed, a bedside table with a lamp and another table with a microwave, surrounded by chairs. At the side of his eye, he caught sight of a curtain. He ripped it aside and pointed his gun at nothing more than a toilet bowl, a sink, and a shower stall.

He strode to the front door, where he heard Young's feet shuffle on the gravel outside.

"He ain't here," Quinn said, as he swung open the door and tucked the gun into the holster under his arm.

Young entered, cursing under his breath. "So what's the call now?"

He had just closed his mouth when a burst of light blinded him. He held up his hand to his eyes, but it could not shield him from the blow that crashed down on his nose.

He cried out and fell to his knees.

Quinn spun around and lunged forward, easily taking down the assailant.

A flashlight slipped out of the attacker's hand and rolled into a corner. It spread a wide circle of light, which showed Quinn that he had his arms wrapped around an almost skeletal, bald, wrinkled old man, who wore only pajama bottoms.

The trembling creature grunted as he wriggled and tried to raise a baseball bat aloft.

Quinn eased the man backward and allowed him to drop his buttocks on the bed. With a tug, he took possession of the bat, and then curved an arm around the old man's shoulder.

"You okay there now, Pops?" Quinn whispered.

Young held his bleeding nose and got to his feet. He marched toward the bed. "What the hell?"

With a wave of his hand, Quinn stopped Young in his tracks. "Shut up and clean yourself up."

Quinn turned his attention back to the pensioner.

"Sorry to give you a scare there, Pops," he said. "We're not burglars. We came to pay a surprise visit to a friend. Except *we* got a surprise, 'cause he ain't here."

The old man looked Quinn and Young up and down, his mouth hanging open as he gasped for breath.

"He told us he lives here," Quinn said. "We were in the neighborhood and thought we'd say hi."

The old man took in shorter, more controlled breaths, but continued to stare wordlessly at the two men.

"A Canadian fella," Quinn said. "About eighteen, nineteen.

Down here all by himself. I mean, he's so far from home, we thought it'd do him some good for us to drop in when he least expected it. Give him some laughs. He's that kind of guy, you know. He'd appreciate something like that."

"Sorry," the old man said, finally. "Thought you fellas came to raid the place. The neighbor half a mile down had a couple break-ins, last month, and I'm here all alone. Gotta defend myself, you know."

Quinn nodded.

"As for your friend, you're too late."

"What do you mean?"

"Seemed like a nice kid, but he's gone."

"Gone?"

"Yeah, just upped and left three weeks ago."

Quinn and Young exchanged glances.

"Did he say where he was going?" Quinn said.

"That's what had me madder than a bull seeing red. He just skipped. Sure he'd paid up for up to the end of last month, but he had to give me two months' notice. 'Stead he just took off, only leaving a note saying he was outta here."

"Any idea where he went?"

The man cackled, his whole bare torso jerking with the effort. "Sure do. I seen service in too many wars to let a young mongrel like that get the better of this old soldier."

Young stepped closer to the bed and growled, "Well, where is he, old man?"

Quinn's eyes narrowed into a penetrating stare. He motioned Young to back off.

"You found out where our friend got to?" Quinn said.

"You betcha. Saw when he brought home a tent, and a sleeping bag, and other stuff a few days before he took off. Didn't take a genius to figure out what he was up to. Still, took me three days of driving 'round in my pickup to every campground within two hundred miles. And, boy, was he surprised as hell when I collared him. Got every red cent he owed me, though." The old man snuffed and rubbed his stubble. "Must have burned up half that money in gas, but it was worth it. No, can't let them young'uns feel they can take advantage of the old soldier."

From the darkness, Young grumbled, "Time's a-wasting, old man."

Quinn ignored Young.

Looking him in the eye, Quinn nodded and smiled at the frail figure next to him on the bed. "So where did you track him down to? Where can we find our friend?"

"Heron's Point, straight down the highway. Gotta miss maybe ten, fifteen exits, but the turn-off's right there after you cross a big, ol' rusty bridge. But yer hav' to look good, otherwise you'll miss it. Nice place too. One of them fancy, new private campgrounds. That was my mistake. I went after him first in the state and federal parks."

Quinn stood up. He rested a hand on the old man's shoulder.

"Hey, thanks, Pop," he said. "You've been a real help. Sorry about the scare you got earlier."

The old man raised his hand and nodded. He seemed suddenly aware of his half nakedness and began to hug and stroke himself, passing thin, veined hands up and down sagging, wrinkled elbows.

Quinn stepped away from the bed and walked toward the door.

The old man didn't see Young's movements in the darkness, and so, he wasn't aware that a Colt targeted his chest.

The single shot exploded; the figure on the bed tumbled forward, crashing onto the floor.

Young strode forward and bent over the body. No sign of breathing.

"Now you won't be telling any tales about whacking what you thought was a burglar with your baseball bat, will you now, old soldier?" he said.

He straightened up, found the torch with his foot and kicked it into the corner. The room went dark, except for a tiny circle of light where the torch touched the wall.

"Let's get out of this dump," Young said.

Chapter 93

We approached a rusting bridge that arched into the dark, early morning sky.

"I think the turn-off is somewhere around here," Parker said.

We zoomed through the metal structure, which clanged and creaked under the weight of the rented car.

"Stop, stop," I yelled.

"Why?"

"I think you just passed it."

The tires screeched and we lurched forward onto our seat belts. In a smooth motion, Parker made a U-turn and headed back.

The road to Heron's Point was narrow and lined with trees. The air smelled of salt, mud, and a certain freshness that reminded me of newly-cracked crab's backs. Through clearings in the vegetation, I caught glimpses of the sea, a sheet of silver in constant motion.

"I think I'll hang back and let you talk to the kid," Parker said.

"I don't know him. Never met him before."

"Well, I have, and let's just say he's not in my fan club."

"I'm not sure how I'd even begin to approach him."

"He's a male around nineteen, going on twenty. Doesn't matter what you say. Just flash a smile, lean in close to him, and I bet you'll get his attention."

Parker chuckled. The grin on his face promptly disappeared when he met my unsmiling stare.

"So what's the plan?" I said after a while.

"First, we make sure we get that video with Eric's confession. Then, we'll try to persuade Jacques to come with us. He won't be safe here, even if he no longer has the video."

"But where will we go, once we get it?"

"If those guys from the airport picked up our trail again, we'd be waltzing right into their arms if we headed back North. We've got to keep barreling South. Key West airport is probably our best bet. Or we could charter a boat to the Bahamas. We'll figure something out."

Parker pulled up close to the registration office. He trotted ahead, and held the door open for me.

Behind the desk, a whale of a man with an unkempt, white beard leaned back in a chair. His mouth was open and his eyes were closed. His snores were as loud as a ship horn.

A large book with handwritten names and dates lay open in front of him.

As I was about to rouse the man, Parked put his finger to his own lips. He tiptoed to the side of the desk. He bent over the register and scanned it. The page crackled faintly as he gently peeled it back. He seemed to become very interested in something he read when the man behind the desk suddenly grunted and shook his head.

The office attendant opened his eyes, then widened them and stared at Parker.

"What the hell do you think you're doing?"

Parker straightened up and stared back at the man.

I stepped forward and cleared my throat.

"We'd like a spot for the day, please."

With his eyes still fixed on Parker, who eased away to the front of the desk, the attendant pulled the register squarely before him. He looked down at the page and frowned, then looked up at Parker with squinted eyes. He noisily turned the page back to the last one.

Parker spun on his heels to face a rack of pamphlets, which he studied intently.

The attendant pulled a pen from behind his right ear and looked at me. "Trailer or tent lot?"

When we finished registering and were about to leave, I flashed a smile at the attendant. "We're hoping to catch up with my boyfriend's brother who came here ahead of us. Can you tell us where we might find him?"

The man shook his head. He rested a protective hand across the register and stared anew at Parker.

"You won't get that kind of information out of me," he said. "Last year, at that state park up the road, a fella walked in, said he was supposed to join his wife and the girl in the office gave him the wife's location. Turns out it was his soon-to-be ex-wife. Beat the poor thing to a pulp. The girl in the office got fired instantly.

No, sir. That's not gonna happen on my watch. You need to find somebody here, that's your affair. Find them yourself."

The sun had now risen, illuminating everything, as if a light bulb had been switched on over the planet.

We drove to our spot and walked the wooded trail up a hill to Section D of the campground. Parker had seen a "J. Taylor" registered in that section but didn't get the lot number. He said Jacques had sent a letter to Dromel in which he said he used "Josh Taylor" as an alias.

"Boyfriend's brother, eh?" Parker grinned as he lifted up a low-hanging branch so I could duck under it.

"It was just the first thing that popped into my head," I deadpanned.

In Section D, we came across a young couple on their knees as they broke down a tent.

"Excuse me," Parker said. "We're supposed to meet up with my brother at this campground, but his phone went dead. Josh Taylor's his name. You seen him around here?"

"We were here only for the night," the man said. "Why don't you ask at the office?"

"Tried that already," I said. "The guy refused point-blank to tell us anything."

"Which one?" The girl looked up at me. "The young one with the long hair, or the slob?"

"The slob," Parker said.

"Doesn't surprise me." The man stopped his work and stood up. "What a jerk! Gave us a hard time for no reason when we registered. But, sorry. We can't help you. We didn't meet anybody here."

"Except for the crazy yoga woman," the girl said. "I think she's been here, like, forever. Tries to get friendly with everybody. She's probably your best bet."

"Where will we find her?" Parker said.

The girl pointed to a trail that led to the beach. "She said the rising sun feeds her soul or something like that."

Reeds along the shore bobbed and bowed as gentle waves rolled in quietly. A light breeze played with the leaves of the bushes and trees that lined the narrow beach.

On a flat rock, a woman sat in a loose, tie-dyed t-shirt and a long, white skirt. Her legs were folded, with her soles pointing skyward; a hand rested on each knee, with the tips of the fingers touching each other. Her frizzy, unkempt hair lifted and fell with the wind. Her eyes were closed, and if she was breathing, she showed no signs of it.

Parker and I exchanged glances. He nodded in the woman's direction.

"Excuse me," I said in a low voice.

The woman didn't stir.

"Can we speak to you for a moment?" I said louder. "We need your help."

The woman remained still for a while again, then flicked open one eye and turned only her head to us.

"Sorry to disturb you." Parker stepped closer to her. "We're looking for my brother, Josh Taylor. He came ahead of us but his phone went dead and the office won't give us his lot number."

"Josh?" The woman shook her head as the rest of her body remained immobile. "I don't think I know a Josh."

"About nineteen years old," Parker said. "A little shorter than me. A Canadian."

The woman opened both eyes and cocked her head. "I'm not getting anything on that name."

Parker bowed and stepped backward. "Thanks. Sorry to bother you."

We had turned to leave when the woman called out.

"Wait!"

She was now on her feet. "Come to think of it, I did meet a Josh, recently. Yes, it's coming back to me. Skinny guy. Short black hair. Forgive me. The old brain doesn't work that good anymore."

"Was his last name Taylor?" Parker said.

"Think so. That one kept mostly to himself. Wasn't too keen to talk to anyone, except for the McKinnon folks down by the creek. Haven't seen him around for days, though."

After asking around, we found the McKinnon trailer on a knoll overlooking a gully. A man who stood not far from the open trailer door sipped from a tin cup and stared at the water that noisily rushed over the stones below.

"Mr McKinnon?" Parker said.

The man turned to face us. "What's it to you?"

"I'm trying to catch up with my brother, Josh Taylor. He's a few days ahead of us. Someone told us you might be able to help us find him."

The man flung the contents of his cup into the creek and stuck out his chest. His jaws twitching, he eyed Parker coldly. "Well, someone told you wrong. I know nothing about your brother."

He walked to the trailer, marched up the steps, and slammed the door shut behind him.

We went to every section of the campground and came up empty. We returned to the car, and as Parker put the key in the ignition, I scratched my head.

"So, what now, Paul?"

"You hungry?"

"I can't even begin to think about food right now."

"Well, I can't think without something in my stomach. How about we get some coffee and donuts, and then try to figure things out?"

I looked at him and shook my head. *Did he have to so precisely fit the cop stereotype?*

"What?" Parker said, apparently unable to read my expression.

He turned the key and the engine purred, and then I heard a child's voice crying out, "Hey, mister!"

A boy, about ten years old, came running down a trail behind the car, waving one hand. Parker wound down his window.

The boy ran up to Parker's door. "Hey, mister, wait a minute."

"What's up, son?"

"Wait." The boy doubled over, panting. "My sister's coming."

In the rear view mirror, I saw a girl trotting toward us, her heavy chest swinging rhythmically with every step, her long hair flowing in the wind.

"You're Josh's brother?" the girl said when she reached the car.

"Yes. We're trying to catch up with him."

"My dad scared him off," the girl said. "Called him a bum. Threatened to kill him because he didn't want him talking to me. Dad's real strict. Doesn't let me have a phone or even a Facebook account."

I saw Parker studying the girl's face. With her braces and smooth skin, she looked to be fifteen, maybe, sixteen; but her body was mature beyond her age.

The boy giggled. "Britney's got two boyfriends. Josh, and Daren, up at the office. Except Dad found out about Josh and now he's gone. But Dad still doesn't know about Daren."

The girl shoved her brother aside. "Stop being a pest."

"Touch me again and I'll tell Dad about Daren."

"You are *so* not going to do that." The girl reached over and pinched her brother's ear, then twisted it sharply.

"Ouch!" The boy tugged away, then shoved the girl so hard, she teetered before righting herself. She raised her hand and the expression on her face signaled her intention to rain down blows, but she was too late.

The boy darted off, laughing.

"Listen, can you tell us where Josh went?" Parker said.

"Bayview, or Fairview — something like that." The girl stared at her retreating brother. She turned again to Parker. "It's supposed to be another camp, further South. Josh said he'd found this funky trailer done up in camouflage for sale. We were going to run away together. But my dad was acting all cranky that day, and, well, in the end, I chickened out."

"Thanks for telling us," Parker said. "You've been a huge help."

The girl bit her lower lip. "When you see Josh, will you tell him I haven't forgotten him?"

Chapter 94

The black sedan rolled into the entrance of Heron Point and paused at a large board with a map of the grounds.

Young studied it and spat out of the window. He was at the wheel; Quinn sat in the passenger seat, and Williams was drowsing in the back.

"It's gonna be a hell of a job finding him," Young said.

Quinn pointed his chin toward the small hut that served as the office. "Pull up over there."

Young followed Quinn inside and the door closed quietly behind them.

The young man with long hair behind the desk kept his head bent and focused on the portable PlayStation which he feverishly jabbed with his thumbs.

Young rapped on the door frame. "Hey, buddy!"

The young man looked up. He paused the game and rested it on the desk. Picking up a pen, he tried to sound interested. "How can I help you?"

Young opened his mouth to speak, but Quinn slapped him in the chest with the back of his hand and stepped forward.

Quinn studied the young man's faded blue shirt, the cigarette packet in his left pocket, the unfinished tattoo sleeves that extended only half-way up his arms. Most of all, he studied the young man's face, and his shifting, green eyes. This was someone he could deal with, he thought.

"We lost touch with a friend of ours, but we know he came here." Quinn fixed a steady gaze on the young man. "A Canadian, about nineteen years old with short, black hair. We need to find him, quick."

Quinn disengaged his stare and let his eyes fall on the registration log.

"Sorry, but we have a strict policy here. We don't give out any information about our guests."

Quinn locked eyes with the young man again, pulled his wallet from his back pants pocket and slid out a fifty-dollar bill. He folded it, leaned forward, and slid it under the PlayStation.

Quinn observed the young man as he eyed the PlayStation and ran his hand through his long hair; he thought he could almost hear the young man's brain working.

"We had one Canadian, recently," the attendant said. "He pushed out about a week ago. My girlfriend knows him. Seems he went to Fairview."

The young man saw the blank expressions on the faces of the two strangers.

"It's another campground, straight down on this highway. You can't miss it. It's bigger than this one."

Behind Quinn's back, Young rolled his eyes. Great, we're back to square one, he thought.

"What's he driving?" Quinn said.

The young man glanced at the register; his eyes roved to the PlayStation, then fixed themselves on the wallet still in Quinn's right hand. He looked up at Quinn.

Quinn pulled out another fifty and slid it under the PlayStation.

The young man smiled.

"A '98 Ford F-150. Dark green," he said. He flipped back through the log book. "But I don't know the plate number offhand. Let's see what it says. Okay, here it is."

He gave them the information, then clasped his hands in front of him on the desk, staring at them. "Is that all?"

Young slipped his hand below his denim jacket. His fingers reached for the gun in his holster. This was not his beloved Colt. It was a SIG Sauer P220, fitted with a silencer.

Stupid punk, he thought. This bum was liable to give up information about them if the cops were to ever come around asking, just like he gave up info on that Canadian.

Well, Young just wasn't going to let that happen.

Suddenly, the door swung open and two small boys burst into the office, giggling as one chased after the other. Adult voices and laughter from outside grew louder as footsteps approached.

Young looked across at Quinn, who jerked his head in the direction of the door. Reluctantly, he let his hand drop to his side and he followed Quinn out.

Chapter 95

By late morning, the sun had fully shaken off its slumber and its rays began to sting. We drove past towering trees and swampland, with no houses in sight.

Our pace was slower now, partly because there was more traffic on the road, but mostly because Parker steered with one hand, while sipping the coffee he held in the other.

A mile or two back, he had pulled into a fast-food drive-thru, but I had refused his offer of breakfast. He got himself an egg muffin and also ordered a half dozen donuts and two cups of coffee "just in case" I changed my mind.

He had wolfed down the egg muffin and three of the donuts. The rest sat in an open box. Somewhere along the way, I relented and picked up the coffee, which I barely drank, preferring to use it as a hand warmer.

The lingering smell of eggs and stale grease that filled the car made me feel both hungry and sick at the same time.

It had been an eternity since I'd had a decent meal. But my stomach was a wreck. The term "butterflies" could hardly come close to describing the queasiness that gripped me.

Here I was with this cop, whose striking good looks and physical presence I'd been forced to acknowledge since circumstances had thrown him right in my face, but whom I hardly knew, and about whom I had some lingering doubts, although at his every move, those doubts were fading fast. Here we were, so far away from home, lying about who we were, speeding down a Florida highway in a mad rush to find a young man with a video of his dead uncle confessing to a crime, and we were trying to reach him before the people who killed Dromel got to him.

The people who killed Ben.

Just the thought of him sent my heart into spasms. But I couldn't let myself become sentimental. Not now, as we were so close to finding Jacques Tremblay and the evidence that the Syron Lake spill was no act of God.

"How do you do this every day?" I said, trying to distract myself.

"What?" Parker said. "You mean have coffee and donuts for breakfast?"

"No. I mean your job."

"Being a cop?"

"Yes. How can you stand it? Evil. Death. The blood. The dead bodies."

"Haven't had much of it these past four years in Syron Lake. Nothing happens there, right?"

He looked at me and smiled. I suppose he was trying to lighten my mood, but I couldn't return the smile.

"Saw some pretty raw stuff during the two decades I was with the military," he continued. "Like any thing, see it enough, you get used to it."

It was just as well that my eye caught something just then, as my brain was too dull to come up with a reply. I lightly touched the hand in which he held his coffee. "What did the girl say the park was called?"

"Bayview or Fairview."

"The sign up ahead says Fairview."

The long trailer that served as the registration office was strewn with rolled-up sleeping bags, tents, and enormous backpacks. Campers crowded around the counter. A young, harried-looking attendant tucked springy, red curls behind her ears and sighed loudly.

Suddenly she shouted out, "Let's get some order here. Checking in, stand on this side; checking out, over there. Okay?"

Like Moses' staff, her words caused the sea of bodies and camping gear to part in two. The check-in line was five deep; the check-out was longer.

Parker motioned me to stand in the check-in. He sauntered over to the other line and sidled up to a couple who were peering over a map.

"The camping's good here?" he said.

"There's a nice beach," the man said. "But otherwise it's no different from any of the other places we've been to. We're doing as many as we can, hoping to get down to Key West, eventually."

"Sounds like a plan. Been here long?"

"Three days," the woman said. "We're on our honeymoon. Got a week left."

"Hey, congrats. My girlfriend and I are doing the same thing, hoping to catch up with my brother along the way. Last we heard, he was coming here. He's got this crazy trailer decked out in camouflage. You seen it?"

"That sounds cool, man. I'd love to see it."

"So you haven't come across it?"

"No. We were on the beach; we didn't do too much exploring around the place." The man cast a knowing glance at his wife.

Parker looked across at me and scrunched up his mouth. He was going to have to go through the whole routine again, most likely with the woman behind the counter. I figured he'd have to wait until the office completely emptied out if he was to have any chance with her.

"I seen it," a voice said, over the chatter in the room.

The triumphal cry came from a near-skeletal man in rumpled clothes who had an unlit cigarette hanging from his lips. He stood in line in front of newly-weds, and held up his hand like a first grader in class.

"Really?" Parker said. "Whereabouts?"

"Up yonder, on the hill in the far corner. Not too many folks goes up there. But I seen it when I went walking my dog. Of course, I had to look really hard to make it out from the bushes, 'cause it's camouflage an' all."

Impressed with his own comic genius, the man leaned forward and cackled, making a thin, wheezing sound that came from deep inside his smoke-ravaged lungs.

"Hey thanks, buddy," Parker said.

With a day pass sticker on the windshield, we parked in our lot. After a long trek to the northern edge of the campground, we climbed a little hill and saw the small, round camper. Covered as much in rust blisters as it was a camouflage design, it looked barely capable of accommodating a grown man. It was on the only occupied lot, and it looked deserted. There was no tow vehicle in sight.

"I'm going to get this," Parker said. "Hide over there in the bushes, just in case there's trouble."

I ducked behind the brush and looked on as Parker walked up to the camper and knocked. No sound came from inside. He tried the door handle. It didn't budge.

He pulled out the key chain for the rented car, on which he'd clipped his own car keys. On it was a small pick, which he applied to the lock.

He then took a step back and reached behind, just under the light jacket that he wore. He pulled out the black and sliver handgun that I'd seen in the glove compartment.

Holding it with both hands close to his ribs, he stood with his back to the camper, on the side of the door where the handle was. With one hand, he turned the handle and flung the door open.

He pivoted and took tiny steps across the path of the entrance, all the while pointing the gun inside.

Nothing happened.

He poked his head in and scanned the camper, then came over and joined me in the bushes.

"Up for a treasure hunt?" he said.

Chapter 96

The tiny tin-can of a trailer had a dank smell of sweaty clothes, stale food and rusted metal. We folded out the bed, unhinged seats, poked around all drawers and cabinets. But there was no video camera, no computer disks or flash drives, no computer, nothing that could possibly hold the evidence we were after.

After straightening the place, we returned to the bushes and sat side by side on a log — waiting.

"What you were saying, earlier, about getting used to blood and gore and killing," I said, breaking the long silence, "I really can't relate to that."

Parker shrugged. "Some people are made for it, I guess."

"I was a crime reporter straight out of journalism school. Covered one murder. But, thank goodness, the body was removed long before I got on the scene. I hated that job."

"A dead body can't harm you."

"Oh yes it can."

Parker arched an eyebrow and stared at me. "How do you figure that?"

"The sight of mangled flesh is enough to do it."

"Come again?"

"It can wound a person's psyche."

"Okay," Parker said, stretching the word out beyond its normal length.

"You see a cadaver and that lifeless mound makes you realize that that could very well be you. And some day it will be you. It's chilling to be reminded of that. Depressing, even."

"That's a very self-centered way of looking at things."

I shrugged.

"The way you think, I'd say you made a good career move by not getting into medicine or law enforcement." The sides of his mouth quivered as if he was forcing himself not to laugh.

It was disarming.

I couldn't help but chuckle. "I guess I'd make a lousy cop or doctor."

"They'd have to order a stretcher and smelling salts for Dr Jacob every time she went down to emergency to admit a new patient."

Parker and I both burst out in laughter and he batted his hand in the air to remind me to keep my voice down.

"Look, Paul," I said after awhile, "I'm sorry if I was a bit hard on you earlier."

"What do you mean?"

"When I blew up about speaking ill of the dead."

"No apologies needed."

"It's just that everything you said about Ben...well, I guess it was all true; and it was all ugly. So it was hard to take."

"Having your illusions shattered is devastating, no two ways about it."

"I mean, it's painful that he's gone. But what's more disturbing is that I was so blind. I had no clue about his true character. How could I have been such a fool?" My voice cracked and I bit my lower lip as I fought back sudden, unwelcome tears.

"Don't blame yourself." Parker patted me on the knee. "Look, I was with a woman for three years. It was three long years of spending almost every off-duty hour with her, sharing our lives, sharing the deepest intimacies. She even went to my father's funeral with me and held my hand before and after I gave the eulogy. Well, I proposed. She said yes and acted as if she was over the moon at the thought of being my wife and the mother of my kids."

Parker paused.

"And?" I said.

"The last day before the wedding, she took off for Mexico with her best friend...."

I raised my brow in sympathy.

"Her girlfriend," he said, "who was a girlfriend in every sense of the word."

"Oh!"

"Oh yeah." Parker nodded. "I never saw it coming. Hit me like a two-by-four in the nose."

"Ouch!" I scrunched my own nose and rubbed it.

We laughed.

"I can laugh about it now, but it wasn't like that for a long time. Couldn't even bear to think about it. In fact, outside of therapy, this is the first I've actually spoken about it."

"Thanks for sharing."

"Just making the point that we all get taken for a ride some time or the other. It may hurt like hell, but eventually, we get over it."

"Hurts like hell sure sums it up."

I stood up as tears welled in my eyes. It felt like I was on an emotional roller coaster and it was about to take me down for a deep plunge.

"I don't understand it," I said. "I can't seem to get this stupid thing called love right. With Peter, my first serious boyfriend, I thought I was doing the right thing. Go slow. Friendship first. Waited ten months before anything happened. That didn't work out. With Ben, I thought, 'Don't hold back. Jump right in and take a chance.' Turns out that was wrong too."

Parker had gone very quiet. He stared straight ahead with glazed eyes as if he had tuned out entirely all of a sudden.

I had thought he would have lent me a sympathetic ear at this moment of obvious emotional crisis. I guess I'd misjudged him. It was yet another thing that I'd gotten wrong.

I exhaled slowly, my spirit deflating along with my lungs. "I can't seem to get life right either."

"Who ever does?" Parker said.

"I feel like...like just a weak, foolish woman."

"From what I've seen of you and read about how you stood up for the community at the hearing, I'd say you're one of the smartest, strongest women I know."

I snorted. "Yeah, well I don't know how smart that was."

Parker tilted his head.

"Look where it's got me." I shook my hands at the bushes around us. "Other people who mind their own business are comfortable in their beds this early morning, curling up next to a spouse. They'll probably wake up to a houseful of kids and a shaggy dog. And look at me! Out here, waiting for some stranger. Scared out of my wits after seeing the man I loved gunned down less than twenty-four hours ago, and after being chased down, myself, by two men in Trinidad, and two more, here, in Florida...."

"Look, I'm not sure who, exactly, we're up against. But I do know they haven't won yet."

I sighed.

Parker continued. "Let's just get this final piece of evidence and take things from there, okay? All your efforts may just bear fruit yet."

"But–"

Parker shot up from the log and held me by the shoulder.

"Shhh." He put his finger to his lips. "I think I hear a vehicle."

Chapter 97

The green pickup rolled up the incline and parked in front of the trailer. The driver's door swung open and a male wearing a baseball cap jumped out. He immediately turned his body back to face the truck as he tugged at white plastic bags on the passenger seat.

The man's stature and the glimpse of his face was enough for Parker.

He motioned me to exit the bushes and approach from the right, while he hung back.

"Jacques," I called out as I neared the young man.

He stood with two bags of groceries slung through his left arm, which also clutched several cans against his chest, while his right hand turned the key to the camper door.

At the sound of his name, he turned around. The door swung open, slamming into his body and causing cans to tumble to the ground.

"Jacques, I need to talk with you about the video your uncle gave you. Your life is in danger because of it."

I looked him square in the eyes. I could see confusion dancing around in there.

"Look, lady, my name is Josh, and I don't know what the hell you're talking about."

His body stiffened, as if he became aware of footsteps on the gravel. But by the time he broke our stare, it was too late.

Parker grabbed him by the collar and jostled him.

"Get in the camper," Parker growled.

Jacques let the grocery bags fall from his hands and threw his weight into Parker.

The two grappled, but Parker spun out of Jacques' hold and swung around behind him. He twisted the young man's right arm behind his back.

Jacques fell to his knees and Parker slammed down on him, pushing the kid's face into the gravel and drawing his right arm further up behind his back. Jacques yelped.

"Are you going to behave, now?" Parker said.

Jacques' muffled groans didn't satisfy Parker. He dug a knee into Jacques' back and yanked the kid's right hand even higher. Jacques' scream made my blood curdle.

"Well, are you going cooperate?"

"Yes, yes!"

Parker eased up off Jacques. He caught him by the scruff, dragged him to his feet and shoved him forward.

"Get in the camper."

Jacques didn't resist this time.

He sat across the table from me, while Parker stood outside, filling up the frame of the open door. Jacques' eyes telegraphed pure terror. I had been stunned by the brute power Parker had released and I, too, was shaking.

"Are you okay?" I rested my hand lightly on Jacques' hand.

He breathed hard, with his mouth open. His head was bent, but he raised his eyelids to look up at me. He nodded.

"Look, sorry about what happened out there. But we need to talk to you. That's Detective Sergeant Paul Parker...."

Jacques lifted his head and looked at Parker with a sneer.

"And I am Stella Jacob. We've never met, but I'm also from Syron Lake and I've been fighting to make the company pay for the spill."

"I thought you looked familiar. I saw your picture in the *Beacon*."

He rounded his lips and blew out a sharp breath.

"We know what your uncle did," I said.

Jacques blinked. He pursed his lips.

"And there's this." I unzipped the fanny pack I carried and pulled out the two printouts from the Trinidad newspapers that Parker had shown me. I unfolded them and laid them on the table.

Jacques read just a few lines from each. His jaw fell and he dug a thumb into his chin.

"Jacques, I was with Benoit Dromel shortly before he died. He told me you have a video your uncle made confessing to causing the spill."

Jacques chewed on his lower lip.

"I saw when he was shot. And I believe I've been followed from Trinidad to here. And we believe that the people responsible for Ben's death will also be searching for you."

Jacques pushed the pages back toward me. He rubbed his nose and shifted his gaze between Parker and me.

"So what now?" he said.

"Where's the video?" Parker said.

"In my truck. I keep it in a bag under my seat that I take with me wherever I go."

Parker walked off. When he returned, he was carrying a small, green, army-issue sling bag. He pulled out a small video camera from among a passport, bankbooks and other papers.

"It's on there," Jacques said. "I lost the cord to connect it to a computer, so I never got around to transferring it onto a jump drive."

Parker flipped out the screen. "There's only one recording on here."

"I've never used it since I filmed my uncle."

Parker pressed the play button. Eric Tremblay's face appeared:

"My name is Eric Tremblay. I have worked with Syron Lake Resources for seventeen years. Currently, I'm employed as a maintenance worker on the tailings site at the former Syron Lake uranium mine. I'm responsible, among other things, for ensuring the dam is sound. But I breached the dam. This was at the request of persons who said the company wanted this done. On that day...."

"It's all there," Jacques said. "It's seven minutes or so."

Parker shut the screen.

"Okay, we'll look at it in the car," he said. "Right now we need to haul it to the airport and get the hell out of here."

"Then what?" Jacques said.

"We put the story together properly and get it to the authorities. Who or how, we'll figure out when we're somewhere safe."

Parker stepped aside and I hopped out of the camper. Jacques followed. He grabbed the bag with his papers from Parker. After locking the camper door, he stepped in direction of his truck.

"Where do you think you're going?" Parker said.

"I'll hitch up the trailer and follow you."

"You're coming with us."

"I'm not leaving my truck and camper. Do you know how much I paid for them?"

"Get this concept, kid. We're going to the airport and we're gonna get on a plane to somewhere. You can't take it with you."

"I know where we're going. I'll pay for long term parking at the airport and pick them back up after we've handed over the video to the authorities. It'll be cheaper than leaving my truck and camper here and having them impounded."

"You'll slow us down hitching this rust bucket."

"I'm not leaving my truck and camper."

I could just see the testosterone swirling.

I held up my hands and made a time-out sign.

"Okay, you guys need to compromise if we're going to get anywhere. How about if Jacques took just the truck?"

Jacques eyed the rusted trailer as Parker approached him with a puffed out chest. I cringed at the thought that there'd be a repeat of the scuffle. Apparently, so did Jacques.

"Alright then," he said.

Chapter 98

Quinn ordered Young and Williams to stay in the car and walked alone to the trailer with the "Office" sign out front.

He was getting tired of Young and his hotheadedness. Young was proving a liability.

He was angry with Young for being stupid enough to let the Trinidad incident happen. That could have scuttled the whole job. It would have been a first for him. Quinn wasn't in the business of taking down non-targets and forfeiting his pay.

They were supposed to have only frightened the man. But, somehow, it all went haywire. What the hell had Young been thinking when he approached the man with a loaded gun? The moron clearly hadn't been thinking at all.

Luckily, though, Quinn thought to himself, Daniel Greene was in too deep to pull out. He was the best kind of client, so compromised that he was forced to extend the job.

Young had made the right call with the old man in that isolated shack in Daytona, Quinn thought. But he was getting too trigger-happy, and seemed ready to take careless chances by mowing down anyone unlucky enough to cross their path, even if that person was in a very public place. Wasting that punk in that first campground office would have been just plain stupid.

They would finish up this job together, Quinn decided. Each would take his share of the payment, though Quinn was tempted to deduct half of Young's as a lesson to him. Then he would lay low for a while, probably make off to Thailand or Cambodia for a few months to cool his heels. If he was lucky, he would probably run into old Army buddies out there; he knew the spots where the US vets hung out because there was cheap beer and cheap women. Maybe he could assemble a new team out there, a smarter bunch.

Whatever, he thought. What he knew for sure was that after this job, he would have to be damned near desperate to even think of calling on Young ever again.

He stepped into the trailer and saw a girl with wild, red curls behind a counter drinking from a plastic cup. People stood in two lines, and others sat on the floor among camping gear.

He joined the shorter line, which filled up behind him as he waited his turn.

"Trailer or tent?" the woman said when he eventually got to the counter.

"Look, I realize you're busy so I'm not going to waste your time." Quinn put on his broadest smile and leaned in toward her. "I don't plan on staying. I just came to find a friend. He's driving a green Ford pickup."

He pulled a scrap of paper from his pocket and handed it to her. "That's his registration number."

She frowned at him, looked at the line behind him, but still took the paper.

"Oh, I know who you're talking about."

"You do?"

"Sure. That's the guy who bought the camouflage camper. The old owner passed away in it and his daughter sold it off. Sleeping in that thing after someone died in it sounds kinda creepy, if you ask me."

Quinn nodded. "Well, my friend isn't just your average kind of guy."

"Funny thing is, you just missed him," the woman said.

"What?"

"Yeah, when I was taking my water break just a while ago. God, I needed that drink. My throat's dry as sandpaper. I've been talking non-stop all morning."

"You're saying I just missed him?"

"Yeah, he drove past at a clip, just as you walked in. I saw him bolt down the road and turn left onto the highway."

Chapter 99

The sky grew black with low clouds that stretched on forever. There was not an inch of blue above, and the sun was completely shut out.

Even though we were barreling down the highway and everything went by in a blur, I saw how the trees swayed and bowed in the steady gusts that came in from the sea. Not a good sign, I thought.

I closed the video camera after viewing Eric Tremblay's confession.

"Explosive stuff," I said as I tucked the device into my fanny pack.

Parker kept his eyes peeled to the road, and to Jacques' truck, which was going way too fast up ahead.

"That'll more than bury that company," he said. "Talk about being caught red-handed."

"Who do you say we should give it to? The CNRA?"

Parker shook his head. "I've got some contacts in the RCMP. I'll call them up when we get somewhere safe. This goes way beyond the CNRA. Besides, one of their own is implicated in all of this."

His words sent a spear right through my heart.

Any investigation was sure to include Parker's theory that Dromel was taking a bribe to go easy on the company after the spill; and then the investigation would come to the fact that he was shot while he was in Trinidad — with me.

For Dromel, violating the *Integrity Act* was a crime. And I was tied up in it.

As a private citizen I was blameless; the law didn't apply to me. But as a public official, Dromel had been obligated to comply with the *Act* by recusing himself from the Syron Lake matter the minute he and I had become involved.

But who would pay attention to such details? I would be cast as the other half in what was sure to be played up in the press as a salacious scandal. My name would be dragged through the mud. And if the novel-writing experiment went nowhere, I would be up the proverbial creek. It would be impossible for me to get a job with any reputable organization after gaining such notoriety.

Parker's voice pulled me out of my thoughts.

"You hear about big business getting away with all sorts of dubious behavior," he said. "But I'm sure this is something that'll stick."

I looked up and shook my head. It took an even more grim prospect to drive away the heavy thoughts that had filled my mind.

"Only if we make it alive to tell the tale," I said.

"Look, I know you're still reeling from what you saw happen to Dromel, but–"

"I'm not talking about that." I gripped the armrest on my door. "It's the speed that could get us killed first."

"Got to keep up with the kid," Parker said. "I should've known he'd drive like a maniac, given half a reason."

Parker suddenly swerved to the right to make way for a black sedan that came out of nowhere, zipped too close on his left, then cut back in front of him.

"Idiot!" Parker shouted and slammed the horn.

I had watched as the car raced by and my heart suddenly pounded fiercely.

"Like a bat out of hell," Parker said. "They must have some crazy emergency to be overtaking us at the rate we're going."

Thunder boomed in the distance and I watched as the car careened toward Jacques' truck.

"Oh my God," I shouted, and my jaw dropped.

"What?"

"It's them!"

"What do you mean?"

"The men who shot Ben."

"What? You're sure?"

"It was quick, but the one in the passenger seat, the one with the long hair. I'm cert–"

I didn't have to finish.

The black sedan raced up behind Jacques' truck and rammed it. The pickup zig-zagged briefly and then took off like a jackrabbit.

Parker floored the gas pedal.

"Hang on," he said.

I gripped the armrest harder, now clutching it with both hands.

The sedan swung into the left lane and was pushing to ride up alongside the pickup. Blaring horns of oncoming traffic forced it back into the right lane.

Parker gained on them, but as he attempted to run into their bumper, the left lane cleared and they swung out, racing to get alongside Jacques.

"They couldn't get him from the back, so now they want to push him off the road from the side," he said. "Well, two can play this game."

He sped up alongside the sedan, the nose of our rental coming up just to the seal of the back door. The gas pedal was touching the floor and there was no possible way he could get further up alongside them.

He slammed his fist on the horn and held it there.

His trick worked. The noise distracted the driver of the sedan. He slowed down just a fraction. It was enough that Parker was now cutting it nose to nose with them.

"Hold on tight," he shouted.

He pulled the steering wheel sharply to the left, but the sedan swerved away.

Parker swung further toward them, and the sedan came on the offensive, veering right. Parker screeched back into his lane and my shoulder slammed into *my* window.

"It's gonna get nasty," he said.

He suddenly made a big arc with the steering wheel. The rental hurtled left. It slammed into the side of the sedan with an unholy bang.

The impact sent both vehicles careening.

The sedan slid right off the road. It bounced off the shoulder, and the front wheels got caught in a reed-lined ditch.

Our rental spun off in the opposite direction. Parker gripped the steering wheel and tried to force it left. But the impact had been too great. The car spun out of control, screeching as it veered off the road and plowed into the bushes.

Our bodies were flung forward into the seat belts and exploding airbags. The front of the car jumped and we came to a sudden halt.

Just inches behind me, a long branch poked through the rear right window. Splintered glass covered the backseat. I shuddered at the sight. Had the car come in just inches at an angle, the branch would have shot through my window.

Parker put the gear into reverse, but the engine screamed. The wheels did nothing but kick up pebbles and dust.

He flung open his door and I realized the front wheels were hung up on a fallen tree trunk. There was no way the rental was getting out of there.

Parker leaned over to the glove compartment and fished out the gun, which he shoved into his waistband. He pulled Dromel's cigar box from under my seat.

"Secure this," he said, handing it to me before jumping out the car.

My door didn't budge. I crawled out through the driver's side, clutching the cigar box against my fanny pack.

Up on the road, a vehicle screeched to a stop near us.

"Get in," a voice called out.

It was Jacques, with the passenger door of his pickup flung open.

I darted into the vehicle.

Parker ran to the other side of the truck and yanked open the door. Grabbing the steering wheel with one hand, he pulled himself into the cab, and shoved Jacques' shoulder with the other.

"Move over!" Parker shouted.

Jacques had just enough time to unbuckle and shift into the middle, when Parker slammed the door and sped off.

In the rear view mirror, I saw two of the men pushing the front of the black sedan, trying to rock it out of the ditch.

Nobody wanted to say anything about the chances of the sedan getting back on the road.

"Floor it!" Jacques shouted.

But Parker didn't need prompting.

Chapter 100

A fast-moving mass of black clouds rolled in from the sea. It changed the quality of light. It was now as if someone had brought down a dark lampshade over a naked bulb.

At the side of my eye, I saw Jacques jerking his chin forward.

"Step on it, man," he grumbled, "or let me get back at the wheel."

"Can it, kid," Parker said.

Jacques Tremblay's attitude clearly irritated him.

"So you've been travelling around a lot, eh?" Parker slammed his knee against Jacques' knee. "Bought this truck and that camper, eh? Where'd you get the money from, huh, Jacques?"

No response.

"I mean Syron Lake's too small not to know everybody's business. And everybody knows your uncle died broke. Some guy named Wilfred Owens said he won the house you used to live in from Eric in a poker game."

Jacques scowled and stared ahead.

"So what would your uncle have us believe?" Parker continued while keeping his eyes on the road. "That he breached that tailing pond for free? He didn't mention anything about any payment on that video."

Jacques clenched his jaw.

"Give it up, kiddo. Tell us–"

"Shut up," Jacques shouted into Parker's ear. "Shut your bloody trap. Just shut up!"

Parker jerked his head back and glared at Jacques. As he took his eyes off the road, the pickup veered into the opposite lane, hurtling toward an oncoming car.

"Paul, look out," I shouted.

The other car blared its horn. Tires screeched. Parker swung out of the way at the last minute.

We drove on in silence for the next few minutes.

"That's a bearer of bad news if I ever saw one," Parker said, casting a glance at the massive, dark cloud just ahead.

He checked the rear view mirror.

"Worse news," he said.

Jacques peered into the rear view and I swiveled my head, wincing as I did. I was sure I had whiplash.

In the distance, a black sedan came charging down the road.

In an instant, large drops began pounding on the roof and pelting against the windshield of the truck.

Parker switched on the wipers and slowed down.

"Floor it," Jacques yelled.

"You want us to get killed?" Parker shouted. "It's bloody raining!"

"You prefer to be done in by those creeps?"

The sedan, which made no allowance for the slick road, was racing up to us.

A turn-off lay ahead.

"We'll never make it to the airport at this rate," Parker said. "We need to get off the highway and hope we can find a good place to ambush them."

I didn't know about the two males beside me, but I was literally shaking. This was taking me back to where I didn't ever want to return: to those horrible moments when the explosion of the gun rang out; people scampering; Dromel falling; me dashing to bear him up by the shoulder; the two of us hurtling through the crowd; darting behind buildings and tumbling into a canal....

Violence and death hung in the air and I could barely handle it. I was a writer, an otherwise mousey girl who thought I could use my keyboard instead of a sword to fight for justice for my neighbors, and for the environment. I didn't sign up for all of this.

"I don't want to die out here," I said to no one in particular.

Parker cut sharply into the narrow side road. The truck crunched gravel and bounced along over potholes.

The rain came down so hard, now, it was difficult to see even with the wipers on the highest speed.

Parker leaned forward and squinted.

"There's something up ahead," he said.

He drove into an overgrown yard and rolled up beside a long building made of rusting corrugated metal sheets. Half of the roof was missing and one side of what should have been a double door seemed to be just barely hanging on by its hinges.

Parker drove around to the back and stopped.

"Jacques, you come with me," he said, popping open the door. "Stella, take to the wheel, just in case."

Parker jumped out into the rain and dragged Jacques out with him before he could protest.

I unbuckled my seat belt and slid over into the driver's seat. I hit the door locks and listened for the reassuring click. Gripping the steering wheel, I leaned forward to see through the rain that lashed the windscreen as fat drops drummed the roof and windows.

I was grateful the handbrake was up. My legs were trembling so violently, I knew I couldn't keep a steady hold on the brake pedal.

Oh God, please don't let me die out here.

I tried to think, but my mind went blank and all I was aware of was the hard curve of the steering wheel in my palms, the paleness of my knuckles, the sound of the rubber of the wipers scraping against the windscreen, and the pounding of the rain on the roof.

Pounding. There was pounding on the driver's side of the truck. I turned and saw the shape of a head outside the window in the pouring rain.

My heart jackhammered.

The figure pressed up against the glass with cupped hands, and I recognized the features.

I switched off the locks. The door swung open and Parker hurled himself in, almost landing on top of me as I scuttled away.

He slammed the door shut and released the hand break.

"You okay?" he said.

"I don't know."

"Don't worry. We'll get out of this. I promise."

He sped to the front of the building, where Jacques held the one remaining side of the door open.

Parker drove into the cavernous structure and steered the truck past empty crates and massive heaps of rusting machinery parts. We went to the far end of the building and stopped behind a tall pile of wooden pallets and metal drums.

The rain clattering onto the metal roof and siding was almost deafening.

"Stay at the wheel," Parker shouted. "We're guarding the door. We'll get them if they try to come in."

Parker jumped out and I was alone again in the vehicle.

If the men did find us and attacked, the truck was our only hope of escaping. And what if I froze again as Parker and Jacques were trying to get in? They'd be easy targets for these ruthless killers. They'd be shot in the back while banging on the glass for me to open the door. I decided to leave the locks off.

I squeezed my eyes shut and braced for whatever hell was to descend upon us. But that would do nobody any good, I thought. I forced myself to open my eyes and stay alert.

Above the roar of the rain on the metal, I thought I heard something. The engine of a car. Wheels crushing gravel. I told myself I was imagining things; my mind was playing tricks on me. It would be impossible to discern those sounds with the rain pounding so hard and the wind rushing through the half-covered roof.

"Hey, God, get us out of this place safely — please!" I whispered.

I hadn't been anywhere near anything resembling organized religion since leaving the high school run by nuns in Trinidad. They had taught me to pray, and if there ever was a fitting occasion to resume the practice, this was it.

Bang!

That was not my imagination.

That was real.

But could the explosion have been just thunder?

I thought I heard crashing noises, then footsteps — running closer and closer toward me.

As I turned to look out the back, the driver's door flung open. A hand reached in the cab and grabbed me by the arm.

Some unfriendly hand was trying to drag me out of the truck.

I held onto the steering wheel and screamed.

A stranger, a young man about my age, came into full view. He gripped my wrists and tried to tear my hands off the steering wheel.

"No, no, no," I screamed.

His fingernails dug into the tender veins just below my wrists. Pain shot up my arm and I released my grip.

The man pulled me out of the seat. My head slammed against the door frame as he tried to drag me out. The blow shot needles of pain into my brain and down my spine.

The man got a better hold of me, and his strong arms wrapped around my chest.

He held me so tight, I could hardly breathe. I felt as if he was cracking my ribs. I wriggled and yelled. But he clamped his hand over my mouth and carried my writhing body around to the front of the pile of pallets.

Over to the left, Parker wrestled another man to his knees and in slid his arm around his neck. The man bucked and flailed to get out of the chokehold.

Further off, Jacques crouched and darted behind a stack of metal drums. The long-haired man got up on his toes and peered from the other side.

"Young," the man holding me shouted past my ear. "He's behind the drums."

I swung my head left and right and managed to budge enough from his clamp-like hold to get my teeth around his thumb. I bit down as hard as I could. I had a sickening feeling as enamel met flesh and bone.

The man yelped and pulled away his hand from my face, loosening his grip around my chest at the same time. I felt myself falling and I bent my left elbow. I flung myself in toward my attacker, aiming for the testicles.

I hit my target, then hit the ground, smashing my elbow. Above my groans, I heard a blood-curdling scream and the man dropped to his knees, clutching his groin.

Parker, too, was now on the ground. He was flat on his back, holding the black and silver gun above his head, while the other man straddled his waist and tried to wrest the gun away.

A short length of metal pipe was in a pile of garbage just within my reach. I stretched out my hand and grabbed it. It was heavier than I'd imagined, but all the better.

I rolled away from my attacker, who was still on his knees. I got to my feet and swung the pipe toward his head, as if taking a wild swipe at a cricket ball. My palms stung as the pipe reverberated on impact. The man's body jerked and collapsed. Streaks of red flowed down the side of his face.

Bang!

The explosion came from behind me. I spun around to Parker's direction in time to see the man who'd been on top of him come crashing down onto his chest. The body knocked the gun out of Parker's hand.

Bang! Bang!

The new explosions came from over to my left. Jacques was nowhere in view, but his voice cried out and a pile of drums came cascading down.

The man with the long hair held up his gun and turned his attention to Parker, who struggled to get out from under the body that had fallen on him.

The long-haired man strode across to Parker's gun and kicked it away.

Parker crawled from under the body. He was on his hands knees, apparently disoriented, and struggling to get up.

The long-haired man took a shooting stance and aimed straight for Parker's head.

"Paul!" I screamed.

Bang!

I dropped to my knees.

I let go of the metal pipe and buried my face in my hands.

"No!" I cried.

My entire body trembled.

Footsteps. Footsteps came running toward me.

A hand rested on my shoulder. A voice I didn't recognize said, softly, "It's all over now."

PART IV

Chapter 101

I opened my eyes and found myself lying in a bed, in an unfamiliar, white room that was bare except for a night stand with a lamp. Dull light filtered through a fading, blue curtain, suggesting it was either close to dusk or just past dawn. I wore some kind of loose-fitting, gray gown that ended around my knees.

I had no idea how I'd gotten there or whether hours or days had passed since my last memory...that horrible sight of Parker struggling to his knees with the long-haired man pointing a gun directly at his head.

I sat up abruptly, and as I did, I found myself unable to move my neck. It was trapped in a brace. I flung the covers off and swung my legs to the side of the bed.

No, that wasn't the last of it. Something else happened.

The effort to rise made my head spin. I felt my brain throbbing against my skull.

After a soft rap, the door creaked open and a young man poked in his head.

"You okay in there, miss?"

"Who are you?"

"Special Agent Ito."

"Special what? Where am I?"

"Somewhere safe."

"How did I get here? What day is it? Where's–"

"It's still Tuesday. And you should take it easy. The doctor said you had a blackout."

"Which doctor?"

"The one who cleared you to be brought here from the hospital. He came by and checked on you again about an hour ago."

"You still haven't explained where I am, yet."

"Please wait a moment. I'll tell them you're up."

He closed the door and his footsteps retreated. The room fell absolutely silent. I wanted answers to my questions but felt little motivation, now, to rise off the bed and cross the floor to get to the door. I sat motionless and stared at the knob.

A short while later, another rap sounded and the knob turned. The door opened again and two men in suits entered.

Then Parker walked in.

I sprang to my feet, rushed over to him, and flung my arms around him.

"Paul!" I cried, burying my face in his chest.

My head spun, my body trembled, and my legs were of no use. Tears ran down my cheeks as his strong arms wrapped around me and bore me up.

"It's okay, Stella," he whispered into my ear. "The nightmare's over."

The memory came flooding back to me. *The deafening explosion...someone touching me on the shoulder...I look up and the long-haired man is down on the ground, bleeding...and Parker is being helped to his feet by strangers.*

I felt suddenly embarrassed at my reaction, and at the intimacy of the embrace. I pulled my arms away, backed off, and dropped down on my buttocks on the bed.

Parker's face was swollen. The left eye, blackened and puffy, almost closed in on itself. A red circle at the right side of his lip formed where the blood had clotted under his skin.

"Jacques," I said. "Is he—"

"He's in the hospital. Took a bullet in his shoulder."

"Is he going to be alright?"

"He's in stable condition. The doctors said he should be back to his old self in no time, fortunately. Or maybe, in his case, that's not such a fortunate thing."

"Paul, that man with the long hair. I'm almost positive he was there when Ben was shot."

"Highly likely. We should find out before long. You did one of those men in pretty badly. He was treated at the hospital, too, but he'll survive. He'll be questioned soon."

"I saw three of them."

"The other two are dead."

The other men in the room whispered to each other. I recognized the slimmer one with a neat haircut; he had chased us all the way to the airport parking lot. I looked at Parker and raised my eyebrows.

"How are you doing, Ms Jacob?" the slim man said.

He smiled and spoke in a mellow tone, but I felt wary of this former pursuer. I bit my lower lip and stared at him.

"Can we get you anything?"

I shook my head.

"She'll be fine." Parker nudged his chin toward the door. The two men left, quietly shutting the door behind them.

"FBI," Parker said. "All of them. The Bureau have been onto us since we landed."

"You mean they followed us all the way?"

"They lost us when we left the airport, but picked up our trail today. Remember that roadblock last night?"

"The one because of the teenage drag racers who crashed?"

Parker nodded. "I found out there was no accident. It was a set-up by the FBI to snag us. Except, it seems the rookie cop that I got out and spoke with apparently didn't get the memo about bringing us in. Still, it worked to slow us down enough that the fibbies could eventually catch up with us."

"So they were the ones who shot the long-haired man?"

Parker nodded.

"But why were FBI agents following us?

Parker raised his shoulders and splayed his fingers. "I spoke on the phone with someone from the Bureau who'll be here soon. Hopefully he'll fill us in."

Chapter 102

Spike Simmons switched off the microcassette player and placed it next to the video camera, which he had already looked at. He sat with Parker and me at a table in the kitchen of the house. A small television on the counter provided somewhat comforting background noise as it indicated that a world outside existed where life went on as normal.

"How'd you get your hands on this?" Simmons said.

"The night he was shot," I said, "Benoit Dromel told me where he hid this recording and asked me to secure it. He'd told the prime minister he'd made it. He was scared that Peabody was somehow behind his shooting and might find and destroy the recording."

"Who else knows about this?"

"Jacques Tremblay recorded his uncle's confession," Parker said, "but I'm sure he knows nothing about Dromel's conversation with Peabody. Unless Dromel was spreading it around, which I doubt, I think knowledge of this doesn't go beyond this room."

"And you say you think the men who attacked you killed Eric Tremblay?"

"It's a hunch," Parker said. "He talks on the tape about Americans approaching him to cause the spill. Could be our same three. Except they had a strange way of showing their gratitude."

Parker shifted in his seat, then leaned in to Simmons. "The FBI and local police are interviewing the guy who survived, right?"

Simmons nodded. He looked at his watch. "I'm heading over there now. Should've been there twenty minutes ago."

"Mind if I tag along?" Parker said.

Chapter 103

Parker and Simmons stood side by side with their arms folded. A short way off in the small, sparse room, the lead detective on the local force leaned against a wall.

"Your cooperation is much appreciated, Sergeant," Simmons said.

The local cop chewed on a toothpick. "Always happy to oblige."

The three watched the scene playing out on the other side of a one-way mirror.

Two interrogators, one short and balding, the other slim with a prominent chin and goatee, pulled up chairs on opposite sides of a small table. Vincent Williams (aka William Vincent, Vince Wallace, and William Wallace) fidgeted in his seat at the third side of the table, in direct view of the spectators behind the glass. Williams' entire scalp was covered in bandages, giving him the appearance of a mummy.

"So we're gonna try this again," the bald cop said.

Since they had got him into the room, they had been relentless, piling him with questions about the attack on the three Canadians in the abandoned warehouse. They had stopped only when Simmons and Parker had arrived. Now, having listened to Parker's hunch, the interrogators returned with a new tactic.

"Your buddies are gone," the bald cop continued. "They're kaput. There's no use trying to protect them, and they sure as hell aren't in any position to cover for you. Come on, Vincent, make it easy on yourself. Maybe we can work something out and get you a plea bargain if you cooperate."

"If not," the cop with the goatee said, "with some of this stuff, you could swing,"

"So let's start again," the first cop said. "This time from the top, literally. Up in Canada. The police from there tell us they can link you to a murder in a place called Syron Lake."

Williams folded his arms and stared at the table.

The bald cop inhaled loudly. "What can you tell us about that, Vincent?"

The cop with the goatee exchanged glances with his partner, and then slapped his palm on the table. "Answer the question!"

Williams jumped. Recovering from the surprise, he pressed his arms more tightly against his body.

"I know nothing about Canada," he said.

"Eric Tremblay," the balding cop said. "That name mean anything to you?"

Williams poked his tongue against the inside of his cheek and sighed loudly, fidgeting more.

The cop continued. "Eric Tremblay drowned at his camp supposedly after having too much to drink. But the Canadian cops say something's wrong with that picture. You see, the man never drank when he went fishing with his buddy like he did the day he died."

"Smarten up, Vincent," the cop with the goatee said. "We understand the Canadian police have evidence to run with."

"Prints lifted off the beer," the first cop said.

"They believe they can place you guys at Eric Tremblay's camp," the interrogator with the goatee said. "Remember your friends aren't here any more. It's just you. So you'll take the full rap."

William shifted noisily in his chair, unfolded his arms and grabbed the edge of the table.

"Liars!" he shouted. "You're trying to trip me up. But I know the tricks you're up to. You got no prints on those cans. None!"

Williams lifted his chin and snorted. "You'll never make me believe you got my prints to be able to pin this on me. You don't scare me. You won't wear me down and make me confess to something I didn't do. Try that on somebody else."

The cop with the goatee held up his hand. "Calm down there, buddy."

"We've got a ways to go still, Vincent," the balding cop said. "Let's get back to where we were, shall we, with the warehouse on...."

Parker turned to Simmons. "It was them; has to be."

"He's denying it," Simmons said. "But that's not saying much. He's denying everything, right, left and center."

"He said 'those cans.'"

"So?"

"We've never released any information about the four beer cans that were found in Tremblay's boat. I told those two investigators to simply mention prints lifted off 'the beer.' That could suggest anything — bottles, or even a single can. But this punk was quite definite in referring to cans of beer."

"He seemed pretty sure you don't have *his* prints."

"We don't," Parker said. "Remember, I told them to simply tell him we found prints and that we believed we could place him and his cronies at Tremblay's camp. I never said we found his prints."

Simmons questioned Parker with a raised eyebrow.

Parker continued. "We found only Tremblay's prints on the cans. Either this guy knew only Tremblay held the cans and was forced to drink, or that the killers also touched the cans but left no prints because they wore gloves or something. At any rate, he demonstrated that he knew without a doubt that cans of beer were involved in Tremblay's death, which is information only the police and the killers were privy to."

Simmons nodded. This Canadian is slick, he thought.

A sudden loud crash caused Parker, Simmons and the local lead detective to jump. They turned to the one-way mirror and saw Williams on his feet with his hands wrapped around the throat of the cop with the goatee. The other cop struggled to get to his knees and throw an upturned chair from off him.

Two new officers burst into the interrogation room and pounced on Williams. He fought with them, twisting about and flinging his arms in the air. In the melee, Parker caught a flash of red at the back of William's left hand and thought Williams had cut himself.

The officers wrenched Williams' hands behind his back as they subdued him. Even so, their light blue shirts remained unsoiled. In fact, there was no dripping blood anywhere as they carted him out of the room.

Parker walked closer to the glass and studied Williams' hand before the officers shoved him out the door. The redness was permanent — a birthmark, it seemed.

Parker's brain tingled. Something about that struck him as important. What was it?

The local lead investigator stood akimbo. He puffed out his chest and creased his face into a scowl.

"That piece of scum is going to get what's coming to him," he said.

Simmons arched his eyebrows and looked at Parker.

Parker stared back at the FBI agent, and his eyes suddenly lit up as if set aflame. "It was them," he said. "Damn! They killed both of them."

"What are you on about?" Simmons said.

Parker let out a sharp breath. "They killed Eric Tremblay *and* Osgood."

"Who's Osgood?"

"Marcus Osgood, Tremblay's fishing buddy. He was at Eric Tremblay's camp the morning Eric drowned. Osgood died of a gunshot wound the same day."

"Oh, the guy in the trailer?"

Parker nodded. "You know about that?"

Simmons grimaced. "We came across his file during our investigations. I saw the pictures. Not a pretty sight."

"It makes sense now," Parker said, shaking his head. "I had thought Osgood's death was somehow tangled up with Syron Lake's local politics. But it looks like Osgood must have seen or heard something concerning Eric and the Americans and the spill. So the Americans snuffed him out."

"How'd you come up with that?"

"An eyewitness picked up Osgood a short distance from Eric Tremblay's camp and gave him a lift home the morning of their deaths. He recalled that sometime later, he saw a stranger parked not far from Osgood's trailer, apparently spying with binoculars." Parker folded his arms. "Someone with a red blotch at the back of his left hand!"

A door opened behind them and a uniformed officer walked over to the lead investigator.

"You won't believe this, Sarge," the officer said. "You know this morning, that report that came in about a mailman who found the pensioner that was shot dead in Daytona Beach?

"What about it?"

"Well, we went through the belongings of these three yahoos from the warehouse and check out what's on this scrap of paper that we found in their car."

He read out an address.

"Same Daytona address," the lead investigator said, nodding.

Parker knitted his brows as he searched his memory.

He leaned over to Simmons. "Jacques Tremblay said in a letter I read that he was planning to move to Daytona Beach and that he was going to send the address in a follow-up letter. When I was at Dromel's house, I saw some goon steal letters from his mailbox."

"You think your goon and Williams and his gang are connected?" Simmons said.

Parker nodded. "They were all after the two recordings Dromel told Stella about. I can only conclude that the men I saw at Dromel's house got Jacques' Daytona address from one of the letters they stole and somehow passed it on to Williams and his buddies."

"So they were trying to track down Jacques and the old man that got killed was just in the wrong place at the wrong time?"

"Highly likely."

Simmons turned to the lead investigator. "Sergeant, we'd be very interested in seeing the ballistics report of that Daytona Beach homicide. Even if it's preliminary. I want anything that could give us more leverage with this twerp."

Chapter 104

Simmons sat on the bed in one of the rooms of the safe house where the two Canadians were being put up. How long they would stay and how exactly they could help tie up the Mahler case, he wasn't sure.

It was the end of a long day and his mind was only on the two calls that he'd been aching to make.

Finishing up the first, he propped his cell phone against his left ear with his shoulder as he undid his tie.

"Okay, good-night, big man," he said. "Remember, Daddy loves you."

He had been ten minutes late, but his ex was playing nice and allowed him to make up the time. Her birthday was coming up and he thought he would play nice, too. Maybe he would get her a bunch of roses to go along with the usual birthday card. Maybe.

Now, he looked at his watch and quickly punched a number. He listened to the ringing on the other end.

"Be there," he said under his breath.

Finally, a voice came on the line. "Sarah Cohen here."

"Good. I was hoping you hadn't left for the day."

"Spike?"

"Yes. It's me. I wanted to be the first to tell you. You nailed it."

"What are you talking about?"

"You called it right about the tailings breach. It wasn't as a result of any storm. I saw a video today with a guy confessing to causing the whole damn thing."

"You said a video? Where's this guy? Can we question him?"

"He's six feet under. He can't help us any further."

"Was he a nut-job out for kicks or did he do it for Greene or Maitland?"

"Don't know. He didn't give us a link to Greene or Maitland."

"Drat!"

"Not directly, that is."

"What do you mean?"

"The guys who lured him into this mess were the ones who killed him. They're the same ones who took down Benoit Dromel in Trinidad."

"Really?"

"The local police are holding one of them. The other two were killed. One by a Canadian cop and the other by one of our guys."

"Getting anything out of the surviver?"

"He's singing like a bird. We told him ballistics linked him to the murder of a pensioner they happened to drop in on in Daytona, and that an eyewitness placed him at the scene of the murder of the guy who was shot in Syron Lake. He knows he's in it up to his neck, so he's cooperating."

"So where's our tie-in to Mahler then?"

"It's very flimsy, Sarah. This guy doesn't know who hired them. He only knows that Quinn, the ring leader, had been taking orders from someone in London, England."

"That's what you've got?"

"Who could it be other than Greene?"

"You're right," Cohen said. "It's flimsy. All just circumstantial."

"Come on. What about that fight in Monaco that Greene had with Mahler over Syron Lake? It shows strong motive. It's our link right there."

Cohen remained silent.

Simmons sighed and kicked off his shoes. He brought his legs up on the bed and leaned his back against the headboard.

"Well, I was afraid to allow myself to go down that path," he said. "But, I guess I have to face it. All this evidence adds up to little more than a big, fat zero for the Mahler case."

"Maybe," Cohen said.

"I feel sure Greene was behind Mahler's murder and the spill."

"I'm with you there."

"It just eats me up to think he could get away with it all."

"But, Spike, why not try the same tactic with Greene as with the guy who's afraid he'll be charged in the murder of the pensioner?"

"We came down hard on Williams with ballistics evidence. In the Mahler case, there's no smoking gun. The killer made some mistakes, but that hit job was as clean as they come."

"But there's enough to lay it thick on Greene. Ask some of

the local boys in London to drop in on him for a bit of tough questioning. See where that gets you. He may just trip himself up."

"Good idea. I should've thought of that."

"I'm a fount of good ideas, Spike. When you need them, you just have to come to the source."

"Don't get swell-headed on me now." Simmons heard chuckling on the line and he cleared his throat. "Don't forget you have an imperfect record."

"What imperfect record?"

"You may have got it right about the dam being breached, but you were way off base in trying to pin this on Angela Roseau."

"Okay, I admit it turns out she has nothing to do with the Mahler case. But I had to explore all possibilities. I was just doing my–"

"I know, just doing your job, as you say. Lucky thing I didn't let you persuade me to take that theory to the director, otherwise we both might have been hitting the street with our resumes by now. Which, by the way, could still happen in my case if I don't get off the phone with you right away and call up London so I can get something to report to the director."

"Go for it, Spike."

Chapter 105

Wednesday, March 09

The elevator doors parted and Director Robert Hutton walked toward his office. It was eleven in the morning and he had already been to three meetings with congressmen out for his head. The encounters hadn't gone well and his face showed it as he passed the desk of a secretary.

"Sorry, Spike," the secretary said into her headset, "the director is just walking in and he has a briefing as soon as he settles in...."

"Is that Simmons?" Hutton said.

"Yes, sir."

"Put him through."

Hutton placed his briefcase on his desk, took off his jacket and threw it on the leather sofa against the wall. He sat and pulled up his chair. He pressed the speakerphone button and clasped his hands before him on the desk.

"What have you got, Simmons?"

"I'm in Florida, sir, and I've been up all night with our legal attaché in London. Fortunately, Scotland Yard has been very flexible and accommodating toward us. We have some developments."

Simmons briefed Hutton on the Florida events, then got to the London follow-up.

"Two Scotland Yard officers went to Greene's London flat to question him, early this morning. Turned out he's disappeared. His secretary said she hasn't seen him in days."

Hutton grumbled something under his breath.

There was a pause on the other end of the line.

"There's more, sir," Simmons said, eventually.

A glance at his watch told Hutton that two of his department heads were now sitting outside his office twiddling their thumbs. He twisted his head from side to side to shake out the pain that had lodged itself in his throat and jaws since early that morning.

"Go on, Simmons," he said.

"When the Scotland Yard officers arrived, they found Greene's secretary arguing with two men. The men had been speaking about giving up on working with Greene and told the secretary they were there, instead, to sell him some files and wash their hands of a project. They identified themselves as Boris Nazarov, a businessman, and one Dr Anton Laschenko, a former Soviet academic."

"Dr Laschenko, you say?"

"Yes, sir."

"As in the academic from the St Petersburg State Mining Institute?"

After a slight pause, Simmons said, "Yes, sir."

Hutton was well acquainted with the case of Anton Laschenko, which was largely unknown to the public. Four years prior, a former girlfriend of the academic had fallen in with the wrong crowd in Moscow and had drunkenly revealed her ex's old exploits as a ghostwriter of doctoral theses. The indiscreet disclosure had traveled to the ears of those who mattered in Russia. It made Laschenko a wanted man and he'd fled. He was presumed dead by his circle of friends and acquaintances. But, as Hutton's CIA contacts had once revealed, the academic was living comfortably under a new identity in California. That was his reward for passing on information about Soviet degree mills that could be tactically revealed by the US to deeply embarrass the very top of Russia's hierarchy.

"So there was some sort of con game taking place there with this 'Dr Laschenko,' then," Hutton said.

"How did you–" Simmons began, but cleared his throat and quickly changed course. "Precisely, sir. The men who called themselves Nazarov and Laschenko are two slippery Russian fraudsters wanted for preying on high net worth individuals in London. There are warrants for their arrest that go back almost a decade. One of the officers who went to call on Greene had been part of Scotland Yard's Fraud Squad a few years back. He recognized them instantly.

"After they left Greene's flat, Scotland Yard nabbed the men on those outstanding warrants. And what did they find on them? Geological surveys, maps and other papers related to Syron Lake."

"Interesting."

"The documents show a massive vein of gold running through the Syron Lake property owned by Magrelma. And, from the looks of things, it's closest to the surface right under the tailings pond that was breached."

"Ah, so that's the reason, then," Hutton said. "That's why Mahler was killed. He stood in the way of Greene's plans to mine for gold."

"Fool's gold, sir."

"Not even that, Simmons," Hutton said. "Fool's gold is a real substance. Iron pyrite. It's a common mineral that inexperienced miners mistake for gold because it's shiny and yellow. But it's actually worthless. In this case, the fake academic would have been selling Greene information about imaginary gold."

"That's right, sir. The documents are forgeries. Nazarov and Laschenko have implicated a third person in their scheme. A retired Imperial College professor. Said they paid him to vouch for the authenticity of the file."

"So where do we go with all of this?"

"Scotland Yard's interrogators were quite accommodating, sir. At our request, they hinted to the Russians they would try to cut a deal on previous frauds if the men told all they knew about Greene. Scotland Yard didn't mention Mahler or the breached dam. But the Russians spilled the beans. They volunteered that Greene had a partner who'd been blocking the project and that he boasted of eliminating him so he could breach the tailings pond. London says the Russians would testify if ever needed."

"That's helpful. Though they don't sound like the world's most credible witnesses."

"Since Greene has gone underground, perhaps, sir, it may be time to ask for Interpol's help in bringing him in for questioning."

"Yes."

"Thank you, sir. I'll get that process in train right away."

"And Simmons..."

"Yes, sir?"

"Excellent job."

Chapter 106

Hutton called Secretary of State Angela Roseau's office and learned the best chance of catching her was as she was leaving the Capitol after a series of meetings there.

He hated the place, felt strong enmity with the "honorable men" who crawled its corridors. But he could endure its rancid odor if it meant he could spend a few moments with her.

He waited in a walkway along which he thought she would certainly pass. Sure enough, there she was. And walking beside her, no doubt planning her next meeting or her next day, was her ever-present chief of staff Kathy Wang.

"Angela," he said.

She looked up and widened her eyes as she recognized him. "What are you doing in these parts?"

"May I have a word with you for a moment?"

She stopped, and with a slight tilt of her head, she sent Wang ahead.

"Robert, it's always great to see you, but I can't linger too long." There was little enthusiasm in her voice. "Hell of a day it is, and we're only halfway through today's agenda."

"There've been some major developments in the Mahler investigation."

Her eyes grew in intensity. He had her full attention.

"We're pretty certain we know who did it and why. I just thought you'd like to know."

She ran her right index finger along the single strand of pearls around her neck.

"Walk with me," she said

He told of what he'd learned from Simmons, but in reverse, starting with Daniel Greene's greed and delusion.

This wasn't how he'd imagined it, this triumphal moment when he would lay the results of his men's superior sleuthing work at her feet to give her at least the comfort of understanding what had led to the demise of her former fiancé. She was forcing him to tell it at a hurried pace, and under circumstances that didn't allow him to see her eyes or the expression on her face.

"So he died for nothing?" he heard her say. "Killed over some cheap fraud?"

"Yes, at the hands of the son of one of the partners with whom he built that company."

She sighed. "It's hard to even begin to grasp how tragic that is."

"Don't worry. Magrelma will not remain in existence much longer. Greene won't have any spoils to enjoy."

Hutton had already been contemplating seeing to it that the plug would be pulled on the company. He had in mind a list of investment bankers among Magrelma's backers that he needed to call. It was time to close up that shop that had long outlived its usefulness, he thought.

Now that the case had been all but tied up, he felt a twinge of disappointment that this connection with Angela Roseau was coming to an end. He wanted to prolong the moment with her. He related the Florida events, and the Trinidad events, and told her about the recordings the two Canadians had shown his agent.

Roseau stopped abruptly when he got to the part about Peabody.

She held on to his upper arm and squeezed it. He saw her fold her lips and look off in the distance, as if her neurons had gone into overdrive.

"Those tapes," she said, "how soon can you get me a copy of them?"

"Right away."

"And this Syron Lake file with the two murders?"

"That, too, is no problem."

"Great." Her eyes brightened for the first time since he had come upon her. "I want everything, and I mean everything, you've got on this investigation, Robert. Can you do that for me? Immediately?"

"Consider it done."

"Who knows about this?"

"So far a couple of agents on the case and the Canadians involved."

"Could you keep a tight lid on this? As in hermetically sealed?"

"I can try."

"You must do better than try. This is important. None of this must get out."

"I'll do my best."

She tilted her head and stared at him.

"I'll see to it," Hutton said.

"Excellent! Thank you, Robert. I'll be anxiously awaiting that file."

A smile began to form on her lips, but she didn't linger long enough for Hutton to see the glee that sparkled in her eyes.

"Call the president and tell him I need to speak with him urgently," he heard her say to Wang. "I'll need to use The Farm. And get someone in Ottawa to visit Danforth and confirm his position on certain issues. I think...."

She was off, doing her thing. Planning her schemes, making her next moves.

All through this encounter she still didn't seem to have really *seen* him.

What would it take?

He shook his head and turned to find another exit so that he would not have to trail her down the corridor.

Chapter 107

It was just past six in the evening. Parker and I sat at the kitchen table, playing gin rummy. The television was showing CNN news, with the volume on low.

We had just finished a dinner of spaghetti and pasta sauce from a tin that I'd found in the cupboard. It was a respite from the pizza and MSG-laden Chinese take-out we'd been fed over the two days we'd spent at the safe house.

I was tired of being in this sterile place. I'd had enough of giving statements to various officers and recounting the ordeal we'd been through. With all the interviews and a visit by a doctor who cautioned me to take things easy because of the whiplash, I hadn't set foot outside.

I was beginning to feel as if *I* was under house arrest and was being punished when I had been the one trying to bring a corrupt company to justice.

Simmons had assured us that this would end soon and we could go back to normal life. I wanted to ask him to give me a timeline, but he had been scarce all day.

He had called an hour earlier and said to expect an important visitor after supper.

Parker shuffled the pack of cards at lightening speed. "So, you really thought I was doing Demetriou's bidding all along?"

I shrugged. "When you're new in a place, it's sometimes hard to know who to trust."

"For the most part, I can't stand the man."

"That makes two of us."

"He's good buddies with my boss. They've been friends since high school. And I can't stand my boss either."

"Lucky you."

We laughed, and I thought about something for a while that made me sigh. "So you're not seeing any connection between Demetriou and Osgood's murder."

"No. This looks like it's all on the company and those three Americans."

"And it had nothing to do with what Osgood said about Demetriou during the election?"

"I don't think Syron Lake politics had anything to do with Osgood's death."

"And you don't think Demetriou was acting for the company when he tried to scare me off doing anything about the spill?"

"From what I've heard about the investigation so far, it seems those three Americans were taking orders from some high company official in London," Parker said.

"In England, you mean?"

Parker nodded. "So this seems like it was way out of Demetriou's league. Can't say for certain, but from the looks of it, I'd say Demetriou was simply looking out for his own bottom line when he wanted to shoot down any alarm you wanted to raise. From his perspective, anything that doesn't paint a rosy picture of Syron Lake harms tourism, scares off retirees, and takes money out of his pocket."

"As much as I dislike Demetriou," I said, "it's a relief to think Syron Lake doesn't have a murderer as our mayor."

Footsteps sounded through the living room and Parker and I turned to look at the open door. Simmons walked into the kitchen, then stood aside, extending his arm toward us.

"They're in here, sir," he said.

A tall, older man in an expensive suit entered, carrying a briefcase. I recognized him instantly. By the glance Parker gave me, he recognized him too.

"Director Hutton," Simmons said, "Detective Sergeant Paul Parker and Ms Stella Jacob."

Simmons stretched his hand and made an arc that took in the three of us. "Paul, Stella, this is the Director of the FBI."

Parker jumped to his feet and his chair noisily scraped the floor.

"Sir," he said.

Chapter 108

Parker looked up from the one-sheet document the FBI director had placed in front of him along with a silver pen. The tiny, windowless room was bare except for a small round table and the two chairs on which they sat. Hutton had requested to speak with him in private and he now understood why.

He tapped the pads of his fingertips noiselessly on the table top and studied the familiar face of the stranger who had him in a steady gaze.

He had seen him countless times in television interviews, and in newspapers and magazines. It had never crossed his mind that he would have ever seen this man in person, let alone that he'd take up the defensive position he now found himself adopting with him.

Parker edged the pen away with his index finger. "With all due respect, sir, why should I sign this?"

"Come now, Detective Sergeant Parker. It's a simple enough document to understand."

"I know what it says. You want me to agree to not say anything about what happened, to anyone — ever. But why should I agree to that?"

"Let's not make this unpleasant. Should I remind you that four weapons were found inside the abandoned building when the FBI rescued you? Your prints were the only ones on the Beretta."

Parker squinted at Hutton.

"That particular firearm was among a cache stolen from the Fort Lauderdale home of a wealthy businessman, six months ago," Hutton said. "We happen to know who's been fencing them. An underground figure whose misdeeds we've turned a blind eye to as he's served as an informant on occasion. It's just a matter of time before he resurfaces. With the long rap sheet he's facing, he'll want a plea bargain. You can be certain that to save his own skin, he'll give you up in a heartbeat as the purchaser of that stolen weapon."

The director leaned back and looked Parker deeply in the eyes. "That would not do much for your career, now, would it?"

Parker matched the older man's stare. The last sentence punched him in the solar plexus. But he didn't flinch; at least he thought he didn't.

"I nearly lost my life getting that evidence. I don't want to see–"

The director held up his palm. "This matter is being handled comprehensively."

Parker rapped his fingernails on the table.

"Listen to me, Detective Sergeant," Hutton said. "You stumbled upon something way beyond your ambit. You did well in protecting Ms Jacob and Jacques Tremblay, and in gathering this evidence. But now it's time to step back. Let those who are best-placed to handle this situation take things from here."

Chapter 109

I had finished doing the dishes and was settling down with one of the numerous potboiler novels that lay about the house when Simmons came to fetch me.

I could understand the director wanting to talk with Parker in private as he'd done earlier. I imagined that they might have discussed law enforcement matters. I couldn't understand why he wanted to now speak with me alone.

Hutton placed a printed sheet of paper and a pen in front of me.

"I'll get directly to the point, Ms Jacob. You've somehow got entangled in some business that's pretty nasty as it is. But you must know that what you've been exposed to is just the tip of the iceberg. It ties in to some serious investigations that are ongoing and which have major ramifications. A lot is pending on this and we can't afford to have any part of it jeopardized."

I glanced at the page before me and my eyes caught the words "in strict confidence."

"What are you asking of me, Director Hutton?"

"For various reasons, which cannot be disclosed, none of what you know can be repeated outside these walls."

"What? I don't understand."

"We need for you to keep all of this strictly confidential, Ms Jacob."

"I don't get it. If nothing is supposed to be said, how will there be a trial to convict that man for Ben's...for Benoit Dromel's murder? How will that company be brought to justice for releasing millions of gallons of radioactive waste?"

"You use the word justice, Ms Jacob."

"Yes, of course."

"Is that what you're after?"

"Absolutely. That's why I got involved in any of this. I didn't want to see the people responsible for the spill getting away with polluting the environment. I wanted justice for our community. And I want to see justice for Benoit Dromel."

"Justice, Ms Jacob," Hutton said in a slow, professorial manner, "is a universal principle that existed long before our legal system was established. It is not confined to the tip of a judge's pen."

I was trying to read Hutton. I studied the features that were so familiar to me from magazines and newspapers. He was a legend, greatly admired by my editor at *The Sentinel*, where I'd first heard of him when I took up the crime beat. There was no doubt that he had a broader understanding of the world than I did. And his air of authority made my mousey self quiver. But what he was asking seemed unacceptable to me. I had gone through too much over the last few hours to simply cave in as I normally would in a situation like this.

"I'm sorry, Director Hutton. But three men attacked Benoit Dromel. Now he's dead. And one of them is still alive. I can't agree to let that man just walk free."

"He won't, I assure you."

"But I'm probably to only witness who can–"

"Miss Jacob, fom what I understand, Trinidad, the jurisdiction in which this incident occurred, doesn't have any information to go on to even begin to link Dromel's killing to the three men who attacked you in the warehouse. It's doubtful the prosecution you're hoping for will ever see the light of day."

I pursed my lips.

"Sometimes it's necessary to be coldly practical, Ms Jacob." Hutton spoke with a patient voice. "Sometimes you need to consider only the objective and remain open to the possibility that it can be achieved in ways that may not be immediately obvious.

"While the Trinidad shooting may be a difficult matter to prosecute, there's a strong case against Vincent Williams in the homicide of a Daytona pensioner. There's also an assortment of other offenses...possession of stolen vehicles, stolen arms.

"There will most certainly be a plea bargain. And he'll get a reduced sentence for cooperating. But he's headed for the penitentiary, and you can rest assured that he'll not be getting out anytime soon."

The tone of the director's voice and the expression on his face took me back to my days at *The Sentinel*. My editor had told me about certain unfortunate convicts who went in, thinking they'd be back out on the streets at the end of their sentence. But then, *things happened*, my editor had said. It would be either through their own hotheadedness, or because a fellow inmate or a prison guard didn't take to them, or it would be at the behest of some higher authority, perhaps the prison warden or some outside figure. The best case scenario was that their run-ins would tack on additional years to their sentence and they would be old, spent forces by the time they got out. A not unlikely scenario was that they would be found face-down on the shower floor, a sharpened screwdriver or some other makeshift weapon driven through their back.

"Did Paul...did Detective Sergeant Parker agree to sign something like this?"

"We had a fruitful discussion."

"And what about Jacques Tremblay? He knows half of this stuff."

"It's all been arranged." The director gave something approaching a smile. "He's agreed to go into a protection program as soon as he's released from the hospital."

I tilted my head and tried to catch the significance of what he'd said.

"If that's what you want, that can be arranged for you as well, Ms Jacob. New identity. Somewhere decent to live. We could set you up in a new career. It would be a whole new life, and you could forget that you'd learned anything about this matter."

I didn't even have to think about it. The last couple of years had been pretty crummy. But it was all part of being who I was. I was not about to give up my identity.

It was a different matter when it came to Jacques Tremblay, though. The teenage girl at the campground with the braces and a woman's body flashed before my mind. Jacques had been lucky to have so narrowly escaped getting into a situation where he could have ended up being arrested for child kidnapping – and worse.

Going into an FBI protection program was perhaps the best thing that could have happened to him. Left to his own devices, he was a tragedy waiting to happen.

I was still not buying this, though. "But all this still leaves the company off the hook. Here we have irrefutable evidence that a mining company breached its own dam and I'm supposed to stay quiet?"

The director looked at me with patient eyes.

"Ms Jacob, you've filed a class action lawsuit concerning this spill, haven't you?"

"Yes."

"Well, if you know anything about the corporate world, you'll understand that few companies would exist without credit. And creditors hate lawsuits with the potential for huge damages. I can't say more, but I can tell you that the parent company of Syron Lake Resources is unraveling as we speak. The real corporate culprit has gotten its comeuppance."

"But–"

My throat tightened. I could hardly form the words. This was it. This was precisely the kind of scenario I'd feared when I'd spoken at the hearing. I'd thought that Syron Lake Resources itself might go bankrupt, but its parent company going bust was much worse. I had not been able to find any information on exactly which entity owned Syron Lake Resources and had given up trying as I'd quickly realized that it was hidden under layer after layer of paper companies. Now that parent company was about to pull off a disappearing act and escape all of its responsibilities.

Hutton studied my face. "What's troubling you, Ms Jacob?"

"If they go bust...."

"The Bureau is not without influence in this area," Hutton said. "The assets of the parent company will be sold off. Remember, the word 'credit,' Ms Jacob. At this level, nothing happens without it. That makes for incredible leverage in a situation like this where the worlds of law enforcement and business collide, and law enforcement has the bigger picture. I'm sure it can be arranged that the new owner is required to agree to a reasonable settlement of the class action."

"Shouldn't my lawyers be in on this discussion?"

"What's there for them to discuss? Their battle is with an Ontario company as it now exists, and their battleground is the Ontario courts. They have nothing to do with the FBI and whatever influence the Bureau may be able to bring to bear in the investment banking community in the US."

"Well, what about the tailings pond itself? Will Syron Lake Resources, or whoever eventually owns it, still be trusted to control that site?"

"That's in the hands of the remaining members of the panel of your nuclear authority. I've been briefed on your presentation at the hearing and I'm well acquainted with your concerns. The Bureau can't control what the panel will decide. But, perhaps, in any settlement to the class action the new owners could agree to relinquish day-to-day management of the site. And even if the nuclear authority doesn't allow that, the settlement could include a commitment to at least bear the financial burden for a period of time, say, twenty years or thereabouts."

I looked at the sheet. None of this was included there, on that a one-sided agreement requiring me to keep my mouth shut.

Hutton seemed to read my mind. He sat back and looked at me unblinkingly. "I give you my word on everything we've said here."

"Yes, but–"

"Miss Jacob, even if you have doubts, put them aside for now. I am certain you will come to realize this is the best outcome that could be hoped for."

He clasped his fingers and rested this hands on the table. The discussion was over.

After he'd gotten my signature, Hutton left me alone in the bare room. I stared at the walls as I tried to process what had just happened.

I'd thought Benoit Dromel had power. This was power of a whole other magnitude.

I'd raised my concerns. But really, there was no negotiating with a man like Robert L. Hutton. I was sure that even if I'd worked up the courage to use them, the womanly wiles I'd learned would have had no effect on him. A woman could not so easily master a man of his position and experience.

He was one of those select few in the world who had only but to give a command, or even merely make a suggestion, and things got done that affected the lives of millions.

There was no reason for him to listen to me And yet he'd answered all of my concerns.

Just like that, he was making it all happen: everything I'd set out to do; everything that Osgood would have wanted.

I understood, now, how this worked.

It was all about Hutton's iceberg.

Things I couldn't see were happening below the surface. The results Osgood and I had sought had been opened up because they somehow aligned with the agenda of a powerful man who could get things done.

Osgood and I were so far removed from anything resembling power, I couldn't even get an eager, cherubic-looking radio reporter to broadcast one sentence about the tailings spill. As the powerless, we could achieve nothing.

And yet, if I hadn't started the process of applying to speak at the hearing or to get class action lawyers at Osgood's prompting, there wouldn't even have been any of Hutton's promises.

The realization was encouraging and daunting at the same time. We had gotten through because, for whatever reason, someone in a position of power wanted the same things we did.

It made me wonder if the powerless ever stood a chance of having their demands met if their goals never somehow meshed with those of the powerful.

I sighed.

And then, another realization about Hutton's confidentiality document suddenly struck me. Everything I'd discovered through this experience, and everything I'd said and done, was going to be kept under a tight lid.

That meant my unfortunate involvement with Benoit Dromel would also never be made public.

My name would be spared.

Chapter 110

The Farm was a sprawling Maine property that had served as a presidential retreat going back three administrations. Fewer than a dozen people knew that the term "The Farm" was also an oblique reference to the tiny shack that straddled the US/Canada border.

The double meaning was shared by only those at the very top of any administration, and it served to facilitate clandestine tête-à-têtes between the two North American neighbors.

The official activity logs would say the occupant of the White House had visited the country residence for some rest and relaxation, and would even record a rambling drive through the Maine countryside.

What would not appear in any official records would be the detour along a long, winding road, whose entrance bore a nondescript sign that said, "Private Property: No Trespassing." There would be no mention of the visit to the property that was guarded 24/7 by officers from an operational unit that did not officially exist.

Hidden among conifers and shielded from satellites by an overhead net, the shack was surrounded on both the US and Canadian sides by two acres of forest enclosed by an electrified fence.

Almost two decades earlier, in the run-up to creating a free trade agreement, an administration under enormous pressure from all sides felt it necessary to meet and talk face-to-face with northern counterparts, away from the public glare. And so, the shack came into being, allowing both sides to secretly craft deals worth billions with the requisite intricate structure to ensure the greatest benefits flowed to those who mattered.

The months of horse trading came and went, and the treaty was eventually signed. But the administrations on both sides of the border saw it fit to keep this channel of communication open for times that required the utmost secrecy.

Riding in a secret service-chauffeured SUV, with only Kathy

Wang at her side, Secretary of State Angela Roseau felt this was such a time.

It was highly unusual that she would have use of The Farm. But she had apprised the president fully of the situation and had persuaded him that it was best that he not get involved, and that she alone could accomplish the required task.

Her old friend, Hutton, had come through for her. In the briefcase that sat on the seat between her and Wang was all the information and evidence from the Syron Lake investigation. During the helicopter ride to Maine, she had rehearsed in her mind every word she would utter, every expression she would let show on her face.

Now that the headlamps of the SUV pierced the pitch-black road as they neared the shack, her heart pounded in her chest and her palms itched at the thought of what she was about to do.

Even in the darkness and privacy of the vehicle, she would not let those human frailties betray her. She held her facial muscles steady as she fingered the strand of pearls around her neck.

Her party was the first to arrive. The room had no windows, only two doors, one on each side of the border. It was bare, except for two green, plastic chairs and a cheap, wooden table that the original users of this place thought amusing to sit at as they discussed billions of dollars in commerce.

The one bulb in the shack was powered by a generator. Roseau listened to it hum softly outside. The cone-shaped lampshade hung low in the center of the room and concentrated light on a small digital audio recorder and a closed manila file which sat on the table.

Kathy Wang and the security detail stood in the darkness, against the wall. Roseau stood behind the chair, on the US side. With her arms folded, she stared in the direction of the door on the Canadian side.

She waited. Far longer than was reasonable. But she was patient. She would not have wanted to miss what was to come for the world.

Suddenly, the door on the Canadian side creaked open. Multiple footsteps followed; minders and security types who would occupy the outer darkness on the other side, Roseau thought.

John J. Peabody marched out of the darkness and stood before her on the opposite side of the table.

He propped his hands on his hips and his jacket flaps splayed open like small wings. "I was in a meeting with First Nations leaders when the president called."

"I think you'll find this a matter of urgency that warrants your attention," Roseau said.

"I think you fail to appreciate how important that meeting was. We've been trying to tie up negotiations that've been dragging on for decades with those people. And where's the president, anyway? Why isn't he here already? I'm half an hour late getting here as it is."

"He couldn't make it." Her voice was cool, bereft of emotion.

She saw his eyes narrow. She had expected that he wouldn't have been pleased to realize that this was between him and her alone. No, he wasn't pleased about that at all.

Peabody huffed. "So what's so important that we have to go to these lengths to meet here?"

"I believe you will want to hear this."

She picked up an earbud that was attached to the digital recorder and held the cord out to him.

Peabody inhaled and hesitated. Roseau did not budge or say anything further, and the cord dangled between them. Finally, Peabody grabbed the cord, then stuffed the bud into his ear.

Roseau pressed the play button. She observed the muscles under Peabody's left eye twitch as he listened to Dromel's recording of their conversation about Syron Lake. Peabody's lips parted and his chest heaved with every breath.

The Canadian prime minister tugged at the cord and the earbud slipped out of his ear. His face turned chalk white as he stared at Roseau. His hard gaze from earlier was now replaced by a wild look in his eyes.

"You know, of course," Roseau said matter-of-factly, "that this official was shot shortly after this discussion."

"I had nothing to do with his death," Peabody said, raising his voice.

Roseau felt the corners of her mouth turning up into a smile, and she held herself back. She had him against the ropes and she was enjoying it. But she had only begun.

"If you care to listen, there's something else on there," she deadpanned. "It's audio from a video confession by a man named Eric Tremblay, a maintenance worker with this Syron Lake mining company. The spill was deliberate, you see."

Peabody jerked back his head. The fact that she'd played his fateful words back to him was enough to convince him that there was indeed such a confession, she thought. He didn't need to listen further to the recording.

She pushed the manila file toward him and opened it. She spread out its contents on the table: photocopies of Dromel's bank book; the Florida police reports on the warehouse attack on the three Canadians, and the murder of the pensioner; photos from the Syron Lake police investigations into Eric Tremblay's and Marcus Osgood's deaths.

Peabody's eyes darted across each piece of the gruesome display. Any blood that was left in face receded completely.

"Rather nasty business," Roseau said. It was like twisting a knife that had been rammed into his throat. "Besides the spill itself, there's bribery of a public official; three, possibly four, murders; attempted murder; illegal arms; auto theft. Not the kind of thing a prime minister would want to be associated with, wouldn't you say?"

"What do you want?" Peabody chewed his lower lip.

She wanted to burst out in a laugh. She restrained herself. The man was so pathetic. He seemed to think he could bargain with her.

"Either you jump or you'll be pushed," Roseau said.

Peabody's eyes told her he didn't understand, or chose not to.

"Go quietly," she said, "and this will be kept under wraps. You'll walk away with your reputation intact and you can salvage what's left of your career."

Roseau glanced down at her watch and then returned her eyes to Peabody's. "You have six hours before this begins to leak out to the press."

Peabody clenched his jaws and fired darts at Roseau with his eyes. She remained immobile.

After a lengthy silence, Peabody snorted. "I've got you figured out, Roseau. You're a bitch! Plain and simple. It's not that you act tough because you're doing a tough job. You're in this job because it gives you an excuse to wallow in your bitchiness."

Roseau allowed her lips to spread into a smile.

"I take that as a compliment, John," she said. "You see, tomorrow, I'll still be occupying one of the highest positions in the most powerful nation in the world. And you'll be out of a job. Sounds to me like you could benefit from learning how to be a bitch."

Without warning, Peabody flung his arms out and sent the table crashing. The digital recorder hit the floor with a metallic thud and papers went flying left and right.

Secret service agents stepped forward into the light and appeared at Roseau's side.

Angus Firestone, who had accompanied his boss and had stood watching from the darkness, dashed forward, placing himself between Peabody and Roseau.

Peabody snorted, stared daggers at Roseau for the last time, then turned and stomped toward the door.

Chapter 111

I was agitated. So was Parker. The director had made it clear that the agreement I'd signed encompassed everybody, including Parker. The director hadn't directly confirmed that he'd made Parker also agree not talk. If he had, I imagined he'd told Parker the same thing about talking with me.

Several times during games of Scrabble and Monopoly at the kitchen table, Parker had skirted the subject of whether I'd had seen the director alone. But with agents milling about the house, I wasn't prepared to test the limits of the agreement.

It was close to midnight. Neither of us wanted to sleep, and we were now into card games.

"You're either no good at gin rummy," I said looking at my winning hand, "or very gallant in letting me beat you every time."

"I just don't seem to have any luck, tonight."

He sounded amused and I looked up at Parker to see whether his words were genuine or whether he was playing with me. Pictures flashing on the television behind him caught my attention.

"Raise the volume, will you. There seems to be some excitement over Peabody."

Parker got up and pressed the volume control.

"...and as I said, Michael," the female reporter blinking into brilliant light in front of a dimly-lit Parliament building said, "Ottawa is reeling from the sudden and unexpected resignation of Prime Minister John Peabody. Nobody, but nobody, not political analysts, nor supporters, nor rivals in his own party, had any inkling that this was coming."

Parker shook his head. "Wow, that's—"

"Shhh!" I put my finger to my lips. "Turn it up louder, will you."

Parker complied and we listened again to the reporter. "Of course in his very brief resignation letter, Peabody mentioned that he was leaving for personal reasons. We have been hearing unconfirmed reports that, perhaps, Peabody's cancer is back, but, as I said, there has been no confirmation on that.

"In fact, the prime minister's...I should say, the ex-prime minister's chief of staff point blank refused to comment when approached by reporters. If you will recall, when the issue of Mr Peabody's health became an issue in his last re-election campaign, he made a statement to the effect that everyone was entitled to privacy when it came to health matters...."

Simmons walked into the kitchen. His eyes homed in on the television.

"Peabody's just quit," I said.

"Huh!" Simmons uttered.

"What are the chances that his departure has something to do with Syron Lake?" Parker said.

Simmons tore his eyes away from the screen. Parker and I looked pointedly at him.

"The answer to that," he said, "is above my pay grade."

Chapter 112

Thursday, March 10

It was the wee hours of the morning. Angela Roseau reclined against the silk-covered settee in the living room of their Georgetown brownstone while her husband, ex-congressman Steve Roseau, sat on the ottoman in front of her, massaging her soles.

He had offered to pour her champagne; she had declined. Not because of the hour, but because she'd always found champagne too light and insubstantial. Instead, she sipped a glass of VSOP.

"I was on the phone with Danforth within minutes of his swearing in as prime minister," she said. "He was appointed as the caretaker until his party can elect a new leader."

"When will that happen?"

"Not for another nine months. He assured me we'll have a softwood lumber agreement stitched up long before then. Even if we don't, he feels pretty confident that he'll get the nod from his party to continue on as prime minister. So the softwood deal is pretty much certain."

"What's the president saying?"

"He's ecstatic. We're going to deliver: he's kept his promises, has a feather in his cap, and those lumber execs are going to open up their coffers to the party — and to the party's next presidential candidate."

"And who might that be?" the ex-congressman said with a wink.

"Oh, I expect there'll be hard nomination battle. The Secretary of Defense has been quite aggressive in lobbying the president for his nod. That's why, before I went up to The Farm, I made sure I got the president to agree that if I secured the softwood lumber deal, I'd have his endorsement."

"It's in the bag, Angela." Steve Roseau chuckled. "You're unstoppable."

"Let's not get ahead of ourselves, Steve."

"Come on, you know whoever the president endorses is a shoe-in for the party's nomination. And I daresay, for the general election itself."

He raised his glass of scotch. "Here's to the next president of the United States. To the first female president of the United States."

Angela Roseau raised her glass and smiled.

"We have a long way to go, yet," she said. "The nomination convention is eighteen months away."

"The other contenders will envy your luck in getting the endorsement instead of them."

"That endorsement didn't come by luck, Steve. It was an opportunity I had to create myself, something I had to spin out of thin air.

"Like everyone around the president who figures they've got a shot at occupying the Oval Office after him, I, too, have been trying to bend his ear. With scant success up until now. Robert Hutton's files gave me the big break I desperately needed.

"If the information Robert passed on to me had fallen into anyone else's hands, nothing would have come of it. But the instant he mentioned Peabody, I saw how I could turn the whole sorry mess into a solution for so many problems."

"President Roseau! Now, there you have two words that belong together. Americans are going to get used to the sound of that."

"Oh, I intend that they will. But we've got a nomination battle and then an entire election to fight first."

Steve Roseau drained his glass and stood up. He had had three straight shots as he had listened to his wife recount the night's triumph. Now he could barely keep his eyelids open. He staggered to the back of the settee. He slid his hands down along his wife's arms and squeezed her just above the elbows. Bending over her, he pressed his cheek against her silky hair and his warm breath cascaded over her right ear.

"That's my girl," he said. "Run. Run, and show them what you've got."

He straightened up and chuckled. "We'll soon be moving into the White House."

Chapter 113

The red Lamborgini raced past a slow-moving Alpes-Maritimes bus on the narrow road that wound down from the French mountain village of Lantosque. Since he'd heard that the Canadian official had been shot, Daniel Greene had fled to the Riviera. He had holed up in a small but well-appointed farmhouse high in the hills, and had made himself invisible to the world, particularly to the Verhoevens.

Now he was headed for Nice, to meet up with Nadia. Things had taken a turn for the worse. But he would let nothing stand in the way of his goals.

He dialed her cell.

"Heard from Nazarov and Laschenko?"

"Not since they left the office."

"Damn, they've probably gone underground now."

"They looked spooked when those men said they were with Scotland Yard."

"Damn that Laschenko and his bloody past. I warned them not to let that nonsense about the fake PhDs interfere with my business. I need to get that file."

"I've tried all the old ways to contact them."

"You shouldn't have let them leave without getting that file."

"I'm sorry, Daniel. I couldn't get you on your mobile."

"I was out of range. Service is spotty up in the hills over here."

"I tried to ask them about the price, but they insisted on talking with only you."

"I would have paid anything, Nadia. Do you realize what we're sitting on?"

"I remember translating the word 'gold' for you that one time that they showed us the file. But you've never really explained."

"Gold and uranium occur together. Often one is predominant and the other isn't in quantities that are economical to extract. But in certain cases, like the mighty Witwatersrand in South Africa for example, you hit the motherlode with both. Magrelma's property in Syron Lake is one of those cases."

"And they never mined gold there?"

"That's because the gold seam that was found has been kept secret in that lost file for decades."

"Why?"

"In-fighting in the company. But it means that the opportunity falls to *me* to develop that gold mine, today. It's about one tenth the size of the Witwatersrand. Even so, we're talking about billions of dollars worth here."

Greene felt his pulse raise just talking about this. "Things are hot right now, but we can't let anything stop progress with developing that site."

"Yes but, Daniel, I checked, and what Scotland Yard came back and told me is true. It's on Interpol's website. You're wanted for questioning."

"Any further information on what for?"

"The website doesn't say. All I know is the police told me it's concerning irregularities in Magrelma's operations."

"It could only be about the spill. Verhoeven and Peabody are probably behind this. I can't get hold of that bloody Quinn to find out about the tapes." Greene snorted. "And what about the Dutch freak?"

"Hans Verhoeven has left five messages since he came by yesterday looking for you."

"Don't want to see that animal ever again. Are you sure no one knows you've come to see me?"

"I chartered the flight over as you instructed. I haven't noticed anyone following me."

"Good. We can do this, Nadia. We'll find Nazarov and Laschenko and we'll get that file. You'll just have to be my proxy and keep behind Maitland so that he doesn't drop the ball with Syron Lake."

"He's worried. Said he doesn't understand why you haven't gotten in touch with the police."

"Who the hell cares what he thinks? He knows nothing about what's really going on here. We just have to work him like a puppet so we can get that gold mine up and running."

Greene heard a sigh on the line and it irritated him. "You still with me?"

"I'm sorry, Daniel, but I'm a bit worried, too."

"Don't go all weak on me, Nadia. I'm trusting you to be steady."

She was silent.

"I've had rotten luck with the people I've trusted so far. Thought Verhoeven senior was a cool customer when I called in the favor he owed Isaac Greene. Now, he's after my scalp. That Canadian official turned out to be much more hard-headed than I expected. It's *his* greed, plus Quinn and his men proving to be trigger-happy idiots, that's landed us in this mess. Only the Russian who took out Mahler did exactly what he was supposed to do."

The line remained quiet.

"Hello? You still with me, Nadia?"

"Yes."

"Look, you've got to trust me, okay? I know what I'm doing. I can handle this. Okay, so I made some mistakes. I thought using people at the top, Verhoeven and Peabody, that is, would have ensured success. But I've learned my lesson. I've got to keep things in a tight circle of people I know really well so I can be sure I can rely on them. And I need to be sure that you're one of them. Are you with me, Nadia?"

"Yes."

"Good. I'll be at the restaurant in ten minutes."

Chapter 114

The Key West airport was throbbing with passengers. With my shorts and fanny pack, and with Parker's flaming orange and blue, palm-covered shirt, we looked like typical tourists heading home. Except I also wore a neck brace and Parker looked like he'd had an encounter with a shark.

Bruised and swollen as it was, his was a very manly face — a handsome face, even if sprouting a rough stubble. The injuries gave me an excuse to let my eyes linger there without having to explain myself or look away quickly when his eyes met mine.

But I was determined not to repeat the last mistake I had made.

Being cooped up in the FBI safe house had given me time to look back and realize that my heart had been in search of a hero and I had fallen hard for Benoit Dromel on the rebound from two-timing Peter Redmill.

There were scars from both those disasters that I needed to let heal. So while Parker had shown himself to be a genuine hero, I would not foolishly rush into anything serious again. Where Parker was concerned, I would tread slowly, and, hopefully, more wisely.

Simmons, who had driven us to the airport, shook my hand briefly. He gave a shallow bow. "All the best to you, my lady."

Then he gave Parker a much longer shake, with both hands.

"So it's back to quiet, small town life for you guys, then?" the agent said.

"Back to writing for me," I said. "And I mean fiction. I think I'll give writing about radioactive spills a break for a while."

"Well, I'm officially on vacation now," Parker said. "I'll be sticking around in Syron Lake only long enough to get a doctor's note for the days I didn't show up for work."

Simmons chuckled. "With the way you look right now, that should be easy."

Parker joined in the laughter. "Then it's off to spend time with the family. Quiet evenings on the patio listening to Aunt Bertha go on about her bunions. Sounds rather appealing now."

Simmons slapped Parker on the shoulder. "Wasn't the best of circumstances, but it was nice meeting...." He furrowed his brow and looked at the television over Parker's shoulder. It was turned on to CNN.

"Hold on. I've got to see this." Simmons strode closer to the overhead screen.

Parker and I followed.

Overlaying scenes of a wreckage were pictures of a man and a woman. The footage looped between a winding, hillside road and a burnt-out car.

"French police are saying very little about the incident." The reporter in a trench coat shouted into the microphone that she held. "What we do know, so far, is that the police had received a tip that the driver of the car, Daniel Greene, had been spotted at a restaurant in Nice and that he fled when approached by the police, who were seeking him for questioning.

"Of, course, as you heard in our earlier report, drivers who were eyewitnesses claimed to have heard a shot or shots fired, then the car exploded and slid off the Moyen Corniche. The charred remains of the vehicle were found in a deep gully with the driver's body burnt beyond recognition."

Simmons' mouth was open. His eyes seemed glazed over. It was as if he was in a trance as he watched the television.

The reporter continued. "Now, there's very little information coming out about the nature of the investigation that led to this encounter with French police. But we are hearing that it had to do with irregularities in the operations of Magrelma Mines, the private mining concern, of which the late Mr Greene was a partner.

"We also understand that an associate of Mr Greene's, one Nadia Imre, had exited the restaurant with him at the time he was spotted by the police. She was taken in and questioned, and later released. News has also reached us that Mr Greene's London apartment has been cordoned off, and that police there have been executing a search since...."

Parker turned to Simmons.

"What's this then, Spike?"

The FBI agent hunched his shoulders and splayed his fingers.

Parker wouldn't let it go. "Williams said the three of them

worked for someone in London. This Greene guy, that was him, wasn't it?"

Simmons took a step back and held up both hands, showing his palms.

"Sorry, pal. From hereon, as far as this case is concerned, it's...." Simmons ran his hand in front of his lips, from left to right, as if closing a zip. "Orders directly from the boss."

He bowed, then turned and walked away.

Parker and I watched the agent's retreating figure.

We turned again to the screen. The news helicopter hovered over the scorched hillside and the camera zoomed in on the charred skeleton of the car.

The reporter said it was a Lamborghini.

"Just imagine that," Parker said.

"What?"

"This is probably him, Stella. The man who was behind everything. And he's just gone down with a Lamborghini as his funeral pyre."

"A wise man told me, recently," I said, "that justice isn't confined to the tip of a judge's pen."

Epilogue

Angela Roseau sauntered down to the office in the basement, relishing the tranquility that dusk brought.

It was Friday and she had the Georgetown townhouse to herself. Her husband and two of his cousins had taken off that morning for a four-day escape to the private Caribbean island owned by a long-time family friend. A boys-only adventure. Wives would only be a distraction on their deep-sea fishing outings, he'd said.

Her husband had an aversion to anything resembling work, and *that* had worked in the favor of their relationship. If the Roseau name were to advance during his lifetime, it would happen through her. He was content with that. As a result, he was reliably discreet, and deeply loyal to her.

Whether those not infrequent, wives-excluded activities included some form of female participation, she could not say. She had certainly made it clear to Steve at the start of their marriage that if he planned to be like his father in seeking outside companionship, *she* would not behave like his mother and tolerate decades of being Mrs Roseau in name only while he flaunted the drawing power his family's fortune had for starlets and assorted desperate females.

As far as the world knew — and as far as she chose to believe — he was a faithful husband.

And a good husband.

What she appreciated most of all was that, apart from her chief of staff, he was the one person in the world in whom she could confide. It was a relief to be able to share her exploits with someone who understood her completely and supported her fully.

Yet, there were parts of herself that she held back. Some things ran just too deep to untangle from her heart and release to another.

In the Tudor style office, she pushed aside a false oak panel to get to the safe behind it. After dialing the combination, she took out two thick, leather-bound journals and a fat, gold pen.

She settled at the large glass desk, which was bare, except for a Tiffany lamp that cast a soft, amber glow in the deepening darkness.

Her palm ran over the smooth, dark brown surface of the older of the two books. She had no need to open it. She was familiar with what filled the pages between the two sturdy covers. It was enough for her to touch the journal for a lifetime of memories and their attached emotions to flood through her.

Somewhere close to the middle was a page on which she had written words she had re-read hundreds of times over the years. She knew the first sentence by heart.

Last night, I met the man who holds the key to my destiny.

Bill Mahler had not been the handsomest or the wealthiest bachelor at the dinner party at which they'd been introduced. According to the "pillow ambition" her mother had instilled in her – by which women ascended in the world through an intelligent choice, and allurement, of a partner – she should have ignored him.

Yet, something had stirred in her when their eyes had met.

The strange mixture of tension and ease she'd felt in speaking with him, and which she had recognized from his somewhat uncertain manner that he, too, had felt, had told her this was no ordinary connection.

He was ambitious and had made great strides in his business. The first few hours they had spoken had been enough to fill her with a desire to be at this man's side as he forged ahead. She saw herself having and raising his children, and supporting him in everything he did.

And he had wanted the same; everything that happened between them had told her as much.

What a shame it was that Fate had stepped in and had forced him to choose between his desire to feel fulfilled as a man by being with her, and his desire for fulfillment as a business titan.

But Bill didn't want to choose. It was the height of his conceit and ambition that he thought he could have both.

Angel Roseau sighed involuntarily.

In her mind, she saw the wild-eyed creature he had been as he sat on the sofa at her Chelsea apartment pleading with her to go along with his plan. They would call off their engagement and he would marry another woman. And he would divorce his wife as soon as his wealthy, ailing father-in-law passed away. He figured it would take two years; maximum, four.

He didn't want her to wait *for* him; he'd asked her to wait out his marriage *with* him.

A meaningless marriage of convenience, he'd called it.

For her, that was untenable. He was asking her to remain in the shadows, a mistress longing for her lover's divorce so she could finally take the place on his arm as his wife.

"I was not born to live in the shadows," she had told him.

She had forced him to choose.

He didn't choose her.

It wounded her deeply.

But ambition knows ambition. She understood his choice, even as her ears burned as he said his goodbyes. Yes, she understood his choice completely, although it took years for her to forgive him fully.

Her words to him had rung in her ears for weeks after: "I was not born to live in the shadows."

And when she eventually crossed paths with Steve Roseau, who was reluctantly set to take on the family tradition of running for Congress and seemed interested in her ideas about campaigning, it felt right.

Gradually, her mother's pillow ambition gave way to Angela Roseau's resolution against living life in the shadows. One son and three miscarriages later, life took a dramatic turn for the couple.

To the surprise of many hangers-on who had surrounded Steve Roseau for years, his young wife commandeered a place at the helm of his campaign and ushered him into the Capitol. He endured what he privately swore would be his single term, which was bearable only because he intended from the very start to bow out of politics and support his wife as his successor.

Half-way through Steve Roseau's term, the death of a Louisiana state legislator created an opening that Angela Roseau seized upon to make her political debut. A stint in the state legislature would give her the credibility to eventually take up the place vacated by her husband in the US Congress

When candidate Roseau stood at the podium for the first time listening to the applause and seeing the thousands of faces eager for someone to lead and represent them, she dared to think that *she* was meant to fill the role.

Not just in the corridors of the Capitol, but, eventually, at another famed Washington, D.C. address, as well.

And why not?

She knew she was as smart or smarter and as tough or tougher than the male politicians of her cohort who would be vying for the highest office in the land, in years to come. Anatomy alone distinguished her from them. For her, that was not a justifiable basis on which she should be excluded from a job that she knew she had all the aptitude and skills to master.

How uncanny it was, now, that Bill Mahler, in his passing, seemed to have played such a key role in her destiny, after all.

His death had set in motion a train of events that had brought her to this moment. People and circumstances had fallen into place. And now she was on the cusp of achieving the greatest desire that she harbored.

It had taken altogether too long for a woman to come so close to holding the reins of power in the most powerful nation on the planet. And now, it was all open to her. Opportunity had knocked, and she had said, "I am ready. I am worthy."

Almost surgically attached to her smart phone at most times, she rarely touched a pen, except in two circumstances — when her signature was needed to make a document official, and when the intimacy of her journal compelled her to set down her deepest thoughts in longhand.

She opened the newer of the two books, and the nib flew across the blank page:

Friday, March 11

My mother fled the confinement of a religious and deeply dysfunctional home, shortly after turning seventeen, and her shadow never crossed the threshold of a church, ever again. Nevertheless, I still think of her as a profoundly spiritual person.

She saw the operation of a divine hand at work in everything around her, from the rising and setting of the sun, to the ebb and flow of the tides, and the birth and death of every living creature.

So many years after she's gone, I remember two of her observations as particularly astute.

The first concerned destiny. In her understanding of life, a divine will offered each one of us a greater and a lesser destiny. She would say that what may seem to small, finite minds as chaos in an irrational world is often the spiritual alignment of people and circumstances in a manner that manifests destiny.

"There's no such thing as luck, neither good, nor bad," she would tell me. "There's only Life presenting a moment of opportunity and asking you whether you have prepared yourself to make good on your greater destiny."

The second observation my mother made was that the world has a habit of underestimating women.

Many men, and even some women, fail to appreciate the ambition to a greater destiny that may throb in the heart of a woman. They do not see a woman's potential because they look at all women through the lens of the limitations they place on the female of our species.

"A smart woman will use this to her advantage," my mother would often tell me.

People's lower expectations allow such a woman to fly under the radar, quietly growing in wisdom and strength, until the moment arrives when she can strike, and claim her higher destiny....

****

A NOTE FROM ALEX: Thanks for picking up a copy of *Run, Girl, Run*. I hope you enjoyed reading it as much I enjoyed writing it. Hey, visit my website and sign up for my mailing list so you can be among the first to know when my next book is available and receive lots of cool, free stuff. You can join me at: ***www.AlexCFranklin.com***.

On a final note, reviews are crucial to allowing other readers to discover books. I would deeply appreciate if you would tell other readers why you liked *Run, Girl, Run* by reviewing it at Amazon.com.

ACKNOWLEDGMENT

I feel so grateful for the wonderful people in my life who gave me tremendous encouragement and support, and enabled me to bring this book into being.

For various reasons, not everyone can be named, but you know who you are, and you know you have my eternal gratitude. First and foremost, to the all-important five of "the original six," I say heartfelt thanks: you have been my rock and this book would never be in readers' hands if it weren't for you guys.

It would be remiss of me not to mention a few others for their special contribution to this project. I must thank Ramsey Hart, former Canada Program Coordinator at MiningWatch Canada, for his input and advice, and the same goes for the "boys in blue," especially Greg and Gary from the OPP and the Ottawa Police Service. I owe a debt of gratitude to Dr. B.-F. for steering me in the right direction and helping me shape vague thoughts into realistic dramatic elements of this story.

My beta readers, editing team (Janice and Cindy), and proofreader, Donna Rich, are absolute gems, as are the book launch team. Thank you for your patience and the skill and loving dedication to your profession that you brought to this project to help a first-time novelist put out a debut that is the best that it can be.

And last, but not least, I must say deep and sincere thanks to you, dear reader, for taking a chance on this Alex C. Franklin, whom you would not have heard of before. As I sat down to write, my intention was to craft for you a tale that would give you hours of pleasure and would leave you itching to call up someone to talk about it. I hope that this is the start of a long and rewarding relationship for both of us.

ABOUT THE AUTHOR

Photo © G.S. Bellamy

Alex C. Franklin is a Canadian author who has had a life-long love affair with words and literature. Alex was a newspaper reporter and magazine writer for over two decades and covered politics and business, among a wide range of other subjects. Over the years, Alex made detours into television reporting and radio talk-show hosting, but the pull of the written word never waned. Now retired from journalism, Alex has finally got around to the childhood dream of publishing a novel, and promises that this debut, Run, Girl, Run, will be "the first of what, hopefully, will be many thought-provoking and entertaining books that you just can't put down."

COMING SOON!

FIGHT, GIRL, FIGHT

THE NEW NOVEL BY

ALEX C. FRANKLIN

For updates on the release, visit:

www.AlexCFranklin.com